THE GUILT OF
AUGUST FIELDING

Another Fawcett Crest Book
by Helen Tucker:

THE SOUND OF SUMMER VOICES

THE GUILT OF
AUGUST FIELDING

Helen Tucker

A FAWCETT CREST BOOK

Fawcett Publications, Inc., Greenwich, Conn.

THE GUILT OF AUGUST FIELDING

THIS BOOK CONTAINS THE COMPLETE TEXT OF THE ORIGINAL HARDCOVER EDITION.

A Fawcett Crest Book reprinted by arrangement with Stein and Day Publishers.

Copyright © 1971 by Helen Tucker

Library of Congress Catalog Card Number: 70-149823

Printed in the United States of America
June 1972

B-288

The Guilt of August Fielding is a novel.
Its characters, however real to me now,
are fictional.

THE GUILT OF
AUGUST FIELDING

PART ONE

1

THE GATE TO BRANDON COLLEGE was wide and tall and made of stone, and a large plaque at the top bore the legend *Brandon College for Men, Brandon, North Carolina, Founded 1834, Pro Humanitate.*

The fact was, it was not a gate at all, but a stone arch which had been presented to the college by the class of 1887. But to August Fielding, an entering freshman not quite twenty years old who had never before seen an arch, it was a gate.

He reined in the team of mules, and the wagon came to a crunching halt on the deeply rutted road in front of the arch. He turned to his father on the seat beside him and was about to speak, then changed his mind. Gervas Fielding's face was expressionless, as much like granite as the arch.

Silently, August surveyed the surroundings. A low stone wall, waist high, extended from each side of the arch around the campus as far as the eye could see. The campus itself resembled a forest, a well-cultivated thicket of giant oak, elm, and magnolia trees. Through the trees August could see traces of dull red, the brick buildings of the college. The nearest was a shade lighter than the others—probably newer, August thought—and from the top of this building a white spire appeared to be climbing toward heaven, towering over the campus and the tops of the tall trees. For a moment August's eyes went upward with the spire. The chapel, he thought, described in the college catalogue as "the center of Christian life for the students of Brandon, and therefore the center of all life." The description, when he had first read it, made little impression on him, but now, looking up at the spire, he suddenly felt small, about the size of a speck of dust underneath the wagon.

He took out his handkerchief, no longer the unwrinkled

white it had been when he carefully folded it into his pocket that morning, and mopped his face. Then he took a small comb from his pocket and ran it through his burnt-orange hair.

"We're here, Pa," he said finally. "This is the college."

His father looked straight ahead, without blinking. "You think you can get the team and wagon through there?" He pointed to the arch. "There ain't even a road on the other side."

"I sure can't get them over the wall," August said, aware that his nervousness was beginning to show in his voice, "so it will have to be through there." He got down from the wagon and went to the arch, walking from side to side, measuring. "I think we can make it." Awkwardly, he climbed back into the wagon. He was six feet two inches tall and extremely thin, and all his movements seemed awkward, almost comical. His height and leanness, topped by the odd-colored hair, gave others—but never August—the impression that he was clownlike and should therefore act like a clown. His innate seriousness had always dispelled the impression.

He clucked to the team. "Gi'up." And the mules began the pull through the arch.

August looked again at his father and saw him relax when the wagon was safely through. On the back of the wagon was a small battered trunk containing all August's possessions, and behind the trunk was a load of wood, stovewood which August had spent the past two weeks chopping because the catalogue had stated that "a small stove is provided in each student room; however, students are expected to furnish their own wood and maintain the fire."

Gervas Fielding's face finally shifted from the position into which August feared its features had permanently settled. He rubbed his hand across his bald head, a gesture August knew meant indecision, and looked at August as though he were delivering his son to an alien altar as a sacrifice.

"It still ain't too late to change your mind, August," he said, carefully avoiding looking at his son. "Nobody'd think nothing much if you went on back home with me tonight. It ain't no sin to change your mind."

"I'm going to be a preacher, Pa," August said, wondering how many times in the past few months he had already made this simple statement of fact to his father, "and to be a preacher you got to go to college."

"I've told you and told you that Brother Johnson never went to college, and he's got a church and been preaching away for just about all his life."

"And I've told you that Brother Johnson is not a good preacher," August said, restraining the impulse to say something stronger about the ignorant little man who screamed hellfire weekly at his congregation. "I know you need help on the farm, Pa, but you've still got Ben. And I guess I never was much of a farmer anyway."

"But you're my son and Ben ain't. You expect a hired hand to be a son for me?" The hurt that had originally been in the words was now lost through constant repetition. "Look, August, if you want to be a preacher, I'm not minding so much. But you don't need to go to school no more. You been to school already. We can find you a church near home, and you can preach on Sunday and still stay on the farm during the week." This, August knew, was the final capitulation, a small concession being held out to him like a gift.

"It's no use, Pa. It's no use even talking about it anymore. I'm going to be a good preacher, an educated preacher."

"You been out of school for three years." Gervas Fielding's voice and argument were getting weaker as he saw his final defeat. "It ain't going to be easy to take up book-learning again."

"I don't expect it to be easy, Pa. But this is 1893, and nowadays preachers are educated. At least, they should be," he added, again remembering Brother Johnson.

He clucked to the mules and looked behind at the tracks the wagon was cutting through the grass. Suddenly he sensed that this was not the route by which he should have entered the college grounds, not the route in more ways than one.

They were now at the center of the campus, and August stopped the team in a small circle in front of one of the red brick buildings. He had had to allay his own personal doubts about the venture in order to be able to uphold the argument with his father. But now, as he looked around him, doubt descended upon him again and enveloped him like a heavy winter coat worn at the peak of summer. He could not look at his father now, for the doubt would show, the slow backing down, and in spite of what Gervas Fielding had said, it was too late to back down.

So he looked around him, feigning an interest that seemed now to be slow in coming, and he tried to remember all the things he had read in the catalogue about Brandon College. Anything, he thought, to keep his mind off saying good-bye to Gervas, that final accusing farewell which would come shortly.

Brandon College, he had read, was founded in 1834 by the Baptist State Convention "to provide better educational facilities for our own people, to establish a Baptist Literary Institution in this State." The convention had purchased a forest containing 615 acres of land, 22 of which were used for the campus site. Around the campus had grown the small town of Brandon, population about twelve hundred.

August looked at the four large buildings on the campus and wondered which was which. The chapel was the only one he could recognize. In the basement, he had read, were class-rooms for the Schools of Latin, Greek, English, and Modern Languages. One of the other buildings, he knew, was a dormitory for one hundred freshmen (upperclassmen roomed in boardinghouses provided by the townspeople). There was also a library which contained lecture rooms and the Schools of Pure Mathematics and Physics, and there was the Philosophy Building which housed the School of Chemistry, School of Natural History, and Schools of Moral Philosophy and Political Science.

As he studied the somewhat imposing buildings, a forbidding paragraph from the catalogue came back to him. "Whereas candidates for the Bachelor of Arts degree are allowed some range of choice in courses, they may in no case omit the more disciplinary studies. It is believed that the present system embraces the most valuable features of both the old curriculum and the new elective system. Solid attainments and true scholarship, rather than showy and superficial accomplishments, are the aims of the Faculty through the whole course of instruction."

Sitting under the maple tree in his front yard at home, he had read the words and thought, I'm not sure I understand it all now, but I will when I get there.

Now he was here, and he was scared. August bit his lower lip; then, conscious that he was doing so, stopped and trained his eyes on the ground, noticing for the first time a sundial in the center of the circle a few feet away from the wagon.

Gervas Fielding spotted the sundial at the same time. "Huh," he said, "if they're still using one of those to tell time around here, you ain't fixing to learn much." This, August recognized, was his father's small attempt at humor, as close as Gervas would come to holding out a conciliatory hand and giving his blessing. He smiled. "Well, I don't have a watch, so I may be using it."

A young man, younger than August, approached the wagon, stood looking at it appraisingly for several minutes, then nodded. "Freshman?" he asked.

August nodded.

"I'm George Cannon. A sophomore. I can show you where you're supposed to go."

August nodded again and climbed out of the wagon. "Thank you."

"You'll be staying over there." George Cannon pointed to the dormitory. "They're giving out room assignments in the parlor now. We can leave your things"—he looked again at the wagon—"and then I'll take you to meet your faculty adviser."

"Mighty kind of you," August said, "but I don't want to put you to any trouble."

"No trouble. I'm on the reception committee. Just follow me."

August pulled the reins over the mules' heads and led them as he followed George Cannon. His father still sat in the wagon, his face expressionless once again.

The procession stopped in front of the dormitory. "If you want to unload now I'll help you take your things in," George Cannon said. "I didn't get your name."

"August Fielding." His face matched the burnt orange of his hair. Already he had committed a social blunder by not introducing himself. He began to pull quickly at the trunk, lowering it from the wagon.

"Pretty strong to be so skinny," Cannon remarked to no one in particular. "I'll help you with that wood."

Gervas Fielding rose up as though emerging from a coma and began to hand down the sticks of wood to the two boys, who stacked them neatly in front of the building. When the last stick of wood was placed on the top of the stack, he sat down again. "Well, I guess you won't be needing me no more," he said to August. "I'll take the team and be going on home now."

August straightened as though he had been caught in a misdeed and was standing before his father awaiting the reprimand. Cannon, waiting patiently at the dormitory entrance, was forgotten. For the first time, the first time since the continuous argument about college had begun six months ago, August felt he knew the reason for his father's almost fanatical denouncement of higher education. He looked at him objectively, really seeing him now: this tall, gaunt man sitting alone in the wagon, his shoulders drooping slightly. August knew. *He's not really opposed to my going to college or being a preacher, and he knows I'd never make a good farmer. He's lonely. And he's afraid of being lonely.*

The discovery, this sudden and fleeting glimpse of something so personal in a man he knew so well that he did not know him at all, was excruciatingly embarrassing. He wanted to look away, but he continued to stare, and in his mind he saw the wagon slowly leaving the campus, rumbling along the dusty road on the long trip back home, stopping under the maple tree in the front yard where grass never grew and where tiny tracks of the wire broom were always visible. He saw his father unharness the team and lead the mules to the barn behind the house, and then walk slowly, bent with fatigue, back to the deserted house. What would he do then? Unlace his boots and fix some supper? Or would he go to the musty parlor that was always closed and stand for a while before the faded picture in the ornate gold frame, the picture of his wife, the mother August hardly remembered?

August approached the wagon. He could say only, "Thank you for the use of the wagon and team and for coming with me, Pa."

"I'll be going on home now," Gervas Fielding said again.

"It's not like I was really leaving home, Pa. I'll be seeing you vacations and all." Now he could look away. "Have a good trip back. Tell Ben hello. And everybody." He started to hold out his hand to his father, then stopped, knowing that it would be the wrong thing to do.

"Take care of yourself, boy." Gervas Fielding pulled the reins and backed the wagon to the circle, then started toward the arch.

"Mr. Fielding!" George Cannon ran quickly to the wagon.
"There's a road down here, the other side of the campus.
You don't have to go that way."

"I come this way," Gervas said quietly, "and I'm going this
way."

August watched the wagon as the wheels creaked over the
grass and through the arch, and even after the wagon disappeared he could still hear the faint rhythmic creaking as it
turned on the road toward home.

He was bone-tired. He stood by the window of his small,
austerely furnished room, thinking that even if he decided
to go to bed, his body would not respond. It was dark outside and he wondered if his father was still traveling slowly
along the road.

After Gervas left, August had followed George Cannon
into the dormitory. The first room was a long parlor, the
largest he had ever seen, and in the center was a line of tables,
obviously set up temporarily, where room assignments were
being given. The parlor was filled with boys who clustered
around the tables. For a moment August looked at the crowd
in dismay, overwhelmed by the knowledge that he was certainly the most confused person there. And then there was
comfort in the thought that these would be his friends, and
he observed the group more carefully.

He had never had friends of his own age because there had
never been time. When he was in school, he had rushed home
every afternoon to help his father and Ben on the farm, and
after he'd finished school three years ago, all his time had
been spent on the farm. Sometimes at night Ben would stay
for supper and they would sit on the front porch talking
afterward, and occasionally there was a church picnic, but
this was as close to conviviality as he had come.

George Cannon took him to one of the tables. "This is
August Fielding, Professor Barringer."

The professor, a small man with rimless glasses and a
dapper gray moustache, looked up briefly. "Fielding?" He con-
sulted a list before him. "Oh, yes. Glad to have you with us,
Fielding. Your room will be 218 and your faculty adviser is
. . ." He hesitated. "I don't believe you specified your course
of study on your application."

"I don't know, sir."

"You don't know?" Professor Barringer stared at him over the top of his glasses.

"I'm going to be a preacher," August said, "but I'm not sure what I ought to study."

"Ministerial student." The professor wrote something beside August's name on the list. "In that case, your adviser will be Professor Eugene Bryant. He's head of the School of Moral Philosophy and you can see him at . . . eight o'clock in the morning. You'll find him in the main reading room of the library. We hope you'll like it here, uh . . . Fielding."

"I'll help you with the trunk," Cannon said. "We have to take it to the second floor."

They moved the trunk slowly up the narrow stairway and down a long corridor to the last room. Cannon opened the door and said, "Well, here you are. Home, sweet home."

August took in the room in one hurried glance. There were two beds, scarcely larger than cots, two desks, a bureau, and a washstand on which stood a basin and pitcher. In the center of the room was the promised stove.

"The dining room is just off campus, right beyond the south side of the wall," Cannon said. "It's a boardinghouse run by Mrs. Larkins, but she won't start serving until tomorrow morning. Well, I'll be seeing you around."

"Thank you for your help," August said. It did not occur to him to ask where he could get supper or who would be sleeping in that other bed. He had completely overlooked the possibility that he would have a roommate.

Now, hungry and tired and with a feeling of strangeness he had never had before, he looked out the window. Below him he heard voices, and he could see the dark outlines of people walking about the campus. Behind him, his trunk sat upright beside the stove, still unpacked.

Pa was right all the time, he thought. I don't belong here. They all talk better than I do, and they're smarter.

He was wondering how long it would take these people to find out that he was just a dumb country boy when the door was suddenly flung open and two boys came in. They looked startled at having startled him.

"This is your room," one boy said to the other, "and I suppose this is your roommate. If you need anything else, just holler. The committee is downstairs and we'll help you if we can." And he was gone.

The other boy dropped a suitcase beside August's trunk. "I'm Ellis Lloyd. I reckon we'll be rooming together."

August held out his hand. "August Fielding." And he thought, Good Lord, he's young; at least two years younger than I am. Ellis's sleek black hair, parted in the middle, had a patent-leather look of sophistication, but his face was child-like, as though his features had not developed much since boyhood.

Ellis surveyed the room. "We're not exactly living in the governor's mansion, are we? How long you been here?"

"Not long," August said. "I came this afternoon."

"Met anybody yet?"

"Only the boy who showed me the room, and the professor in the parlor. I see my adviser in the morning."

Ellis scowled. "I just saw mine. Said I had to take Greek. Now, can you tell me why in the name of God a doctor should know Greek?"

"You going to be a doctor?"

"Yep. My old man thinks that's where all the money is. How about you?"

August hesitated, not knowing why. Then he said, "I'm going to be a preacher."

"Good God from Goldsboro! Imagine me rooming with a come-to-Jesus man." Ellis laughed and August flushed, knowing then why he had hesitated. "Well, I've got nothing against preachers, long as they keep their religion to themselves."

"I'm not a preacher yet," he said finally.

"No, but you've got the call, huh?"

"Don't say that," August said. "You make it sound like I took a purgative."

Ellis sat down on the nearest bed and rocked with laughter. "Maybe you're not going to be an ordinary, everyday, run-of-the-pulpit preacher. So you never got the call, huh? All of the preachers I know spend hours telling you about how they got the call."

"No, I guess I never got it," August said slowly.

"We'll get along fine, then. I don't believe in all this rah-rah God business myself."

"Are you an atheist?"

"Nope. I'm just not anything—don't have time to think about things like that, Brother Fielding."

Again Brother Johnson came to August's mind. "I wish you

wouldn't call me that," he said. "I know some people call preachers brother, but I'm not a preacher yet."

"All right friend. We'll forget the brotherhood." He picked up his suitcase and threw it on the bed where he had sat. "Think I'll go outside and look around a bit. Want to come?"

"No, I don't think so. I want to unpack tonight."

Ellis started for the door. "I'll be back later, Bro—August. Say, why weren't you named July? It's always ahead of August." He went out, still laughing.

I don't think I'm going to like him, August thought, knowing that he already disliked his roommate.

He opened the trunk and began to remove the few clothes he owned, the books, and from the bottom tray the black-bound Bible from which Gervas Fielding had read nightly to his wife and infant son—the Bible that had not been opened since Caroline Fielding's death.

"You'll be needing this, I reckon, if you're going to be a preacher," Gervas had said the night before, holding out the Bible as August was packing. August had nodded and put the Bible in his trunk without a word.

So you never got the call, huh? August went about the business of unpacking with a vengeance, ignoring his hunger and fatigue, trying to ignore his thoughts, but unable to cast aside the embryo of guilt that was slowly forming in his mind. He had been so sure of his motives for going into the ministry that he had been able to win the argument with his father about college. He had even been able to stand still, without showing his disgust, last Sunday when Brother Johnson had approached him after the service.

"So this is your last Sunday with us, August?" August had known he was in for a private sermon now. "Words cannot express what this means to me—to know that a member of *my* congregation got the call. I tell you, August—and you know already—there ain't nothing like a religious experience. When you know your whole heart and soul belong to Jesus and that you have been chosen to lead others in the paths of righteousness for His Name's sake. Praise God, there just ain't nothing in the world like it."

August held out his hand, wanting to shake hands and get away as quickly as possible. "Good-bye, Brother Johnson."

But Brother Johnson grasped the proffered hand and held

it. "My boy, you can go happy in the knowledge that we back here will be praying for you night and day. And you must pray night and day, too, August. Pray to the good Lord to keep your feet on the path . . ."

"Yes, sir." He tried to disentangle his hand.

"I tell you, August, a religious experience is something that ain't vouchsafed to many of us. Only those who are chosen by God . . ."

August had never had a religious experience in his life. At least not the kind Brother Johnson meant.

He took the sheets from the trunk and made up his bed. Even when he joined the church, at the age of nine, he had not felt anything special—just a certain discomfort and self-consciousness when Brother Johnson ducked him three times in the river.

He had made up his mind to join the church for the simple reason that he was the only one in his Sunday school class who had never been baptized, and Mrs. Bonner, the teacher, had embarrassed him one Sunday by asking, "August, don't you think you ought to join the church now? Don't you think you're old enough to be a Christian?"

Two weeks later on a Sunday afternoon in early spring, there was a baptizing. The church members stood on the bank of the river, and the choir, robed in white, stood knee-deep in the water in a semicircle around Brother Johnson. Seven people had already been baptized when Brother Johnson waded slowly to the bank.

"Is there anyone else?" he called. "Anyone else who is not afraid to send the Devil out of his life and believe on the Lord Jesus Christ? Oh, come, brethren! Come to Christ! Cast out sin and lead a new life."

And the choir began singing.

> Just as I am, without one plea,
> But that thy blood was shed for me,
> And that thou bidd'st me come to thee,
> O Lamb of God, I come! I come!

It might be a long time before another baptizing, so he'd walked slowly down the bank to meet Brother Johnson.

Brother Johnson held out his hand and led August into the water with him.

"I have to . . ." August began, wanting to tell the preacher that he had to take off his shoes and stockings, but it was too late—he was already ankle-deep in the water.

"Yes, we all have to, dear child. We all have to confess we are sinners and let the light shine through the darkness. You want to renounce the Devil and his ways?"

"Ye-es."

"And you believe on the Lord Jesus Christ as your personal saviour?"

"Yes, sir."

"Praise God! Another lost soul has been saved."

He slipped a white robe, which was really a sheet with a hole cut in the center, over August's head and led him to deeper water. Then he placed one hand in the small of August's back and the other on his head.

"I baptize you in the name of the Father—" And suddenly August's head was thrust under the water. It was unexpected and the water was cold. He choked. "And the Son—" He was pushed under again. This time he came up coughing. "And the Holy Ghost—" This time he was ready and held his nose as he went under. "Amen."

The choir began to sing.

> Just as I am, though tossed about
> With many a conflict, many a doubt,
> Fightings within, and fears without,
> O Lamb of God, I come! I come!

August waded from the water, his feet squishing in the sodden shoes. He pulled the sheet over his head, and someone gave him a towel.

"Let us give thanks to God . . ." Brother Johnson began, but August did not hear the rest. He dried his head and left the bank, walking slowly home down the dirt road, his drenched clothes chafing him.

Gervas was sitting in the yard, whittling. He looked up as August approached, then looked again and stood up. "What in the name of peace happened to you?" he asked. "I told you not to play around that river. Like as not, you could get drowned."

"Brother Johnson had a baptizing," August said. "I'm a Christian now."

"Humph." Gervas sat down again, and August could not tell whether his father was displeased or merely surprised. "You'd better go get out of them wet clothes before you catch your death."

So you never got the call, huh?

August folded a blanket across the foot of the bed. A few minutes ago he had silently condemned Ellis, who was going to be a doctor because "my old man said that's where the money is." What right had he to sit in judgment of Ellis when he was so unsure of his own motives?

Ellis came back into the room. "Not much going on. Just a lot of people milling around—all freshmen. The others come tomorrow. You had any supper?"

"The dining room don't open until tomorrow, I was told."

"Doesn't," Ellis said. "Dining room *doesn't* open."

August looked away.

"Here." Ellis held out a brown paper bag. "There was a store open over there in town. I brought you a sandwich."

Surprised, August took the bag and pulled out a chicken sandwich. "Thank you," he said, touched. "That was mighty nice of you."

Ellis flopped down on his bed, then got up immediately and opened his suitcase, took out a box and placed it on one of the desks. "I've got to write to my girl," he said, sitting down. "You got a girl back home, August?"

"No," August said, then added, "I never had a girl." He bit into the sandwich.

"Too bad." Ellis stared at the ceiling for a few minutes and then began to write.

August lay down on his bed and turned his face toward the wall, not wanting to intrude upon Ellis's thoughts while he composed the letter.

I never had a girl, he thought. *Unless you could count Rosemary, which you really couldn't.*

Rosemary Tippett, Ben's sister, was a year younger than August and he had known her all his life, but he had never known her very well. The Tippetts had the farm next to the Fieldings', and as a child, August had seen Ben and Rosemary, though they had not been companions. Ben, three years older than August, had been too old for a playmate, and Rosemary was a year younger and a girl besides. But during the last two years he was in school he had seen more of Rosemary, and when the weather was good, he had sometimes walked her home from church. Rosemary was tall and thin, like August, and she had long dark auburn curls which she always wore tied back with a blue ribbon. Her eyes were brown and her skin was milk-white. Even in summer when August turned red and peeled, Rosemary's skin never changed. It never occurred to him that she was pretty, or not pretty. She was just Rosemary.

They might have been friends, August thought, or maybe even sweethearts if it had not been for that afternoon in the woods. They had taken a shortcut home from church, leaving the main road and turning through the woods. When they reached a gnarled old oak tree, Rosemary suddenly stopped him.

"Let's sit down a minute, August. You don't have to rush right home, do you?"

"No." He sat down on the thick green moss beside her.

"August . . ." She looked at him, here brown eyes narrowing. "Have you ever been in love with . . . with anybody?"

He was so surprised that he stammered, "N-no. Why do you ask?"

"Just wondering what it would be like," she said. "I think Ben's in love with Sarah Hanright. Has he said anything to you?"

"No. He's mentioned her, but he's never said he was in love with her."

"He goes over to her house two or three nights a week," Rosemary said. "I asked him what they talk about, and he said, 'Nothing much.' I guess," she added matter-of-factly, "they must kiss a lot."

August felt his face growing hot, and he knew the color was creeping all the way up to his orange hair. "Oh, I don't think Ben would do that," he said quickly. He had never before heard a girl mention what went on between the sexes, and it embarrassed him.

It wasn't that he didn't *know*, and he supposed Rosemary knew, too, but you just didn't talk about it like that.

He had seen horses together, and once, several years ago, his father had taken him with him to the Mayberrys' farm when he took the heifer to the bull. He had watched from behind the fence while the bull pawed the earth several times and then charged upon the squealing heifer. That was the way it was with men and women, too, he knew, but still he could not quite believe it. He could not imagine himself doing it to a girl. Or, as far as that went, a girl letting him do it.

"I'll bet he does kiss her," Rosemary said. "And what's more, I'll bet she likes it. I heard Mama tell Papa that that Sara Hanright was fast, and she wished Ben would stop going to see her."

August surveyed the thick green moss carefully, pulling up little tufts and placing them in a neat pile.

"Have you ever been in love, Rosemary?" he asked.

"No. Mama says I'm too young to think about things like that. Do you think fifteen is too young, August? After all, Mama was fifteen when she married Papa."

"Then I guess it isn't too young," August said. He was suddenly very much aware of Rosemary. In the past few minutes she had ceased being just Rosemary.

"Rosemary." He leaned over a little. "May I—would you mind if I kissed you?"

She looked surprised and did not answer. He took her silence for acquiescence and leaned farther until his face was right beside hers. He kissed her quickly on the cheek, and then, taking her by the shoulders, drew her closer.

Suddenly she pushed him away and was laughing. Peal after peal of laughter. Laughing as though she would never stop. Laughing at *him*.

"Oh, August," she gasped. "I'm sorry, but you looked so *funny*." And she was laughing again.

He got up, stunned, and looked at her. "Rosemary, I better go now." He turned and fled, looking back only once. She was still sitting on the moss, doubled up with laughter.

No, he certainly could not count Rosemary. He raised his head and looked at Ellis, who bent over the desk, sucking the end of his pen, thinking.

August closed his eyes. When he opened them again the room was dark, and from the other side he could hear Ellis's light snoring. He did not know how long he had been asleep. Quietly, he got up and began to undress. He put on his nightshirt (ever since the day he was baptized his nightshirt had reminded him of the sheet with the hole in it), and before going back to bed, he looked out the window.

The campus was dark and still now. From the window he

could see the black outline of the library and beyond the library was the long stretch of grass over which he and Gervas had come in the wagon. And beyond that was the gate that said *Pro Humanitate*. And beyond the gate was the road leading home.

"Strange" seemed to be the only word that would come to him. He wished he were at home with Gervas.

Then he looked up a little and caught his breath. A thin stream of moonlight had touched the chapel spire. It rose sharp, white, and painfully beautiful against the dark sky. August's loneliness, his feeling of strangeness, was lessened.

This is my home now, he thought. I *am* home.

2

AUGUST HURRIED TO THE LIBRARY building, his long legs covering the ground quickly. He had overslept; it was already eight o'clock, time for his appointment with Professor Bryant. He had awakened with a start, sleepily scrutinizing the room. Always on waking, his preliminary chore for the day was solving the small mystery of Who Am I?, that split-second wonderment of who is the me that now is conscious?

Ellis was still sleeping, his knees drawn up, his fists balled up under his chin. He looked even younger than he had last night. August was unsure whether he should wake his roommate, then decided to let him sleep. Ellis had already seen his faculty adviser.

August dressed quickly. There was no time to look for the boardinghouse and eat breakfast, for it was unthinkable to be late for his first appointment.

The library was a large building which looked as though it had not been constructed but had grown out of the ground to fit in with the landscape. The entrance jutted out slightly from the rest of the building, and as August opened the door, he sensed rather than saw its sober, academic atmosphere. It was cool inside, a completely different climate from the rest of the campus, and, August thought, there was a smell of oldness.

There were two lines of tables on both sides of the main reading room, each with a large printed card bearing the name of a professor. There was no particular need to obey the large SILENCE sign over the front desk now; the conversations emanating from the tables were in hushed tones. Like a home where someone had died, August thought.

He looked down the rows of tables for a card with Professor Bryant's name and saw it on the table next to the main desk. He went to the table quickly, immediately made self-conscious by the noise of his boots on the hard floor. He tried to ignore the heads that turned to look at him, and for the first time in months he was made aware of how he must appear to others. I'm funny-looking, he thought, unconsciously using Rosemary's words.

He stopped at the table, and the man sitting there looked up at him. He was a big man with broad shoulders and dark hair which was graying at the temples and in a small patch just above his forehead. He wore thick glasses through which he squinted with watery blue eyes.

"Professor Bryant?"

The man nodded and stood up, and this surprised August because he did not expect a professor to stand up for a student. Professor Barringer had not done so yesterday.

"You must be . . ." He looked down at a list on the table. "August Fielding." He held out his hand.

"Mighty nice to meet you," August murmured, not quite sure what he should say.

"We're glad to have you here, Mr. Fielding." He shook hands with August and motioned to the chair beside him.

There was a moment of confusion, followed by a certain elation. August had never in his life been addressed as "Mr. Fielding."

"I see here," Professor Bryant pointed to the list, "that you are a ministerial student."

"Yes, sir. I'm going to be . . . I want to be a preacher."

The professor nodded. "A worthy ambition." And then he stared straight into August's eyes. "Why do you want to be a preacher?"

August swallowed. "Because . . ." He looked down at his

hands, folded tensely in his lap. It would be impossible to explain to this strange but direct man why he wanted to be a preacher. "Because, I think . . ." It was no use. "I don't know, sir."

"You don't know! Then how do you know you want to go into the ministry? Did you have a vision? Did the Lord send angels down a golden ladder to impart the information to you that you were elected to save your fellowman?"

Was the man laughing at him, making fun of him from behind those thick glasses? August could not tell. "No, sir. Nothing like that."

"Then why did you decide to be a preacher instead of a lawyer, or a doctor, or a merchant, or a farmer? They are all worthy professions." Professor Bryant was no longer looking at him. He was absently flicking the corner of the list as though he had lost all interest in the conversation.

"I want to be a preacher, a good preacher, because I think good preachers are needed." What right had this man to question his motives? "I don't think there are many good preachers around."

"And that brings up the question of what you mean by 'good,'" Professor Bryant said quietly. "But it's a philosophical question, and I don't suppose you yourself know what you mean." He smiled slightly, and August had the impression that Professor Bryant lived entirely in another world, this world of books and ancient wisdom. He could not, for instance, know about things like river baptizings or shouting preachers or picking cotton in the fall or what bulls did to heifers. And yet he was laughing quietly at August who did know about these things.

"I think," August said, his face reddening, "that religion should have dignity, and I ain't—haven't—seen much dignity in it. I don't think whooping and hollering and carrying on is any way to worship God. That is, if God is the kind of God He's supposed to be. The way some people carry on, it's like spitting in the face of an old man who never done nothing to deserve it."

Now Professor Bryant was staring at him intently.

"I think," August went on, calmer now, "that people ought to . . ." He stopped. "Like I said before, I don't know."

"You seem to know a great deal, Mr. Fielding."

"No, sir. That's what I came *here* for—to learn."

"To learn to be a good preacher who will restore dignity to religion." Professor Bryant opened a catalogue on the table, and August was still unsure whether the man was, in a quiet way, making fun of him. "Well, let's see what courses of study we can find for you. As a freshman you don't have too much choice, you know."

August relaxed, thankful that the discussion had ended. He watched the professor write English, Mathematics, History, Physics, and Latin on a piece of paper, along with the location of the classrooms. "This should keep you occupied, Mr. Fielding."

"But, sir . . ." August looked at the paper. "There isn't anything on here that will help me be a good preacher."

Professor Bryant smiled openly now, and his whole face was changed. The otherworldly look vanished, and for a minute he looked to August like an ordinary man, one you could josh a little if there was ever an occasion. "Unfortunately, we do not offer a course in how to be a good preacher, Mr. Fielding. But I think you will find that these courses, each in its own way, will help you."

"But what about a course in Bible study? I thought that was required."

"You can't take every course listed in one year, Mr. Fielding. Do you suppose you could wait until your sophomore year to try some of the others?"

"But I wanted . . ."

"Well, if you're determined, you may take my preliminary course in moral philosophy. It includes a study of both the Old and New Testaments."

"Thank you."

"But I think you're overloading your schedule. I don't recommend . . ."

"I'll do my best, sir. I'm wanting to be a good student as well as a good preacher."

Professor Bryant nodded. "I hope you will. Tell me, Mr. Fielding, have you always been of the opinion that religion lacks dignity? Your theory interests me."

"No, sir. I never thought about it much until . . . recently. It just sort of came to me."

The professor sighed. "Then I was right in the beginning. It doesn't necessarily have to be angels on a golden ladder. It could be almost anything. You suddenly have a new feeling which, for lack of any other explanation, you attribute to coming from On High. You believe you 'got the call,' I think the expression is."

"I never got any call," August almost shouted. "I never got any call at all. I ain't . . . I'm not even sure what that means."

Professor Bryant threw back his head and laughed loudly, so loudly that people at other tables turned and stared at him. "Thank God for that," he said, removing his glasses and wiping his eyes. "You know, August, you may very well turn out to be a good preacher at that." Still smiling, he gave August the paper on which he had been writing. "You may give this to the registrar now. I'll be your adviser until you are graduated, unless, of course, you change your course of study to another field. If I can help you at any time, if there is anything you do not understand, you are to come to me."

"I'm much obliged to you, sir. I . . . Good morning, Professor Bryant." The interview was at an end, and he knew he should not take any more of the professor's time trying to explain himself. But he felt that Professor Bryant did not understand at all, and therefore at some time or other he should try to make himself clear. He rose and walked away slowly, as though he expected to be called back. At the door he looked back. Professor Bryant, still smiling warmly, was watching his departure.

Outside he was momentarily blinded by the bright sunlight, and his nostrils were filled with the smell of evergreens, the small box cedars carefully spaced around the library. Although it was not yet nine o'clock, the sun burned down with such force that August wondered why the thick grass was not parched.

As did the other walkways across the campus, the path from the library to the stone wall on the south side had stepping stones—large flat stones placed on the path with no thought of design or symmetry. Some were so close together that they almost touched, whereas others were spaced so far apart that it would have taken a leap to cross without stepping on the scraggly grass that tried to grow between them. The stones reminded August of a game, he had played during recess at school when he was a child. Take one giant step forward and now two baby steps. And if you forgot to say "May I?" you had to go back to the point of beginning. He

followed the stones to the edge of the campus and then stood
by the wall looking for the boardinghouse.

There was a large white frame house across the street. It
had a wide porch which extended all the way across the front
and around one side of the house. He crossed the street and
went up to the porch, uncertain whether he should knock or
go in and look for the dining room. Since there was no one
in sight, he decided to knock.

A large woman with the roundest face he had ever seen
came to the door.

"Is this Mrs. Larkins' boardinghouse?"

"Yes, I'm Mrs. Larkins."

"I'd like to make arrangements to eat here if I could."

"You don't have to make arrangements in advance," Mrs.
Larkins said. "Just about everybody at the college eats here,
so you just come on."

"Could I have breakfast now?"

"Lord, boy, no. Breakfast is from six to eight. How come
you so late?"

"I had an appointment and I overslept," he said.

"Well, I'm sorry, but we're getting ready for dinner now.
You come back then. Dinner is served from eleven thirty to
one thirty, and supper is from five to seven."

Go all the way back to the point of beginning, he thought
as he went back to the campus. I forgot to say "May I?"

The campus was alive with students now. He watched them
as he walked along, some rushing up to others and shaking
hands; others like himself, walking alone and looking slightly
mystified and a little lost.

He sat down on a stone bench in front of the chapel,
glancing at the six tall white columns which matched the tall
white spire. It was beautiful here; a beautiful place for forming friendships.

In his mind he, who had never had friends, knew exactly
what the ideal friend would be like. Someone who knew
everything about him and liked him without trying to change
him and make him into something he wasn't. Someone he
could tell everything to—even his most serious thoughts—and
know that he would not be laughed at. Someone who could
look at him without noticing that he was funny-looking.

Of course, he knew there were private things that you could
never tell another human being. Because if you told, you

would lose dignity in their eyes, and losing dignity was the same as losing self-respect.

A heavy sadness filled him as he realized that probably in his whole life he would never feel really close to anyone. But, then, preachers must be close to everyone, or how could they preach love and fellowship and brotherhood? How many sermons had he heard Brother Johnson preach on the theme of "We Are Our Brother's Keeper"?

No, he could not imagine revealing himself to anyone—not even to God, though he supposed God knew all about him anyway. He would not have dreamed of going down on his knees and saying, "Look, God, this is the way I am. I am selfish and I don't think much about other people because I'm not concerned with them. And sometimes I think dirty things, like how it would be to lie down with a girl, and sometimes I'm impatient with my father and Ben. But, God, I'm not asking forgiveness because, You see, I don't really want to change because I'm pretty well satisfied with me the way I am. This is the way I am, God, and you've got to like me in spite of it. And anyway, God, didn't you make me this way . . . ?"

If he couldn't explain things to God, how could he be expected to explain to someone less than God? He could not even explain to Professor Bryant why he had decided to be a preacher. Nothing could have made him tell Professor Bryant about that night last March when he had decided that he must leave his father's farm and "be about his Father's business." The professor would have looked at him incredulously. Or worse, he might have laughed.

All my reasons for wanting to be a preacher, he thought, are negative rather than positive. And most of the reasons had come from that night in March, six months ago, when under a brown canvas tent his disgust with man-made religion had become so overwhelming that he had been violently ill.

Brother Johnson apparently considered himself a herald angel. Every Sunday for two months before the revival was to begin, he made the announcement. And every Sunday the announcement was longer.

"Brethren, we are in for a religious experience the likes of which this community has never seen before. And maybe never will again. This is something we have all been waiting for, something we can share. Rich or poor, dumb or smart, saint or sinner, this reawakening, this soul-saving experience, is for *you*." He pointed a stubby finger toward the congregation as though he was getting ready to announce the Second Coming.

"On the eighteenth of March in this here community, Brother Galen Manly is going to pitch his tent. Now, some of you already know what that means. For those as don't, I'll tell you. It means the end of sin. A time for repentance. A time for love—real honest-to-God Christian love. Now, Brother Manly will only be here one night. After all, we are not the only ones in the world the Lord has called him to talk to. And I know every one of us will be there to hear him. The tent will be right across from Brother Jones's store. Come and bring a friend with you. And bring a clean heart, a heart ready to repent and see God. Because I tell you, brethren, only the clean in heart will see God . . ."

August did not think about going or not going. He just assumed that if he wasn't too tired, he would go. A revival was, like weddings and funerals, a social occasion where you went to hear the Word and afterward mix a bit with your neighbors, ask about their crops and their children. Sometimes revivals lasted all day and well into the night. August did not like sitting so long, and most of the time his attention wandered, but he did like the picnic lunches—fried chicken, roast beef, ham biscuits, potato salad, deviled eggs, sandwiches, and pies and cakes of every description, all spread on tables outside the church at noon.

August asked Gervas if he was going to hear Brother Manly, and Gervas shook his head. Since August's mother had died, Gervas had not even been going to church on Sundays. So on March the eighteenth August went alone to the tent across the road from Herbert Jones's general store.

The tent was large. The big flap in front was tied back to stobs, and August could see that the tent was crowded even before he entered. He was a little late because Ben was ill and he had had to feed the mules and milk the cow before he left home. The night was warm, much too warm for March, and had all the promises of a false spring. There was a full moon and the air carried a heavy, sweet odor. As he approached the tent, he heard voices within raised in song.

Stand up! stand up for Je-sus!

Ye sol-diers of the cross;
Lift high his roy-al banner,
It must not suf-fer loss.

He went through the flap and looked about him for a seat.
In front of him, on a raised wooden platform, stood Brother
Johnson, hymnbook swaying in his hands in time to the
music, and beside him was Brother Manly, a big man with
wavy hair which tapered off on the sides of his face in white
sideburns. The tent was filled with chairs, straight hard-
backed chairs borrowed from Sam Rimber's Undertaking
Parlor. The chairs were parted in the middle to make room
for a narrow aisle leading to the platform, and along the aisle
someone had carefully spread the crinkly shavings of sawdust.

There were only three vacant chairs left in the tent, two
in the front row and one near the back. He went to the chair
near the back, and a woman in a tight-fitting pale blue dress
with circles of dried perspiration under the arms gave him a
hymnbook.

Stand up! stand up for Je-sus!
Stand in his strength a-lone;
The arm of flesh will fail you;
Ye dare not trust your own.

August moved his lips, silently reading the words while
others loudly and proudly lifted their voices to the Almighty.
If volume had anything to do with it, August thought, the
Almighty must be hearing every note.

He looked around the tent, wondering where so many
people had come from. Judging from the number of buggies
and wagons outside, they had come from all over the coun-
tryside to hear Brother Manly preach. Here and there among
the crowd he spotted his neighbors. Mr. and Mrs. Mayberry
and the six young Mayberrys were near the front. On the
left side of the aisle near the middle were Mrs. Tippett and
Rosemary, both singing lustily. Mrs. Tippett was a stringy
woman with a long face and limpid brown eyes, which had
always reminded August of calf eyes. He had not been able
to look at Rosemary, really look at her, since that afternoon
in the woods three years ago. Now as he saw her thin straight

back, he thought, She's going to look just like her mama
when she gets old.

The hymn was finished, and with a great scraping of chairs
on the hard dirt the congregation sat down. Brother Johnson
remained standing and held out his hand for silence.

"Praise ye the Lord," he thundered. "Both young men and
maidens; old men and children: Let them praise the name
of the Lord: for His name alone is excellent; His glory is
above the earth and heaven."

He looked solemnly over the sea of faces. "Brethren, tonight, like I promised you, we are blessed with the presence
of Brother Galen Manly, who is going to bring us a message.
A message that may well tear at our souls, for we all are
sinners. But remember, brethren, there is plentiful redemp-
tion, and Brother Manly will show us the Way."

Brother Johnson retreated to a chair well back on the
platform, and Brother Manly stood up. He walked to the
edge of the platform and leaned over so far that August
thought he would lose balance and fall. For a moment there
were short spasms of coughing throughout the tent and then
the noise subsided, followed by a silence so all-consuming
that one forgot the sound of voices. Still Brother Manly did
not speak. And then, just as August was becoming accustomed
to the silence, Brother Manly lifted his right arm and bell-
owed, "I say unto you!" and August jumped as though he had
been hit by buckshot. The bellow had the same effect on the
rest of the congregation. Everyone sat bolt upright.

"I say unto you!" he cried again. "Enter ye in at the strait
gate: for wide is the gate, and broad is the way, that leadeth
to destruction, and many there be which go in thereat: Because strait is the gate, and few there be that find it."

He paused again, letting the words echo through the tent
and come to rest. Then he held out both arms.

"You are doomed!" His deep voice pronounced the words
like a heavy axe splitting wood. "It says in the Good Book,
brethren, that you are doomed. Doomed because you are
sinners. Now, don't look at your neighbors and start counting
their sins and feeling sorry for them. Look deep in your own
black, sinful hearts before you cast the first stone. You there,
I mean." He pointed accusingly. "You think the little things
don't matter. So you talked bad about your neighbor and
excused yourself because you thought your neighbor deserved

it. You think it don't matter. And you there. You looked at your neighbor's wife with lust in your heart and you think it don't matter because you didn't do anything about it. And you. Maybe you cheated your neighbor just a little and said it don't matter because he's richer than you are anyway. Well, I'm telling you, brethren, it does matter. It matters to God. You are digging your way straight to hell, using your own evil deeds as a shovel. You are doomed and there ain't any power on earth that can save you."

He scowled again, still pointing his finger first left then right. "The only power that can save you is in heaven, and why should heaven bother with the likes of you? God abhors a sinner and you are all sinners."

Across the aisle from August, on the back row, an old woman began to cry.

"You think you are different, not like the others, that when you die God is going to pass a miracle and take you right up into heaven with Him while He condemns your neighbor to everlasting hell. It ain't so, brethren. *You* are going to be burning right alongside your neighbor. Why should God do you a personal favor? What have you ever done for Him?"

The old woman bent forward in her chair, her bonnet tilted on her head. "Oh, save me," she sobbed. "Lord, save me."

"That's right, cry to the Lord. Cry and hope it ain't too late to be heard. Wide is the gate that leadeth to destruction, and many there be which go in thereat."

The cry was taken up from the other side of the tent. "Lord, save me."

"You are not promised eternal life like a gift on a silver platter; you got to *earn* it. Do you ask yourself every night before you go to bed, 'What have I done to earn eternal life today?' No, you don't. Like as not, you gloat over the little sins you committed and think you've gotten away with."

"Help us, Brother," called a man near August. "Show us the way."

"There is only one Way," Brother Manly thundered. "Jesus Christ is the Way, the only Way. He is the only one that can save you. You got to renounce your sinning ways and become again as a little child, pure and innocent and loving."

August wiggled uncomfortably in his chair. He was getting terribly warm; not a breath of air stirred in the tent. He took out his handkerchief and mopped his face. The fat woman

beside him took out a handkerchief at the same time and
blew her nose loudly. Tears were coursing down her round
cheeks. Suddenly she sat up straight and called out, "Tell
us what to do, Brother."

"Confess your sins and profess faith in Jesus Christ. Ask
Him—no, *beg* Him—to show you the strait gate and the
narrow way that leads to eternal life. Lay your sins on Jesus."
He motioned to Brother Johnson, who came forward with
the hymnbook, and the people rose again.

I lay my sins on Je-sus, the spot-less Lamb of God;
He bears them all, and frees us from the accursed load . . .

"Mean it when you sing it," Brother Manly called over the
singing. "God don't listen unless you mean it." The voices
and the pitch went higher.

I bring my guilt to Je-sus, to wash my crimson stains
White in his blood most precious, till not a stain remains.

"Sinners, come forward," Brother Manly cried. "Come
forward and repent and go home tonight easy in your souls.
Go home filled with love. I tell you, friends, love is the only
way. The love of Jesus Christ has to grab a-holt of it and
never let it go. We've got to have honest-to-God Christian
love around here." He looked meaningfully at Brother Johnson, as though the two of them were winning allies in the
war against sin. "Come forward and confess your carnality,
the lust in your hearts. Confess your lying tongue that bears
false witness. Who'll be the first? Who'll be the first to get
right with God?"

The woman beside August got up and moved her heavy
bulk slowly down the sawdust aisle. She stopped in front of
the platform. "Save me, Brother."

"Get down on your knees and pray with me," Brother
Manly said. He jumped from the platform and stood beside
her, placing his hand on her head. "Save this sister, O Lord,
from her sins and bring her to everlasting life. Amen." The
chorus of "Amens" was taken up throughout the tent.

With difficulty she got up from her knees, her hands
clasped together, her eyes focused on the top of the tent.

"Thank you, Jesus," she cried, and her eyes rolled back so only the whites were visible.

"Come forward, sinners," Brother Manly called. "Are you going to sit there and be eternally damned? Are you going to let this woman bear the whole burden of your guilt? Come forward while we're singing."

Brother Johnson led the singing again.

I am coming to the cross; I am poor and weak and blind;
I am counting all but dross; I shall full salvation find.
Humbly at the cross I bow; save me, Jesus, save me now.

There was now a steady procession going to the platform and kneeling. A low, terrible moan came from the aisle, a wailing voice crying, "God, have mercy! Save me, Jesus." And then the moan, too, became a chorus.

August listened to the moaning and watched as men and women and even small children went to the platform and dropped to their knees. No, he cried out inside, it should not be like this! He sat firmly in his seat, not moving in spite of the fact that everyone around him was getting up and going to the platform. He looked at the chairs across the aisle where a few people still sat awaiting their turn to be saved. Can't they see? August thought. Can't they understand that they are not worshipping God, they are only fearing the Devil?

Then he saw Rosemary and Mrs. Tippett rise and follow the line. Mrs. Tippett pushed Rosemary forward and knelt beside her at Brother Manly's feet.

"Come and cast your sins away," Brother Manly said. "Let Jesus take over your life."

He placed his hand on Mrs. Tippett's head, and August saw her shiver and look up at him with her big calf eyes. "I'm coming, Jesus," she cried. And when she got up, August saw her face plainly. To him she looked exactly like the heifer that day the Mayberrys' bull had charged upon her.

August felt sick with embarrassment. How could she let people see her like that? He was suddenly choking for breath in the warm tent. Brother Manly had turned to Rosemary now, and August could not bear to watch. He got up quickly and stumbled out of the tent. But there was something hypnotic about the scene. Outside, he peeked around the flap and saw Brother Manly put his hand on Rosemary's shoulder.

"Go and sin no more, daughter. Open your heart to God's love."

Rosemary returned to her seat, her face a replica of her mother's.

August mopped his face. It wasn't right. It just wasn't *right*. There was something sensual, almost sinful, about the way they were casting out sin. But, then, how else did you go about it? He remembered a lesson from Sunday school about a man being told to go into his closet and close the door and pray. Pray privately. While being stripped of their sins, his neighbors were also being stripped of their dignity. And how could you worship a dignified God in such an undignified way?

He walked over to the nearest wagon and leaned against it, feeling as though he were suffocating in the heavy night air. Tomorrow, he wondered, would those people be embarrassed when they remembered their actions, as embarrassed as he was for them tonight? Would he ever be able to look at them again and not see them as they were tonight?

He was going to be sick. His stomach was churning, and even though it was cooler outside the tent, he felt feverish. He put his head down on the side of the wagon, and as he did, he felt a slight movement and heard a muffled voice.

"Ben, oh, Beh-en."

Startled, August drew back. There was someone under the seat of the wagon. Ben Tippett? Ben was sick that day. He had left the farm early and August had done his chores.

But it was Ben. He could see, now that his eyes had grown accustomed to the darkness. Ben was lying under the seat and there was a girl with him. He could not see who the girl was. Did they know he was right beside the wagon?

Apparently not. "Beh-en," the girl said, "you're being bad again."

"Shh," Ben said. "We're going to be saved tonight. Didn't you hear that preacher say love was the only way."

"Oh, Beh-en."

August moved away from the wagon as stunned as if he had just received a blow on the head. He crossed the road to Jones's store and sat down on a green bench in front. Then he put his head between his knees and vomited. And all the while the words kept going around in his mind: You've got

to grab a-holt of it and never let it go, you've got to grab a-holt of it and never let it go.

He got up and walked slowly down the road. Maybe they didn't know any better. Maybe that was why they were so easily led by a man who also didn't know any better. But how could they have gone to Sunday school or read their Bibles and not have known that God was not the way Brother Manly said.

He stopped and held on to the trunk of a tree while he was sick again.

This argument in his mind, this sermon he was preaching to himself, was only a coverup. He was trying to keep from thinking about what he really *thought*. He had been disgusted to the point of illness for one reason only: Tonight he had seen that it was possible to use a public worship service as a means of sexual satisfaction. He had seen the look on Brother Manly's face as he screamed from the platform about lust and carnality; he had seen the people squirming and writhing in their chairs as they called for God to save them. It was not a religious but a sexual experience they were having. Whatever inner frustrations they suffered were relieved in one evening of excited moaning, crying, praying, singing, and finally climaxing the evening by kneeling abjectly in public and saying, "I am a sinner; do to me what you will."

If he were a preacher, he wouldn't try to scare the hell out of them.

He walked unsteadily, overcome by weakness and the horror of what he had witnessed. He had bee̶ ̶ ̶ ̶ ̶ls before, and he had sat through Sunday aft̶ ̶ ̶ ̶ Brother Johnson's shouting evangelism, but s̶o̶ of it had affected him the way tonight's spectac̶ ̶ he becoming more aware of people and their ṟ̶ ̶ ̶ knew only that emotionalism was something you sh̶o̶ẉ̶e̶d̶ ̶o̶n̶l̶y̶ at the price of self-respect. He could remember when he was a child crying over some trifle and Gervas saying to him, "Don't show yourself, August. Don't go around showing yourself." It had made a profound impression upon him.

If he were a preacher, he would calmly and quietly try to influence his congregation by appealing to reason and logic rather than to emotions. Let them keep their dignity. It was the one thing man had that raised him above the animals.

If he were a preacher . . .

August looked again at the columns of the chapel. That was it, he thought. He was drawn to the building because it had dignity. And the spire had become in his mind almost a living thing. This was not a place where people whooped and hollered and screamed "Jesus, save me."

"Well, Mr. Fielding, are you musing over the problems of mind and matter?"

August started, and looked up into the face of Professor Bryant. The professor's mouth was twitching slightly at the corners, and again August was not sure whether the man was laughing at him or with him. It was almost as though they shared some small joke.

August stood up. "I was just thinking, sir."

"And the thoughts of youth are long, long thoughts." His eyes had a faraway look.

"I reckon so."

"Don't let me interrupt the thinking process," Professor Bryant said. "After all, that's what you're here for. And I think you'll find, Mr. Fielding, that your most serious thinking will be done outside the classroom—if you're not careful." His mouth twitched again, and he continued his stroll across the campus.

August reached into his pocket and pulled out the list of courses which had at the bottom the tiny, almost unreadable signature of Eugene Bryant, School of Moral Philosophy. Now he must find the registrar's office and present the list.

He walked toward the building in the center of the campus and ▮▮▮▮▮ to himself when he realized that unconsciously ▮▮ ▮ imitating the unhurried stride of Professor

3

August had never known an autumn like that one in Brandon, and looking around the town and the college grounds, he realized that he had never really seen autumn before. On the farm the fall of the year meant long days of picking cotton, or chopping larger supplies of wood, of putting in the winter feed for the mules and cow. In Brandon it also meant an extra stir of activity, but the activity was mostly mental and social, seldom physical. And instead of looking out over fields with long, even rows of cotton, he looked out over the spacious campus, blazing with red and gold fire from the flaming trees. Never had he seen such color, or so much of it. It was all he could do to force himself to sit in the classrooms listening to the lectures when there was so much color outside.

He had been at Brandon nearly two months now, and he could hardly remember ever having been anywhere else. It was even hard to remember that he had felt like a stranger here. He had made friends; it had not been difficult at all to meet and get to know a great many of the students. He liked his roommate very much. He did not understand Ellis at all, but it wasn't necessary to understand him in order to like him.

His only worry was his courses. In almost every class he remained in constant fear that he would not be able to keep up with the other students, since they seemed to know more than he. Most of the time he did not know what his professors were talking about; consequently he spent hour after hour studying, sometimes in the cool, musty library, sometimes on the bench in front of the chapel.

Ellis spent almost no time studying and even less time worrying about passing his work. This made August even more conscious of how little he himself knew. Where Ellis breezed through his classes, even the hated Greek, and always had an answer when called on to recite, August trembled in every class, afraid that if called on, he would display his vast store of ignorance.

If he had a favorite class, it was philosophy, though in many ways it was more difficult for him than the other classes. There was no way to arrive at a direct answer to anything, and the lectures left him filled with questions about things he had never thought of before.

"Philosophy is the love of wisdom rather than the pronouncement of truth," Professor Bryant had said, and August was convinced that Professor Bryant loved wisdom more than anything else in the world. He had, August thought, made a religion of wisdom. And his love of Plato was second only to his love of wisdom, for to the professor, Plato epitomized all wisdom. Even though Plato supposedly had no place in the freshman philosophy course, the professor referred to him constantly and sometimes read excerpts from the *Dialogues*. Finally, August felt compelled to read all of Plato.

"I don't think I understand it, sir," he said to Professor Bryant after class. "There's too much here. I can't take it all in."

Professor Bryant's mouth gave the inevitable twitch. "I think you may have stumbled onto the beginning of wisdom, Mr. Fielding. No matter how often you read them, you will always find something you had not seen before. The *Dialogues* are divided into two categories, the metaphysic and the humanistic." And seeing that he was only adding to August's confusion, he added, "Perhaps next year you will be ready for the course on Plato."

"Yes, sir. I hope so." He started to leave the classroom.

"Oh, Mr. Fielding. Mrs. Bryant and I are having a few students—mostly my philosophy students—in for tea next Sunday afternoon at five. We would be delighted to have you join us."

"Thank you, sir. I'd like that." He left the room, enormously pleased at the invitation.

On that Sunday in late October—August's birthday, a fact that he kept to himself—he walked down the treelined street to Professor Bryant's house, marveling once again at the most beautiful street he had ever seen. It was like an exaggerated picture, splashed with too much paint. The trees covered the street like an arch, their colors mingling at the center. The street's official name was North Main Street, but because of all the college teachers who lived there, it had become known as Faculty Avenue, and even the townspeople seldom remembered that it was North Main. Most of the houses were white frame structures with wide front lawns, and as August passed, he looked at the circles of chairs on the lawns, chairs occupied by people dressed in their Sunday best. At several of the houses some of the people, strangers, waved or nodded to him as he passed, and without self-consciousness he returned the salute.

The only strangeness he found in Brandon now was in himself. Before, his actions and reactions had been predictable; few thoughts had come to him unbidden. Now he found himself reacting to people and situations in ways that he would never have thought himself capable of.

The change had been a gradual one, but the realization of the change came suddenly. Only recently had it dawned on him that he was no longer afraid and uncertain, and that the new August was someone whom on better acquaintance he could like.

Someday, he thought, maybe when I'm too old to preach, I would like to come back here to live. Live in one of the big white houses on Faculty Avenue and be touched every year by the miracle of autumn.

That thought brought to mind another: He would have to leave Brandon someday—when he finished his work at the college. How could the seniors bear it, knowing that this was their last autumn at Brandon? But, then, he had four years ahead of him and that was a long, long time.

Professor Bryant's house was on a corner lot four blocks from the campus. Unlike most of the houses on Faculty Avenue, it was cream-colored and had only a small front porch, which made it seem compact despite the fact that it was actually quite large. It had three stories, or rather, two stories and on top of the second a small round room which made August think of a castle tower. The window of the tower room was almost completely obscured by the foliage of a tall sycamore tree. August studied the tower for a minute. That was probably where Professor Bryant had his office, where he kept the scores of books over which, August was sure, he pored during every waking minute when he was not teaching.

August rang the bell and waited on the porch, listening to the sound of voices from within. A large Negro woman in a black uniform with a white apron and cap came to the door and led him through the hall to the living room. It was a large room with the highest ceiling August had ever seen, and his first impression was that all the furniture was red velvet. Actually, it was not. There was a thick, red rug on the floor and a red sofa and one matching chair. The other furniture was of a nondescript color, which blended with the red.

Professor Bryant rose from his chair on the far side of the room.

"Ah, Mr. Fielding. Glad you could come." He ushered

August into the room in which approximately a dozen young men were seated, with the exception of three who stood before a tall fireplace, resting their arms on the mantel while they talked.

There was one woman in the room. She sat very straight on the red sofa, a silver service on a small table in front of her. Professor Bryant took him to her. "This is Mrs. Bryant, Mr. Fielding. Angela, this is the new student I was telling you about."

August had not thought about Professor Bryant as a family man. Had he done so, he would have pictured Mrs. Bryant as a thin middle-aged woman with gray hair and a kindly expression on her face. Angela Bryant was nothing like that. She was probably in her mid-thirties. Her hair was the color of pale honey, and she had blue eyes which seemed to both twinkle and snap. Her features were good and she had all the ingredients of beauty, yet she was not beautiful nor even pretty. High on her left cheek, just below her eyes, was a large brown mole which gave her face a coarse look. Under the bright green skirt she wore, August could see that her legs were crossed and he noted this with some amazement. Most of the women he knew sat either with both feet planted firmly on the floor or with their ankles sedately crossed. Mrs. Bryant definitely had one foot off the floor, and at least four inches of the other leg showed above the ankle where her skirt hiked up.

"Welcome to the meeting of the minds, Mr. Fielding. Lemon or cream?"

Professor Bryant laughed good-naturedly and said, "I wouldn't exactly call it that," and at the same time August said, "Very glad to meet you, ma'am. Cream, please."

She gave him a cup of tea and the professor said, "Now, come meet the others."

All conversation had stopped when August entered. Now, as he was taken from student to student, August wondered how he would ever remember all their names. Some of them he had seen before on campus; others were strangers. They were all upperclassmen, he decided. He was asked the usual polite questions: "How do you like Brandon?" and "What is your course of study?" and he learned that, like himself, most of the young men were ministerial students.

After shaking the last hand, he looked around for a place

to sit to drink his tea, which he had been holding nervously in his left hand, with the deadly fear that he would spill it on the rich red carpet. The only seat left was on the sofa beside Mrs. Bryant.

She was watching him closely and seemed to read his mind. "Come sit beside me, Mr. Fielding. Everyone else seems to have shunned me this afternoon." Her voice was deep and mellow, and a titter of embarrassed laughter went around the room at her words.

"Oh, no, Mrs. Bryant," a tall student by the mantel said quickly. "It's just that none of us wanted to hog the place of honor."

Angela Bryant smiled and patted the cushion beside her and August sat down.

"I believe my husband said you were a freshman," she said. "You don't look like a freshman."

"I'm the oldest in my class," August said. He almost added, "Twenty today," but decided not to. "You see, I waited a while before coming to college. I finished school three years ago."

As he talked, his eyes went back to the fireplace, and for the first time he noticed the portrait above the mantel. It was the most beautiful girl he had ever seen, a child really, for she couldn't have been more than twelve or thirteen. She had long pale blond hair, which seemed almost to have a halo around it, and deep eyes, which stared out in perpetual innocence.

Mrs. Bryant followed the line of his vision. "My daughter," she said quietly.

"She's beautiful," August said. He noticed that Professor Bryant across the room, was also staring at the portrait. He turned quickly back to the two students with whom he was talking.

"Her name was Angela, too," Mrs. Bryant said. "She died two years ago."

"I'm—I'm so sorry." August was stricken, unable to believe that death could touch anything so beautiful.

"She was thrown by a horse," Mrs. Bryant continued in a curiously toneless voice. "Her back was broken. She was thirteen years old."

"I'm sorry," August said again, feeling inadequate, wanting to change the subject. Professor Bryant did it for him. "Mr.

Fielding hasn't tasted your cookies yet, Angela. Perhaps he'd like one."

Mrs. Bryant immediately passed the silver tray to him.

"As I was saying, Professor," a student by the mantel said, "I just don't think I'll ever understand that part in *Ion* where Socrates—"

"Now, Clarence," Mrs. Bryant said. "None of that this afternoon. Save it for the classroom. For once, let's discuss trivialities and not go off on philosophical tangents. Besides, I wouldn't give you that"—she tried to snap her fingers and failed—"for Socrates."

She was teasing, of course, August thought as Professor Bryant looked at his wife in amusement. "I didn't know you were well enough acquainted with Socrates to give that." He snapped his fingers.

"I know enough about him to know I don't want to know any more," she replied.

Now the professor did not look quite so amused. "The logic of the female mind sometimes astounds me," he murmured.

"I know he was a man who went around arguing with everybody in sight in the hope of making everybody else appear idiotic," she said. "He couldn't even get along with his own wife."

The student she had called Clarence laughed. "I understand Xanthippe was not an easy woman to get along with."

"Unfortunately," Mrs. Bryant said, "we've never heard Xanthippe's side of the story. Socrates thought he was God and," she looked around the group challengingly, "I dare any of you to try living with God day in, day out."

Professor Bryant, his eyes on the red carpet, was quiet. The bantering conversation had taken on overtones that August knew were there, but could not define.

"I've been reading *The Republic*," he said quickly, "and I don't understand it. I'm not even sure I understand the parts I think I understand."

Professor Bryant looked up and laughed. "Keep reading, Mr. Fielding," he said. Then he turned to another student. "Mr. Farris, I hear you have a church now."

A heavyset young man sitting by a window said, "I'm a supply pastor for Corinth. They'll probably get someone within the next few weeks. It's good experience, though."

August looked at the young man with interest. "Are you a ministerial student?"

"I am."

"Mr. Fielding has ambitions in that direction also," Professor Bryant said. "He wants to bring dignity to religion."

August thought the professor obviously had in mind starting a discussion—an argument perhaps—with that statement. But whatever his intentions, they were lost immediately as Mrs. Bryant turned to him. "A preacher, Mr. Fielding? You?"

"Yes, ma'am. I want to be."

She smiled. "I would never have guessed it. You don't exactly look like a preacher. But I should have known, since most of the boys here are ministerial students. Eugene seems to gravitate to them. He was once a ministerial student himself."

August looked up in surprise. "I didn't know that."

"Yes, indeed. Then he decided that teaching was more his line."

Now Professor Bryant smiled at him. "I never got the call either, Mr. Fielding."

"What it was," Mrs. Bryant said, "was Socrates. He decided the highest goal in life was to emulate Socrates. And now he's looking for a pupil to be his Plato. Can any of you qualify?"

The boy named Clarence said suddenly, "I'm enjoying this very much, but I have a quiz tomorrow and I'm not as well prepared as I should be. If you'll excuse me . . ."

And that began the exodus. The others rose and thanked the Bryants and left. August was last in the line by the door.

"Thank you for asking me, Professor Bryant," he said. "I certainly enjoyed myself, and—"

"And did you enjoy anyone else?" Mrs. Bryant was laughing again.

"Yes, ma'am, I—"

"Oh, don't look so serious," she said. "I'm only teasing you a little." She took his right hand in both of her tiny hands. "I'm glad you could come, August—may I call you August?—and I hope we'll be seeing you often."

"Thank you ma'am. I hope so." He went out and hurried to catch up with Farris, who was walking just ahead of him.

"How did you like our little gathering?" Farris asked him.

"Fine" August said. "Very sociable. Do you go there often?"

"About once a month." Farris said. "Sometimes Mrs. Bryant comes in, sometimes she doesn't. When she's there we usually end up talking about happenings around the campus, but when it's just Professor Bryant we have some good discussions."

August nodded. "I guess she doesn't like philosophy too much."

"One could say that, yes. By the way, have you affiliated with the M.S.A. yet?"

"What's that?"

"The Ministerial Students Association," Farris said. "I think it might help you to join—put you in touch with others with the same interests, and all. We meet once a month—just had a meeting last week, so it will be the end of November before we meet again. There'll be a notice on the main bulletin board."

"I'll try to be there," August said, trying to sound enthusiastic. The ministerial students probably got together to tell each other about their religious experiences, and he wanted no part of that. "I'll try to be there," he said again.

"This is where I live." Farris turned in at a large white house. "Nice meeting you, Fielding. See you again."

August went back to the dormitory. It was time, past time, to go to Mrs. Larkins' for supper, but he was not hungry, so he went instead to the library and sat at a corner table reading Plato until the librarian told him it was time for the library to close.

As he left and started down the stepping stones toward the dormitory, he felt a hand on his shoulder. "Mr. Fielding, you are working late tonight."

The night, without a moon, was black but he recognized the voice of Professor Bryant. "Yes, sir," he said. "There was a bit of reading I wanted to do."

"I also had a bit of reading," the professor said. "Mr. Fielding, I would like to say to you . . ." He broke off and began again. "Mrs. Bryant still gets very upset when she thinks about our daughter. You see, she has never recovered from the shock of Angela's death. Therefore, if she seemed a bit, well, unnerved this afternoon, I hope you will understand."

"I understand, of course, Professor Bryant," August said. "I'm sorry I mentioned the portrait, but I didn't know . . ."

"No, of course you didn't. We both hope you will come back to see us again." He took off his thick glasses and cleaned them with his handkerchief as though by doing so he would be able to see better in the darkness.

"Yes, sir. I'd like to." August waited for a minute, but the professor said nothing else. "Good night, sir," he said finally.

"Good night, August." And Professor Bryant moved away from him down the stepping stones toward the north side of the campus. August stood listening to the footsteps as the sound faded, and thought that suddenly, for no reason he could understand, Professor Bryant seemed to August a man who had suffered for a long time from ills that were indefinable. August felt tears behind his eyes and turned to go back to the dormitory. Ridiculous, he thought. I hardly know the man . . .

Ellis was already in bed when August entered the room. He undressed in the dark and went to bed, listening to Ellis's heavy breathing as he tried to sleep. But his mind kept going back to the tea at Professor Bryant's. There was something very wrong in Professor Bryant's life, something wrong with Mrs. Bryant, and August was not sure that whatever it was could be blamed entirely on the death of young Angela. Something, he did not know what, gave him the idea that Mrs. Bryant hated her husband and would belittle him at every opportunity. But why on earth should she? He was kind, the kindest man August had ever met, and he had certainly treated his wife with affection—until she had begun the teasing about Socrates.

Finally, he slept. But it was a restless sleep, filled with dream fragments in which Eugene and Angela Bryant acted out a pantomime. First they smiled, then they frowned, and then they clawed at each other. Their mouths moved constantly, but August heard no words. And although he knew it was Professor Bryant, the man took on the appearance of a curly-bearded Socrates, while Angela, the woman, became a shrewish, faceless Xanthippe.

4

AUGUST WENT TO THE NOVEMBER meeting of the M.S.A.
and took Ellis with him. He had given the matter no further
thought after Farris mentioned it to him until he saw the
notice of the meeting on the main bulletin board. He discovered he had a mild curiosity about what went on at the
meetings, and also, he reasoned, it would be a good opportunity to get to know the other ministerial students on campus.

It would never have occurred to August to invite Ellis to
go with him, but Ellis, who had been staring at the ceiling of
their room for quite a while out of sheer boredom, insisted
that he'd even go listen to a bunch of "come-to-Jesus" men
instead of study.

The leaves had long since fallen from the trees, and they
walked across the campus with a cold wind cutting through
them.

When they got to the Greek classroom where the meeting
was being held, every seat was taken. In the back of the room
students stood between the last row of seats and a wall blackboard. August and Ellis found a place beside the blackboard
and rested their elbows in the chalk tray.

August looked around the room in amazement. It had not
seemed possible there were so many ministerial students en-
rolled at Brandon. There were more than one hundred boys
in the room, mostly upperclassmen. Seated at the lecture desk
was Farris, who looked out over the group with a benign
smile on his face.

"Glad to see a turnout tonight," he said, "especially since
we'll be electing officers for the coming year. As your outgoing president, let me say that it has been both a privilege
and an inspiration to serve. And now, Brother Barber, will
you open the meeting with a prayer?"

Brother Barber, an obese student in a black suit suitable for

50

pallbearing, stood up and bowed his head. "O Lord, look down with favor upon those who are gathered here tonight to do Your work. Help us by our good example to show others the Christian life . . ."

The prayer went on and on. August, his head bowed, opened his eyes and watched Brother Barber while he beseeched the Lord to bring all sinners to Christ. It was almost, August thought, as though Barber thought this particular group knew exactly what the Lord wanted, whereas others foundered in uncertainty and misdeeds. His prayer soon lost all qualities of prayerfulness and became a monologue that Barber was delivering to his good friend God. August stopped listening and studied the others. Apparently everyone except himself, and possibly Ellis, was in complete accord with Barber. Finally, after about ten minutes, Barber ended his prayer, "for Jesus' sake. Amen." There was a shuffling noise around the room as the group straightened up.

"And now Brother Haynes will read the Scripture for the evening," Farris said.

Brother Haynes made his way to the front of the room and began reading in a high-pitched voice: "Now I beseech you, brethren, by the name of our Lord Jesus Christ, that ye all speak the same thing, and that there be no divisions among you; but that ye be perfectly joined together in the same mind and in the same judgment. For it hath been declared unto me of you, my brethren, by them which are of the house of Chloe, that there are contentions among you . . ."

Again August's mind wandered. All speak the same thing, he thought. No divisions among you. Join together in the same mind and in the same judgment. That seemed to be what the group wanted. He looked to see what effect the meeting was having on Ellis, but Ellis was, or appeared to be, deeply engrossed as were the others in the room. These will be the preachers of tomorrow, August thought. No divisions among them. *And every one of them reminded him of Brother Johnson.*

The scripture finished, Brother Haynes resumed his seat and Farris made announcements about future meetings and went on to the election of officers. August did not listen; he had no interest in future meetings and did not know the men nominated for office. Then Farris said something that made him sit bolt upright. "I think it would create more interest in the association among freshmen if one of their class held office. I see a freshman with us tonight and I would like to nominate Brother August Fielding for the job of sergeant-at-arms. Do I hear a second?"

The nomination was seconded and the group had elected him before August fully grasped what was going on. He felt a sharp nudge in his ribs and saw that Ellis was enjoying himself immensely.

"Ah, Mr. President." August pulled himself away from the blackboard. "I appreciate the nomination, and all that, but I'm afraid I must decline . . ."

"It's too late to decline, Brother Fielding." August cringed. "You have been elected. There's not much involved in being sergeant-at-arms. You just stand by the door and . . ."

"I'd rather not hold office," August said. "If you don't mind." How could he tell them that he never expected to show up for another meeting?

"I tell you what we'll do, Brother Fielding," Farris said. "We'll hold the office open until the next meeting. You think about it and pray over it, and I'm sure you'll come back next month and tell us you'll be our sergeant-at-arms."

"There's no need to wait . . ." August began. But Farris had turned back to the group and was asking Brother Smith to close the meeting with a prayer.

As he and Ellis walked back toward the dormitory, August's mind kept repeating: Brother Johnson with an education. They spoke better and in softer tones than Brother Johnson, but underneath they were all Brother Johnsons forcing their fundamentalism on the world.

He had thought that religion would be different away from the Pine View Community; now he felt it must be basically the same everywhere. Didn't the students realize that they were going against the Bible they professed to believe when they publicly thanked God that they were not as other men? And how could they have the audacity to pray to God to make all men as they were?

He looked at Ellis in the darkness. "Well, why don't you say something?"

"Nothing to say," Ellis said. "I asked to go—nobody made me."

"But you won't go again." It was a statement rather than a question.

"No," Ellis said quietly. "I'm not a ministerial student."

"Neither am I," said August. "Not anymore."

Ellis stopped walking. "Why not?"

"I'm not sure," August said. "I guess I just wasn't meant to be, and I had to go to that meeting tonight to find out."

"I can't see why that meeting should make you change your mind. I've been to that sort of thing before and tonight wasn't any different."

"That's what I mean," August said. "I want something different."

"I don't see how it could have been," Ellis said. "They prayed, they read the Bible. What did you expect a bunch of preachers to do——handsprings and magic tricks?"

"Ellis," August said, "I think I'd like to walk around some."

Ellis started to protest, then shrugged his shoulders. "All right. See you later." He moved off in the direction of the dormitory. August, standing in the center of the campus, thought, So now I'm not going to be a preacher, and my coming here was a waste of my time and Pa's money.

And the alternative? He wasn't about to go back to the farm and tell Gervas that he had been right all along. Preaching might not be right for him, but neither was farming. He put his hands to his temples and pressed hard. There did not seem to be a place for him anywhere in the world.

He walked slowly across the campus, wanting desperately to talk to someone who would know and understand and tell him what to do. But there was no one who could help him now——except, possibly, Professor Bryant.

Professor Bryant had been a ministerial student and had changed his mind. And he was August's faculty adviser. He found himself walking very fast down Faculty Avenue, feeling suddenly very close to the professor who had the reputation of being the most remote man on campus.

As he approached the house, he saw a light flickering in the tower room. He hurried to the porch and pulled the bell, listening as it jangled inside.

Mrs. Bryant came to the door. "Yes? Oh, Mr. Fielding—August— come in."

He knew at once that he should not have come, that the hour was late—he had no idea how late—and that he was intruding upon the professor's private life. He should have waited until tomorrow.

"Come in," Mrs. Bryant said again.

He stepped inside, feeling ill at ease and foolish. "Could I—I wanted to see Professor Bryant for a minute. Maybe it would be better if I waited until tomorrow."

Mrs. Bryant smiled, and August noticed that when she did, the mole under her left eye moved slightly. "I'm sure he'll be delighted to see you tonight," she said. "Let me take your coat." Almost reluctantly he took off his overcoat, and stood numbly while she went to the foot of the stairway. "Eugene," she called. "Eugene, August Fielding is here to see you."

There was only the slightest pause, then, "Send him up here."

She turned to him, still smiling. "Go up to the top of the steps here, then turn right and go up the second flight."

At the top of the second stairway Professor Bryant waited for him.

"Good evening, Mr. Fielding," he said as though the late visit were a nightly occurrence. "Come in."

He followed the professor into the tower room. The room was exactly as he had imagined it. It was round, with only one window. Beneath the window was a rolltop desk which was open and a masterpiece of disarray. Huge piles of papers, manuscripts, and books completely obscured the surface. There was a swivel chair in front of the desk and one other chair in the room, a worn leather wing chair. There were two bookcases, the shelves of which sagged visibly beneath the weight of their overload, and books were piled on the floor, stacked neatly around the round walls.

"Sit down." Professor Bryant motioned to the wing chair. August sat down, thinking, If he says, "What can I do for you?" I'll know I shouldn't have come. It will mean he wants me to state my business quickly and get out.

But the professor said no such thing. He reached behind some books on the desk and picked up a pipe, which he lighted slowly and with great concentration. August suddenly realized that he himself had not uttered a word.

"I don't like to bother you," he said. "I wanted to talk to you, but I could wait until tomorrow after class."

Professor Bryant puffed at the pipe, then took it out of his mouth. "You have walked to my house on a cold night, Mr. Fielding. I would be both mystified and disappointed if you left so soon."

"Professor Bryant," he began miserably, "I decided tonight that I'm not going to be a preacher after all."

He expected a reaction appropriate to the bombshell he had dropped, but he got none. The professor continued to draw on the pipe, quietly studying August. The silence became embarrassing.

"You see . . ." He started again, then stopped. It was as impossible to explain his reason for not being a preacher as it had been to explain why he wanted to be one.

Professor Bryant turned in the swivel chair and beat the ashes from the pipe into a large receptacle on the desk. Then he faced August again.

"I came to Brandon," he said, "something like a hundred or so years ago with the idea that I wanted to be a minister. I went through four years of college thinking that I would go on to seminary and thence to the ministry. At the end of my senior year, I changed my plans completely. Instead of going to seminary, I got married. And in order to support my wife, I returned to Brandon as a teacher. What kind of preacher I'd have made, I don't know. The High Calling had a nice sound to it, but when I met Angela and it came to choosing between the ministry and her—well, my calling was not so high as I thought. I chose marriage because I was sure that Angela would not wait. Am I sorry now that I gave up the ministry so easily? Who is to say? There is, I'm sure, as much satisfaction in teaching the young as there is in preaching to the old. At least, I think the minds of the young are more receptive. . . . If you have given a great deal of consideration to the matter and have truly found that the ministry is not for you, then you are fortunate to have discovered this so soon. On the other hand—"

"I don't know what I want," August said, his tone indicating the annoyance he felt at himself. "I only know what I don't want."

"A few weeks ago you knew what you wanted and you expressed it very well. You wanted dignity in religion."

"I still want it," August said. "I want it more than ever, but . . ."

Professor Bryant leaned forward in his swivel chair. "Would you like to tell me about it, August? What led you to this decision—both decisions?"

And then August found himself talking. He felt a compul-

sion to justify himself to Professor Bryant. He told him about
the revival and the long walk home during which he'd
decided to become a preacher. He told about the months of
arguing with Gervas about college. And then he told about
the M.S.A. meeting and his disappointment. "I don't know
why I feel the way I do," he finished. "I simply think that
things should be different. All during the meeting I had the
feeling that those students were not really sincere in what
they were doing. They were doing it for show—a see-how-
righteous-I-am attitude. And the worst of it is, I don't think
they even realize it . . ." he broke off.

Professor Bryant sat back in his chair. "I gather from what
you say that these people—in your church at home as well
as here at Brandon—don't think as you do."

"No, sir, they certainly don't."

"Then, of course, they are all wrong and you are right."

August felt his face reddening. "I don't say they're wrong.
The truth is, I don't know. Do you think I'm wrong?"

"No, I don't. But neither are they. Many things are done
in the name of religion. Have you ever been to a revival where
the congregation, children as well as adults, fell on the floor
in a convulsive state and babbled like mental defectives?"

August shuddered. "No, sir. It wasn't quite that bad at
Pine View."

"They do this because this is the religion they are taught,
August. And they are sincere in it. For the short time that
the spell lasts, they honestly believe that they have been
touched by the Holy Spirit. And, since they believe it, who
is to say they haven't?"

"But they haven't been touched by anything but ignorance,"
August said.

"How do you know? These people who fall on the floor
are satisfied with their religion. Do you think they would be
happy at a service, say, here at Brandon, where we remain
fairly calm and, for the most part, dignified?"

"No, I suppose they wouldn't be."

"To them, we would seem irreligious—just as they are to
us."

"You are saying," August said slowly, "that everyone should
find the way of worshipping God that satisfies him personally.
But how do we know that that way satisfies God?"

Instead of answering, Professor Bryant asked him a peculiar question.

"Do you pray, August?"

"Yes, sir."

"And do you ask God in your prayers to increase the faith of everyone in the world?"

"Yes, sir."

"Then are you not, in fact, asking God to make others as you are? To give them the same beliefs?"

"I never thought about it that way."

"Can you honestly say—and know—that the men at the meeting tonight were not sincere?"

"No, sir," August said softly. "But at the time I was sincere in thinking they weren't. Now, to tell you the truth, I don't know who is right."

"In twenty, thirty years, if you keep an open mind, you will still be wondering who is right." He stood up and leaned over the desk, looking out the window at the white sycamore. "So you've decided you're no longer a ministerial student," he said.

"That's what I thought when I came tonight, but now I'm not so sure. I think I would like to give it more thought."

Professor Bryant turned away from the window and smiled at him. "As I said that day in the library, I think you might make a good preacher."

"Thank you, Professor." August stood up. "I'm much obliged to you for talking to me—for taking so much time like this . . ."

Professor Bryant went with him to the door of the tower room. "I enjoy talking to students," He gave a little laugh. "I guess you could say I enjoy talking. Come back any time you feel like it. I'll be glad to see you."

August went down the two flights of stairs, found his overcoat, and had started out the front door when he heard his name called.

"August, you're not leaving so soon, are you?" Mrs. Bryant came down the hall toward him.

"Yes, ma'am. It's late, I reckon. I didn't mean to stay so long."

"Nonsense! You've had your visit with Eugene, now come on in the kitchen and have a cup of hot chocolate with me."

"Thank you, but I should be getting along now."

"It's a cold night," she said. "You need something to warm you before you walk back to the campus."

He followed her to the kitchen, where he noticed that two cups had already been placed on the table. "Is Professor Bryant going to join us?" he asked.

"Eugene? Mercy, no." She laughed as though he had said something very clever. "He'll stay up in his ivory tower most of the night reading. Plato, no doubt."

He watched her as she took the cups to the stove and poured out the hot chocolate. She was not wearing a dress, he noticed, but a thin pink wrapper, and involuntarily his thoughts went to what she was wearing underneath the wrapper. He had never seen a woman in this state of dress, or undress, before.

She smiled at him as she set the cup in front of him again, and he looked away in embarrassment, sure that she could tell what he had been thinking.

She filled her own cup and then sat down across the table from him. "How are your courses going, August? I hope tonight's visit to Eugene doesn't mean you're having trouble in his class."

"No ma'am. Professor Bryant's class is my favorite, even if I don't always understand what he's talking about."

She laughed, and this time her voice held genuine amusement. "I'll tell you, August, I don't always understand what he's talking about either."

He had the momentary feeling that they were allies, but he was unsure what they were allied about. "I have more trouble with my other courses," he said quickly. "I don't understand physics very well."

"Why should you bother, if you're going to be a preacher?"

"It's required."

"You know, I still can't quite picture you as a preacher. Almost anything, but not a preacher."

He shifted in his chair uncomfortably, then straightened immediately as one of his long legs inadvertently rubbed against hers under the table. He looked at her, embarrassed again, and noticed that she had not touched her chocolate. A thin skim had formed across the top.

"Professor Bryant seems to think I could be one—a preacher, that is."

"Yes, he has a lot of confidence in you," she said. "Don't

misunderstand me, I think you can be anything you want to be. It's just that I'm not sure why you want to be a preacher."

"I'm not quite sure myself," he said quickly, and she obliged him with the laugh again. "I mean," he added, "my reason is not always the same. I guess that doesn't make too much sense to you."

"It's refreshing to find someone who doesn't spend all his time trying to make sense of everything. Some things can be explained so much that they lose what sense they made in the first place."

He nodded and finished his chocolate. "I'd better be going," he said. "I certainly thank you for the chocolate."

She went with him to the door. "Don't think that you have to wait for a special invitation to come here," she said. "Come back anytime, August."

"Thank you, ma'am. I appreciate that." He left and went quickly down the walk to the street, glancing back as he reached the street. She was still standing in the doorway, looking at him. She waved as he turned, and he waved back.

Professor Bryant was certainly not like the other professors in one respect, August thought as he walked toward the campus. The others were teaching him not only how to think but also what to think. Professor Bryant stimulated but never directed thought.

He reached the stone wall and started down the path of stepping stones. Professor Bryant could not tell him what to do, of course. No one could. But the professor had shown him how to think independently and had expressed faith in him. It was up to him now to see that the faith was not misplaced, for without knowing why, he felt that Professor Bryant cared—cared terribly and in a personal way—about his decision.

I understand a lot of things that I didn't understand before, he thought, but I never seem to understand the *why* of anything. He knew that tonight was a turning point, and he knew that there would be no turning back from the decision he made this time.

He stopped in the center of the silent campus and looked around him. The ground was covered with a heavy frost, as white as the spire tapering above him. He turned to go inside.

She never did take even the first sip of that chocolate, he thought.

The following morning, between classes, he saw Farris going down one of the long halls in the Philosophy Building and called to him. Farris stopped. "Good morning, Brother Fielding. What can I do for you?"

"Call me August," he said quickly. "I just wanted to tell you that I'm much obliged to you for nominating me last night at the meeting, and if you haven't changed your mind, I'll be glad to serve as the sergeant-at-arms."

5

BRANDON CLOSED FOR ONE WEEK at Christmas, and August went home. He had been aware during the past three months of certain changes in himself, but only after returning to the farm and Pine View Community did he fully realize how sweeping the changes were. He tried to fall back into his old routine of helping Gervas with the chores and later talking with him at the kitchen table at night after the dishes had been done. But now, when it seemed to August that they should have more than ever to talk about, they had less. The silences between them seemed interminable. Finally, they stopped all pretense at conversation about anything but affairs on the farm.

On the Sunday before Christmas they went to church together—and this surprised August, he could hardly remember when Gervas had last been to church—and as they left, Gervas stood behind while Brother Johnson clasped August's hand and welcomed him back.

On Christmas morning August and Gervas exchanged gifts —each gave the other a shirt—and then went to the graveyard behind the church and placed a wreath of holly by the headstone marked "Caroline, beloved wife of Gervas Fielding." And then, in silence, they walked home.

That night, the night before his return to Brandon, August made one last effort to establish contact with Gervas. There was something about the way his father sat at the table, bending over as though studying each familiar board in the table, that struck him as being pathetic.

"You know, Pa," his voice shattered the silence like the crash of hailstones on a tin roof, "there won't be too much for you to do around here until spring. Why don't you take yourself a little trip? Come to Brandon with me. I'd like for you to meet my friends."

Gervas shook his head slowly. "No, I guess I'd better stay here. There's always something needs tending to."

"Ben could take care of the stock for a few days."

"I'd best stay here," Gervas repeated.

"Well—maybe you can come before college lets out in May. Or maybe next fall."

Gervas looked up suddenly. "You figgering on going back next year?"

"Sure, Pa. It takes four years to get a degree."

Gervas continued to stare at him. Finally he said, "But, August, you can't go another year."

"But, Pa, you can get along without me, you and Ben. You've already proved that."

"It ain't that, August. There ain't any money."

"What do you mean? The crop was good this year. You said so yourself."

"It takes more than one crop to pay for that school, August. I only had enough money laid by to pay for one year."

"Why didn't you *tell* me that before I went last September?"

"I never figgered you'd want to go more than one year." Gervas' finger traced a crack in the table. "In fact, I didn't hardly think you'd want to stay a whole year. I thought after you got there you'd change your mind and come home."

August felt as though everything inside him had suddenly come loose. His first impulse was to lash out at Gervas for ruining his plans—wrecking his life. But then he thought: What's the use? Gervas was the way he was, and getting angry at him would change nothing.

"I guess," he said slowly, "there's no point in my going back at all. If I can't finish, there's no use going on with it."

"But there's enough money for you to stay until May," Gervas said, as though this made up for everything. "And you know you're welcome to the money, boy."

He can't understand, August thought. He knows he's done

something to upset me, but he'll never understand what. "I don't know." He got up from the table and walked to the back door. "I just can't see any point in going back at all."

"You said you'd already paid them for half of the year in advance," Gervas said. "You might as well get your money's worth."

August leaned his head against the cold pane of glass on the upper part of the door. Never to see Brandon again, never to walk on the funny stepping stones or see Faculty Avenue in autumn or hear Professor Bryant expounding on the wisdom of Socrates . . .

Professor Bryant. He had to see Professor Bryant again to explain to him about the money. He couldn't just drop out of college and leave the professor thinking that his faith in him had been misplaced.

He turned back to Gervas. "Yes, you're right. I'll go back. I'll go back and stand my examinations for the first half-year. But after that, I don't know."

August's first night back at Brandon reminded him of that first night there nearly four months ago, reminded him not because of similarities but because of differences. This time there was no feeling of strangeness, no gnawing hunger pains, no loneliness. Boys on the hall popped in and out of the room at irregular intervals, and Ellis amused each new group by imitating various relatives that had infested his home during the holidays.

August laughed with the others, but the heaviness inside him seemed to weigh down even his laughter.

On the way back to Brandon he had made up his mind that he would try not to think about what he now thought of as "the end of it all." He would study hard for his examinations and do the best he could. After that, he would withdraw from school. He had also decided that he would say nothing to Ellis until after the exams were over, but as he watched Ellis entertaining that night, he changed his mind.

When the last student had left their room, August went to the window and looked out. A light snow was falling, small flakes pirouetting through the air, taking a small eternity to reach the ground. August sighed and turned away from the window.

"Ellis," he said, "I think you ought to know something, but I'd be much obliged if you wouldn't mention it to anyone."

"Let me guess." Ellis, still in a playful mood, controlled his face. "You got a girl in trouble during vacation."

"No, nothing like that. I'm leaving Brandon after examinations."

Ellis looked at him, his expression suddenly dead serious. "But why?" he asked. "Why in God's name should you leave? You're passing your work—"

"It isn't that," August said. "My father needs me on the farm." Then, as Ellis continued to stare at him, he said, "The truth is, there's not enough money. Oh, there's enough for me to finish out the year, but I don't see any point in staying on when I can't finish the whole thing. I thought I should tell you so you can be thinking about another roommate."

"But, August, I don't want another—look, why couldn't you get some kind of work, or something? A lot of the boys are working their way through."

"I thought of that," August said. "I thought of getting a job somewhere this summer, but I couldn't make enough to pay for a whole year here, so what's the use?"

"Maybe you could get some work around the campus to help out."

"There isn't time. I have to spend all my time studying just so I can pass." He smiled ruefully. "I'm not like you. I guess it takes me a long time to catch on to things."

"Jesus, August, there ought to be something—"

"There isn't," August said, wanting to end the conversation right that minute. "I've thought and thought, and there just isn't anything."

"What a shame! It just isn't fair." Then he smiled. " 'Scuse me, preacher. I didn't mean to be a long face, but I've kind of gotten used to you and . . ."

August smiled back at him and went to bed. His thoughts took on a monotony that should have lulled him to sleep, but instead only made the sadness grow inside him. Over and over the words went through his mind: I'm going to leave. I'm going to leave Brandon.

Finally, when the world outside his window was completely white, and dawn came like a gray streak, soiling the white, he slept.

The weeks ahead were arduous ones. August, who thought he had been having to study much too hard before, now doubled his efforts. He became single-minded in his desire to make a good showing on his examinations, as though by doing so he could prove to himself that if given the opportunity, he could have gone ahead with his life as he had planned.

Once, after attending the January meeting of the M.S.A. and hearing a talk on "Why God Sends Us Trouble," he wondered briefly if God had given him this obstacle for a reason. Then he dismissed the thought. The student who gave the talk had made it sound as though God passed trouble around neatly gift-wrapped, and those whom He loved the most got the biggest packages. None of it made much sense to August, and he was too busy studying to find time to worry about the size of the package he had gotten or the reason for getting it.

During the week of examinations he was extremely nervous, suffering from too much steady concentration and lack of sleep. He marveled at Ellis who had spent no more time studying than usual, and yet remained calm and cheerful, still a cutup. He came in from each exam whistling, whereas August returned with the feeling that all his hours of study had been in vain.

The week finally ended, and then came what to August was the worst of all—the three days of waiting for the papers to be graded and the grades posted.

August and Ellis went together to the main bulletin board in the Philosophy Building. August hung back, afraid to look at the board, but Ellis went straight up and looked at it for a long time, hunting for his grade in each subject. Then he turned away with an explosion.

"Good God from Goldsboro! Jee-zus!"

"What is it?" August could hardly speak.

"I failed two, got two D's, and only made one C. Ah, Christ, I'll be sent home for sure and my old man will kill me."

August felt sick. If Ellis had failed . . . Quickly his eye went down the columns of grades. And only after seeing the last grade did he relax and lean against the board. He had passed everything. Not brilliantly, but he had passed. There were two B's, two C's, and two D's. He grinned broadly, but then felt he had no right to feel so good when Ellis was so miserable.

"Oh, God, God, God," Ellis was saying. "I'll be leaving the same time you do, and I wish money were the reason. Boy, what I wouldn't give to change places with you."

But August was thinking: Take one giant step forward, then return to the point of beginning.

That night he went to the Bryants'. He had put off telling Professor Bryant until after the exams, but now it had to be done. He could have told him in the classroom, but since Mrs. Bryant had been so nice to him, he thought he should tell them together.

As he listened to the bell jangle inside he thought, This will be the last time. For the next two days, the days he would spend packing and getting ready to leave, there would be many "last times."

Professor Bryant came to the door. "Good evening, Mr. Fielding. Come on in."

August was still not sure when he was "Mr. Fielding" and when he was "August" to Professor Bryant, but, too late now, he was beginning to see a pattern. "I hope I'm not interrupting your supper," he said.

"No, we've finished. Would you like to go up to my study?"

"I wanted to see both you and Mrs. Bryant."

The professor nodded and ushered him into the living room. "Angela," he called, "we have a guest."

Mrs. Bryant came in immediately. "August, how nice to see you. You've been neglecting us lately."

"I didn't mean to." August began an apology, then realized she was probably only being polite. "I was busy with exams."

"Of course. Sit down. Did you have a good holiday at Christmas?"

"I missed Brandon," he said. "The fact is, I've come to say good-bye to you both and to thank you for being so kind to me."

"Good-bye!" For once, Professor Bryant's face showed plainly what he felt, and that was shock. "I don't understand."

"I'm leaving Brandon," August said. "There—there isn't enough money for me to finish my education, so I'm leaving now."

"Has something happened?" Mrs. Bryant asked. "Have you had trouble of some kind?"

"No, ma'am. The fact is, there never was enough money, but I didn't know it until I went home for Christmas, I could stay on until the end of the year, but there doesn't seem to be much point in it."

Professor Bryant was quiet. He looked at August as though he still did not understand what it was all about.

"But you should stay on and finish out the year," Mrs. Bryant said. "Then maybe you can come back later . . ."

August shook his head. "I don't think there'll ever be enough money," he said. "I guess you can't pay for an education by farming." He looked at the professor, still waiting for him to say something.

Finally, he spoke. "You say you have enough to finish this year?"

"Yes, sir."

"How were your grades for the term, August?"

"I passed everything. And I want to thank you for the B, sir."

Professor Bryant waved the remark aside. "Don't thank me, you deserved it. Have you thought of applying for one of the Lea scholarships? If you get one, you can have your tuition paid for the next three years, and you'd be given up to ten years after graduation to repay the loan."

"I wouldn't be eligible," August said. "My grades—"

"You don't have to have superlative grades to get a Lea scholarship," Professor Bryant said. "You only have to maintain a C average. The scholarship was set up for students who deserve it financially. If you'd like to apply for one, I'd be glad to recommend you."

For a moment August felt like standing up and shouting with joy. Then he said, "I appreciate that, sir, but I'm afraid it wouldn't be enough. I'd still have to pay for room and board and books and . . . and I couldn't manage even that."

Mrs. Bryant had been watching him thoughtfully. Now she clapped her hands like a child. "I know," she said. "You can stay here. We need someone to do things like taking care of the stoves, seeing the coal is brought in, taking care of the yard. You could do that, August, and it wouldn't take much of your time. And in return there's an extra room in the basement that we could fix up for you."

Overjoyed again, August looked at Professor Bryant for confirmation of this arrangement. The professor said nothing.

"And as for your meals—you eat at Mrs. Larkins', don't you? Doesn't she still use students to wait on the tables?"

"Yes, ma'am."

"Well, I'm sure if you spoke to her now—told her you would like to start next fall—she'd be delighted."

It was too good to be true. Tuition, room, and board—if he got the scholarship, and he was sure that a recommendation from Professor Bryant was tantamount to getting it. It seemed so easy now, and all his worrying had been for nothing. There would be no "last times" after all.

"I think," Professor Bryant said quietly, "that you may be rushing August into plans before he has had a chance to think them over."

"I only wish I had talked to you sooner," August said.

"Yes—well." The professor went to the mantel and selected a pipe from the rack there. "I'll speak to the scholarship committee tomorrow. They may want an interview."

"Don't I have to do anything to get the money?"

"Only sign a paper agreeing to repay the committee within ten years."

Ten years was forever. "I'll be glad enough to do that," he said. Then he hesitated. Professor Bryant had still said nothing about the room arrangement, and he wanted to know what his silence meant. "About my rooming here, sir—"

"Oh, don't say you can't, August," said Mrs. Bryant. "We need someone to help out, and—"

"I don't want to put you out any." He looked straight at the professor, almost demanding an answer.

"Yes, August," he said. "You may stay here if you like. But if you find something that would suit you better before next fall, we'll understand."

"I'm sure I won't sir," he said enthusiastically. "This is just perfect. I don't know how to thank you. Both of you."

"Yes—well." Professor Bryant replaced the pipe without lighting it. He seemed to have a lot on his mind, and so August did not prolong the visit.

He ran all the way back to the campus, his feet having difficulty keeping up with his quick, happy thoughts. He was going to stay! He was going to finish! He was going to be a preacher! And he owed it all—his whole life—to the Bryants.

Just before reaching his room he remembered Ellis and *his* dilemma. He slowed his steps and put on what he hoped was a properly solemn expression.

But when he opened the door, he was greeted with a rousing "Hey, preacher, where have you been?" Ellis was lying flat on the bed with his feet propped up on the wall. He swung his legs around and sat up. "Come listen to the glad tidings."

August waited by the door wondering if Ellis's bad news had caused him to take leave of his senses.

"I ain't gonna leave no more, no more; I ain't gonna leave no more," Ellis sang. "You know what, August? I saw my faculty adviser tonight and he said I won't be sent home for failing, that I can stay on if my grades show an improvement this term. But," and now Ellis appeared a bit crestfallen, "he also said I'd have to have a C average for the *whole year* by the end of the next term or I won't be able to come back. That means I'll practically have to make all A's."

"That's good, Ellis. I'm glad it worked out for you. I saw my faculty adviser tonight, too, and I don't think I have to leave either."

"You mean he gave you money?"

"No, but he thinks I have a chance of getting a scholarship that will take care of the tuition."

Ellis stood up and did a clog dance. "Boy, we got to celebrate. We got to celebrate this night. Let's go downtown and have a soda."

August stuck his hand in his pocket and rubbed two dimes together. They were all that was left of the spending money he had allowed for January, but suddenly he felt very rich. "Let's go," he said. "We'll flip to see who buys."

Even though August had been almost sure he would get a scholarship with Professor Bryant's recommendation, there was still that small area of his mind that refused to believe anything so good could actually happen to him. Therefore, it was with a mixture of surprise and expectancy that he listened as Professor Bryant told him he had been approved by the committee and that beginning with the fall term he would receive a total of four hundred dollars a year for the next three years.

"I'll pay it back," he said fervently, "every penny of it—if it takes the rest of my life."

"You'd better see that it doesn't take but ten years of your life," Professor Bryant said.

The next two months were cold and gloomy, and August had no trouble settling back into his routine of study. There were few distractions, not even from Ellis. Fears of his father's wrath had inspired Ellis to become, if not a scholar, at least a student.

Spring did not touch Brandon until well into April, and by the time the trees began to bud, August discovered that he was very tired. Not tired in a physical sense, but mentally restless, as though he was waiting for something to happen, something that would break the routine of the past few months.

It was almost the way it had been back on the farm—waiting for the first sign of spring so that the early planting could get under way. And when spring finally came, he found that for the first time he was a little homesick. He pictured Gervas, rising early and hitching the mule to a plow, out working in the earth, shouting across the field to Ben who would also be behind a plow. Sitting in his classes, August sometimes caught himself looking longingly out the window. For one who had spent so many months indoors, there was much to be said for breaking new ground, watching a new crop rise and struggle through torrential spring rains and parching summer droughts and live.

He wondered if the professors at Brandon felt the same about the new crop of students every year. Did they derive the same satisfaction from watching the boys come in, helping them through the four years until harvest, and seeing the men go out?

At what age, he thought, does a person reach maturity? In six months he would be twenty-one years old, and yet he felt no older and no wiser than he had at fifteen. Although he made an effort to seem mature, he was never without the feeling that he was only trying to fool others into believing he was.

These were the things that occupied his mind as he tried to focus his attention on a lecture or as he sat on the stone bench in front of the chapel or as he walked around the town looking absently at the tiny buds appearing on the trees.

It was on an afternoon in late April, on his way back to the campus from the soda shop, that he saw Mrs. Bryant. She came out of a grocery store, a bundle under each arm, and hurried past him, then turned and smiled. "August! I haven't seen you for such a long time that I almost didn't recognize you. Where have you been keeping yourself, and why haven't you been to see us?"

"How are you, ma'am? I've meant to come, but I've been busy studying. May I take your packages for you?"

She gave them to him. "The buggy is right over here. Just put them in the back and—are you busy right now?"

"No, ma'am. I was just going back to the campus."

"If you're in a hurry I'll drop you off there, but I thought perhaps you'd like to see your room." She climbed into the buggy and picked up the reins while the black gelding stirred restlessly. "I have it all fixed up now and I'd like to get your approval."

"That's mighty nice, Mrs. Bryant. I'd like to see it." He got in beside her and watched as she adeptly pulled the horse around and maneuvered the buggy from the hitching area to the street. She was wearing a bright blue silk dress—she always seemed to wear vivid colors—and a matching blue ribbon was tied, little-girl style, around her honey-blond hair. She was probably very pretty years ago, August thought. Now her whole face was dominated by the mole under her left eye. Perhaps no one but him particularly noticed the mole. He was, he thought, peculiarly sensitive to defects.

She took the small whip from the stand beside her and cracked it over the horse's back. August wondered why she was in such a hurry. He would have enjoyed riding around Brandon in the warm afternoon sunshine.

When they reached the house, she hopped out of the buggy almost before it had stopped, and tied the reins over the hitching post. "Eugene can put Socrates away when he comes," she said.

"Socrates?"

"Yes," she said, patting the horse on the flank as she passed. "Because he's always turning around and looking at me as though he would start an argument if he could."

August laughed and followed her into the house. "I think Professor Bryant would say that description fit Xanthippe better."

"Wrong gender," she said. "Would you like a cup of tea?"

"No, thank you. I can't stay long. I have a Latin test tomorrow."

She patted his hand in much the same way she had patted Socrates' flank. "Always thinking about your work, aren't you? You're so conscientious, August. Well, come along, I'll show you your room."

She opened the door behind the hall stairway and led him down the dark narrow steps to the basement. At the foot of the stairs she opened another door. "Here it is," she said. "I haven't put up any curtains yet. I thought I'd wait until just before you come."

The room was quite small, and in spite of a tiny window near the ceiling which opened on the ground, there was not much light. On one side of the room was a large brass bed and beside the bed was a leather chair, companion to the one in Professor Bryant's tower room. In a corner under the window was a small table which could be used as a desk, and in another corner a huge chiffonier with a cracked mirror above it. The large pieces of furniture made the room look even smaller than it was.

"The furniture is some we had right after we were first married," she said, apparently reading his thoughts. "I had it moved down from the storage room upstairs. It isn't very elegant, but perhaps you won't mind."

"No, ma'am. It's very nice," he said. "And I want to thank you again for letting me come here. If it hadn't been for you and Professor Bryant—"

"Now, August," she said. "You'll be doing us a favor, you know. And it will be good for me to have someone in the house I can talk to occasionally. Eugene stays over at the college all day and shut up with his books all night. Sometimes it gets so lonely around here. So very lonely." She was standing in the center of the room, looking up toward the light from the window. "It will be good to have you here."

"It's mighty nice, Mrs. Bryant."

She did not move for a long time, and when she finally turned around, her eyes were misty. "August, I wish you'd call me Angela. 'Mrs. Bryant' is so cold and formal."

"Yes, ma'am, but I don't think I could . . ."

She sighed. "I get so lonely that sometimes I think it would be a singular blessing just to hear someone call my name."

She sat down on the coarse mattress cover on the bed and gave him a faint smile. "You're nice, August. Such a nice young man."

"Thank you," he said uncomfortably. "I expect I'd better get back now. There's a Latin—"

"I wanted to ask you," she said, "do you want another chair in here? Another big chair, I mean. I could have one brought down."

"No, ma'am, it's just fine as it is."

She was looking straight at him, and he felt red color creeping over his face because suddenly, for no reason at all, he was thinking about the way she had looked in the filmy pink wrapper the night she had served him hot chocolate.

"August, sit down a minute. Just a minute." She looked up and her eyes showed the same frightening loneliness he had seen in Gervas's eyes the day he first came to Brandon. It was a loneliness without hope, hideous and endless.

He sat down. "I shouldn't stay," he said. "I have a test."

"We all have tests, August. One kind or another every day." The tears were flowing freely down her face now.

He thought about her dead daughter. Professor Bryant was right; she had not recovered from the shock yet. He wanted very much to say something to her, but any words he could think of seemed completely inadequate.

"Please talk to me, August. Just talk to me."

He started to say something, but she was looking at him as though he weren't there and she continued talking as though she were talking to herself. "I need people," she said. "I need to be needed. Oh, God, how I need someone who needs me. No one ever has, not in my whole life. Eugene's completely self-sufficient; he doesn't need another soul in that world of his—and he won't even let another soul in that world." Her eyes were suddenly focusing on him again. "Are you self-sufficient, August? Have you locked yourself up inside yourself so the world can't get in and you can't get out?"

He sat there, frozen in an agony of embarrassment. She put her hand to his hair, and before he could answer she pulled his head down and kissed him, moistly, full on the lips.

"Oh, God, August, kiss me." She clung to him like a child, holding him around the knees as he stood up suddenly.

"Don't leave me now. You don't know how it is, you couldn't know. Please, August, just kiss me once."

He could not move without kicking her away, and he could no sooner kick her away than he could a whimpering puppy. He sat down on the bed and she released his knees and took his face in both her hands, pulling him nearer. And then for one wild minute he expected to hear her laughter, derisive laughter, and her voice saying, "Oh, August, you're so *funny-looking*." But she did not laugh. Her face was grave, still marked by grief and loneliness. She did not laugh at him. He put his arms around her and bent over her slowly, slowly until their mouths touched, and then she pulled him urgently, opening her mouth under his as though to devour him. The brown mole under her left eye seemed almost to be moving, and he closed his eyes quickly, trying not to see it.

He pulled away from her quickly, gasping for breath, and moved farther down on the bed. She let him go. "Please, August," she whispered.

"I can't," he said. "Please, ma'am, I just can't."

"Can't you just call me Angela? Can't you even say my name?" Then she began crying again, with great heaving sobs, as though she would never stop. Her hands covered her face.

He knelt beside the bed and patted her shoulder. "Please don't," he said. "Don't cry, Angela. It's all right now." It was like trying to quiet a small child.

Slowly, she took her hands away from her face and held out her arms to him. He sat on the bed again, letting her cling to him, and then her arms tightened about him and her hands caressed him as though he were the one to be comforted.

Then her hand found him. "Please, August, please." She pulled at her skirt until it was out of the way. "Please, August. Here, I'll show you. Let me help you. Oh, please, please, please."

But she did not have to help him.

He lay beside her, spent, his mind curiously blank, thinking only, What will I think when I think again? He raised up on his elbow and looked at her face, at peace now. But the mole was still there, the big brown mole under her left eye.

"Oh, my God!" He got up quickly, almost falling over the chair.

"August." She sat up. "August, stay with me."

But now he could not look at her. He turned around and saw instead his own distorted image in the cracked mirror above the chiffonier. "Oh, my God!"

He ran from the room without looking back and stumbled up the dark stairs to the floor above and then out the front door, letting the screen door bang shut behind him. Outside he stopped, imagining that he heard her calling him, but then he hurried to the end of the walk where Socrates waited patiently beside the hitching post. The horse looked at him, almost questioningly he thought, as he ran past him to the street.

Once in the street he stopped running. It was almost dark, and the pale green of the new leaves looked a darker green in the dying light. He walked up Faculty Avenue toward the campus, still not daring to think, to remember.

It was at the first corner that he saw him coming. Professor Eugene Bryant, one arm curved around some books, the other swinging loosely with his stride, was going home.

No! August breathed, no! He crossed the street, walking at a normal pace so he would not be conspicuous, and from the other side he watched the professor. At that moment Eugene Bryant seemed to him the epitome of all that was good in the world. He walked, August thought, as though he was in pursuit of truth and virtue and goodness, as though, momentarily, he expected to catch up with them.

He stopped and looked at the horse and buggy by the hitching post. "How long have you been standing here, old fellow?" August heard him say. Then he untied the reins and led Socrates behind the house.

August moved on, past the big white houses to the stone wall. He sat down on the wall and stared into the gray light of dusk until it became black, until the blackness enveloped him. And all the while, his mind could only repeat the phrase he had uttered in horror: Oh, my God, Oh, my God. Then, slowly, he got up and walked again, all the way around the stone wall encircling the campus, until he came back to where he had started. Take one giant step . . .

But there was no way to go back now—not all the way back to the point of beginning. He looked down to the first curve in the wall where the arch stood like a black sentinel, and he tried to imagine that he could read the words on the arch from where he was. *Pro Humanitate*. And he tried to remember the feeling he had had that first day when he had driven the team and wagon through the arch. But he could not remember. He could see only Professor Bryant, gently leading his horse back to the stable to put him away for the night.

Again he left the wall, this time walking through the campus. Several times he stumbled because he was not watching the uneven stepping stones. When he reached the chapel, he looked up, but there was no moon tonight. The spire was there, he knew, up beyond the sheltering tree branches with their new leaves, up beyond the trees themselves, hidden by the black night, lost to him.

He went to his room and prepared for bed, trying not to awaken Ellis. And trying not to touch his body as he undressed.

When he was in bed, he closed his eyes tightly and tried to pray, but no words would come. There was nothing, nothing in the whole world that he could say to his God now.

He burrowed deeper under the cover, balled up his fists and held them against his eyes. Oh, my God, oh, my God!

And then his hands relaxed, fell slack across his face, and he wept. Wept for Professor Bryant, the gentle man who had befriended him, wept for himself because he knew he would never again feel the way about himself he had before this afternoon, and, finally, wept for Angela.

6

TWO WEEKS AFTER IT HAPPENED Ellis said, "August, what in the Sam Hill is wrong with you? You've been creeping around here like a spook."

They were on their way back to the dormitory from Mrs. Larkins' boardinghouse. When August did not reply, Ellis continued, "If you've been carrying on any conversations, they've all been with yourself because you certainly haven't said two consecutive words to anyone else lately. It's getting so my Greek book is better company. And speaking of books, I suppose you know that final examinations begin next week?"

"I know," August said.

"You think maybe you'll spend a few minutes studying? You haven't exactly hurt yourself lately."

"I'm going to the library now," August said, turning down the path that led to the center building. "I may be late getting in."

He entered the library and sat at one of the tables in the main reading room, but he did not open the philosophy book he had with him. Ellis was right, he knew. He had been shamefully neglecting his studies. And Ellis, unknowingly, was right about something else. He had been carrying on many conversations with himself.

Shamefully neglecting . . . Shame. No matter where his thoughts went, they always ended with the same word. He wondered if it was possible to learn to live with shame. Only if reparation could be made. If you stole money and later confessed and paid it back, it might be possible to live with the knowledge that you had stolen. If you cheated on an examination and then told the professor and accepted a failing grade, you might be able to stand the thought that you had cheated. But he could not confess, could not make reparation without hurting others and thus compounding his sin.

His mind went back to that first morning in class, the first morning after it happened. Professor Bryant had walked into the room, laid his books on the desk, and then pulled his chair around to the front of the desk and sat down.

"I think," he said, "that instead of discussing today's assignment, we will read together Plato's dialogue on the nature of virtue, *Meno*. Mr. Wiley, you will read the part of Menon, and Mr. Fielding, you will be Socrates."

August looked closely at the professor's face, trying to read it. Was it possible that Professor Bryant knew? Automatically, he reached out for the book that the professor gave him.

Wiley began to read. "Can you tell me, Socrates—can virtue be taught? Or if not, does it come by practice? Or does it come neither by practice nor by teaching, but do people get it by nature, or in some other way?"

August, in panic, began reading the words of Socrates mechanically, trying not to listen to his own voice. ". . . So far from knowing whether it can be taught or can't be taught, I don't know even the least little thing about virtue, I don't even know what virtue is . . . and when I don't know what a thing is, how can I know its quality?"

He read on, the words taking on two meanings for him, both excruciating.

Socrates: ". . . But some men desire bad things?"

Menon: "Yes."

Socrates: "Thinking the bad things to be good, you mean, or even recognizing that they are bad, still they desire them?"

Menon: "Both, I think."

Socrates: "Do you really think, my dear Menon, that anyone, knowing the bad things to be bad, still desires them?"

Menon: "Certainly."

On and on he read, and with each sentence he read his own condemnation, and with each sentence he thought: He knows.

The hour and the dialogue seemed interminable, and August read Socrates' closing words almost without realizing that he had reached the end. "Then from this our reasoning, Menon, virtue is shown as coming to us, whenever it comes, by divine dispensation; but we shall only know the truth about this clearly when, before inquiring in what way virtue comes to mankind, we first try to search out what virtue is in itself."

Professor Bryant closed the book in which he was following the reading. He took off his thick glasses and cleaned them with his handkerchief, then put the glasses on and replaced the handkerchief in his pocket with slow deliberateness. "You will have quite enough to study," he said to the class, "if you spend your time before we meet again thinking about what you have heard today." Then he left the room.

In bed that night August tried again to pray. This time he began by praying for others—for the whole world, for Brandon College, for Gervas, for Ben and Rosemary, for Ellis, for Professor and Mrs. Bryant, then, finally, like a small postscript in place of "Amen" he said, "Forgive me."

He tried to turn off his night thoughts and go to sleep, but his mind was too crowded. He would come back to Brandon in the fall and go on with his studies. He would take advan-

tage of the scholarship money and prepare himself to be a
preacher, and for the rest of his life, while preaching to a congregation or walking down a street or dressing or undressing
or reading a book, he would go on saying constantly, "Forgive me."

But he knew that when the fall term began, he could not
go to the Bryants' to live. There was no other place; he had
no excuse to offer Professor Bryant, and it was too late now
to announce a change of plans, especially when there were
no other plans. But he *could not* go back to that room.

August had his last examination on the twenty-ninth of
May; on the thirteenth he left Brandon without waiting to see
his grades posted. The grades would be sent to him later, and
he was eager, as he thought of it, to get back to the earth
again, to look down long furrows and see the cotton plants
break through the ground. He realized that his newly ac-
quired interest in watching the crop had no connection with
a love for farming; he merely wanted to get away from Brandon.

And yet as soon as he returned to the quietness of Pine
View Community, he knew that he was homesick for Brandon.

His last week at the college had been a frantic one. There
had been an examination every day, and since he had spent
so little time beforehand preparing for them, he had stayed
up far into the night before each examination, forcing himself
to stay awake, forcing himself to learn. The examination in
moral philosophy had been the last one, and as he turned in
his paper to Professor Bryant, he paused beside the desk.

"I am leaving tomorrow," he whispered, in order not to
disturb those students who had not yet finished. "I want to
say good-bye, sir, and to thank you again for all you have
done for me this year."

The professor stood up and extended his hand. "I hope you
will have a good summer, Mr. Fielding. Mrs. Bryant and I
shall be expecting you in the fall."

August lowered his eyes. "Please give my regards to Mrs.
Bryant, sir. I hope you both will have a pleasant summer."
And he bolted from the room.

Saying good-bye to Ellis had been almost as difficult.
Timidly he had held out his hand. "It's been fine rooming
with you, Ellis."

"Look, preacher," Ellis said. "I've sort of gotten used to you and I don't want to room with anybody else. I've got a room at Mrs. Barry's for next year, and I told her I was expecting a roommate and not to let anybody else move in with me. So if you change your mind . . ."

"You know I'd like nothing better. But . . ." And there he left it. At Mrs. Barry's he would have to pay ten dollars a month for a room and that was out of the question.

Gervas met him at the Pine View station with the wagon. As soon as he got off the train he found himself remembering, with a sinking feeling, the long silences, the awkward hours, of his Christmas vacation. But as they drove from the station to the farm, Gervas was more talkative. He seemed to be making polite conversation with August, as though he were a stranger who had come to visit.

"Well, it's good to have you home again," he said. "Ben has been asking when you'd get here."

"It's good to be back," August said, and then, carefully, "Did you get my letter about the scholarship?"

"I got it," Gervas said. "Does that mean you'll get to finish college?"

"Yes, I'll be going back in September."

"I'm glad it worked out that way," Gervas said, "if that's what you want. You know, August, you may amount to something. Something more than if you stayed on the farm."

August thought he detected a certain amount of pride in Gervas's remark. Certainly he seemed finally to be reconciled to the fact that August had left the farm for good. For this, August felt relief and gratitude.

"Ben doing all right?" he asked quickly.

"Yep, he's a natural-born farmer, Ben is. Don't know how I'd get along without him." Then, as though afraid he had said something wrong, "But I reckon I could. He said he'd be over tonight to speak to you."

Ben came that night after supper. At first he seemed quiet, almost shy, and August realized that he had attained a new status in Ben's eyes.

"You really like it over there at Brandon?" Ben asked.

"More than like it, Ben. It's not like anything I've ever known before." He realized he could not explain his new life to Ben, for Ben would think he was putting on airs. "How're your mother and Rosemary?"

"They're doing along," Ben said. "Rosemary said she wanted to see you. I told her you'd more than likely be at church Sunday."

"More than likely," August said. He saw again Rosemary's face close to his own and heard her laugh. And then he saw that other face, close to his own, and the brown mole coming nearer, nearer.

He looked out across the road that went by the house. Would he ever stop thinking about it? Would there ever be a morning when he could get up and go through the entire day without once thinking about it? For a few minutes when he and Ben first sat down on the porch it had been like the days before he went to Brandon. It was hard to believe that he had ever left home. But then pictures of the past nine months went through his mind like those on a stereopticon, and he knew only too well that he had been away.

"You know, August, I always hoped that maybe you and Rosemary . . ." Ben left the sentence unfinished.

"Is Rosemary going with anybody?"

"Nobody in particular. I think Ma worries about it some."

"She's only nineteen," August said.

"Most of the girls her age are already married."

Again August wanted to change the subject, but he didn't know how without doing it abruptly, so he remained quiet.

"Would you like to call on Rosemary, August? I don't think she'd object if you did."

"I don't know, Ben. She might get the wrong idea if I did. You see, I've still got three more years of college and then seminary, if I can manage it."

"Well, I just thought I'd ask. You don't mind my asking, do you, August?"

"No, I don't mind. But the fact is, Ben, I don't think Rosemary would be much interested if I called on her. I don't think she likes me very much."

"I think you're mistaken, August. She's always liked you."

Now August did change the subject, and abruptly. "You've sure been a big help to Pa this year. He said he didn't know what he'd have done without you, and I want you to know how much I appreciate it."

Ben dismissed the compliment with a wave of his hand. "It ain't like he didn't pay me, August. You know that. And besides, this farm is like my own. Sometimes it's hard for me to remember that it ain't my own." They were off then on a discussion of the farm and the crops, and August relaxed. In a few minutes Gervas joined them, and once again August had the feeling that he had never been away.

After the first few days at home, the rest of the summer stretched before him endlessly. He tried to fill his spare time by reading, and he borrowed book after book from the inadequate Pine View school library. But there was still so much time to think—long, lonely hours when he tried to control his thoughts and then, finally, let them go where they would.

Somehow the long days of June passed and then the dry days of July. He went to church each Sunday and listened to Brother Johnson, and each Sunday night after church he walked Rosemary home, not because he wanted to but because he thought Ben expected it of him.

The month of August was even hotter and drier than July had been. The earth was hard and parched, and although Gervas remarked that this kind of weather wouldn't hurt the cotton crop, might even be good for it, August could not imagine how it could be good for anything but lethargy. He spent more time sitting under the big maple tree in the yard with a book, and finally, when the heat reached what appeared to be maximum intensity, he even gave up trying to read.

"I think those people at the college have softened you up," Gervas said when August complained of the heat, but there was no malice in his voice.

It was during the second week of August that the weather and everything else became secondary in his thoughts.

He was returning from the store in the late afternoon with the week's supply of groceries, walking slowly because he did not want to stir up any more dust than necessary. As he reached the edge of Gervas's property, he saw Ben running across the field.

"August, August!" He waved his arm frantically. "Come quick," he yelled. "It's your pa."

August was panting when he reached Ben.

"He's over there," Ben said and pointed to the long rows of cotton. "I was on the other side of the field and I saw him fall. I waited a minute, but he didn't get up. I tried to move him, but I couldn't manage by myself. He must of took sick and passed out."

August, running, scarcely heard the last words.

Gervas was lying face down between the furrows, his head elevated slightly on a small mound of hard, baked earth.

"Pa." August knelt beside him and turned him on his back. Then he stared into the distorted face. The mouth hung open loosely and the eyes, also open, were rolled back. Plastered against the sweat on his forehead were tiny bits of grit and dust from the mound where his head rested. The dirt had made a weird design on his face, not unlike the outline of a fish.

"My God, August, he's gone!"

"No, he's not, Ben. He can't be," August said quickly, knowing even as he said it that Gervas was dead.

"Pa, can you hear me? Pa!" He took out his handkerchief and gently wiped the dirt from Gervas's forehead; then he sat down and looked again into the face of death.

"August, there ain't nothing we can do," Ben said, kneeling beside him. "He's gone."

August looked away, down the long row of cotton now in full bloom. Next week they would start picking it, pulling the soft bolls away from the prickly green leaves. It was a middling-good crop, Gervas had said last night. Not as good as last year's, but better than some he'd seen.

"August . . . You hear what I'm saying, August? We better get him in the house."

Slowly, August stood up. "I'll do it myself, Ben. I want to take him home." Ben helped him raise the body of Gervas to his shoulders and followed him back to the house, where he laid Gervas gently on the bed.

I wonder, August thought in that rational way one thinks just before the full impact of a blow renders all irrational, I wonder what we're supposed to do now.

"August, do you want me to go for Brother Johnson? And I could stop by my house on the way and tell Ma to come over here."

"I'd be much obliged if you would, Ben."

Ben, obviously relieved at being able to spring into action, left quickly, and August sat down beside the bed to wait. Wait for the neighbors to come in and take over the ministrations of death as they had done when his mother died. A sea of tearful faces would hover about him; muted voices, which had once spoken in hushed tones of Caroline, would now speak of Gervas. August could hear them as clearly as though they had already crept into the room: "He was a good man, August. Your pa was a good man." "Gervas Fielding never done a wrong thing in his life." "He was a hard worker, your pa. Sunup to sundown." "He was a good man, even if he didn't hold much with churches."

August put his head down on the bed and tried to cry, as he had tried to pray.

The service in the Pine View church lasted for nearly three hours. It was as though Brother Johnson, once he got Gervas back in the church, was making the best of it. August sat unhearing, his only thought being, Pa would have hated this. August had suggested just having a prayer spoken over the grave, but Brother Johnson had merely looked at him as though he understood well a time of grief when the mind does not function normally.

"No, August," he said, as though explaining to a child, "it just wouldn't do. I know Brother Gervas wasn't what you could call a regular churchgoer in his last years, but he wasn't one for defying God either. And not to have a service for him would be defiance. It wouldn't even be Christian, and I'd be surprised at you, a man of God yourself, proposing such a thing, but I understand—you're just not yourself right now."

After the service, Mrs. Tippett came up to him. "August, we'd be pleased to have you go home and eat supper with us. And spend the night if you want to. I know going home to an empty house ain't worth much."

Rosemary picked her way across the graves beside the Fielding plot. "Yes, come with us, August."

"Thank you, but I reckon I'd better get on home," he said. "There's so much food in the house now I doubt if it will ever get eaten. You were all mighty nice to bring in so much."

"Well, if you won't come, we'll possibly be over to your place later tonight," Mrs. Tippett said. "It ain't good for you to be by yourself now, August."

August, who wanted nothing more than to be by himself, said, "I don't want you to put yourself out any. I'll manage."

Mrs. Tippett gave him a weak smile and moved on as other neighbors crowded about August.

That night he heard the inevitable knock at the front door and was relieved to find only Ben standing on the porch, still dressed in his funeral suit and looking uncomfortable. It seemed strange to see him there; he usually came in the back door without knocking, like one of the family.

"Come on in, Ben," August said, trying to put him at ease. It seemed that for the past two days he had done little more than try to put others at ease, to cover their embarrassment at his grief.

Ben started toward the parlor when the straight-backed chairs were still arranged in a circle to accommodate callers, but August said, "Come on back to the kitchen. I'm not quite through cleaning up."

"I'll help you," Ben said eagerly. August started to refuse, then saw that Ben would feel better if he thought he was being of service.

"I'm trying to find a place to put all this food so it won't spoil," August said when they were in the kitchen. "There isn't enough room in the icebox. Would you mind washing those dishes for me? There aren't many."

Ben nodded and set to work. "August, I guess you won't be able to go back to college now, will you? I mean, there ain't nobody to look after the farm now."

August stopped in the center of the room, holding a platter of fried chicken in his hands. "I've thought of that," he said, not admitting that he had thought of little else since early this morning when it had occurred to him that his future, once more, would have to be rearranged. The past year had been like an obstacle course, and Gervas, who had not wanted August to go to college, had by his death placed the final obstacle in his path.

"Ben," he said, "do you think maybe I could rent the farm out?"

"Get a tenant, you mean?"

"Something like that," he said. "Only I would want someone who would rent the house, too. If I do go back to college, I won't be needing the house and I'd like to know someone was living in it."

Ben was quiet for a long time, then he said, "August, if you don't think you'd ever want to come back here to live, would you consider selling the farm—to me?"

August looked at him in surprise. "You want to buy it, Ben?"

"Sarah and I are thinking about getting married this fall,"

he said. "Only thing is, Sarah don't much want to move in with Ma and Rosemary. She wants us to have a place of our own. I don't know how much you'd want for this place, August, and I couldn't pay you no big amount all at once, but maybe if you'd let me pay you a little bit at a time, when the crops come in . . ."

August didn't answer immediately, so Ben went on, "I've been working this farm ever since I was a kid and it's always been like home to me. And I think Sarah'd like living here."

August turned his back so Ben could not see his face. "It's the answer to everything, Ben. Of course you can buy the farm—and pay for it a little at a time. I think Pa'd rather you have it than anybody in the world."

"Except you," Ben said.

"Yes, but he knew I was no farmer, and you know, I think he finally got so he didn't mind too much."

"He was proud of the way you made good over at Brandon," Ben said. "He talked about it a lot."

"I wish he had told me," August said.

"He told me. Sometimes when I'd come over here to sit a spell at night he'd say, 'Got a letter from August today, Ben, and . . .'" Ben stopped, and August knew the conversation was becoming awkward for him. "Look, August," he said, "I've got pretty near a thousand dollars. I've been saving up all my life for something—I wasn't sure what at the time— but if you'd take that as a beginning, I can pay you some more, maybe next year."

"That will be fine, Ben. I'm not even sure what the farm is worth. I'll have to ask around, and we can go over to the courthouse and sign the papers, or do whatever has to be done."

Ben hung the dish towel beside the pan. "Lord, August, I never thought I'd end up owning this place. It's almost like I was making hay out of your bad luck."

And me? August thought. I can pay for my tuition, without borrowing from the scholarship fund. And I can room with Ellis at Mrs. Barry's . . . "It's not that way at all," he said. "You're helping me, Ben. You just don't know how much."

Later that night, after Ben had gone, August sat alone on the porch, once again conscious of the oppressive heat. He looked out over the front yard and was suddenly very tired. He knew what it was like now, in reality rather than imagination, to sit alone on the porch and hear only silence and expect only silence. For those few minutes he felt that he was Gervas and that August was a stranger who had gone away.

7

YEARS LATER WHEN HE THOUGHT about his student days at Brandon, there was no clear memory of those last three years. Except for certain isolated incidents, he could not have said with certainty that such and such a thing happened during his sophomore or junior or senior year. He had no difficulty remembering any part of that first year, even though there were parts that he tried desperately to forget, but there was a sameness to the last three, a repetition of pattern which caused them to blur and run together on the screen of his memory like raindrops merging on a windowpane.

But there were incidents he could place in the correct year and season, like his first meeting with Professor Bryant. He had left his suitcases at Mrs. Barry's as soon as he arrived and had immediately gone to the campus to find the professor. He found him, as he had the year before, seated at a table in the library, waiting to talk to the incoming freshmen.

"August, it's good to see you. We've been wondering when you would arrive."

August shook his hand. "It's good to be back, sir. Do you have a minute?"

"Sit down. Sit down. How was your summer?"

"I meant to write to you, Professor, but—well, there just hasn't been much time lately. My father died two weeks ago and . . ."

"I'm sorry to hear that, August. Was he ill long?"

"No, sir. It was quite sudden. He wasn't sick at all—at least, if he was, he never mentioned it. He just—died one afternoon while he was out in the field." He paused and

Professor Bryant nodded. Thank God, August thought, he hadn't said, "Well, my boy, it's better that way—better to go quickly," or, as Brother Johnson had said, "It's the Lord's will, August, and we can't question that." Whatever his philosophy about death, he kept it to himself and August was grateful.

"You see, sir," he said, "after Pa died, I changed my plans somewhat. I've sold the farm to a neighbor and now I won't have to borrow from the scholarship fund. I can pay my own way."

"That's fine, August. When you finish here, you can start your career with a clean slate, without having to worry about repaying a debt."

"Yes, sir. And I made another change in my plans." Telling him this would be more difficult. "I have decided to room with my former roommate at Mrs. Barry's. I want you to know how much I appreciate you and Mrs. Bryant offering me a room but—well, I'd like to room with Ellis again and now it's possible. Will you tell Mrs. Bryant for me?"

"Yes, I'll tell her. I think this will be a much better arrangement, in any case. You'll enjoy it more, being with someone your own age."

So telling Professor Bryant had not proved to be difficult after all. For a minute he had even thought the professor seemed relieved.

Three weeks after his return, he met Angela Bryant unexpectedly on the steps of the Brandon post office.

"Why, August! Hello."

He could feel his color changing as the blood rushed to his head. "How are you, Mrs. Bryant?"

"Quite well, thank you. Eugene told me about your father's death. I'm sorry."

August tried to hide his discomfort. "Thank you for your sympathy. I . . ." What in the name of heaven could he say to this woman with whom he had spent that afternoon in the room with the cracked mirror?

"Wonderful fall weather, isn't it?" She gestured about her as though pointing to something tangible. "Brandon is beginning to get beautiful. By the way, we'll be starting our Sunday afternoon tea parties soon, and we'd like to have you come as often as you like."

"I'll look forward to it," he said formally.

She went down the steps, then looked back and said, like a little girl remembering that her mother told her to "make her manners" before leaving, "Nice to see you again."

He stood where he was for several minutes, stunned. He wondered if he was shaking visibly. They had spoken like a student and a professor's wife who scarcely knew each other. She had not even mentioned the fact that he had not taken the room she had fixed for him, and he had expected her to bring that up at once.

He watched her as she walked down the street to where Socrates and the buggy were waiting. How could she remain so calm and cool? How could she have been so untouched by an experience the mere thought of which caused a violent churning of his insides?

At the end of his sophomore year August made the honor roll, which both surprised and pleased him, and during his senior year, there were two events he remembered clearly.

Early in the fall he was elected president of the Ministerial Students Association. His first impulse was to decline, but after thinking about it it became a challenge to him. He had never liked the organization as it was; this was his chance to try to change it. During his first month as president he instigated two new programs.

One was to send supply pastors to churches in the vicinity that needed them. Most of the churches responded favorably: during the year there was seldom a Sunday that one of the students was not called upon to preach, and some were even asked to help with revivals. August gave the assignments out like a professor announcing homework, but he himself never took one. He felt he was not ready yet to tell his fellowmen how to find faith or how to live by it.

His second program consisted of holding services on Sunday afternoons at the Brandon County poor farm. Most of the residents were too feeble to attend church in Brandon, and in these services August was a willing participant. There was something about the loneliness of the old men that reminded him of Gervas, and preaching to them was almost the equivalent of bringing Gervas back to the church—or rather, taking the church to Gervas.

"Remember one thing," he told the M.S.A. members. "These men have not attended church for years and they may resist your efforts. But they are old, and even though they may not be aware of it, they are thinking more and more about the next life, and maybe wondering if there is one. Don't go out there with high and mighty sermons about the peace of God which passeth all understanding. If it passeth all understanding, then you don't understand it either and you're fools to try to explain something you don't understand. Tell these people something that has meaning for *you,* and, chances are, it will mean something to them."

Both programs were a success, but August took little credit for them. He knew that they had stemmed as much from his discontent with the way things were as from any high purpose of his own to do good.

The second event that stood out in that senior year was the day Professor Bryant asked August to be his assistant. "You would grade papers from the freshman and sophomore classes," he said, "and act as proctor during some of the examinations. The position doesn't pay anything, but fifty dollars is deducted from your tuition."

August turned his head away, afraid Professor Bryant would see his emotion.

"I realize you have a heavy course load," the professor said, "and that the M.S.A. takes a good deal of your time. If you say No, I'll understand."

"I want it very much. It will be a privilege to be your assistant. I don't know how to thank you."

"I think you'll find that thanks are not in order," Professor Bryant said. "It's a lot of extra work with very little reward."

"Your asking me means more than you can possibly know," August said quickly.

Professor Bryant did not reply, for which August was grateful.

During the last term of his senior year, August spent less time with his books and more time just walking about Brandon. His love for the town and the campus bordered on what Ellis called the maudlin. But during those last few months he began to remember how he had felt at the end of his first term when he had thought he would not be returning, how he had walked down Faculty Avenue for the "last" time, how he had looked at the spire, in his mind already missing it. The thought of leaving Brandon made him almost physically ill.

"You know, August," Ellis said one afternoon in early spring, "I think I know what's wrong with you."

"I didn't know anything *was* wrong with me," he said.

"I mean this nostalgia you're suffering before you even leave this place. You're just plain scared to leave here—you want to stay inside the stone wall and forget there's a world outside."

August smiled. "You could be partly right," he admitted, "but not entirely. There is something about this place," he gestured around him, taking in all of Brandon, "that—I don't know, I can't explain it. But I know I'll never feel this way about anywhere else."

"You'll be just as maudlin about the seminary. Have you decided which one yet?"

"No, not yet. And I'm not sure I'm going to seminary."

"Money again?"

He nodded. "I could probably manage it if I worked part time, but—well, I want to think about it some more."

"You're not giving up the idea of bringing in the lost souls again, are you?"

"No." He didn't want to talk about it until it was clearer in his mind.

A buggy went by them, and August recognized Socrates even before he saw Angela. She sat very straight and did not look at them as she passed.

Ellis stopped walking and stared after the buggy. "I guess we're the only two upperclassmen who never made it," he said dolefully.

"Never made what?" August asked.

"Mrs. Bryant's boudoir."

"What do you mean?" August grew pale.

"The story goes she has a steady procession of students going in her bedroom—while the good professor is on campus, of course. Only qualification seems to be that they be upperclassmen. Freshmen and sophomores just can't make the grade."

Now August felt his face turning red. "That sounds to me like a lot of dirty gossip made up by people who have nothing better to talk about."

"Well, I got it from one of the boys who claims he's been there," Ellis said. "You know how Professor Bryant is about Plato. Well, it seems he carries some of the old boy's theories to extreme. I'm told the good professor doesn't believe in going to bed with his wife except for one reason—to beget children. And since there isn't any begetting going on, he won't even sleep in the same room with her. Hasn't for the past fifteen years. She doesn't like this arrangement too well, so she makes other arrangements more to her liking."

"Ellis, that's the most farfetched thing I ever heard. Even if it was true, how would anyone know for sure?"

"Well, I can imagine her telling it to some student. Just think about it for a minute. Did you ever see two more different people? The only thing I can't understand is how they ever got married in the first place. Good God from Goldsboro!"

"They had a child," August said. "A little girl who died."

"Yeah, I heard."

"Let's not talk about it anymore."

"Jeezle-peezle, August, you sound as stuffy as old man Bryant. I know you like the man, and it's nothing against him if his wife has to have it." He laughed. "And that's nothing against her, as far as I'm concerned."

August remained quiet for the rest of the walk. Ellis was talking about something he could not possibly know for a certainty—people did not reveal things like that about themselves. And yet, even as he rebuked Ellis for telling the story, he knew it was true. And he felt sorry for Professor Bryant, who, though August tried to convince himself differently, seemed somehow less a man to him now, and for Angela, who by her indiscretions had emasculated her husband in the eyes of his students.

I wish, August thought, that I had never found out. I wish that I would never have to find out anything like this again.

Knowing could be heartbreaking. And in that moment he realized that in the years to come he would know many things about people and that his heart would ache with that knowledge many times.

"You can get a church without going to seminary, August," Professor Bryant said. "But I thought seminary was your goal after graduation."

August looked out the window of the professor's office across the newly green campus. "It's a matter of money again. I have a little left from the sale of the farm, but it's not

enough to see me through two or three more years of school.
Ben, the neighbor who bought the farm, still owes some on
it, but he can't pay but a little each year. I don't want to divide
my time between working and studying. I suppose I have a
single-track mind."

Professor Bryant nodded. "Have you thought of borrowing
the money?"

"Yes, and although I was willing to do that three years ago,
I'm reluctant now. I don't want to come out of seminary in
debt. I'd rather preach for maybe two or three years, and then
go to seminary."

"You can, of course. But the great fallacy there is that
once you leave school, you'll probably never go back. Then,
too, I'm sure you know something about preachers' salaries.
Do you think you could save enough in two or three years to
put you through seminary?"

"I could try. With what I have left now I think I could
manage."

"In one respect it would be a better plan," Professor Bryant
said. "After a few years of practical experience, your work
in the seminary would have more meaning for you." He
tapped a pencil absently against the side of his desk. "I keep
in close touch with some of the churches in the state, since
so many of my former students are ministers. If I hear of an
opening, I'll let you know."

"Thank you, sir. I'd appreciate that." He rose and started
for the door. "I hear of vacancies through the M.S.A. supply
program, but they are only temporary. I'd like something
permanent."

Three weeks later Professor Bryant kept him after class.
"Have you changed your mind about wanting a church now?"

"No, I haven't. I'm not sure I'm ready for a church, but,
then, I have no assurance that I would be ready in three years
either."

"You think by waiting you might work up a good case of
pulpit fright?"

August smiled. "Something like that."

"I don't think your congregation would ever know," Professor Bryant said. "You have a positive knack for concealing
your emotions. In fact, for a young man, you sometimes seem
quite unreachable. That's a rare quality in the young, and

I'm not sure but what it might prove to be detrimental to a minister. A minister has to be reached, August."

He nodded, suppressing a smile at being called remote by the most remote man on campus. "I'll try to overcome it," he said.

"I'm not sure you should," the professor said seriously.

"I don't much think I could be anything but what I am anyway," August said.

"However," Professor Bryant went on as though he had not heard, "I didn't keep you to discuss personality differences. Would you be interested in an opening at the Fairmont church? It's a small town about seventy-five miles from here. The pastor for the past twenty years died last week, and the deacons are looking for a replacement."

"But I won't be through here for another month."

"It's unlikely that they'll find anyone before June," Professor Bryant said. "For the next few weeks they will be having ministers come in for trial sermons, and then the deacons will select a pastor."

"You mean I'd have to go preach to them?" He had known that this was the procedure, but it had never occurred to him that he would be judged on one sermon.

"If they like you, they may ask you to go back for a second sermon. The church, of course, will pay your expenses to and from Fairmont."

August knew nothing about Fairmont, had never even heard of the town before. But he could not afford to let any opportunity slip by. "I'd like to try it, sir," he said.

"I was sure you would," Professor Bryant said. "Knox Maddry, the chairman of the board of deacons, was here in Brandon yesterday—that's how I heard about the opening—and I told him about you. He wanted to know if you could go to Fairmont next Sunday."

August swallowed. "I suppose I could."

"You'd have to go on Saturday, of course. Knox said one of the deacons would meet your train and that they'd have a place for you to stay Saturday night. Forgive me for making your arrangements for you, but I thought you'd be interested and Maddry didn't have time to stay over to meet you."

"I appreciate it, sir." He rose to go.

"Good luck, August," Professor Bryant said. "I wish I could hear your first sermon."

August smiled and closed the door behind him. He was thankful, *very* thankful, that Professor Bryant would not be in the congregation. It would be bad enough facing strangers without having someone he knew also sitting in judgment. If you're going to make a fool of yourself, he thought, it's better to do it before strangers, because they forget quicker than friends.

As the train pulled into Fairmont, August closed his notebook and peered through the window, but there was little he could see through the darkness and probably, he thought, little to see even in daylight.

He stepped from the train, holding tightly to his small valise, and looked around the almost deserted platform. A voice close to him said, "Mr. Fielding?" and he turned.

A stout, balding man held out his hand. "I'm Knox Maddry. Welcome to Fairmont."

"Thank you, Mr. Maddry." August put the valise down and shook hands. "Professor Bryant has spoken very highly of you." Actually, Professor Bryant had been neither complimentary nor uncomplimentary in mentioning the chairman of the board of deacons.

"Eugene and I were classmates at Brandon," Maddry said, and bent to pick up the valise. "I'm partial to Brandon men, of course. Always been sorry I didn't have a son so I could send him to Brandon."

He led the way around the small smoke-grimed station to the street where his buggy waited. "You're spending the night with Deacon Marlowe and his family, but I told Staley—Staley Marlowe—that I wanted to meet your train, since I was responsible for getting you here."

August was not sure whether he was expected to express gratitude at being invited to Fairmont or whether Maddry should be the one to thank him for coming, so he said, "That was mighty nice of you. I appreciate it."

On the way to the Marlowe house, Maddry suddenly stopped the buggy. "You can't see too much now, but that's the church." He pointed to a square white frame building which was dwarfed by two large, completely unnecessary columns in front.

"It looks like a new building," August said.

"Not new, but recently remodeled and painted. We're

proud of our church. It's the biggest in Fairmont, and we keep it up. You know, Baptists are usually good givers, and about fifty percent of our members tithe. We think that's quite a record."

"It is indeed."

"Especially for a rural community. Eugene tells me you come from a small town yourself. We had a city fellow here last week to preach and afterward most of the members said they couldn't understand what he was talking about, and what they could understand they didn't like."

August wondered what Maddry would be telling next week's preacher about him. "Actually, I'm not from a town," he said. "I lived in the country all my life—on a farm near Pine View Community."

"Never heard of it," Maddry said cheerfully. "Well, I'm glad to see a farm boy, after last week. And I think it's just as well you haven't been to seminary. I'm not against education—far from it—but some of these fellows come out of seminary with some mighty peculiar notions, especially about religion. As somebody once said, a little learning can be a dangerous thing."

August made no comment. When the buggy stopped again, a deep voice boomed at them.

"That you, Knox? Supper's ready—I told Miranda you'd take the young man on a tour of the town."

"Train was late," Maddry said. "We came straight from the station. Mr. Fielding, this is Staley Marlowe."

August got out of the buggy and shook hands with the gaunt, Lincolnesque man who waited at the end of the walk. "Pleased to meet you, Mr. Fielding," Marlowe said. "You coming in, Knox?"

"Not tonight, Staley. Here's his bag. I'll see you tomorrow."

August thanked Maddry again for meeting the train and went into the house, where he was introduced to Mrs. Marlowe, a beautiful woman with dark hair and pale, creamy skin, and the four young Marlowes. Miranda Marlowe appeared to be at least twenty years younger than her husband. She gripped his hand warmly—a strong grip, he thought, for such a fragile-looking woman—and said, "We're so pleased to have you staying with us, Mr. Fielding. We do hope you'll like Fairmont."

August smiled, feeling more relaxed after his somewhat

tense ride with Maddry. "I hope Fairmont will like me," he said.

"I'm sure you have nothing to worry about," she said. "Staley, show Mr. Fielding to his room. He probably wants to wash after his trip. But don't get too clean, Mr. Fielding. Supper is on the table."

August had planned, after supper, to excuse himself and go over his sermon one more time, but he found himself reluctant to leave the family. He had never been exposed to family life like this. Mrs. Marlowe kept up a stream of conversation that was both light and all-inclusive, even calling for occasional comments from the children. Unlike most women he knew who talked a lot, she came forth with thought-provoking statements from time to time. Staley Marlowe was a quiet man who looked at his family like a proud impresario watching his protégés perform, and when he spoke, his dry wit made his family and August laugh uproariously. He thought he had never seen a closer, happier family, and it was not until Mrs. Marlowe looked at the children and said, "Time to say good night, chickens," that he remembered the sermon and excused himself.

The Marlowes took him to the church a half hour before the service the next morning, and he met the other five deacons. His nervousness had returned and he wondered how he would ever remember all the names, and then realized that he had not even heard most of the names as he was being introduced. Questions were going through his mind: Do they think I'm too inexperienced? (The last preacher had died at the age of sixty-three after being in Fairmont for twenty years.) Do they think I'm too comical-looking to be a preacher? (He had had an unusually hard time managing his orange cowlick that morning.) Will they think I'm cold, a preacher they could never get close to? (And this caused him to keep a foolish grin frozen on his face.)

"What hymns do you want to use, Preacher?" one of the deacons asked.

This was something he had not anticipated. "What are your favorites?" he asked.

"Well, we like 'On Jordan's Stormy Banks I Stand,' and 'Work for the Night Is Coming.' "

August at that moment could think of nothing worse than

being in a stuffy church on an unseasonably warm Sunday singing "Work for the Night Is Coming."

"I think," he said quickly, " 'Love Divine, All Love Excelling' might fit in with the sermon better. And perhaps 'Blest Be the Tie That Binds.' "

The deacon hurried away to post the hymn numbers on the board beneath the pulpit.

He felt as though he were in a daze when he went to sit in the huge chair beside the pulpit and faced the steadily filling church. He tried to remember the opening lines of his sermon. All he could remember was that they had something to do with love. And then he panicked. Dear God, what do I know about love? he thought. Why didn't I choose sin as a topic? At least I would be on home ground.

But after years of hearing Brother Johnson bellow the negative side of religion, he wanted the positive. He stood up quickly as weak chords arose from the out-of-tune piano under the choir loft.

After the opening hymn he walked stiffly to the pulpit, spent what he felt was an eternity leafing through the Bible to find his text (something he should have done beforehand), and then before reading it, looked out over the congregation, desperately wanting a reassuring smile from the Marlowes. Instead, he saw only Knox Maddry, his round face looking up expectantly.

August read, his voice deepening as he moved from "Though I speak with the tongues of men and of angels, and have not love . . ." to "And now abideth faith, hope, love, these three; but the greatest of these is love."

He closed the Bible and stood silently for a minute, looking out over the faces without actually seeing them. What could he tell them of love? He thought back over his entire life, trying to find one person he had truly loved, and could find none—himself least of all. Oh, there had been Gervas, but now it seemed that what he had felt for Gervas had been not love but rather a tolerant affection. He was genuinely fond of Ben and Ellis and Professor Bryant—Professor Bryant especially—but was there one single person in all the world whom he loved?

He began to speak. "I came to you today with a sermon prepared, carefully written and memorized, on love, and now I realize that my understanding of the word is small, and I have put aside the sermon. Perhaps I am not alone; perhaps there are others who grope for meaning in the word.

"Count to yourselves the number of people you love. It is a word we use lightly with many shades of meaning. We say of a friend, 'I love him, but . . .' and then we enumerate his faults. Love thinketh no evil and rejoiceth not in iniquity.

"How many times have you estranged a friend because you thought in some way he had failed you. Were you not, in reality, failing him, proving that no love ever existed? Love never faileth.

"I think the truth is that we are afraid of love." He had forgotten the congregation now as he searched his mind, reasoning the cause of his own inability to love. "We are afraid to give love because we are in terror of having that love rejected or made light of. And in our small minds we think of personal rejection as the worst tragedy that can befall us. When we give love to others, we do it with reservations, for we are afraid of giving ourselves, our souls, away irretrievably. We give love like an investment—only letting it go if we are sure the return will be greater than the original investment . . ."

He went on, talking to them quietly, condemning himself with every word he uttered. Occasionally while he talked the congregation came into focus and he was aware that he was standing before them, preaching, and that the experience was not so terrifying as he had expected it to be, but through most of the sermon he was almost unaware of the presence of others.

"We have faith," he said. "Faith is such that we can make of it what we want; therefore, we have faith. And hope—it is natural to hope even when all cause for hope appears to be gone. But love . . . love which seeketh not her own, which rejoiceth in the truth, which beareth all things, believeth all things, hopeth all things and endureth all things . . . Love—we have it not. And the greatest of these is love. Since only God can know perfect love, our only hope of attaining love is through a knowledge of God."

He stopped speaking and went back to the big chair, sitting motionless while the piano tinkled out the offertory anthem and the ushers took the collection. And then he arose and gave the benediction. "The Lord bless and keep you; the Lord

cause His face to shine upon you and give you peace, now
and ever. Amen."

As the congregation rose and sang the closing hymn, "Blest
Be the Tie That Binds," he made his way down the aisle to
the door and waited to greet the people.

One by one they filed by him shaking hands, murmuring
nice comments about "a fine sermon, Preacher. Enjoyed it
very much." He wondered if enjoyment was the purpose of a
sermon. If so, he did not think his would be rated very high
in entertainment value.

When Miranda Marlowe stood before him she took his
hand and pressed it and said only, "Thank you, Mr. Fielding,"
and moved away from the door to make way for others.

Perhaps, he thought, I said something that reached them
after all. But when Knox Maddry was pumping his hand, his
round face still looking expectant. "Very nice, Mr. Fielding,
very nice. But you forgot to issue the invitation."

"Invitation?"

"The invitation for those who want to profess faith in Jesus
Christ to come forward and join the church. We'll never get
any new members without issuing the invitation now, will we?"

August felt like a small boy who had been told he recited
very well but had left out most of the lines. "Yes," he said,
"I forgot the invitation."

The Marlowes waited for him in front of the church and
took him to the depot. "I'm sorry your train leaves so soon,"
Mrs. Marlowe said. "We were hoping you could have dinner
with us."

"I'm sorry, too," he said. "Visiting your home has been
one of the nicest things that ever happened to me."

"We hope you'll come again," Staley Marlowe said.

"He will," Mrs. Marlowe said quickly. "He'll come often
when he comes back to Fairmont."

"I don't think I will be coming back," August said. "I forgot
to issue the invitation."

Miranda Marlowe laughed. "Next time you can issue it
twice to make up for your omission."

As the train pulled away, August looked out the window at
the six Marlowes standing on the platform waving. Then he
sank back into the seat, so exhausted that even breathing
seemed to require a monumental effort. But, inadvertently,
his thoughts returned again and again to Miranda Marlowe.

For two weeks he waited hopefully, and then less hopefully, for word from Fairmont. He had thought he would hear something—if no more than a note thanking him for taking the time to go to Fairmont—from Knox Maddry or the other deacons. He had even half expected to be invited back to preach another sermon.

"I guess they weren't very much impressed," he told Professor Bryant. "It wasn't much of a sermon, although at the time, judging from the reaction, I thought it wasn't too bad. But, then, I forgot to issue the invitation and that seemed to bother Mr. Maddry."

Professor Bryant laughed the way Miranda Marlowe had. "That would have been the real test of your silver-tongued oratory," he said.

"But it wasn't an evangelistic sort of sermon," August said. "Anyway, I forgot."

"Don't worry about it," the professor said. "They may issue another invitation to you yet."

Meanwhile, there were final examinations—his last at Brandon—and all the added chores that went with graduation. While Ellis feverishly addressed graduation invitations, August wandered disconsolately about the campus. Was it possible that he would ever get over missing Brandon? Oh, he could come back in the future, attend the class reunions, go over the "remember whens," but it would be different then. He would not belong. And, thinking about it, he doubted if he would ever return. It would hurt too much.

Examination week, no longer the terror it had once been, came and went, and then there were only three more days before the end of the term, before he would be an outsider.

"Have you made any plans yet, August?" Professor Bryant asked him as they sat side by side in his office grading freshman papers.

"Nothing definite," August said. "I think I may stay in Brandon during the summer. I can have my old job back at the hardware store. And during the summer I'll look for a church."

"You'll find one." He spoke with more confidence than August felt.

The last morning had even less reality for him than he had imagined possible. He went, with his class, to the basement of the Philosophy Building and put on his black robe and mortarboard. There was chattering all around him, but he could think of nothing to say. And then they were in line and it was suddenly quiet. The academic procession moved slowly across the campus from the Philosophy Building to the chapel. Far ahead of him, near the beginning of the line, August saw Professor Bryant, and it occurred to him that for four years he had been following this man figuratively, and now it was entirely fitting that on this last day he should literally be walking behind him.

The morning became dreamlike. He heard the choir sing, he half heard the speeches, he marched to the front when his name was called and held out his hand for the diploma. And all the while he felt as though he were outside himself, watching himself perform with mildly interested detachment. It was much the way he had felt at Gervas's funeral.

Afterward the campus seemed to be overflowing with people. Ellis, standing in the center of a group, called to him and introduced him to his parents, an aunt and uncle, and a few stray cousins who had been rounded up for the occasion. August talked with them briefly and then went back to Mrs. Barry's. Soon Ellis came in to get his things. He took his suitcase down to his family's waiting carriage and returned and stood awkwardly in the center of the small room.

"Well, I guess I'll be going now," he said finally. "Lord, August, I hate leaving you here by yourself not knowing what you're going to do."

"Don't worry about me," August said. "I'll be all right. You'd better start concentrating on medical school."

"I reckon."

There was another silence and August thought, I am saying good-bye to my best friend. Maybe I'll never see him again, and yet I can't tell him what I really want to. I can't say to him, "Ellis, rooming with you these four years has meant more to me than you can possibly know. There were times when your clowning made life bearable. There were times when, without you, I would have given up in despair. We are different, you and I, and the difference has been to my advantage. Thank you for your understanding and your friendship." Oh, no, he could never say that to Ellis, for Ellis would be embarrassed beyond words.

"It's been great, Ellis, rooming with you. Good luck, and

don't worry too much about med school. You'll do just fine, if I know you."

Ellis grinned and slapped him on the back. "Tell you what, Preacher. I'll let you be the one to bury my mistakes for me." Then he was quiet, still staring awkwardly around the room and at August.

He's going to miss me, too, August thought, but he can't say it either. Why, in God's name, can't people *talk* to each other?

Ellis went to the door. "I guess this is good-bye," he said. "Family's waiting."

"Good luck, Ellis," August said again.

The door closed and Ellis was gone. And then it opened immediately and Ellis stuck his head in. "You know, Brother Fielding, there were times when you *damn near converted me.*" He banged the door without waiting for a reply.

The tension was broken and August laughed. Maybe after all it was not necessary for people to be so exact in expressing themselves. Ellis knew what he had wanted to say, and he knew what Ellis would have said to him.

The room seemed deathly quiet, but the quiet was short-lived. Mrs. Barry's voice called up the stairs, "August Fielding, you've got a visitor."

He hurried downstairs and saw Professor Bryant standing in the parlor.

"I wasn't sure where I'd find you," he said, and for once his face seemed expressive. He looked as though he could hardly contain good news. "When I went home I found a letter waiting from Knox Maddry. He wrote to me because he didn't think just Brandon College for an address would reach you. He—they—want you at Fairmont."

"They want me to preach another sermon?"

"No, they want you for their pastor. Here, you may keep the letter. It has all the particulars about the salary and so forth. Maddry wants to know how soon you can assume the duties, if you're still interested, that is."

"I can leave tomorrow morning," August said. "But I thought I'd have to go back for another trial sermon—if they liked the first one."

"He didn't mention it. That must have been quite a sermon, August."

And so the last member of the class of 1897 to leave the campus found himself on the train the following day, bound for Fairmont, apprehensive but not nearly so nervous as he had been when he made the first trip.

He had said his good-byes and the pain of them still ached inside him. It had been all he could do to control his emotion when, just before leaving, he had stopped by Professor Bryant's office. He might never again see this man whom he respected and admired more than anyone he had ever known. And it touched him even more when he noticed that the professor seemed equally moved by this last good-bye.

Professor Bryant said, almost brusquely, "Much luck to you, August, and keep in touch. I want to hear how you're getting along."

"I certainly will, sir." He hesitated. Somehow he could not get the long good-bye speech out which he had planned to say. "I want to thank you, Professor Bryant . . ." He stopped and began again. "I can't begin to say—"

"Please." The professor looked as embarrassed as he did. "I was just leaving. I'll walk out with you."

They went downstairs together, and neither spoke until they were outside.

"Good-bye, August."

"Good-bye, sir."

They shook hands in front of the Philosophy Building, and the professor left him, striding across the campus as though for the first time in his life he was in a terrible hurry.

When the train left Brandon, August turned in his seat for one last look. Now, at this minute, he could not think of what was ahead of him, only of what he was leaving behind. But from the tracks there was no clear view of Brandon, the college or the town. All he could see was the white spire rising above the trees, puncturing heaven.

PART TWO

8

KNOX MADDRY, AT FIFTY-SIX, was the richest man in Fairmont, which is not to say that he was wealthy, merely that he had more money than anyone else in town. He owned several farms which were tended by tenants, the town's only drugstore managed by its only registered pharmacist, and Fairmont's only office building. This he managed himself, collecting rent each month from the two doctors, one dentist, and two lawyers who had offices in the building.

In addition to his business interests, he was chairman of the town board of commissioners, president of the Baptist Brotherhood Fellowship, and, of course, chairman of the board of deacons.

He had inherited the farms and office building from his father, but the drugstore had been his own venture. Being a civic leader had followed in the wake of being a business leader. And no one felt his importance more than Knox Maddry himself.

Early in their marriage, Hattie Mae Maddry had felt a certain amount of that importance, but now she no longer thought about it, primarily because Knox's domineering personality left her little time to think about anything but pleasing him.

Pleasing Knox consisted mostly of keeping his house spotless, his meals hot, and listening, but never answering, when he felt like talking. Also of keeping Harriet, their daughter, from getting on his nerves.

This latter was the hardest part of Hattie Mae's job. Harriet was twenty-five years old, unmarried, and (as Knox had been known to note in her presence) as homely as a mud fence. She was a sullen, moody girl, and was apparently the only resident of Fairmont neither impressed with nor afraid of Knox Maddry.

106

She was the reason (though she had no way of knowing it) that Knox seldom went to bed with his wife. He had been so repelled by the thought that this oversized and awkward human being was the result of sleeping with Hattie Mae that by the time Harriet was four years old he had taken the big double bed out of the master bedroom and replaced it with twin beds. He had had to send all the way to the state capital to get them, because at that time twin beds were virtually unheard-of in Fairmont.

Harriet was also the reason (and she had no way of knowing this, either) that August Fielding was pastor of the Fairmont Baptist Church.

Knox Maddry had, years ago, given up all hope of having Harriet taken off his hands by marriage. No man in his right mind would ever join hands (or anything else) with Harriet. One by one the girls she had grown up with were married, and with each marriage Knox's hopes sank a notch lower. At first he had thought of the marriages as taking one more girl out of the field of competition. But then it occurred to him that with each wedding, one more eligible man was also eliminated. And now there was not an unmarried man anywhere near Harriet's age left in Fairmont.

A preacher would not, under ordinary circumstances, have been his choice for a son-in-law, especially a stringy orange-haired one who looked at people as though he were looking right through them. But Knox was the first to admit that the circumstances were not ordinary and he was ready to grasp at any straw, even a stringy orange-haired one. God knew that with Harriet's looks, *she* could not afford to be choosy.

The idea of August as a possible suitor for Harriet had come to him during his sermon on the subject of love. Love to Knox meant physical love, and so the meaning of the sermon escaped him, but while the young preacher was holding forth on love, Knox was wondering if it would be possible for him to love Harriet. Everyone knew that preachers were not supposed to concern themselves with what people looked like, but with what they were inside. Maybe if he could just keep young Fielding from finding out what Harriet *was* like inside, at least until the knot was safely tied . . .

During the month he listened to four other trial sermons. But three of the preachers already had wives, and the fourth, a widower, was too old. And so when the deacons met at the end of May to talk over the candidates for the job, Knox said without hesitation, "To my way of thinking, the young preacher from Brandon was the best we heard."

"I couldn't agree more," Staley Marlowe said. "That was a powerful sermon. He even had Miranda in tears. Furthermore, he seems a likable sort, one who'd fit in well in town. He's young, but I think it's time we got some young blood in the church."

"One thing is certain," Knox said. "He'll get over that—being young, I mean—or my name ain't Knox Maddry." He was frequently ungrammatical, not because he did not know better but because he felt it made him seem folksy.

"He was good, all right," Broadus Nichols said, "but for the size of our congregation, I think we need a man with some experience. Now that last one we had here, Thomas Coonce, he was a good preacher and also has had experience —three churches already, I think he said."

"We don't know why he left those churches," Knox said. "Maybe the people didn't like him. No, I think we'd do well to go along with Fielding."

So the board voted unanimously in favor of August, and Knox smiled, seeing his troubles diminishing. Eugene Bryant, buried among his everlasting books over there in Brandon, would never know the favor he had done his old classmate by suggesting that this odd-looking boy be given a trial sermon.

But now, one year later, Knox had all but lost hope again. During the past year he and Hattie Mae had invited August to dinner any number of times. He had taken August on long drives in his buggy, always managing to have Harriet with them. And though August was always polite and attentive to Harriet, so far as Knox could see he could not have been less interested in becoming her suitor. He never came to call without a special invitation, and although he did not look particularly uncomfortable when Knox left him alone with Harriet, his visits were noticeably briefer on these occasions.

Knox was forced to admit that August was a good preacher —or, as he told Staley Marlowe, "He ain't bad, as preachers go." His sermons seemed to inspire those who wanted to be inspired by that sort of thing, and he even had some of the members who had not been inside the church in years attending regularly now. And he did his duty when it came to calling on the sick and the old people and taking care of the bereaved. One thing that Knox could not understand was the fact that August spent an uncommon lot of time with Staley Marlowe's children. He took them fishing frequently or out for walks, and those children went in and out of the parsonage as though it were their own home.

August seemed to have time for everything and everybody but Harriet. There was only one hope left now. Knox gave the matter considerable thought and decided that during his first year, August had been busy making an impression. He was establishing himself in the church and in the town. Now that he had been accepted and had made his impression, he could relax and give more time to personal things—like finding a wife. Somehow Knox would have to get this thought into August's mind.

August stood at a window in the parsonage, unconsciously fingering the curtains that Miranda Marlowe had hung for him the first week he had been in Fairmont, looking out at the unexpected early summer rainstorm. He had promised to take the young Marlowes fishing that afternoon, but it was obviously out of the question now and he wondered if their disappointment could possibly match his. He had taken to fishing at the same time he had taken to the little Marlowes, and he would be hard put to tell which he found more relaxing. There was something so natural and at the same time so invigorating about the children that he had almost come to prefer their company to that of adults.

With a sigh he moved away from the window and went to the desk he had built for himself. It wobbled slightly because he had never been able to get the legs the same length, but it served its purpose not only in its function but in taking up space in the almost empty room.

He had arrived in Fairmont without one stick of furniture, having sold his own to Ben along with the house. The big, barny parsonage offered only a kitchen stove, an old icebox, and two or three coal heaters in the living room and bedrooms. He had bought some furniture, and the women in his flock had come to his rescue by providing some of the essentials, but the rooms still had a bare, unlived-in look. Miranda's curtains, more than anything else, had softened the rooms a bit.

He picked up his pen and began a letter to Professor Bryant.

"When I look back over the past year," he wrote, "I am appalled at my ignorance in church matters when I came here."

He put the pen down and smiled to himself. His ignorance still covered many subjects, but not quite as thickly. He had arrived in Fairmont with the idea that his work would consist of preaching a sermon every Sunday morning and Sunday night, conducting prayer meetings on Wednesday night, calling on the sick, and burying the dead. It had not occurred to him that he would be called upon to referee a bout between two women who disagreed on a flower arrangement. ("I say, Lucy, that tiger lilies are completely out of place in front of the pulpit. They're gaudy and sacrilegious, that's what they are." "And I say, Ernestine, that they are flowers made by God and therefore completely in place in God's house.")

Nor had it occurred to him that he would have to settle disputes among the choir members about which anthem to sing at the offertory, or plan church bazaars, or give his opinion about minor disagreements among the deacons. (These were usually minor because the deacons, for the most part, went where Knox Maddry led them like sheep following a shepherd's staff.)

There was one thing he did, not because it went with the job but merely because he wanted to. He occasionally called on people who were not members of his church. There were fifteen hundred people in Fairmont (seven hundred of whom were listed on the books as being members of his church, although there were seldom more than three hundred in church on any given Sunday), and three churches. The Methodist church, second largest, claimed four hundred souls for its own, and the Presbyterian church only one hundred. ("There ain't enough of them to do us any harm," Knox Maddry told him, "but you got to watch out for them Methodists. They're sneaky.")

August picked up the pen and started writing again, then stopped as he heard footsteps on the porch. When he went to the door, he was surprised to see Knox Maddry, his round face beaming pleasantly as he brushed the water from his coat.

"Afternoon, Preacher." He stepped inside. "I had started to

one of my farms, but then the rains descended and I decided to pay you a little visit."

"Come in," August said, and led the way back to the living room. The call, though unexpected, was not entirely a surprise, for Knox had dropped in on him several times since he had been in Fairmont.

Knox took off his coat, carefully hung it over a chair, and sat down in his shirt sleeves. "Hope you don't mind, Preacher. I'm soaked."

"Not at all," August said, wondering what the purpose of the visit was. Usually when Knox came, he had something on his mind. The last time, it had been plans for the annual revival, and August, who was unalterably opposed to revivals, had managed to stall him. Now, he thought, Maddry had probably come to renew his campaign.

"It's nice and quiet here," Knox said, settling back against the cushions of the divan. "A pleasant change." He was silent while August tried to think of an answer to this profundity. "But you know, Preacher," and he sat up suddenly, "I'll bet all this peace and quiet gets on your nerves at times."

"No," August said. "I hadn't noticed."

"It's nice for a change," Knox repeated. "But there's nothing like going home at the end of the day and finding the family waiting. Of course, I don't suppose you'd know much about that kind of satisfaction."

"No," August agreed.

"How old are you, August?"

He heard his given name so seldom now that it startled him. "Twenty-four," he said. "I'll be twenty-five in October."

"I was twenty-four when I got married," Knox said. "That's about the right age, I think. You're still young enough to have your youthful enthusiasm and yet old enough to have some sense. I don't hold with these young marriages. Young folks get married so early now that by the time they're thirty they feel as though they've been married all their lives. I've always said to Harriet, 'Take your time, daughter. Enjoy life for a while. You've got long enough to be married.' Not," he added hastily, "that you don't enjoy life after you're married. It's just that if you wait until you're twenty-four or so you're more likely to choose a mate who wears well. Don't you agree, Preacher?"

"Oh, yes," said August, who had never thought about any

age as being either good or bad for marriage. "Yes, I think you have something there."

"You ever thought about betting married, Preacher?"

"No."

"Why not, fine young man like you?"

"I think that before getting married, one should be able to support a wife," August said, "and until the past year, I've been a student."

"Well, you ain't a student any longer." Knox laughed and slapped his thigh. "Maybe it's time you thought about it."

"Why?"

"Well, you know, Preacher, folks somehow don't put their trust in a single man the way they do a married one. Oh, I'm not saying anyone don't trust *you*, Preacher, but you know how it is. You figure a man who has a wife and family to take care of is going to be more serious, a hard worker. Not that a single man don't work hard, God knows, but . . . You know what I mean."

August nodded, trying to keep his expression appropriately serious. "I expect I'll marry someday," he said, "but . . ."

"But you want to do it in your own good time." Knox laughed mirthlessly. "Can't say I blame you. Oh, by the way, I almost forgot the reason I stopped by here. Hattie Mae told me to tell you to come by Sunday after church for dinner. We'd be pleased to have you."

"And I'd be pleased to come," August said. "Give Mrs. Maddry my thanks."

Knox stood up. "I'll do that. Well, I guess I'd better be getting along. We'll be looking for you Sunday."

After he had gone, August returned to his desk and the letter, shaking his head in bewilderment.

The dinner was similar to the countless other Sunday dinners he had had in the Maddry home during the past year. Even the food seldom varied: fried chicken, mashed potatoes, green peas, stewed tomatoes, ice cream and cake. But today, instead of ice cream there was strawberry shortcake, which August complimented highly and watched Hattie Mae blush with pleasure.

He had long since formed his opinion of the Maddry family, and it bothered him sometimes to think that his opinion was lacking in Christian charity. Apparently, Knox Maddry had at one time ruled his family with an iron hand, although the iron hand was no longer necessary, for both of the Maddry women seemed by now subdued and colorless. Harriet, possibly, was capable of small rebellions now and then, but Hattie Mae—never. She seemed to be afraid of both her husband and her daughter, and she seldom spoke except to repeat irritatingly something Knox had said.

Knox had a way of talking over both of the women as though they were not present and he was addressing his remarks only to his visitor, and, August thought, if no visitor was present, he would merely talk to the atmosphere around him.

Harriet was the feminine counterpart of Knox, although there was little about her that would give rise to the word "feminine." She had Knox's round face and stocky figure and his heavy features which seemed to protrude at jarring angles from her face. Even her eyes seemed to bulge.

The conversation was almost as invariable as the meals. It would begin with Knox saying, "Now, eat hearty, Preacher. Hattie Mae don't like to see people picking at their food like birds." And Hattie Mae would smile slightly and look down at her plate. Then Knox would say, "Well, Preacher, how do you like Fairmont by now?" And Hattie Mae would echo, "Yes, by now." Whereupon August would assure them that Fairmont was a veritable garden spot, and Knox would beam happily and let the conversation rest while he ate like a bird, perhaps a three-hundred-pound ostrich.

Today, however, he carried the conversation a step further. "It's not a bad place," he said. "Not a bad place at all to settle down in. I reckon you know you could do a lot worse."

August nodded.

"A lot worse," Hattie Mae said.

"How and where?" asked Harriet, and was rewarded with a scowl from Knox.

He turned back to August. "She has quite a sense of humor."

August nodded again, wondering where she kept it hidden.

"You thought any more about the revival, Preacher?" Knox found it safer to change the subject. "You know we have one every year. It's customary."

August was sure that this was not the time to plunge in

with his opinion of revivals, but obviously an answer was called for.

"How are your revivals usually conducted here?" he asked.

"We get a visiting preacher who comes for a week and preaches high-powered sermons every night. Our revivals are always a success.

"We bring in right-much money for the church that way— souls, too, of course. Last year there were thirty-some-odd people who joined the church during revival week."

"Some odd people," Harriet said in perfect imitation of Hattie Mae, and August decided that maybe after all she did have a sense of humor. He smiled but cleared his face immediately when he noticed Knox again scowling at his daughter.

"I don't know," August said. "I haven't thought too much about a revival."

"I think we better get cracking on it," Knox said. "We usually have it in April, and here it is June already."

"Mr. Fielding is such a good preacher," Hattie Mae ventured, "that I don't see we need to get another one to come here. I'd much rather hear him than anybody else."

"Thank you," August said.

"I think you've got something there." Knox beamed at his wife as though she were a child who had suddenly performed well without having to be prodded. "How about it, Preacher? Think you could manage this year's revival all by yourself?"

August looked down at his plate. There seemed to be no way of getting out of a revival. But at least if he handled it himself, he could have control over the kind of revival it was. None of what Ellis would call come-to-Jesus-or-go-to-hell sermons.

"Yes," he said slowly. "I think I could."

"Good!" said Knox. "You know we'll come out even more ahead this year, because we won't be paying a visiting preacher. Glad I thought of it."

He pushed his chair back from the table with a flourish. "August, why don't you young people take the buggy and go for a ride? I know you don't want to spend the afternoon sitting around here talking to us old folks. Want me to hitch up old Bessie for you?" He left the room without waiting for an answer.

Hattie Mae rose and began to help the maid clear the table.

August followed Harriet uncertainly into the living room and then to the front of the house, where they waited for Knox to bring the buggy.

"Harriet," Knox said when he appeared, "if you all don't have anywhere in particular to go, you might go out to the Ridge Road farm and give this check to Tamini. Tell him it's to pay for the stuff he bought last week." He gave her the check. "Tamini," he explained to August, "is one of my tenants. An Eyetalian who came here years ago looking for work. Mostly I'd rather use niggers on my farms, but Tamini's all right. Knows farming."

August was about to help Harriet in the buggy when she went to the other side. "I'll drive," she said. "I know the way." And she climbed in before August could reach her.

They rode in silence, listening to the steady *clop-clop* of Bessie's hoofs on the wide dirt road. Harriet handled the reins expertly, like a man, August thought as he stared at her thick square hands.

"We'll make this as fast and painless as possible," Harriet said finally, "then I'll leave you at the parsonage."

August looked at her, not comprehending. "I'm not in any pain," he said, "unless it's from overeating."

Harriet laughed. It was a raucous, rusty sort of laugh, as though she didn't use it often. And then she was silent again.

They reached a small road, hardly more than a path, and Harriet turned Bessie into the road. They passed through a grove of trees before reaching a small farmhouse with a wide front yard where no grass grew and where he could plainly see the tracks of a wire broom. It reminded him so much of his home that for a moment he felt he had traveled backward in time. There was even a large maple in the yard.

At the side of the house was a small brook which seemed to spring from beneath a huge rock, winding beyond the house into the woods. August surveyed the course of the brook for a full minute before he saw a girl sitting on its tiny sloping bank. At first he thought it was Miranda Marlowe, then he realized that he had never seen the girl before. She had thick wavy black hair and a light-olive complexion. She wore a bright-red skirt and white blouse; the skirt was pulled up almost to her knees, and her bare feet were in the brook. The scene was like a pastoral painting, so well did the girl blend in with her surroundings. Something one of those French painters would do, he thought, and call *Summer Afternoon*.

Harriet pulled on the reins and called, "Mr. Tamini, you home?"

The girl by the brook got up and walked slowly and unself-consciously toward them. August had never been greeted by a barefoot girl before, and he didn't know whether to avert his eyes modestly or pretend he did not notice and look only at her face. He did neither. He stared openly at the delicate little feet, and only when she was beside the buggy did he look at her face. Now, close up, she did not resemble Miranda at all, except for the black hair. She was younger—about nineteen—and her expression was more serious than Miranda's. Grave—that was it. Grave but nevertheless beautiful.

"Good afternoon, Miss Maddry," she said. "My father is not at home right now."

"Good afternoon, Mary. This is Mary Tamini," she said to August. "Mary, Mr. Fielding, our preacher."

"How do you do." She held her hand up to him.

"I'm very glad to meet you, Miss Tamini." His eyes went back to the bare feet and she followed his glance and smiled. "It's a warm day," she said. "I'm sorry my father isn't in. He should be back soon, though. Would you like to come in, or could I give him a message?"

Harriet gave her the check. "My father sent this—it's for the supplies Mr. Tamini bought last week."

"Thank you, Miss Maddry. I'll give it to him."

"Poor things," Harriet said as they turned out of the rutted path onto the road. "Giuseppe Tamini takes care of the farm, barely ekes out a living for himself and his six children, and thinks he's lucky. Well, maybe at that, he is. Maybe he has more here than he had in Italy. But still, I think he'd like to go back to the old country—if he had the money."

"Where is his wife?" August asked.

"She died about four years ago, leaving him six children to bring up. Or rather, leaving five for Mary to bring up. She's taken over as mother now, even though she's a frail little thing."

"She speaks very good English," August said.

"All of the children were born here. I don't think any of them speak Italian, except Tamini. He goes from one language to the other without noticing the difference."

"I've never seen any of them at church," August said. "Do they go to one of the others?"

"They're Catholic," Harriet said, "and since there isn't a Catholic church anywhere near here, they don't go to church. Every year at Christmas and Easter, they hitch up the wagon and drive all the way to Raleigh to church. It takes two days and it makes Daddy furious—especially at Eastertime when there's so much to be done on the farm—but nothing he says makes any difference. They go to church, no matter what."

August had read about Catholicism some, but most of what he knew was what he had heard Brother Johnson say in sermons against the papists. The Catholics, he had declared, not only were trying to take over this world but also thought they could buy their way into the next. "Just give a little money to the priest," Brother Johnson had shouted, "and they think their sins are all gone and they're as white as snow. Brethren, I'm here to tell you you can't buy your way out of sin, and when you see a Roman Catholic, you ought to take out and run like the Devil is behind you—because he is."

There was certainly nothing devilish-looking about Mary Tamini, who, August decided, had the face of a Madonna. He could imagine her seated with the five younger Taminis around her, looking like the picture on a Christmas greeting.

August had not noticed that they were back in town until Harriet stopped the buggy in front of the parsonage and said, "Well, here we are."

"It's been most enjoyable, Miss Harriet," he said. "Thank you for taking me along."

"You couldn't very well have gotten out of it, could you?" She pulled out the rusty laugh again. "When Daddy makes plans, he expects them to be carried out—to the letter. It will be interesting to see how you react to his plans for you."

"What plans? He hasn't mentioned any plans to me."

"These are not the kind he would go around mentioning. To put it bluntly, Mr. Fielding, you are supposed to see a lot of me—all by Daddy's arrangement, of course. And then you are to get the idea that someday I'll be a wealthy woman and therefore might possibly be a good match. Oh, I know what Daddy's thinking almost before he does. And believe me, that's what he's thinking."

August's face became redder and redder as she talked. "I—

I'm sure you must be mistaken, Miss Harriet," he stammered. "I—"

"I'm not mistaken. And I'll tell you something else, Mr. Fielding. I'm on your side. I don't want to marry you any more than you want to marry me. Not that I have anything against you, understand. I just can't quite see myself as a preacher's wife. So would you like to make a little deal?"

He swallowed. "What's that?"

"Now that we both know what he's up to, we could pretend to go along with it. I mean, like today, when he sends us off together, or goes off and leaves us alone, we can grin and bear it and share our own little joke on him. How does that sound?"

August grinned now. "It sounds all right to me, Miss Harriet."

"Good. We'll have the last laugh after all. Well, good-bye for now. I'll see you next time you're hauled in for Sunday dinner—probably next week on the pretense of planning the revival."

She drove away, leaving him staring after her. Knox Maddry, it suddenly occurred to him, was not the only manipulator in the family.

9

"*I* HAD SOME BATTER LEFT OVER," Miranda said, "so I made a little cake for you."

"Thank you," August said, taking the cake and pulling out a chair for her.

"I can only stay a minute," Miranda said. "Staley's going to a meeting tonight, so I've got to round up the children and have an early supper. It's a deacons' meeting," she added, "so I suppose you are going also."

"No, I only go to the meetings when I'm invited. Tonight they're going over the plans for the revival—my plans—so an invitation was not forthcoming."

"Staley said you were going to do all the preaching."

"I am."

"Thank God," Miranda said. "I shouldn't feel the way I do, but I don't hold much with revivals. The sermons are always the same, and frankly, I have a hard time staying awake."

"I'll talk softly so I won't disturb you," he said.

"I didn't mean *your* sermons. You're the best preacher we've ever had here, August. I find myself listening to every word you say, sometimes even when there are other things I had planned to think about during the sermon."

He laughed. "I'm getting the impression that I distort your image of what a preacher should be."

"No, not really. It's just that you aren't much like the others we've had here. Although to tell the truth, I can only remember the last one—and the revival speakers, of course. They were all old and talked constantly about death and sin and hell and eternal life. You talk about living, August. I wonder if it's because you're young. When you're older, do you suppose you'll be like the others?"

"I hope not." he said. "But we'll just have to wait and see. By the way, Miranda, I'm thinking about buying a horse. Would that jolt my flock too much?"

"Of course not. Your predecessor had a horse and carriage —a very fancy carriage, I might add. You really need one to get around."

"I'm not getting a carriage," August said. "Just a saddle horse."

Miranda laughed. "You think seeing the preacher on horse-back will cause comment? I doubt it. Of course, Knox Maddry probably will say you look like a Methodist circuit rider, but don't let that bother you."

"It won't," he said. "Miranda, do you know Harriet Maddry very well?"

She looked at him intently for a minute, a small frown puckering her eyebrows. "I don't think anyone knows her *very* well, August. Why do you ask?"

"No special reason. I just wondered if she had any friends here. She seems to be a lonely person."

"She has acquaintances; I wouldn't say friends. Folks here got the idea a long time ago that she preferred her own company. I think, in a way, it's Knox's fault, but I'm not sure how it's his fault. Actually, the few times I've been with

Harriet, I've found her quite pleasant—except when Knox was around. Then she almost never says a word. Hattie Mae is exactly the same way. Are you getting interested in Harriet, August?"

The directness of the question startled him. Then he smiled. Miranda was the one person in the world he could relax with and say what he thought without being afraid of being misinterpreted or having his words come back to him later by way of town gossip.

"I'm interested in her, but not the way you mean," he said. "I find her very entertaining—as you say, when Knox is not around. She has a good mind. It's a shame she isn't allowed to use it constructively."

"Knox couldn't stand the competition, especially from within his own family. She's a lot like him, you know."

"I know."

She stood up. "Time to find the little ones. Staley thinks I let them run wild, so I try to have them at home, washed, and with their best company manners polished by the time he gets home. Can you come for dinner Saturday night, August? It's ages since you've been to see us."

"Do you think that invitation will keep until after the revival?" he asked. "I'm using every available minute this week on my sermons."

"Of course," she said. "Come anytime. But you're working too hard, August. Slow down or you'll be old before your time."

After she had gone he went to his desk and picked up his notes for the sermons. He knew he was working hard—harder than necessary—and he had been ever since he arrived in Fairmont. He didn't know why he steeped himself in work; if there was none demanding his immediate attention, he promptly invented some. It was as though he was trying to keep busy constantly in order to keep from thinking. But what was he trying to keep from thinking about? This was the thing that worried him. Soon, perhaps very soon, he was going to have to stop long enough for a mental accounting with himself. Meanwhile, there was work to do . . .

He laid the notes aside and restlessly pushed his chair back from the desk. The fact was, he no longer knew himself. At Brandon when Professor Bryant and others had called him remote, he had known that although others had not been close to him, he had been close to himself. Oh, there had been times when it was hard to analyze his thoughts and his reactions, but still in the long run he had *known* himself.

Now he was almost a different person. He had not consciously tried since coming to Fairmont to make himself warm and outgoing (he remembered too well his conversation with Professor Bryant on the subject), but the fact remained that in subtle ways he had changed. He was with people more, a part of their lives, and they had become a part of his. More and more he found that he was giving himself to others—or, as he thought of it, giving himself *away* to others. And in the giving he had retained very little of himself for himself. Was it always like that? When you gave yourself away, was there nothing left for you to keep? In being known by others, did you necessarily have to become a stranger to yourself?

He thought for a moment of the horse he was going to buy. The idea of long rides into the country alone suddenly appealed to him as a means of becoming reacquainted with the person who had once been August.

The first service of revival week went, August thought, very well. The church was packed, and the people sang lustily and listened to his sermon. True, when he gave the invitation at the close of the service, no one came forward, but this did not surprise him. He had been to enough revivals to know that it was during the last few nights that the people trooped forward, eager to lay their sinful burdens on the Lord and receive His absolution.

He thought it had gone very well, until the following morning when he met Knox Maddry on the street and stopped to talk. Knox came right to the point.

"I was at church last night, Preacher, and I'm wondering if that's the kind of sermon you're aiming to preach all week."

August had chosen the Beatitudes for his text for the week and had planned to use a different beatitude each night as a sermon topic. Last night's had been the first one: "Blessed are the poor in spirit; for theirs is the kingdom of heaven."

"Why?" August asked bluntly.

"Because that was not a revival sermon. You won't get any new members that way."

August was suddenly angry, very angry. "Maybe I gave the old members something to think about," he said.

"They're already Christians—and Baptists," said Knox, to whom the two words were synonymous. "The business of a revival is to make Christians out of heathens."

"Don't you think that sometimes Christians forget that they are Christians?" August asked, trying to control his temper. "Do you really believe that after a man is baptized he sins no more?"

"I'm not going to stand here on the street and go into a ridiculous argument on theology with you," Knox said impatiently. "I'm fifty-six years old, August, and it stands to reason that I know more than you do, about people anyway. I know that at a revival you've got to hit them with evangelism. They expect it and they want it. If you don't, the revival is no damned good."

"I don't tell you how to manage your . . ." August began, and trailed off. Aside from the loss of dignity, he did not want to be rude to Knox, who, after all, was merely expressing his convictions.

Knox, of course, knew what August had left unsaid; his face became red, and the veins in his forehead bulged out. "Why of all the—" Then he too stopped, and, surprisingly, smiled. It was a tight, forced smile at first, but gradually his face relaxed with it. "No hard feelings, Preacher," he said amiably. "Just thought I'd make a suggestion. The sermon last night was all right—in fact, Harriet seemed very much taken with it. She commented on it several times after we got home. I only meant that it wasn't exactly a revival sermon."

August nodded silently, not trusting himself to speak.

"Well, I'll see you in church tonight," Knox said, and ambled off down the street.

August went in the other direction to McAllister's Stables and bought himself a horse, paying more than he had intended to, but doing so cheerfully because McAllister was a Presbyterian.

That night, however, he changed his sermon somewhat. He used the beatitude "Blessed are they which do hunger and thirst after righteousness: for they shall be filled." And it could almost have been called a revival sermon.

Harriet stopped at the parsonage the following day to see

the new horse. "I heard at church last night that you bought an animal yesterday. May I see him, please? I love horses."

This statement came as much a surprise to August as her visit. He sometimes saw the ladies of Fairmont in their long black riding habits clinging to the side saddles as they rode through the town, but he had never seen Harriet riding.

"Of course," he said, and led her to the shed behind the parsonage. He slipped a rope around the animal's thick neck and brought him out of the shed.

"My goodness, he's huge," Harriet cried.

"Sixteen hands," August said proudly.

"A beauty, a real beauty." She patted him on the neck, and the horse flicked his mane as though trying to get rid of a fly. "What's his name?"

"Brandy," August said, and Harriet burst into laughter. August had never heard her laugh like that, and even the horse turned his head as though trying to see what the joke was.

"Brandy!" she gasped and then started laughing again. "Imagine a preacher having a horse named Brandy. August, you do beat all."

August turned red. "I didn't think about that. Mr. McAllister said his name was Brandy and I didn't want to confuse him with a new name."

"Very sensible, I'm sure." She stopped laughing, but the corners of her mouth twitched.

When she laughed, August thought, you could almost forget she wasn't pretty. Her heavy features seemed to rearrange themselves, and she looked quite different.

"You didn't get a buggy, did you?" she asked.

"No, I don't think I need one."

"Would you like to try him with our buggy sometime?"

"That would be very nice," August said, putting Brandy back into his stall. "Mr. McAllister said he could do most anything, but I'd like to try him with the buggy."

"McAllister is a horse trader," she said, "but I think you got a good one. I guess he wouldn't cheat on a preacher."

They walked back around to the front of the house, and August debated about inviting her in. Had it been Miranda he would not have hesitated, but somehow with Harriet it did not seem quite right. She settled the question herself by saying, "I just wanted to see him. Why don't you bring him over Sunday after church? We can try the buggy after dinner."

August hesitated. He did not want Sunday dinner with the Maddrys to become a habit, but he did not have a reasonable excuse ready.

"Fine," he said. "I'll do that."

She hurried down the walk then, without a good-bye, as though she were off on an important errand and had already wasted too much time. August went back into the house to work on the rest of his sermons for the revival.

The last day of the revival, in late June, was hot and sticky. Summer had come suddenly and with a vengeance, making up in one day for the late spring and giving promise of nothing more than long, hot days to come. August had slept little the night before, and when he awoke he felt as though he had not slept at all. He had had fitful and restless dreams, but he could not remember what they were. He knew only that he was exhausted and depressed. Depressed because he was sure that in the eyes of Knox Maddry and possibly others the revival had been a failure. His sermons had seemed to be well received, but the fact remained that during the week fewer than twenty persons had come forward to join the church. On this the last night, there should be more, although he could still not bring himself to preach a hellfire and damnation sermon.

Late in the afternoon the sun disappeared behind a dark cloud. The humidity was even more oppressive than the temperature, and August was afraid it would rain. In bad weather his congregation was almost nonexistent. But when he went to the church at seven o'clock, although the sky was black, there was no rain, and by seven thirty, when the service began, the church was once again full of people. (He noted, with a small feeling of triumph, that McAllister was in the congregation. Not that he expected the Presbyterian to renounce his own church, but it was gratifying, a small personal victory, to see him there.)

In deference to Knox Maddry and possibly the other deacons he had selected "Almost Persuaded" as the opening hymn, although he personally did not like it. He sang with the congregation automatically, thinking of his sermon while he mouthed the words.

"Almost persuaded" now to believe; "Almost per-
    suaded," Christ to receive.
Seems now some soul to say, "Go, Spirit, go thy way,
    Some more convenient day, on thee I'll call."

The Marlowes, Staley and Miranda and the four children,
sat near the front, and only a few rows behind were Knox
and Hattie Mae and Harriet Maddry. He saw Harriet looking
at him as she sang and wondered what she was thinking—
not about the hymn, obviously. But then, neither was he.

He opened the service, for the sixth time that week, by
reading all the Beatitudes. Suddenly, he felt as he had the day
he had preached his trial sermon. He didn't want to preach
to them. He wanted to talk to them and preach to himself,
though he knew they would put their own interpretations, not
his, on the things he said.

"I am a little sad tonight," he began, "because this is the
last night of our meeting. I am sad because I feel that I have
not entirely pleased you, and I am even sadder because I feel
that I have not entirely pleased God either. When Jesus was
baptized, a dove came down and the voice of God was heard
to say, 'This is my beloved Son, in whom I am well pleased.'
I suppose few of us can know God's pleasure on earth, and
yet that is what each of us is striving for."

A crash of thunder suddenly vibrated through the church,
and the startled congregation looked toward the windows.

August hesitated, then went on, his thoughts turning inward
again to his reflections of a few days earlier. "And yet, we
also seek to please God through our fellow man. We seek the
approbation of our fellow man, yet still we pause before
revealing our natures to him. We are afraid of becoming too
close to him, lest we be disappointed in him and he in us.
But when you think about it, what else is there in life if we
do not give or receive this closeness?"

Another roll of thunder, long and threatening, claimed the
attention of his congregation.

"Men sometimes seek immortality in strange ways," August
said. "The artist thinks he is leaving his soul behind for the
ages in his painting, the writer in his words, the philanthropist
in his good deeds. But are these things really monuments? Do
they have the warmth that you find when a man says of his
dead friend, 'I miss him. Nothing is the same without him'?

Our lives themselves should be the monument and not our feeble efforts at immortality. For it is by our lives that we are judged both now and on the last day that the world shall stand."

A jagged fork of lightning went across the church from the windows on the right side to the choir loft on the left, and there was a loud crack as the wooden panel in front of the loft split. One of the choir members screamed, a scream lost in the roar of thunder that followed. A few sparks fell from the split wood while the congregation watched in mute horror. Then the sparks died, the thunder subsided, and there was silence.

The silence did not last. A rumble of voices rose from the pews, and slowly people began to get up and move toward the door. Slowly at first, and then driven by panic they rushed, pushing their way to the double door.

"Wait!" August cried. "You're safer in here. Don't go outside." His voice was lost in the noise of the crowd. "The storm will not hurt you," he shrieked. "Don't leave. There's so much I want to say to you. Oh, please!"

But the last of them had gone through the door, and he was alone in the church. Now the only sound he could hear was the noise of buggies being driven away from the church, and then that, too, abated.

You could not watch one hour with me, he thought, and walked away from the pulpit to the first pew. "No," he said to the deserted church. "No." He looked back at the empty pulpit, standing like a grotesque symbol before him, and knelt where he was. He remained on his knees a long time, neither praying nor thinking, until it occurred to him that this was his Gethsemane. The comparison fanned his guilt to flame; he arose from his knees and walked slowly down the aisle and out of the church.

He stood beside one of the columns of the church, watching the rain which splashed against the earth with the noise of a waterfall. The churchyard was deserted now, except for Brandy, who stood by a hitching post, his head down between his front legs, his saddle soaked. August went out in the rain and untied the reins. "Poor old thing," he said. "I'll take you home now."

He was starting to mount when he felt a tug at his coat. "Please, mister, I'm lost."

Beside him in the darkness was a small boy, not more than six or seven years old, whose dark wet hair was plastered against his head and whose clothes were as wet as Brandy's saddle.

"My name is Gaetano Tamini, and I'm lost," the little boy repeated.

"Tamini—are you Giuseppe Tamini's son?"

"Yes. But he left me. I looked for him and could not find him. We came to town today in the wagon, and when it was time to go I could not find the wagon. It was dark." He began to cry. "They left without me: I want Mary." And then he was crying in earnest.

August put the child on the horse and then mounted. "Don't cry," he said. "We'll find Mary for you." He put his heels into Brandy's flanks and cantered down the road where Harriet had taken him to the Tamini house. Tonight the trip seemed to take much longer. After a while he slowed the horse to a walk, afraid he would pass the path that led to the house. The child had stopped crying and occasionally looked up at August, but he did not speak.

August was turning Brandy toward the path when his eyes fell on a figure crouched beside the road. He pulled Brandy over and the figure stood up.

"Stop, please stop," the girl said unnecessarily, for Brandy had already stopped. "Please help me; my little brother is lost."

Mary Tamini's long black hair fell like seaweed about her shoulders, her skirt clung to her, and her blouse stuck to her shoulders, so that even in the darkness he could see the pale flesh beneath it. "Gaetano!" She had seen him on the horse. "Where have you been? I've looked everywhere."

"I found him outside my church," August said. "He told me he was lost."

She looked at him now, really seeing him for the first time. "Mr. Fielding, is it? We went to town today, all of us, and when we saw it was going to storm we hurried home. We didn't notice that Gaetano was not with us until we got here, and then we didn't know whether he had not been with us at all or whether he had jumped off the wagon on the way home. I've been so frightened . . ." She had her hands on Gaetano's shoulders, helping him off the horse. Then she reached down to take his hand, as though to lead him home, and as she did, she crumpled and hit the ground before August was aware that she was falling.

"Mary!" Gaetano screamed, and began crying again. August bent over her, and gathered her into his arms as he tried to calm the little boy. "Hush, Gaetano. She has fainted. We will take her home now—take you both home. Can you lead my horse?"

The boy nodded and took the reins. Mary's body felt strangely light as August walked down the rutted path, feeling his way with his feet, stepping from time to time in mud-holes with water going over the tops of his shoes. Gaetano followed close behind with Brandy.

Finally they reached the house, and with his head August motioned for Gaetano to open the door. He went inside with Mary still limp in his arms and found himself staring into the eyes of Giuseppe Tamini, who looked as though he, too, had just come in from the rain, and the four other Taminis.

"Dio!" Giuseppe cried. "My Maria, she is dead!"

"No," August said quietly. "She has fainted." He looked around the little room with its crude furniture and then put her on a sagging couch.

"Gaetano," Tamini said, noticing his son for the first time, "where have you been. What has happened to your sister?"

"Get me a towel," August said to one of the gaping children, and when the little girl returned with it, he dried Mary's face. "Do you have smelling salts?" he asked, and they all looked at him as though they did not understand. "Never mind," he said, "she's coming around now."

Mary whimpered once and opened her eyes. "Gaetano," she whispered.

"He's here," August said. "We brought him home. You'd better get out of those wet clothes and into bed. Everything is all right now." He turned to the little girl again. "Can you help your sister?"

She nodded, and as Mary stood up shakily, helped her into the bedroom.

Tamini still looked bewildered.

"I found Gaetano outside my church tonight," August said, "and I was bringing him home when we found Mary out near the road. She fainted as we started back to the house."

"She was looking for him," Tamini said. "My Maria will be much sick, I think. So easy she gets sick. She is not strong.

I do not want her in the rain but she say, 'I find Gaetano,' and she go. *Grazie*, Mr.—"

"Fielding," August said.

"*Mille grazie*, Mr. Fielding. You bring them both home to me. I will remember you."

August suddenly noticed the puddle of water around his feet, and the water still dropping from his clothes. "I must go," he said.

"To town you cannot go in this rain," Tamini said. "You stay the night with us."

"No, my horse is outside. I'll be all right."

The bedroom door opened and the little girl said shyly, looking at August, "She wants to see you."

August went into the bedroom. Mary was in bed, shivering slightly under a rose-colored spread.

"Thank you," she said. "I wanted to thank you for bringing Gaetano home and," she smiled weakly, "for bringing me home."

"You get some rest," he said. "The lost sheep are all in the fold now," Looking pale and tired against the white pillow-case, her face was still incredibly beautiful. He thought again of a drawing of the Madonna. "I will see you soon," he said, "to see how you are getting along."

He left the house quickly to begin the endless ride back to town.

The next morning August preached his Sunday sermon as usual, making no reference to the storm and the chaos in which the revival had ended. But at the close of the service he did not stand at the door to greet the congregation. He did not feel like waiting for a pointed remark from Knox Maddry on the subject of the revival. Instead, he slipped out of the side door beyond the choir loft and went back to the parsonage for Brandy. Then he rode, in bright sunlight this time, to the Taminis'.

The family, with the exception of Mary, was having a picnic lunch by the brook. Giuseppe Tamini came to him as he was tying Brandy and said, "*Buon giorno*, Mr. Fielding. You eat with us, yes? We have the sandwiches today because Maria she is not well."

Gaetano, recognizing his rescuer, rushed over and hugged August. "You eat with us," he repeated his father's invitation.

August laughed and rubbed Gaetano's hair. "I see you survived your night in town," he said. "Yes, I'd be happy to eat with you." He looked around him. "You say Mary is not well?"

"She caught a cold from getting wet," Gaetano said, "but I didn't. Mary always catches a cold."

"She is not strong," Tamini said.

August went with them back to the brook and joined the picnic. Someday, he decided, he would bring the little Marlowes out to see the young Taminis. He enjoyed talking with Giuseppe, finding him warm and friendly and, August thought, almost too emotional where his family was concerned.

"It is my dream," he said, "to go someday back to my country and take my children. They do not know how beautiful is Italy. They do not know Italiano, but they learn fast when we are there."

"You would take them for a visit?"

"Not for a visit, but to stay," Tamini said. "For a young man a new country, a new home, it is all right, but I am not a young man yet, and I think of the old home now. My brothers, they are in Italy, and my sister, and I think of them more and I wish my children to know them."

After they had finished eating, August asked if he might see Mary.

"Cristina, go say to your sister that Mr. Fielding is here," Tamini said, and the young girl scampered to the house. She returned a minute later and said, "Mary is asleep, Papa. Do you want me to wake her?"

"No," August said quickly. "I'll see her some other time." He thanked the Taminis for their hospitality and went to Brandy.

"You come again," Tamini said. "You come to see us more."

He waved to them as he rode back down the path where water still stood in the deep ruts. Being with the Taminis had lifted his spirits, and he was aware that he felt this way whenever he was around a happy family. He thought again of the Marlowes, and suddenly he wanted a family of his own. He had never really thought about it before, except as something that might occur in the faraway future, but now he wanted to move the future up, to have his own family picnic and take his own children fishing as he did the Marlowes. His daydream lasted all the way back to town, and it was not until he was back at the parsonage that he remembered he was supposed to have gone to the Maddrys' for dinner, that Harriet had invited him to bring Brandy over and try him with the buggy.

10

KNOX MADDRY WAS UNHAPPY, and that meant that unless the cause of his unhappiness was cleared soon, there more than likely would be others in the same state of mind. He usually managed to see to it that he never suffered alone.

The summer had begun with great promise (Harriet and August seemed to get on well together, and that both surprised and delighted him), but now the summer was almost over and the promise remained unfulfilled. Now that he thought about it, the turning point had been fairly early in the summer, during revival week. That the revival was a fiasco there was no doubt. Oh, some of the women and a few of the men had had nice things to say about August's preaching, but they were just being polite. Staley Marlowe called the storm an act of God and said nobody could help something like that. But Knox was convinced that if God had been pleased with the way the revival was going, he would not have pointed His finger of fire at the church. August Fielding might just as well take that storm as a warning from above.

The second thing that went wrong came right on the heels of the first. Harriet had invited August to Sunday dinner the day after the revival and not only had he not come, he hadn't even had the grace to send his regrets. True, he came around the next day to apologize, said someone had been sick unexpectedly and he had gone straight from church to call, but Knox knew every member of the congregation and could verify the fact that there had been no sudden illness among them. He personally believed that August had gone to see a

Methodist. More and more he was hearing reports about the Baptist preacher fraternizing with the Methodists, and as chairman of the board of deacons, he was duly alarmed. Lord only knew where a thing like that might lead.

But that was only the beginning. During the entire summer August had had only two Sunday dinners with the Maddrys, although he had been invited almost every Sunday. He always pleaded a previous engagement. Knox knew that he had been to the Marlowes' once or twice, but he could not find out where he was on the other Sundays.

The strangest thing that had happened, though, was that day in July when Knox had been making the rounds of his farms. He had driven the buggy up to the Tamini house, where he saw August sitting by the brook with the six Tamini children. All of them, including the oldest girl, were wading in the brook, and August was watching them and laughing. He saw Mary splash some water toward August while August, still laughing, moved farther back on the moss. Hardly a pose befitting a preacher. He found Tamini in the shed behind the house and lost no time in asking what the preacher was doing there.

Tamini shrugged as though he gave the matter no importance and said, "He came to see the children."

After his initial surprise at finding him there, Knox decided that August was trying to convert the family. In his young mind August probably thought that Catholics who had no Catholic church in the vicinity would be fertile ground in which to plant the seeds of Protestantism. But Knox knew better. The Taminis were not only Catholics, but Italian Catholics, straight from the Pope's own country.

On two other occasions during the summer he had seen August's horse tied to the tree in front of the Taminis'. He decided not to say anything until the end of summer. When the weather got bad, August would probably give up his trips to the country anyway, and he might become discouraged with his missionary work before then.

He did, however, decide upon a course of action. Along with everything else, Harriet's disposition had deteriorated with the summer. She was never easy to get along with, but now she seemed particularly feisty and became more old-maidy every day. August was still the only solution to the problem, but as a matchmaker he, Knox, did not seem to be making much progress.

The course of action he decided upon was to elicit help from Hattie Mae. His confidence in her ability was not overwhelming, but he thought that this was probably something in which a woman's strategy might be more effective than a man's.

So after the Sunday school picnic in early September, he talked to Hattie Mae about it on the way home. Harriet, pleading a headache, had not gone with them.

"I hope Harriet's headache is better," Knox said. "Lord knows she's hard enough to get along with when she feels well."

"I don't think she wanted to go to the picnic," Hattie Mae said. "I wonder why not."

"I'll tell you why not," Knox said. "She didn't want to see the preacher."

"Oh, I don't think so, Knox. I think she likes him well enough."

"That's just it, Hattie Mae. She likes him too much, and he don't pay her much attention anymore."

"Harriet likes the preacher! Oh, Knox, not that way. I think you must be mistaken."

"I am not mistaken," he said emphatically. "Don't you think I know my own daughter? I've been meaning to speak to you about this for some time, Hattie Mae. August was nice enough to Harriet when he first came, but this summer he just seemed to lose interest, and her pride is hurt. I think we ought to do something to bring them together again," Knox went on, choosing his words carefully. "We ought to help this thing along or Harriet will become even more unhappy."

"I don't know what we could do," Hattie Mae said. "Of course, we could invite the preacher to the house more often, but lately he hasn't been accepting our invitations, so—"

"No, we've got to try something else," Knox said. "Think for a minute. Harriet's whole future," he gestured expansively, "depends upon it."

Hattie Mae thought and thought and then said, "I wouldn't want Harriet to do anything that would make her seem like a brazen hussy, and I wouldn't want us to do anything that would be encouraging her in brazenness. No, there's nothing else we can do."

Knox clucked to Bessie and slapped the reins over her back. Should have known better, he thought. It was easier to get blood from a turnip than to get anything sensible out of Hattie Mae. If you want to get something done, don't go to a woman for help; do it yourself.

The early October sun was still warm when August left the Taminis and rode back to the parsonage. It was Wednesday afternoon, and he had not yet prepared his talk for prayer meeting that night. His thoughts kept pace with Brandy's easy gait. He was aware that he was spending a great deal of time at the Taminis'. It had started with occasional visits during the early summer, then as the summer progressed, so had the visits. At the time, he had told himself he enjoyed being with the family, and they, apparently, enjoyed his company. Only now, today, did he admit to himself his real reason for continuing the visits.

There was no longer any doubt in his mind; he was in love with Mary Tamini. He wondered if he had been in love with her all along—since that first day he had seen her sitting beside the brook resembling a delicate painting—and was only late in realizing it. He had not been alone with her more than two or three times in the past few months. Today, however, had been one of those rare occasions. They had gone into the woods to gather bright-colored leaves to decorate the house, and each of them seemed more aware of the other than before.

When they both had their arms filled with the small branches of red and gold and rust, she looked at them and said sadly, "They are so pretty here. In the house they will look different—not so pretty."

"I suppose taking them away from their natural habitat has something to do with it," he said.

"Yes. It's the same with people, isn't it? They are not themselves when they are away from their natural habitat. Something goes out of them, just as it does the leaves."

He waited for her to go on, but she said nothing else. "Are you talking about yourself?" he asked finally.

"No, about Papa. This is my home, this country. I have never known another. But Papa—I think the longer he is away from Italy, the more he misses it. I remember when I was a little girl he would say something now and then about taking us to Italy for a visit. Now he talks about it all the time, especially since Mama died—only it isn't to visit anymore, it's to stay."

"But if he went back, Italy wouldn't be home to him," August said. "He's been away too long."

"Perhaps. But his family is still there, and there is nothing to keep him here except that there isn't any money to go back."

And then the idea came to August. If going back to Italy was Giuseppe's heart's desire, he wanted him to have it. Somehow he would raise the money. The family had given him so much friendship, so much warmth, that he wanted to do something in return. But there were two barriers in his way. He could never save enough money to pay the passage for seven people, and even if he could, Giuseppe would never accept it as a gift. And a third barrier entered his mind at that moment: he did not want Mary to go away. Not ever.

"Do you—you and the others—want to go?" he asked.

"Papa has told us so many stories about his old home that the children would think it the answer to their prayers to be able to go."

"And you?"

"I am not so young as they," she said. "I would go to make Papa happy, but I am not unhappy here." She gave him a warm look which caused him suddenly to feel the pounding of his heart.

"I would miss you, Mary." He tried to sound casual, to hide the mounting excitement within him.

She stopped walking and looked at him seriously for a minute, and then she smiled. "You are strange, August. Sometimes I think I know your thoughts and other times I don't know you at all. You are very complex, I think."

He put down the branches and took her arms, ready to draw her into his arms, about to tell her that he was not complex at all, about to see her lift her face to him to be kissed . . . But suddenly he dropped his arms and picked up the leaves. Without looking at her, he knew she was staring at him, hurt and mystified.

They took the leaves back to the house and he left immediately. On the way back to the parsonage, he could think of nothing but the bewildered expression on Mary's face as she had said goodbye to him.

He wanted her. He desired her as he had never desired any other woman. But as he was about to embrace her he had seen in his mind the picture of a basement room and his own distorted image in a cracked mirror. Would not the guilt of that April afternoon always be over him like a shadow?

But perhaps he might be able to make her happier *because* of that April afternoon. Was he not more aware now? Was he not . . .

No, he was rationalizing. He wanted Mary and he was trying to salve his own conscience to make it possible for him to have her. It was as hopelessly wrong as trying to make a bargain with God—and as futile.

That night at prayer meeting his talk was briefer than usual, and although the small group's attention did not seem to wander, his did. When he concluded the talk, he opened the Bible to the Book of Psalms and read one at random, forcing his attention on the reading as he had forced it on the talk. And then suddenly the words seemed to jump up at him, and he was convinced that he had been led to that particular Psalm.

"Delight thou in the Lord, and he shall give thee thy heart's desire. Commit thy way unto the Lord, and put thy trust in him, and he shall bring it to pass."

He thought about the Psalm again that night after he was in bed and decided that tomorrow he would go again to the Taminis' and talk to Giuseppe.

"So you are wanting to marry my Maria. And is my Maria wanting to marry you?"

"I don't know," August admitted. "I haven't spoken to her yet. I wanted to talk to you first."

"That is right," Giuseppe said. There was another long silence, then he said, "It is not what I wanted for her. I wanted for her to go to Italia and find a husband there."

"But Mary is an American," August said. "Perhaps she would rather have an American husband."

"You are maybe right," Giuseppe said. "And I want for Maria what she wants, but who can know what is the best thing? You are a good man, August, but you are not Catholic and Maria is. I do not want for her to marry out of the church."

"But she has lived most of her life away from the church," August said.

"Yes, but it is not her doing because there is no church here for her. She is one of the faithful; she goes to church when she can. And I think you would try to make her something else."

August was silent for a minute. This was a matter that had not occurred to him, or possibly he had assumed that if Mary married him, she would naturally go to his church. But if Mary preferred another, he would offer no argument on the subject. From Eugene Bryant he had learned that there might be a few souls in heaven that had not been immersed as Baptists on earth. As far as he could see, a person should be allowed to worship God in the way that best suited his own religious needs.

"I would not try to change Mary's religion," he said.

"And your children?" Giuseppe asked. "What about them?"

August hesitated again. "I think," he said slowly, "that our children can decide for themselves."

"No! That is not right! The children must be as Maria."

August smiled. "Very well—and may they turn out half as good."

"You are not like other preachers," Giuseppe said. "You do not hate Catholics."

"I hope," August said, "that I don't hate anyone."

"My Maria is very frail," Giuseppe said, as though making a last point in an argument. "She has never been strong like the others."

"I'll take care of her always," August said, "and do everything in my power to make her happy."

"You may speak to my Maria, and if she say so, you can marry her, but you must marry her in her church, not yours."

"Thank you, sir," he said, and hurried to the house to find Mary.

She was in the kitchen, preparing lunch for the children. "You will eat with us," she said without greeting him or turning toward him.

"Mary, I want to talk to you. Now."

She turned away from the table at the urgency in his voice. "Before we eat?"

"Yes."

They went to the porch, and he sat down beside her on the

squeaking swing. Suddenly he realized that he had no idea
how to begin. He had thought talking with Giuseppe would
be more nerve-racking than anything he could imagine, but
he had remained strangely calm until now.

"Mary, I . . . I have just spoken to your father, and I have
his permission to speak to you."

She drew back, almost imperceptibly, and said, "You want
to marry me, August?"

"Yes." He could not conceal his surprise.

"And Papa said it was all right?"

"Yes. He said it was all right with him if that was what
you wanted. Will you marry me, Mary? I'll try . . ."

"That's very strange," she said, interrupting him. "When
we talked of it, Papa and I, he was very much against it."

"When you talked of it . . . You mean you—"

She laughed. "It was several weeks ago," she said. "He
said I could not marry you because you were not Catholic."

August thought the expression on his face must be unusually stupid. "But several weeks ago . . ."

"I know, it had not entered your mind then. But I had
thought about it and I knew if I thought hard enough eventually you would, too. You see, it worked."

Now August laughed, too. She was accepting him, but it
was probably the strangest acceptance a man ever had. He
laughed and laughed, and she joined him, until the other
Taminis crowded to the door to see what was causing the
merriment on the front porch. "Come and speak to August,"
she said. "He is going to be your brother."

They came out with grins on their faces and each in turn
solemnly shook his hand. None of them looked very startled
at the announcement. August decided that he was probably
the only one to whom it had come as a surprise.

Marrying Mary was not a simple procedure. First, there
was the question of who would take care of Giuseppe and
the children when Mary left home. The logical one was
Cristina, the second-oldest daughter, but she was only
thirteen and Mary wanted her to remain in school. August
had suggested that the family come to the parsonage to live
with them, but Mary told him Giuseppe would never give up
the farm and his independence.

Another complication, though not quite so serious, was

seeing a priest. Mary told him that he would have to talk to a priest and he was willing enough to do it, but the nearest Catholic church was in Raleigh, and even if he went by train, it would mean being away from Fairmont for two or three days.

"I think," Mary said finally, "that we should wait until next summer to get married. School will be out and there won't be as much responsibility for Cristina."

August demurred, but even as he did, he saw the wisdom of her decision. And so, restlessly, and yet in resignation, he settled down to another winter in Fairmont similar to the past one, with only his frequent trips to the Taminis' to break the monotony—and also to add to his growing frustration.

Knox's original plan had been to leave August and Harriet at the house after supper on Christmas Eve while he and Hattie Mae made the rounds of the neighbors' houses delivering gifts. The spirit of Christmas Eve, Knox thought, must get through to August, and then Harriet had, unconsciously, aided the plan by looking and acting most un-Harriet-like. She wore a soft red velvet dress and even had a sprig of holly in her mousy hair. She would never be pretty, but there were times, and this was one of them, when she was not entirely unattractive. And before they had gone in to supper, she had been in quite good spirits. She had offered August a glass of eggnog which, surprisingly, he had drunk.

"It has brandy in it," Harriet had said, "and I know Brandy is your weakness."

Knox had been a bit perplexed until he realized that Harriet was talking about the preacher's horse. Jovially, he added, "You got any other weaknesses, Preacher?"

"A great many," August said, laughing. Knox *could* have been mistaken, but he thought August looked at Harriet when he said it.

But during the meal he was not sure the original plan had been a good one. He did not know what happened to change the atmosphere, but *something* went wrong, and in the space of a few short minutes August became preoccupied. He seemed to go away from them mentally, and his answers to the simplest questions were forced and monosyllabic.

Afterward, when they went back to the living room, Knox tried to figure out what had happened. The conversation had

been harmless enough. He had mentioned that he had taken
Christmas baskets to all his tenants that afternoon and that
it really made him feel good to see the food and fruit going
where it was needed.

"It's not that I object to contributing to the baskets the
church sends, Preacher," he had said. "But it makes a difference when you actually deliver them yourself and know that
the people appreciate them. I think some of those folks who
get church baskets take them for granted. They *expect*
charity."

"Expect charity," Hattie Mae said.

August looked interested. "It's a nice thought," he said,
"to remember all of your tenants at Christmas."

"Well, not *all* of them, exactly. But it ain't my fault if the
Taminis go away every Christmas. They have to go find a
priest, you know, and pay him to pardon their sins. But I
guess I can't complain about that to much. Tamini is a good
farmer, even if he is a Catholic."

August was concentrating on his food.

"How'd you get along with your summer campaign there,
Preacher?"

"What do you mean?"

"Your campaign to try to make Christians out of the
Taminis. I could have told you you weren't going to get
anywhere. One thing about those Catholics, you can't change
them. Their minds are closed up tighter than a jug and they
ain't about to let any air in. Why, you know when Tamini
first came here, I invited him and his whole family to our
church, since there ain't a Catholic church around here, and
you know what he said? He said he couldn't go to any other
church. Now how's that for being narrow-minded?"

"The Taminis are Christians," August said, and Knox
detected a certain stiffness in his tone.

"You still going out there to see them? If you ain't trying
to convert them, just what are you doing?"

"I enjoy their company," August said.

Knox let the subject drop and went on to something else,
but he made a mental note to remember to have a talk with
August about his choice of friends. Just being a preacher did
not place him above gossip. A preacher had to be as careful
as anybody else, maybe more so, and it wouldn't do August

any good in the town to spend his time with a tenant-farm family, and Catholics at that.

But the mood that had existed before supper had been wrecked. Try as he might, he could not get August back into his earlier frame of mind. And now he wondered if it was a good idea after all for him and Hattie Mae to go out.

It was Harriet who came up with a plan that, he had to admit, was a stroke of genius.

"You haven't delivered the gifts yet, have you?" she said to Hattie Mae.

"No, we were going to do it tonight," Hattie Mae said.

"You've been busy all day and so has Daddy, I'll take the things around and you can stay here and rest. Would you like to go with me, August?"

Knox almost chortled out loud. August, of course, could not say no and let Harriet go out alone. And as they went from place to place, the neighbors would see them together and get the idea . . . Oh, it was perfect, just perfect. Pretty soon people would start asking August about Harriet and including them in social affairs as a couple.

"That's mighty thoughtful of you, daughter," Knox said quickly. "Hattie Mae and I are a bit frazzled. You two young people go and have a good time."

After they left, he turned gleefully to Hattie Mae. "It's turned out to be a nice Christmas Eve, hasn't it? Don't know when I've had so much Christmas spirit. I think when they come back, we'll all have a glass of brandy to celebrate—without the damned eggs in it this time."

"I think August is lonely," she said. "He misses the Taminis."

"Why in God's name should he miss them? It ain't like they're his family." Hattie Mae was the beatingest woman he ever saw for bringing up nonsense. "Just because he goes out there sometimes don't mean he's adopted them."

"I've seen that oldest Tamini girl," Hattie Mae said, "and she's quite pretty."

"What's that got to do with . . ." Knox stopped, remembering the first time he had seen August at the farm. Mary Tamini had been barefoot—barefoot and showing part of her legs—in the brook.

"You think he goes out there because of her?" The thought was so monstrous that he felt ill.

"I can't think of any other reason. Can you?"

He slumped in his chair and was silent. Hattie Mae had never had an idea of her own in her whole life, and he could not believe she could be right. But the more he thought about it, the more it seemed there would be no other reason.

He had sowed a few wild oats of his own when he was young and he certainly could dismiss a young man's follies with a wink as quick as the next fellow. But the *preacher* with that girl? Surely it wasn't too much to expect the man he had picked out for his own daughter to have some conception of moral behavior. The *preacher* at that.

Tomorrow, without fail, he would have a long talk with August.

11

AUGUST DREAMED HE WAS FALLING, and jerked awake with a start. He had no idea how long he had been asleep; the room was the black dark that means daylight is still hours away. He sat up in bed, fully awake now, and pushed back the covers. His body was drenched with perspiration and his nightshirt clung to him. He got out of bed and went downstairs to the kitchen for a glass of water. The clock on the kitchen table said one-thirty.

Christmas Day, he thought. He had been dreading the arrival of the holidays because it meant that Mary would go away from him, and though she and the family would be gone only three days, the thought that she was not there in the accustomed place was disturbing.

Christmas Day. He had spent lonely holidays locked inside himself before, but this particular Christmas seemed lonely in a new, special way, even though he would not spend the day alone. There was his Christmas sermon at eleven, followed by dinner with the Marlowes, and then he would visit the shut-ins, and after that . . .

He went back upstairs, but he did not go back to bed. Sleep seemed as far away now as Mary.

It had been a disturbing night. He found that the more he saw Knox Maddry, the more irritated he became with the man. He tried to tell himself that Knox meant no harm in the things he said; it was just his way. But the irritating thing was that Knox did not know he was irritating and therefore would never make any effort to change.

Tonight, while he and Harriet were delivering the gifts, he had seen her in a completely different light and had guessed what her trouble was. She had affected gaiety on their rounds, laughing often with the neighbors over nothing. And between houses, when they were alone, she was quiet, like a tongue-tied young girl.

The trouble was, he decided, Harriet was a bundle of nerves after all these years with her father. Knox, apparently, used the same tactics with Harriet that he had with Hattie Mae in killing whatever spirit she had, but being of a different temperament, Harriet had reacted in a different way. He felt sorry for the girl, terribly sorry, because he could see no way out for her. Only a miracle would get her away from Knox's influence, and the day of miracles seemed to have passed long before the printing of the King James Version.

He went to the window and looked out into the blackness. These hours of wakefulness, once rare with him, were becoming more frequent. The thing, whatever it was, that had for months been resting in the back of his mind was slowly pushing itself to the front. That was why, instead of marshaling his thoughts into a straight line to proceed to a logical point, he let them straggle like unknowing soldiers without a commander. Later, he promised himself (it was always later), he would take charge. Meanwhile, there were the duties of his church, his people, to see to. And perhaps right now . . . sleep.

As he turned up the walk, after making his calls, August saw Knox Maddry leave the porch. "Merry Christmas," he called out.

"Well, Preacher," Knox said. "I declare you're a hard man to get a hold of. This is the third time today I've been here and I thought I had missed you again. Merry Christmas," he added as an afterthought.

"Come in," August said. "I hope nothing is wrong."

"No," Knox said as they went into the house. "At least, I hope not."

August knew at once that his chief deacon had not come to bring him season's greetings. The round face was puckered into worry wrinkles.

"Sit down," August said.

"Preacher, what I wanted to see you about—maybe I shouldn't have come on Christmas Day, but it's something that's been bothering me a bit—uh, I hardly know how to say this." August waited.

"You see a great deal of the Taminis, don't you?"

"Yes."

"Why?" The word went through the air between them like a shaft.

"I enjoy being with them," August said quietly.

"The whole family—or one particular member?"

"Both. The whole family *and* one particular member. May I ask why this inquisition?" Although he was trying to control his temper, he knew that before Knox left, he was probably going to be very angry indeed.

"Then it's true," Knox said softly. "August, you are a young man, and I'm willing to give the devil his due. I know sometimes even preachers are tempted, but you don't have to forget discretion."

"I don't think I understand you," said August, although he was beginning to understand perfectly.

"That girl—Mary—she is a foreigner, a Catholic, and the daughter of a sharecropper. How do you think it looks, in the eyes of the town, for you to go sneaking out to see her?"

August sat up very straight. "She is not a foreigner, she is an American. I can find no disgrace in her being a Catholic. She is a fine, Christian girl. As for her being the daughter of a farmer—well, you seem to forget that my father was also a farmer."

Knox looked at him and shook his head. "You are overlooking the one point that you, as a preacher, should certainly be aware of. Or are you in favor of immoral situations?"

August stood up, his face very red. "Are you implying that there is something immoral about—"

"Why else would a man in your position go to see a girl like that?"

He sat down again, biting his tongue, struggling for composure. "I have not, as you said, been sneaking out to the Taminis'. I have been going openly. It is no secret, and I will tell you now. Mary Tamini and I are going to be married."

Knox's mouth flew open, but he said nothing. He stared at August, and the silence between them stretched on and on. "I don't believe it," Knox said finally. "You are making a joke, and not a very good one."

August did not answer. Now he remembered what Harriet had told him early last summer, the day they had first gone to the Taminis'. He had not taken her seriously at the time, but now he wondered. Was it possible that Knox Maddry really had plans for him and Harriet?

"No, I am not joking," he said.

"Have you forgotten yourself completely? You're a Baptist preacher, for God's sake!"

"I hope so."

"You hope what?"

"That I am a preacher for God's sake."

"Don't try to twist my words!" Knox was shouting now.

August sighed. "Mary and I will be married during the summer. I cannot see why that should cause you or anyone else any anguish. Your last preacher here was a married man, I believe."

"That has nothing to do with it. Next summer, you say?" Knox, for some reason, looked a bit relieved.

"Yes."

Knox stood up and walked across the room several times. Finally he stepped beside August's chair.

"You know, August, you're young enough to be my son. In fact, you *are* like a son to me, and I'm going to talk to you that way—as though you were my son. I know the temptations that face a young man—maybe it's hard to believe now, but I was your age once. And there was a girl out in the country I went to see occasionally." He winked, and August felt like striking him. "But when it came to getting married, I had sense enough, after some advice from *my* father, to pick a proper girl. You've got to think about that, boy. You've got to take that into consideration. You know a preacher's wife has to be like Caesar's wife. She has to be an example for all of the women in the church. And Mary Tamini doesn't even *belong* to your church."

He paused, but August said nothing.

"You are probably going through a bad time now," Knox continued. "I know it gets lonesome for you around here sometimes. Just work ain't always enough. But I want you to think about this, think about it for a long time—and pray over it. You're a bright young man, August, but I'm fifty-seven years old and I *know*. You think about it and you'll see that marrying that girl will ruin your life. It's a long time before next summer—six months—and I know you'll come to the right decision before then. Mind you, I'm not saying you shouldn't get married. I think you should *if* you marry the right girl. You think about it, August, and pretty soon we'll be laughing together about this little crisis, and you'll thank me for setting you straight."

"I have thought about it," August said, "for a long time, and I have prayed about it, and my decision is, and will remain, the same."

Knox frowned, and then smiled and patted his shoulder. "Let's just wait and see what you'll think a few months from now." Then his sober expression returned. "I would hate to have to bring this up before the deacons," he said, "because it would be a serious matter to them. So we'll keep it quiet, and wait and see . . ."

"As you like," August said.

Knox started toward the door and August followed him. "No, I won't say anything to the deacons—yet," he said as he went out. On the porch he turned around and called, "Oh, yes, Preacher, a merry Christmas to you."

It was another sleepless night, but not because of Knox Maddry. That night August found that the thing in the back of his mind had reared again, like a stallion about to take a jump.

And it did. He knew what he supposed he had hidden deep in the recesses of his mind, because thinking about it meant self-condemnation. He was living a selfish life, a life that purported to be for others, but had no real purpose to it except to exist day by day and satisfy his own needs. He prepared his sermons to the best of his ability, not to glorify God but because it pleased him to do the best he could and possibly to gain the approval of his congregation. He went about his other duties because they kept him busy. Possibly by serving himself in this manner, he inadvertently rendered some service to his fellowman. But he was not serving God.

The worst of it was that where he had once been so sure how it would be when he was a preacher, he now had no idea what God expected of him or even what he expected of himself.

Professor Bryant had once asked him if he had ever considered atheism, and the thought had amused him. It was not possible for him *not* to believe in God. But how easy life could be, he thought, if we owed no allegiance, no gratitude, no reverence, to anything divine or human. There would be no fear of the consequences of sin—for sin, as such, would not exist. No more religion, only philosophy. Or perhaps it was possible to make a religion of philosophy. Professor Bryant apparently had.

Professor Eugent Bryant . . . his friend. His betrayed friend.

He got up at intervals during the night and put more coal in the stove, then sat down again and contemplated his fear and his sin and his guilt.

As the day and night passed, so did the winter. He spent even more time at his church duties, seeing the members of his congregation, and also finding time to see those who were not in his congregation. He expected to hear from Knox Maddry on this score, but Knox remained jovial, backslapping, and patronizing. Their Christmas night conversation was not referred to, and both studiously avoided any subject that might bring it up again.

August would have liked to talk to someone about it, but since he could not tell Mary, he decided he would tell no one, although on one or two occasions he found himself close to confiding in the Marlowes.

He saw less of Mary during the latter part of the winter. There were two big snows, and the last one stayed on the ground for what seemed like weeks, making the road to the farm too dangerous to attempt with Brandy.

Spring brought signs of hope, but the hope was short-lived. It was a cold, gray spring with much rain and finally turned out to be a continuation of winter. It was not until June that he felt the season had really changed and that summer, at last, had come.

But summer brought a problem of its own. Three days after

his last visit to the farm, during which he and Mary had decided to be married in July, Mary sent him a note informing him that Cristina had typhoid fever and that he must stay away until she recovered.

August saddled Brandy and rode immediately to the farm. As he went up to the porch he saw the large yellow quarantine sign on the door. Before he knocked, the door opened, and Mary, looking pale and tired and half sick herself, said, "August, I told you not to come. You can't come in."

"Can you come outside?"

"No, I'm afraid to get near you."

"What about the others?"

"I have Cristina in the front bedroom and I'm trying to keep everyone away from her."

"But you're going near her. You might get it."

She shrugged. "I hope not. Someone has to take care of her. Oh, August." Suddenly she was crying. "I'm afraid she is going to die."

"Mary." In spite of her warning he opened the screen door and took her in his arms. "Mary, let me do something for you. Let me help. What about food, supplies from town, medicine for Cristina? There must be things you need. Make a list and I'll take it back to town."

After that, he went to the farm every day and talked to Mary on the porch and took her the things she needed. In their concern for Cristina, neither of them mentioned what her illness had done to their wedding plans. For nearly two weeks Cristina hovered between life and death, and then one morning, after what had been her worst night, she seemed better.

"I can't believe it," Mary told him. "Last night we thought we were going to lose her, and this morning she seems better than she has yet. But, oh August, her hair is all coming out. She's almost bald. If she looks in a mirror—how can I keep a mirror from her?"

August laughed. "If all you have to worry about is keeping a mirror from her, I think our worries are over."

"We'll have to postpone our wedding again, August. It will be a long time before Cristina will be able to be up and around again. Maybe September."

"September is fine," he said.

"That really isn't so far away," she said. "And August, this would be a good time for you to talk to the priest."

He went the following week and he did not like the priest at all. Had he not considered himself more enlightened, he would have believed all that Brother Johnson and Knox Maddry had said about Catholics.

Father Kegan was middle-aged, with dark hair growing low over his forehead and black, bushy eyebrows. He spoke with a slight Irish brogue, and being unaccustomed to it, August found it hard to understand.

Father Kegan made it clear from the beginning that he did not approve of mixed marriages, and the marriage of a Catholic to a member of the Protestant ministry was worse than mixed. It was in the priest's words "something of a catastrophe, or at least, has the making of a catastrophe." He soon realized, however, that this approach was the wrong one for August, so he tried another, and then another. He covered, August decided, all the ground Knox Maddry had covered Christmas night, plus a few acres more.

But there was a difference in Father Kegan the next day. He had apparently decided there was nothing he could do to prevent the marriage, so he spent the morning telling August about his duties and obligations as the husband of a Catholic. August relaxed somewhat and listened with interest.

When he left, the priest gave him two books and some pamphlets about the church. He shook hands with August and said, "Tell Mary to let me know about the banns."

"The what?"

"Banns," he repeated, then smiled. "She'll understand."

With Cristina's recovery August's problem was how to break the news of his approaching marriage in Fairmont—and to Knox Maddry. Telling Knox would lead only to unpleasantness, and August wanted his news to be received with joy. He decided to tell the entire congregation at once.

On the second Sunday in September, two days before he and Mary were to leave for Raleigh to be married by Father Kegan, he was nervous during his sermon. After the offertory, before the singing of the closing hymn, he went back to the pulpit.

"I have an announcement to make," he said. "It is a personal announcement and I hope that you will feel something of the happiness on hearing it that I feel in making it, for you are all very close to me, and it would increase my joy to know that you rejoice with me. On Wednesday of this week, Miss Mary Tamini and I are to be married . . ."

"Who is she?" he heard a male voice whisper loudly.

"I regret to say that we will not be married here," he said, "because I would like to have you with me on that day. However, we shall return to Fairmont on Saturday." He smiled and went on as though making the regular weekly announcement: "And services will be as usual next Sunday."

He left the pulpit and went back to his chair to await the singing of the closing hymn, which was to be "Gently, Lord, O Gently Lead Us." But the pianist began playing instead "Love Divine, All Love Excelling." He smiled and nodded to her, appreciating her little joke, and waited while the congregation found the right hymn in their books.

Then, as he had not dared to do before, he searched the individual faces. Miranda Marlowe, the first one he sought out, was smiling and singing. Beside her Staley sang also. He did not look perturbed. By the aisle, near the center of the church, Knox Maddry held a hymnal in front of him but made no pretense of looking at it or singing. Hattie Mae held the hymnal in trembling hands, her face registering nothing but surprise, and beside Hattie Mae Harriet stood like a statue, her eyes trained on the head in front of her as though she were in a trance.

During the singing of the last stanza, August went to the door to await his congregation, and as they left the pews the restraint that had marked their reaction to his announcement vanished. They rushed forward, eager to shake his hand, to ask questions: "Who is Mary Tamini? Why didn't you let us know before? Oh, you're a sly one, Preacher." They shook his hand, slapped him on the back, wished him well. "We'll have a pounding for you when you get back."

"I'm so glad, August, so happy for you," Miranda Marlowe said, "but also a little hurt that you didn't tell us."

Staley shook his hand and said, "I wish you well, Preacher. I know Giuseppe Tamini and he's a fine man."

And then the Maddrys were at the door. Hattie Mae paused, but Knox, right behind her, took her arm and ushered her by August before she could speak. Knox neither looked in his direction nor said a word. Harriet met his eyes for a moment and then looked away. He had plainly been snubbed by the leading deacon and his family, and those behind the Maddrys, waiting their turn to congratulate him, showed that they were puzzled.

When the last one had left the church, August closed the door and went to the parsonage. It had, on the whole, gone off very well. He wasn't sure what he had expected—possibly for Knox to get up in church and make a scene. But now he was over the last hurdle. It was reasonable to suppose that Knox could not make a scene now without making a fool of himself, and knowing Knox, that would be the last thing he wanted.

As Knox had once thought that August would get used to certain ideas and change his mind about the marriage, so August now thought the same of Knox. By next Sunday the marriage would be accomplished, and Knox had a week to reconcile himself to that fact.

But each of them had underestimated the tenacity of the other.

An hour later he was saddling Brandy to go to the farm when he saw a woman walking around the side of the parsonage, approaching the shed. He thought at first that Miranda had come to see him, then as she drew nearer he recognized Harriet. He put the saddle back on the side of the stall and waited.

"Hello, August." Her tone of voice could have been mistaken for that of a shy schoolgirl.

"Hello, Harriet. This is a surprise." It was indeed, after the way she had walked out of church without a word to him.

"I wanted to talk to you."

He did not invite her into the house. There was something about her manner that frightened him a little. Even though she seemed to be in perfect control, she gave him the impression that at any minute she might lose control.

"Yes, Harriet?"

She looked at Brandy and then at the saddle August had just replaced. "You were getting ready to go see her, weren't you?"

"Yes, I had started to the Taminis'. But I can certainly

wait to hear whatever you have to say, Harriet. If there's anything I can do for you . . ."

"Don't go, August." Her voice was so low that he had to bend slightly to hear her. "I can't believe you really meant what you said in church. Not if you had had time to think about it."

"No, Harriet. I've thought about it a great deal. I'm going to marry Mary. I don't understand why you—"

"I think you do, August."

"What I understand is that you're upset about something and therefore might say something you'll later wish you hadn't said. Perhaps you'd better think about it for a while, and then maybe later when you're feeling better we can talk about it."

"I've thought about it for two years," she said. "Oh August, didn't you know how I felt? How could you *not* have known?"

"I'm sorry, Harriet. I—"

"Don't apologize to me, August. Don't you dare apologize to me." The anger in her eyes was replaced by tears. "Think about yourself, August, if you can't think of me. You *can't* marry her. You don't love her. It's only a momentary infatuation because she's different. She's the kind men make jokes about to each other. Why—"

"Harriet, that's enough. I love Mary very much and we're being married this week." His anger drained away as he looked at the hurt, confused girl standing before him. "I'm sorry this distresses you. I've considered you a very good friend ever since I've been in Fairmont, and I hope we can always be good friends."

For a long time she stared at him silently, her eyes narrowing as apparently many thoughts went through her mind. She turned and started back around the house, then stopped again. "You're a fool, August Fielding," she called. "She's nothing but the daughter of a tenant farmer, a foreigner, and a Roman Catholic at that. Why, her father *works* for my father. You're a *fool* to marry her."

She grabbed at her skirt to get it out of the way, and held it up several inches as she ran, disappearing around the house. August stared after her, his only thought for the moment being how exactly like her father that last speech was. Pure Knox Maddry in thought and in wording.

She had surprised him, and yet, as he watched her go, he

felt that he should have been more surprised than he was. Did that mean he was in some way guilty, had in some measure unconsciously contributed to Harriet's hoping when there was no cause for hope? Could he have wanted her to fall in love with him, perhaps as a means of revenge on the world for that long-ago time when a girl had laughed at him and called him funny-looking?

He picked up the saddle again and threw it over Brandy's back and led the horse out of the stall. Of course he had done nothing to give Harriet hope! Lately, he had a way of making too much of everything, of giving motives to himself and others that never existed, of over-explaining in trying to explain to himself. It had become like a sickness in him and he was unsure about the cause and therefore could think of no cure. It could be, he thought, that he had so much guilt left over from that early sin that he was constantly seeking new causes to which he could assign the guilt.

August and Mary were married at ten-thirty Wednesday morning by Father Kegan at a side altar in the church (because August was not a Catholic, they could not be married at the high altar). Watching the brief ceremony were Giuseppe and Mary's five brothers and sisters, and, in a way, August himself might have been called a spectator at his own wedding. It was the first time he had been inside a Catholic church and the wedding ceremony left him slightly mystified. He understood the English, so far as it went, but the English did not go very far. Father Kegan lapsed into Latin almost immediately, and August watched Mary closely in order to know when to kneel and when to stand.

It was during the talk, when they were being reminded—rather sternly, August thought—of their obligations to each other and to God, that August reproached himself for his lack of reverence at his own wedding. This was not at all the way he had expected to feel. He had thought he would feel such gratitude, so much emotion, and finally, on realizing that his marriage to Mary was actually taking place, a sort of adoration of Mary herself. Instead, he was only half aware of the words the priest was saying, only half conscious that Mary was beside him. His eyes went from statue to statue, from the crucifix above the altar to the candles. He had not been prepared for the ornateness, the elaborateness, of it all. He

had not expected a Catholic church to be so very different
in appearance from a Protestant one; certainly there was not
much difference in the exterior appearance. Once again, and
very much against his will, Brother Johnson's words came
back to him: "They bow down to statues and worship idols.
They burn incense even as the pagans did."

And then it was over and the priest was giving his benediction in Latin. He and Mary arose from their knees and
went back to the pew where the Taminis were also getting
up from their knees. Giuseppe opened his arms to Mary and
embraced her, then held out his hand to August.

August was suddenly choked up and he felt tears well into
his eyes. The obstacles were past, the long wait ended. Mary
was his wife. "I'll spend my life trying to make her happy,"
he promised, and Mary, looking smaller, more fragile and
childlike than he had ever seen her, smiled up at him.

On the steps of the church they said good-bye to the
Taminis, who were leaving for Fairmont. He had thought this
would be a bad time for Mary, that final good-bye with the
realization that when she returned she would not be going
back to her family. But Mary kept smiling.

They watched and waved as the wagon rumbled off down
the street, then he and Mary walked slowly to the end of the
block (as though out for a midday stroll, he thought), past
the capitol building, and to the hotel where he had made
reservations.

He awoke in the middle of the night, slowly, as though
consciousness would take a while in returning. First he looked
around at the strange surroundings, and then when he had
got his bearings (the furniture looked black and grotesque,
almost animated in the darkness), he listened to the breathing
of Mary beside him. He was not used to sharing a bed, and
he had gone to sleep on the very edge lest he disturb her. Her
dark hair was matted against the white pillowcase, and he
could make out her features. He raised himself on one elbow,
his face just above hers.

He could not understand how it was possible to love so
much. Last night when they had returned to the room after
dinner, he had taken her in his arms and said gently, "I love
you, Mary," and realized with something akin to horror that
this was the first time he had said that to her. How was it

possible? During all those months he had not told her he loved her. And she had looked at him with an expression he had never seen before and said simply, "I love you too, August." And he knew that no matter how long he lived, no matter what transpired in the future, no moment would be better or more memorable than this one.

Later, he had been surprised by her passion. She had turned to him naturally, with no false modesty, her love-making as direct and welcoming as her manner of speaking. And his own passion—it was as though he would never get enough of her. The feel of her arms around him, her soft body beneath his . . . Mary, Mary, Mary, the name went through his mind repeatedly as though all the love and all the feeling in the world were in that one word. He had never imagined that love could be like this, all-consuming, all-enveloping. And even when the peak was past, he still held her tightly, lost in the wonderment of it all.

Now, he put his face closer to hers, trying to discern whether she was dreaming and if her dreams were happy ones, and he was so overwhelmed with a feeling of tenderness for her that he thought he could not bear it. Without moving, he tried to will her awake. He could not bring himself to awaken her, but surely if he concentrated she would awaken by herself and put her arms around him and . . .

But she did not wake up. Once she stirred slightly and he cupped her shoulder with his hand, but she settled back upon the pillow and slept.

Mary, he screamed silently. I am adoring my wife, he thought. Then: Oh God, I thank thee. Thou hast given her to me, and I shall try to be deserving.

The sky outside the window was streaked with rose when she opened her eyes. The arm on which he had been leaning was numb and he fell on his side, smiling at her, waiting for the strangeness which she must feel to vanish.

But almost immediately she returned his smile and laid her hand on his chest. "August," she whispered.

He kissed her forehead and her cheek and paused above her lips, savoring the moment.

"August, do you know what?"

"What?" Talking seemed impossible now.

"I have an American name now. Mary Fielding."

He could stand it no longer. His mouth was on hers, and

once again he had the feeling he would die of love for her. "Mary." Over and over like a litany. "Mary, Mary, Mary."

On Sunday morning when August went to unlock the church before Sunday school, he was astounded to see a large piece of cardboard tacked to the door printed unevenly in black paint: Due to Special Meeting of Deacons, There Will Be No Service Today. He stared uncomprehendingly at the sign for several minutes, then went to the side door where he was confronted by an identical sign.

He could not imagine what had happened during the short time he had been away that would call for a special meeting —and a meeting during the church hour was unheard-of. He went at once to the Marlowes', where Miranda was just clearing away the breakfast dishes. She looked surprised when she saw him at the door.

"August, come in," she said. "Welcome back—to you and your bride. What brings you out so early?"

"That's what I want to find out," he said. "Is Staley here?"

"No, he went out just a few minutes ago." She stared beyond him. "I'm not sure what time he'll be back."

"What's going on?" he said. "Tell me, Miranda."

She was silent for a minute, then she said, "I can't, August. I promised Staley I wouldn't say a word to anybody—at least not until . . . Oh, August, I wish I could tell you what little I know about it, but I can't. I will tell you this, though. The deacons have met twice since you left, and apparently they're expecting you to be at this meeting because they're having it in the choir room during the church hour."

"Where is Staley now?"

"When he left the house he said he was going to see Knox Maddry before the meeting. He and Knox are . . . in disagreement about something, and Staley wanted to try to clear it up."

He made a move to leave and she grabbed his arm. *"Don't* go to the Maddrys', August. Please give Staley a chance."

"A chance for what, Miranda? None of this makes sense."

"It doesn't to me either," she said. "But promise me, August, that you won't try to see Knox or Staley before the meeting."

August turned away, both mystified and alarmed.

"Tell Mary I'm going to see her very soon," Miranda said, then added, "perhaps this afternoon."

He nodded and left the house, heading back to the church, where Sunday school was in progress. He went to the empty choir room and waited.

At five minutes to eleven the deacons began arriving. They did not seem particularly surprised to see him there, but they seemed distant. They inquired politely about his new wife and said that of course the meeting could not begin until Knox arrived. August asked to be told the nature of the meeting, but got no answer except "a business matter. We'd better wait for Knox—and Staley isn't here yet either." August did not volunteer the information that Knox and Staley were together settling a disagreement.

At quarter past eleven they walked in together. Staley's long, gaunt face looked like a thunderstorm that would break momentarily; Knox seemed his venal self.

"Well, Preacher, I see you're back. I wasn't sure you'd be at this meeting," Knox said.

Staley nodded to August and sat down in a corner, two seats away from the nearest deacon.

"I wasn't sure I was supposed to come," August said, "but since it is taking place during church hour, and since someone took the liberty of informing the congregation there would be no service . . ."

"Yes, we meant for you to be here," Knox said quickly.

"May I ask what this is about—and also why it was necessary to have two extra meetings last week?"

The board registered surprise at his knowledge of the meetings.

Knox sat down in a chair directly opposite August. "First of all, Preacher, I suppose we should congratulate you on your marriage."

August nodded. "However, I don't think that was the purpose of this meeting."

The room was quiet for what seemed a very long time. Then Knox said, "On the contrary, that is exactly the purpose of this meeting."

August looked from face to face, expecting one of the others to say something, but they sat like statues, their eyes fixed on their spokesman.

"August, you and I had a little talk some months ago, if

you remember," Knox said. "I have told the board about my conversation with you, though I waited until this past week. Until the last minute, I hoped you would come to your senses."

"I wasn't aware that I had lost my senses," August said coldly. His deacons continued to stare at Knox.

Knox went on. "Not in the history of this church, and I dare say not in the history of any Baptist church in the country, has a minister so defied his board of deacons and gone against the trust of his congregation by marrying a Catholic. When we hired you we had great faith in you, in spite of the fact that you were a young man utterly without experience in the pulpit."

He paused again, apparently waiting for August to say something but August remained quiet. Finally, he said, "So?" and met Knox's gaze.

"So we find it an abominable, thoughtless action on your part," Knox said. "One which we cannot in any way condone. I explained to you last fall, very patiently, all the reasons why a marriage to a Catholic would be out of the question, and you chose to ignore my advice. Therefore, the other deacons and I are asking for your resignation as pastor of Fairmont Baptist Church."

August looked again at his deacons, and they all nodded solemnly, with the exception of Staley, who kept his eyes fixed on some point behind August.

"I'm sorry, Preacher, that it has to be this way," Knox said, "but you'll have to admit you brought it on yourself."

Still August said nothing.

"We have already let it be known that we are looking for a new preacher."

August cleared his throat. "And suppose I refuse to resign?"

"You have little choice," Knox said. "Your salary was stopped as of last Sunday, and next Sunday we have a preacher coming in for a trial sermon. By the following Sunday we may be needing the parsonage, so you have two weeks, Preacher, to find another place to live."

"Is this the decision of the board or did Mr. Maddry decide upon this course of action independently?" August asked.

There was no answer, but the deacons switched their gaze

from Knox to August, and then to whatever objects in the room seemed most convenient at the moment.

"I believe," August addressed Knox, "that your reasons for demanding my resignation have nothing to do with the fact that my wife is Catholic. Can you honestly deny that personal considerations entered into it?"

"Don't try to make excuses for yourself, August," Knox said. "We all know—I told the others—how you refused to listen to reason in this case. It ain't like I didn't warn you, you know."

"And what would happen," August said, "if the matter were placed before the congregation, if all the church members were allowed to vote."

"I can tell you what would happen," Knox said heatedly. "It would be very embarrassing for you—and your wife."

"I don't doubt that," said August. His anger had been slow in rising because he was not entirely surprised by the result of the meeting, but now, thinking of Mary at home, happily awaiting his return, he was furious.

"You have my resignation," he said, "and as far as I am concerned, you may all go to hell at your earliest convenience."

Knox gasped, as did the rest of the board. Staley, however, stood up and looked contemptuously around the room. "You have my resignation also," he said. "I want no part of this board."

"Now wait a minute, Staley," Knox said. "You'll cool off. Why, by next Sunday . . ."

"Next Sunday," Staley said, "will find the Marlowes in the Methodist church."

Even in his anger, August had to smile at the expression on Knox's face. Going to the Methodists, in Knox's opinion, was even worse than going to hell.

Staley walked out of the room and August followed him. He did not try to talk to the deacon who had championed his cause, but let him go silently and determinedly out of the church.

He stood for a minute looking at the empty pulpit facing the empty pews, then he, too, left the church. Never before, Knox had said, had a minister so gone against the trust of his congregation. Well, they could chalk up another first

for him, for he'd venture to say that never before had a
minister told his deacons to go to hell.

12

AUGUST'S MAIN CONCERN NOW was to keep Mary from finding
out what the town of Fairmont had known for a week. He
had told her nothing of Knox Maddry's talk with him months
ago because he did not want her to think that by marrying
her he would jeopardize his job. But now the job was gone,
and there seemed to be no way to keep the reason from her.
There was one thing in his favor: the ladies of the church
were not coming to call, as would have been customary. Only
Miranda—who was as good as her word and came to see
them on Sunday afternoon—had been inside the parsonage
since that fateful deacon's meeting. And Miranda had understood immediately that Mary did not know and therefore
avoided the subject.

In a way it was odd. He and Mary had spent so much time
worrying about her church and the possibility that it would
stand in the way of their marriage that they had given no
thought to his church. He was sure it had never entered
Mary's mind, and even he had been naïve enough to think
that once his marriage was an accomplished fact, Knox
would forget their personal differences.

By Thursday he had written to every Baptist church within
two hundred miles of Fairmont, and he had even written a
long letter to Professor Eugene Bryant, telling him all that
had happened and asking if he knew of any vacant pulpits.

It was on Friday night that he finally brought himself to
tell Mary. She took it very well. He led into the subject gradually, pretending great restlessness on his part, telling her that
he had done all he could in Fairmont, that he and the deacons
did not see eye to eye on a number of matters, with her help
he would like to try something new—a new town with more

challenge. She listened in silence, staring at him all the while as he paced the floor. Finally he looked at her, saying, "What do you think of the idea, Mary?"

"Whatever you want, August. It is for you to decide."

He went to her and held her in his arms and he thought of asking, "Are you really sure?" but he could not press the matter. If he did, she might have second thoughts about leaving Fairmont. So all he said was, "I'll try to find a church not too far away, and we can visit your family often and they can visit us."

"How soon do you think we'll be leaving?"

He hesitated, then said, "By the first of October—a week from Sunday. I've already preached my last sermon here."

"Why didn't you tell me before, August? Is there something wrong?"

"No, no," he said. "Nothing is wrong. I just thought that now would be the best time to make the break. I should have told you before, but I wanted to be very sure about—about everything before I did." Regardless of what happened, Mary must never know that he had been dismissed and that she was the reason.

On Sunday during the church hour he left the parsonage, telling Mary he was going for a walk, knowing—and hating himself for it— that at some point during the walk he would pass by the church. It was like touching a new scab on a sore, wanting to keep the fingers from pulling at it, but being unable to do so. By the time he reached the white frame building with its overly large columns, the service had begun. He stood in front looking at the closed door, listening to the congregation singing "Jesus Keep Me Near the Cross."

The cross now being borne by the congregation of the Fairmont Baptist Church consisted solely of having to listen to a trial sermon today by a man who, regardless of his qualifications or lack of them, would be invited to be the new pastor. Knox Maddry would consider the quick hiring of another man one more strike at August.

He thought of his one ally, Staley Marlowe, and wondered if Staley had really taken his family to the Methodist church today.

"Why are you standing outside?"

He turned quickly toward the voice, which belonged to Harriet Maddry.

"Because I don't belong inside," he said. "And why aren't you inside?"

"I have no wish to be," she said. She hesitated a moment, her eyes seeking the ground as though for relief, then she looked at him again. "I've been wanting to see you, August, but I was afraid to."

"I shouldn't think I'd be a figure to inspire much fear in anyone right now," he said.

"Perhaps afraid was the wrong word. I should have said ashamed. You see," she went on quickly, apparently wanting to get something out before he could speak, "after the other day, I . . . August, can we forget about that, pretend it never happened?"

He started to answer her brusquely; he was in no mood to dispense charity, something that had been utterly denied him, but when he looked at her face he said gently, "It never happened."

"Thank you. I've wanted to see you, to tell you how sorry I am that all of this has happened."

He thought immediately of her father, but even so, he believed her. "Thank you, Harriet."

"I feel responsible," she said. "My father being what he is, it probably would have happened sooner or later for one reason or another, but since it happened when it did, I feel it's my fault."

"No," he said slowly, "it is not your fault. I think you are probably right. It would have happened sooner or later anyway." He had not thought about it before, but now he was certain she was speaking the truth. It would only have been a matter of time. He and Knox Maddry had been at cross-purposes ever since he had come to the church.

"I know I can't really do anything to make amends," she said, "but I'd like to try to do *something*."

"There's nothing you can do, Harriet."

"I think there is," she said. "I've thought about it a great deal during the past few days. August, I've known the Taminis for a long time and I know that more than anything else in the world Giuseppe wants to take his family to Italy. I have some money, enough to get them to Italy, and I want to give it to him."

Startled, August was blunt. "He would never accept the money from you—or anybody else."

"I wouldn't do it as a gift," she said. "I could tell him there had been a mistake in my father's bookkeeping over the years and that in going over the books he found the farm had made more money than he had thought. I could tell him I was bringing him his part of the money at my father's request."

As she talked, August felt his spirits lifting. It was possible; it was logical. But then he had a second thought. "And how are you going to keep your father from finding out? He certainly would not allow you to do it, and I'm sure Giuseppe would go rushing to him to thank him."

"I think I can manage that part of it," she said. "I can tell him my father is out of town and won't be back for a long time. I don't care if Daddy finds out—after the Taminis have gone."

"Why are you doing this, Harriet?"

"I thought perhaps you'd understand," she said, her voice flat. "But you don't. Oh, August, how can you understand so little?"

"I'm sorry, Harriet," he said. "Perhaps my ability to understand has become a bit dulled in the past week. It is a fine thing you are offering to do, and I appreciate it. It will mean a lot to Giuseppe, more than you can know, and it will mean a great deal to Mary, too. It will be easier for her to leave here, knowing that her family will also be leaving shortly. I hope your plan works, but even if it doesn't, it was a kind thought."

"It will work," she said. "I'll see that it does. I suppose," she added, "that I should congratulate you on your marriage, but I can't. Good-bye."

She walked away quickly, leaving him standing in front of the church.

"I thought you were going to church," Mary said when he returned. "But you didn't, did you?"

"No."

"Why not? Even though you weren't preaching today, wouldn't your people expect you to be at church anyway, especially since it's your last Sunday in town?"

August did not answer. He walked over to his desk and

picked up several letters which were to be mailed tomorrow. These were to churchmen in other states, in the event there were no openings in this one. By next Sunday they would have to be out of the parsonage. The panic grew within him.

"August?" She was waiting for an answer.

"I've been thinking," he said, "that it might be just as well if we went to a new place, even if I don't find a church right away. I can look around from another town as easily as here."

She got up from her chair and went to him. "When are you going to tell me?"

He paled. "Tell you what, Mary?"

"Tell me what's wrong. Oh, no, don't shake your head. I know. You haven't been yourself since we came back to Fairmont. Either that, or I never really knew you before. You're always thinking about—I don't know what—about things that seem far away. And they're not pleasant thoughts, and you're changing. I can see a difference in you from day to day. You are becoming colder—maybe that isn't the right word—more withdrawn."

He put his arms around her. "I am not withdrawn from you."

"I wasn't talking about the way you are to me. But I can tell just by the things you say, and more by the things you don't say, that—"

He held her tighter. "Hush, Mary," he whispered. "There is nothing to worry about. Changing churches has unsettled me, but it will be all right as soon as we go somewhere else. I promise you everything will be all right then."

She seemed to believe him.

In the middle of the week he received a letter from the pulpit committee of the Lakeview Baptist Church asking if he could arrange to preach the evening sermon on the following Sunday. He sent an affirmative answer immediately and wrote to the hotel in Lakeview for reservations for himself and Mary. He did not want the pulpit committee to know that when he arrived in Lakeview, he would be bringing all his earthly possessions and would be staying there until he found a church. Neither did he want to think about how much depended upon the sermon he would preach Sunday night. And there was the thought that had haunted him ever since his dismissal. Would he find the deacons of every church like those in Fairmont? Would he be turned down in church after church because his wife was Catholic? He was sure he would never be told that was the reason—how would he ever know whether his inability to get a church was because of his own inadequacy or because he had married a girl who did not worship a Baptist God? And if he could not find a church, what then? He tried not to think about it, but in trying, he thought about it constantly. No wonder Mary found him withdrawn and changed. There were too many things that had to be kept secret from her.

He went to Staley Marlowe to learn what he could about the town he prayed would be his new home. Lakeview, Staley told him, was about forty miles from Fairmont, a slightly larger town but still a small agricultural community.

"I know a few of the people in the church there," Staley said. "I don't think you'll have anything to worry about, August."

"I can't hide the fact that Mary is Catholic," he said.

"No, but you don't have to let it be known until after you've been accepted. I'm not going to say it won't make some difference, but I don't think it will make the difference it did here."

Most of the furniture and furnishings in the parsonage had been provided by the ladies of the church, so there was little for August to take with him. But he decided to buy a wagon from McAllister—he and Mary would make their grand entrance into Lakeview with Brandy. After all, he had gone to Brandon in a wagon and now he looked upon it as a good omen.

On Friday he drove Mary to the Tamini farm to say goodbye to her family and waited in the wagon while she went into the house. He would see the Taminis, of course, but he wanted to give her a chance to be alone with them first. He got out of the wagon as Giuseppe came from the house.

He stood before August with tears in his eyes, then embraced him. "It is bad that we will be so far apart. We will miss Mary, and you also, August."

"We'll see you often," August said.

"No. There is news. We leave soon for home. We are going to Italy. Only this week did we decide."

Harriet had lost no time. "That's wonderful news. When are you going?"

"As soon as we can make it possible," Giuseppe said. "There is money, money I did not know about. I do not understand too well, but it is true."

Mary came out of the house, followed by the little Taminis. "Did Papa tell you?" she asked breathlessly.

"Yes." He turned his head as Mary kissed her brothers and sisters. The awareness of what she was giving up for him broke over him like a sudden excruciating pain. And if he had to give up the ministry for her, was that not small repayment for a large debt?

She whispered something to Giuseppe that August did not hear, held him close for a minute, then turned to be helped into the wagon. As they drove away he looked back at the line of Taminis watching them and raised his hand in salute, but Mary did not look back.

She gave him a little smile when she saw that he was looking at her wet eyes. "Forgive me if I cry a little," she said. "I am not really unhappy, but . . . well, Italians are emotional people, I suppose you will get used to it."

He would never forget how strong she was at this moment, nor would he forget the restraint of the farewells—a restraint maneuvered, he felt sure, by Mary, who knew him well enough to know that a long, tearful scene would have caused him not only anguish but also embarrassment.

"I love you," he said quietly, and even that seemed inadequate.

August, who had thought after his leave-taking from Brandon that he was inclined to be sentimental about any departure when it was a final departure, felt very little upon leaving Fairmont. It could have been a pleasant place, was his only thought. It could have been different.

At four-thirty Saturday morning, he hitched Brandy to the wagon. Four people came at that early hour to see them off: Staley and Miranda Marlowe, Tom McAllister, and Jonas Downs, the Methodist minister. This last surprised August very much and he was touched when the Reverend Mr. Downs grasped his hand and said, "I am sorry to see you go, Mr. Fielding. I wish we could have become better acquainted."

McAllister shook his hand and said gruffly, "Well, Preacher,

I hope you have a good trip. You've got a good wagon to make it in."

Staley Marlowe extended his hand and said, "Good luck to you and Mary, August. You deserve it."

But Miranda kissed him on the cheek and said, "Oh, August, I hope we'll meet again. I shall miss you, and I think the children will miss you most of all. Don't forget us."

August thanked them all for coming, helped Mary into the wagon, then sat beside her on the broad wooden seat and clucked to Brandy. The wagon rumbled down the street, and August did not look back, not once, as they left the parsonage and then the town behind.

13

As THE MORNING passed, the day remained gray and overcast, and the stiff, cold October wind seemed to herald a bleak November. They made several stops along the road for Brandy to rest and to eat the lunch Mary had packed the night before. By four o'clock in the afternoon a light rain was falling, and within the hour it had turned into a steady, freezing-cold drizzle. August looked in vain for a farmhouse, a barn, any kind of shelter that would get them out of the rain. At noon they had passed through the only town between Fairmont and Lakeview and they were now nearer to Lakeview than the town. He urged Brandy on, faster, knowing that the horse was exhausted.

Their clothing was soaked. August felt Mary shiver beside him and saw her pull her cape more closely about her, and after that he could not bear to look at her. Finally he said, "We'll stop and take the things out from under the seat and you can lie down there. It won't be comfortable, but at least it will be some protection from the rain."

"No," she said. "I'm all right. I'd rather stay here." He knew no amount of persuasion could make her move.

Within another hour even her cape clung to her, its wet
folds plastered over and outlining her thin body. Her hair,
which had been carefully done up that morning, now streamed
to her shoulders. He himself was shivering audibly, but he
gave it no thought.

"Mary, I'm sorry," he said.

She gave him a laugh which was meant to be reassuring
but which ended with the sound of her teeth chattering. "You
sound as though you planned this, August. It certainly isn't
your fault. We'll soon be there."

He cracked the reins over Brandy's back. Giuseppe's warning came back to him now: "She is not strong like the others,
my Maria," and he remembered the night she had looked for
Gaetano in the rain and had fainted and had later had a
terrible cold.

It was nearly seven o'clock when they arrived in Lakeview.
In front of the hotel he tied Brandy to the hitching post and
helped Mary out of the wagon. She was so stiff that he picked
her up bodily and set her down at the hotel door.

An elderly man with sparse white hair ran from behind
the desk in the lobby and met them just inside the door,
looking at them with alarm. More, August thought, because
of their disheveled appearance and because their clothing
was dripping on the dark brown carpet than because he was
concerned about them.

"My name is Fielding," August said. "My wife and I have
a reservation here."

"Fielding—oh, yes. We have been expecting you. You
chose a nasty night to come."

"It couldn't be helped," August said. He signed the register
and they were shown to a small room dwarfed by a huge bed.

He went back downstairs to be sure that Brandy had been
put away and fed. When he returned, Mary, still in her
soaking petticoat, was half lying across the bed. Without a
word he opened her suitcase, took out a nightgown, and
undressed her. Then he put her in bed and pulled the blankets
around her. She was still shivering.

"I'll see if I can get a hot-water bottle downstairs," he said.
"And I'll have some supper sent up. Is there anything special
you'd like?"

"I'm not hungry, August. And you'd better get out of those

wet clothes. You can't afford to have a cold when you preach tomorrow night."

His trial sermon was something he had not thought about for hours. It seemed unreal and far in the future.

He changed his clothes and went back to the lobby where he asked for a hot-water bottle and told the clerk to have some hot soup sent to the room. When the soup arrived Mary would not touch it. He put the hot-water bottle to her feet and bent over her anxiously. "You're still cold, Mary. Try to eat a little of the soup. It will warm you."

She allowed him to feed her a few spoonfuls, then shook her head. "I'm just not hungry, August. But tomorrow, you'll see—I'll eat a big breakfast, a field hand's breakfast."

After he finished his own soup he set the tray outside the door, undressed, and got into bed. He was still too tired to think about his sermon. That would have to be done tomorrow. He reached for Mary and held her shaking body in his arms.

"Are you all right?" he asked. "Why don't you get warm?"

"I will now," she whispered. "Just hold me, August. Hold me tight."

He could hear the beat of her heart through the flannel nightgown as he brought his head down on her breast, and then he was asleep.

It must have been hours later when she awoke him—not with words, but with the continual tossing of her body.

"Mary?" He sat up. She did not answer. Her whole body seemed on fire. Quickly, he got up and lit the lamp, blinking as the tiny flame sputtered, then grew brighter. Her face was flushed and her hands continually pushed at the cover, trying to remove it.

"Mary!"

Her eyes were open now, and fever-bright. He raised her gently by the shoulders. She mumbled, but her words were unintelligible. He threw on his clothes and ran from the room to the lobby below. The clerk was reared back in a chair behind the desk, his head resting on the wall.

"Wake up!" August reached across the desk and shook him. "My wife is ill. We need a doctor, quickly."

The man jumped up suddenly, still not quite awake. "Yes, sir, you wish to register?"

"Get a doctor," August shouted. "My wife is ill. Get a doctor right now!"

The clerk was finally spurred into action. He put on a coat and started across the lobby, mumbling as he went, "It's no wonder, coming in here in the pouring rain, wet as dogs." To August he called back over his shoulder, "Dr. Badin lives a few blocks from here, but I can get him to come—if he ain't already out on a case."

August waited, an endless wait, beside the bed, staring at Mary in panic, not knowing what to do for her, afraid to do anything lest it be wrong.

Finally there was a knock at the door and Dr. Badin walked in, a little man with a small head and a black moustache which was so large that it tended to obscure his features. He nodded to August, set his bag down beside the bed, and looked at Mary.

"Niles tells me you people had quite a ride in the rain," he said after a little while.

"Yes."

"It didn't do her any good." He turned back to Mary, saying nothing else. August walked from side to side of the small room nervously. When he could stand it no longer, he stopped beside the bed. "What is it? What's the matter with her?"

The doctor stood up. "Looks to me like she's going into pneumonia—there's not much we can do about it but hope and pray." He took a bottle of medicine from his bag. "You give her a spoonful of this every hour." He pulled an oversize watch from his pocket. "It's five o'clock now. I'll be back a little before eleven. I'll tell you, your wife should never have traipsed around in this weather."

August felt the blood leaving his face as he looked from Mary to the doctor, then back to Mary. "We had to move yesterday. There was no time left." He neither knew nor cared that his words made no sense to the doctor.

The doctor closed his bag. "Well, maybe I'm being too pessimistic. There's a chance—a small chance, but still a chance—that this may be the result of becoming overchilled and she'll get over it in a few hours. We'll know soon, if the fever goes away."

"Help her," August said simply. "You've got to help her."

The doctor, on his way to the door, stopped and patted

August on the shoulder. "I'll do all I can, son. But there's a lot that has to be left to the Great Physician."

August sat down beside the bed, afraid to breathe, afraid to pray, his only thought being: Mary, be all right, you've got to be all right.

"Pneumonia," Dr. Badin said when he returned. "She must be unusually susceptible. It doesn't often happen this fast. Was she sick when you left . . ."

"Fairmont," August said automatically. "No, she wasn't sick."

"She needs a nurse. I'll send Mrs. Grannis over. She can help you out during the day. Do you have any family here in Lakeview, any friends?"

"No." He shook his head, his mind framing the question he was afraid to ask: Will she be all right?

As though he read August's mind, the doctor said, "She's mighty sick, Mr. Fielding, but you can't tell about pneumonia. It could go either way. We won't know for a while yet. I'll look in again this afternoon."

August had never felt so helpless, so completely at the mercy of strangers. The hotel clerk gave him a room across the hall, but he spent no time in it; he would not leave Mary, not even when the stolid Mrs. Grannis arrived and with hardly even a "Good afternoon" to him, took over.

"You might as well get some rest," she told him. "There's nothing we can do here now except wait for the crisis." Still he refused to leave.

That night Mary looked up at him as he sat beside the bed. "Am I very sick, August?" Mrs. Grannis, on the other side of the bed, immediately placed her hand over Mary's forehead.

"Too much rain," August said. "You'll feel better tomorrow."

"Is this Sunday?"

"Yes, Sunday night."

She tried to raise herself on the pillow, but Mrs. Grannis held her back.

"How was your sermon, August? Did they like you?"

August gasped. It was now nearly midnight. He had forgotten that he was to have preached, had forgotten even to get in touch with anyone in the church to say that he would be unable to preach.

"It went very well," he said, but Mary had lapsed again into unconsciousness.

The following day Dr. Badin held her limp hand as he took her pulse. He shook his head slowly, and August, who was standing at the foot of the bed, felt his own head jerk suddenly. His fatigue was so great that his head seemed an unnecessary weight too heavy for him to carry.

"I'm going to have two patients here," the doctor said, "if you don't get some rest. There's nothing you can do, Mr. Fielding, and she may remain this way for hours, possibly days. You are going to bed now."

And so August, unprotesting because he no longer had the strength, allowed the doctor to lead him to the room across the hall.

When he woke the room was dark. For a moment he lay there trying to remember . . . Then he jumped up and ran back across the hall.

Mary was conscious and whimpering his name. Mrs. Grannis was trying to get her to take her medicine.

"I was just going to call you," she said. "She's been awake about five minutes."

"August." Mary's voice was so weak that he had to bend over her to hear. "August, I want a priest. Please find a priest."

"I'm here now, Mary." He stroked the damp black hair away from her forehead. "I won't leave you again."

"A priest," she whispered. "Please send for a priest."

If it would make her feel better, set her mind at ease, he would get a priest. "Is there a Catholic church in Lakeview?" he asked Mrs. Grannis.

Her eyebrows went up briefly, and then the impassive expression returned as though she was saying to herself, Well, nothing really surprises me anymore.

"No, the nearest one I know about is in Raleigh. You a Catholic?"

August ignored her and rushed to the lobby. "Is it possible," he asked the clerk, "for you to get in touch with Father Kegan, the priest at the Catholic church in Raleigh? Can you get word to him to come here?"

As the clerk's white eyebrows shot up, Mrs. Grannis appeared at the top of the stairs. "Mr. Fielding!"

August left the desk and rushed back to the room. Mary, once again, was unconscious and her breathing filled the room—heavy, labored gasps as though there was not enough air in the world to fill her lungs.

"I've already sent for Dr. Badin," Mrs. Grannis said, but August did not hear her. He knelt beside the bed, clutching Mary's hand.

"Mary, Mary, Mary . . ."

The room was suddenly quiet. He raised his head and looked at her. She's gone, he thought. O Christ, she is gone.

But she was breathing still. She opened her eyes. "August, I have loved you so."

He strained to hear.

She raised her hand slowly and placed it upon his head. "The priest?"

"Father Kegan is coming," he said. "He will . . ."

But she was speaking again. Her eyes were closed and her head dropped back to the bed. "O my God, I am heartily sorry . . . for having offended Thee . . . because I dread . . . the loss of heaven . . ."

She sat up then, bolt upright, her eyes wide, staring at him. There was a long breath, like the sigh of one who is very tired, and she fell back to the pillow.

He found that the worst part of his grief was waking up with it in the mornings, his eyes opening to an empty world, and memory of the past few days returning. Woodenly, he got out of bed and dressed each morning, though he could not have said why. There seemed no purpose, no meaning, to any of his actions.

Giuseppe had gone alone to Lakeview, leaving the children at home. Unable to look into Giuseppe's eyes, August had waited for the accusing words that did not come. Giuseppe asked only two questions: "How did she die?" and "Did she die unconfessed?" August answered him, and Giuseppe said: "She will be buried in holy ground."

So they went to Raleigh for the requiem mass and Mary was buried in the new Catholic cemetery. Then Giuseppe, after a long talk with Father Kegan, returned to Fairmont. There was no good-bye to August and yet no animosity. He said only, "Next week we will go to Italy, and you—what will become of you?"

"I don't know," August said. "I don't know."

Giuseppe left, and August went back to his hotel room in Raleigh, trying futilely for the oblivion of sleep.

And so the Taminis had gone out of his life as quietly, as unobtrusively, as they had come in.

Lately, he had been thinking a great deal about his father. As Gervas had lost, or misplaced, God when Caroline had died, so August could not now bring himself to look to heaven for help. His religion, which had failed Mary at the last— had she not died calling for a priest while her husband, a man of God, stood beside her?—had failed him also.

Mary. Even now, so soon, she was a stranger to him. He remembered her laugh, the sound of her voice, but in his mind there was no clear picture of her face. He had memorized each dear feature, but he could not put the features together and make her face.

Had he ever known her? Had she not always been as mysterious, as strange, to him as the surroundings of her church? He had known her for a short while as the girl he had courted, and for those three brief troubled weeks as his wife. But he had never known her as a person in her own right. It was for that that he grieved now. What had she really been—the beautiful, acquiescent, and passionate girl he had married? As the priest stood over the coffin at the cemetery, August had wanted to cry out, "Wait, not yet. I must know who she is." He had started forward, then stopped, almost hypnotized, as Father Kegan made the sign of the cross. He did not understand the alien words and gestures.

It is not possible, he thought, to know a person without knowing his God, and he had never known Mary's God.

He did not know how long he had been sitting in the chair, but it seemed that the knock had been sounding at the door for a long time before he was aware of it. He roused himself and went to the door, then stepped back, stunned. "Professor Bryant!"

Eugene Bryant entered the room and without a word grasped August's hand. August felt tears come into his eyes.

"I came as soon as I heard," Professor Bryant said. "I had trouble finding you."

"How did you know?"

"Knox Maddry's daughter heard about your wife's death and sent word to me. I went to Fairmont, and a Mrs. Marlowe told me you were at the hotel in Lakeview. When I arrived in Lakeview, the people at the hotel told me you were here. August . . ."

August held up his hand, stopping him. "Thank you for coming," he said.

"I could not have done otherwise," Professor Bryant said. "You have been in my thoughts a great deal, August, since you left Brandon."

Mechanically, August said, "Two years and four months ago. And now I can hardly remember ever being at Brandon." He looked at Professor Bryant, really seeing him now as he tried to connect him with that recent—and yet long-ago—past. In the space of two years the professor had become an old man. His hair, which had been streaked with gray, was completely white, and his face was lined. Even his eyes were different. Though he still looked out at the world from behind the thick glasses, the twinkle that had sometimes seemed almost patronizing was gone, replaced by a look of indefinable sadness.

"Have you had lunch yet?"

August thought. "No, nor breakfast."

"We'll go to the dining room and we can talk while we eat."

They ate in silence for a long while, then finally Professor Bryant said, "I know the whole story, August. You had written me much of it, and Mrs. Marlowe told me the rest. It was a bad business—there in Fairmont, I mean."

"It's over," August said. "I'd rather not talk about it, if you don't mind, sir."

"There's no point in talking about it," Professor Bryant said. "It's past, and now you have to think about what's to come."

August stared at his plate.

"I understand you did not preach the sermon in Lakeview."

"No."

"And you are not committed to any church at present?"

"No. I am not committed to anything. Once you asked me, Professor, if I had ever considered atheism and I told you no, and you said that probably would come. I think it has."

He sighed deeply and waited for a response, something that would tell him the professor was deeply shocked at his words, but he continued eating as though he had not heard.

"Do you remember when I was in college, there were at least two occasions when I decided that I should not go into the ministry?"

Professor Bryant nodded.

"I should have taken whatever obstacles were before me then as a sign. I should not have become a minister."

"A sign from whom, August?"

"From God," he said without thinking. Then he smiled. "You opened the door and I walked right into that one, didn't I?"

"August, you are no more an atheist than I am, and you never will be. You see, you *are* committed. It will take you a while to get things sorted into their proper place in your mind, and I am not here to comfort you with platitudes. I came to tell you that you are needed at Brandon."

August smiled again, ruefully. "I am not needed anywhere, Professor."

"Brandon has grown tremendously in the past two years. There is a new dormitory and a new classroom building. The faculty also is much larger."

"I'm glad to hear it." Actually, it made little difference to him.

"We also have separated the study of religion from the Philosophy Department. August, we could use another teacher in religion. Would you consider coming back?"

"To teach? I'm not a teacher. I've never even taken graduate courses."

"You could be an instructor in the department and work toward your master's degree at the same time. Since most of the students in the department are preministerial, your experience in the field would be as valuable as another degree. Also, August, there is a small country church near Brandon that has been without a pastor for several months. I talked with one of the deacons before I left and he asked me to tell you that they would consider it a favor if you'd fill in until they get a pastor."

August was quiet. Professor Bryant, as he had done several times before, was offering him his future. But now, unlike the other times, he no longer cared. "The school year began nearly two months ago," he said.

"That doesn't matter," Professor Bryant said. "You are needed now."

He shrugged. It was easy, so easy, to let someone make decisions for him.

"Will you came back to Brandon with me, August? There is a train leaving this afternoon."

Suddenly he was practical about the details even as the major decision escaped him. "I can't," he said. "I have a horse—a horse and wagon."

Professor Bryant laughed. "We'll go to the nearest livery stable and sell them," he said. "If you need a horse and wagon in Brandon, there's Socrates and the buggy. And August, you can live at my house as long as you like."

It came back then, that April afternoon, the room with the cracked mirror.

"Mrs. Bryant?" August said. "I haven't even remembered to ask about her. I've been so . . ."

The professor's eyes clouded and he looked beyond August, out across the dining room. "I don't know where she is," he said slowly, as though every word caused him acute physical pain. "Angela disappeared about a year and a half ago."

"Disappeared!"

"I returned home from the campus one day and she was not there. I thought perhaps she was visiting. Late that night when she still had not returned . . ." He broke off suddenly, his eyes meeting August's now. "I took a leave of absence to look for her, but I never found her." He did not go on.

"I'm so sorry," August said. "I—was fond of Mrs. Bryant."

It was after midnight when the train arrived in Brandon. "We'll leave your baggage here at the station tonight and come back in the morning with the buggy," Professor Bryant said. "Do you mind walking to the house?"

August shook his head. He looked beyond the station to the road and across the road to the stone wall. They walked together down the incline from the tracks, crossed the road and came to the arch. *Pro Humanitate*. He stopped and waited as a cloud passed over the moon. And when the thin moonlight was again visible, he looked beyond the arch to the spire, unchanged and unchanging.

It was after midnight, the beginning of a new day. An arrival, he thought, and stopped again, remembering that it was more than a new day. It was his twenty-sixth birthday.

PART THREE

14

IT HAD BEEN A LONG DAY for August, and as the afternoon shadows lengthened across the yard he piled the leaves he had been raking into a wheelbarrow and took them behind the house. Tomorrow he would burn them. He replaced the rake in the little shed that had once been Socrates' stall, Socrates having long since gone to his eternal pasture.

This was the end of the leaves. The trees, now bare, took on their distorted winter forms. Faculty Avenue had been like a raging autumn fire, burning itself out, the leaves finally relinquishing their color like slowly dying embers. Each year he was reminded of his first autumn in Brandon, when he had hoped that someday he would be able to retire there.

Sometimes he chuckled to himself when he remembered. He had come back to Brandon fifteen years ago, and he had come back to anything but retirement.

In those fifteen years, he thought now, his attitudes had changed even more rapidly than the seasons. First of all, he had had to adjust to the new relationship with Eugene. They were no longer student-teacher, and although August had thought he would probably make other living arrangements once he settled into college life, he had soon admitted to himself that he needed Eugene's companionship, his understanding, and sometimes just his silent presence in those first weeks after his return. It was not until he began to feel again —for others as well as for himself—that he realized Eugene needed him as much as he needed Eugene.

He had begun teaching at once and confessed to Eugene after the first month that he found himself liking it. He also preached every Sunday at the little church in the country, an assignment that was to have been temporary but that lasted for ten years. He had given up the church only five years ago, long after he had been made a full professor in the Department of Religion.

Autumn, he thought, as he walked back toward the house, had always been for him a time for taking inventory, a time of beginning as well as ending. Last year, at this time, he had become head of the Department of Religion upon the retirement of Professor Marris.

Since he never spoke about those years away from Brandon, it seemed now as though they had never been. He had come back in resignation, thinking, at twenty-six, that his life was over. But he had known on the night of his return that he had not been meant to live for himself alone, that resignation was not something he cultivated, but a way of life that came to him naturally. Then he found there was little time to brood over a past that he had thought had drained him of all feeling.

There were his students with their problems, their familiar demands ("Professor Fielding, I've given a great deal of thought to it, but I'm still not sure if I should go into the ministry . . .") There were his church and the demands of his congregation, and there were his own studies as he worked for an advanced degree.

And, of course, there was Eugene who in his quiet, subtle way had steered him along his own carefully chosen course of resignation. Now he worried about Eugene. Three years ago he had given up his classes at the college, had moved his things out of the master bedroom into the tower room, and told August, "This is what I've been wanting for a long time. I can stay in my tower and watch the world, a limited world to be sure, and write my book." August knew little about the book except that it was about Plato, and that after three years, Eugene was still working on it.

The afternoon ended with the sinking of the sun behind the shed as he went in the back door of the house. Mayline, the Negro housekeeper, said, "About time for the professor to return from his walk, ain't it? Reckon I can start the biscuits now?"

August put another log in the living-room fireplace and sat down to wait. Almost immediately he heard the front door open.

Eugene came in, taking off his overcoat as he came. He looked even more tired today than usual. "It's getting colder," he said, and sat down stiffly in front of the fire. "This feels good."

"Supper will be ready soon," August said. "Mayline just put the biscuits in."

Eugene was staring into the fire. Finally he took a letter from his pocket and placed it, without opening it, on the side of his chair. "This came in today's mail," he said. "Angela's sister died a month ago and this is from the executor of her will. It seems odd that I wasn't informed of her death at the time though. I never knew her—only saw her once, at our wedding. Anyway, she left a seventeen-year-old daughter, and this Mr. Claymore wants to know if Ann can come to live with her Aunt Angela and me. Apparently he never heard about Angela . . . I'll have to write him."

Eugene was silent for a long time, then he chuckled softly. I don't imagine you and I could very well bring up a young girl." Then he was thoughtful again. "Poor little thing, I wonder what she'll do now."

"Her father?" August asked.

"He died several years ago. Well," Eugene go up from the chair and took his cane, "I'll write a letter tomorrow. I wish there were something I could do—I think Ann was named for Angela—but I don't think . . ." He left the sentence unfinished as he limped out of the room.

After supper Eugene went immediately to his tower and August went back to the living room. He pulled his chair closer to the fading fire and propped his feet on the andirons. Eugene had not said a word during the meal. Probably, August surmised, he was brooding over the letter about Angela's niece, and, of course, anything connected with Angela necessarily precipitated brooding about Angela herself.

He stirred in the chair and moved his legs, which were becoming cramped from pressing against the andirons. It was at moments like this that the past sometimes came too close. Why must I keep thinking about it? he asked himself. I have lived through remorse, and I have lived through my punishment.

It was only at moments like this that he thought of the events in Fairmont as his punishment. He had preached, and still did occasionally when he was called to fill in at a church, that God was a merciful God and not a God of vengeance. But no matter how convinced of this he might be rationally, when he thought of Mary's death he was not nearly so sure.

"Good night to y'all," Mayline called from the kitchen. He heard the back door slam as she went out.

He went upstairs to his room to prepare his lectures for the next day. Above him, he heard Eugene pacing in the tower with the irregular, halting step of an old, old man.

Actually, August thought, sixty-three was not an ancient age, but Eugene had long ago dismissed any sign of youth as though it had been an unwelcome visitor. August found it hard to remember him in any way other than the way he was now.

At breakfast the next morning he found out the cause of Eugene's pacing.

"August," he said, looking down into his cup of coffee, "I did a great deal of thinking last night about that child. She has no one, absolutely no one. I think Angela would want me to do what I could for her, and so," he paused a moment, "I have written Mr. Claymore that she may come here."

Somehow, August was not at all surprised.

The train had been at the station for several minutes before she got off. Ann Elizabeth Randolph was the only passenger for Brandon, but even if there had been dozens of passengers, August would have known her immediately.

The conductor helped her down the steps. In the dim light from the station he saw her face and he gasped. She was someone he knew. Where? And then he realized that he saw her every day, in Eugene's living room. She had pale-blond hair and deep-violet eyes which stared out in perpetual innocence—the daughter of Eugene and Angela, young Angela, whose portrait was over the fireplace. For a minute he felt frozen to the ground, and then when he could think again, his first thought was, What will this do to Eugene? In the two months since the letter had arrived, they had thought of her as a child, but she was not a child at all. She was a young woman, a tall, beautiful young woman standing expectantly beside the train while a porter brought out six large bags. He went to her.

"Miss Randolph?" All along he and Eugene had spoken of her as either "Ann" or "the child." Suddenly she became Miss Randolph.

She looked at him, the dark eyes boring into his face. "You're not Uncle Eugene."

"No, I am August Fielding. I live at Professor Bryant's." His hand was cold as he held it out to her, but hers was warm in his. "Your uncle is waiting at the house. He gets around rather slowly now and—"

"I've never seen him," she said quickly, "but I knew you weren't he. You have red hair." As though this were the reason he could not have been her uncle.

August smiled, thinking that the orange of his hair had faded with light touches of gray. "Mr. Mosby's taxi is waiting to take us to the house," he said. He took her arm and steered her beyond the station. "He'll take care of the bags." He helped her up to the running board and then got in beside her.

"I didn't want to come, you know," she said. "But nobody could think of anything to do with me—so here I am. If I had been twenty-one . . ." She stopped and looked at him. "What do you do?"

"I teach at the college."

"What do you teach?"

"Courses in religion." For some reason, he did not tell her he was head of the department.

"Oh, God, wouldn't you know!" She pursed her lips in an I-told-you-so expression. "I told Ward—Ward Claymore—that this whole thing would turn out to be a total disaster. But he said—well, it doesn't matter what he said. I was in school until Mother died, but after I knew I would have to leave Richmond I couldn't see any point in going on. Anyway, I didn't like it. But," she looked around her as Mr. Mosby cranked the car, "I suppose this won't be any better. Sometimes I think I've outlived myself." The long pale hair bobbed as she nodded her head.

August did not know what to say to her. He had never spent much time around young girls, except for the daughters of his colleagues, and Ann Elizabeth Randolph was certainly not at all like the quiet faculty children. As they drove away from the station he asked, "Did you ever see your cousin Angela—Professor and Mrs. Bryant's daughter?"

"Mercy no! She died before I was born. My mother told me she was thrown from a horse—that's why I was never allowed to ride."

"You look very much like her," he said. "Almost identical."

"But she was just a *child* when she died, and I'm . . ."

Certainly not a child, he thought.

"I suppose you're very religious," she said.

"I used to preach—still do, sometimes," he said, as though that answered her question.

"We'd better have an understanding right now," she said, "if we're going to be living in the same house. I don't believe in organized religion. If people want to worship God quietly, without making a fuss about it, that's their privilege. But churches do more harm than they do good. Frankly, I don't worship anything—or anybody."

"That's *your* privilege," he said stiffly, and then was annoyed at himself for letting this child irritate him. And now he was convinced that beneath her fast-talking façade she *was* a child. And it occurred to him that she was probably a very scared and lonely child, arriving at a new place to live with people she had never seen.

"Your uncle and I—have been looking forward to your arrival," he said, hoping to put her at ease before she met Eugene.

"I didn't know about you," she said.

Mr. Mosby drove the taxi to the side of the house to unload the baggage. August got out and helped Ann. As they went to the porch, the front door opened and Eugene came out. He went to Ann and took the hand that she brought out, almost reluctantly, from her muff.

"Ann, my dear, welcome. We hope you will feel very much at home here." Stiffly he kissed her cheek, and then he looked at her closely. August hoped that she had not noticed the expression that crossed his face.

"Thank you," she said.

Eugene held the door for them and August saw that his hand shook. Ann looked around her as they went into the house; August could not tell from her expression whether she approved or disapproved. She was suddenly very quiet.

Mayline emerged from the kitchen, wiping her hands on her apron. "This Miss Ann? We mighty glad to see you, honey. Lord, ain't she pretty!"

"This is Mayline, Ann," Eugene said. "We couldn't get along without her. She'll show you to your room and help you with your unpacking, then we'll have supper."

"I ate some fruit and candy on the train, but I suppose I could eat again," she said. As she was following Mayline up the stairs, she turned. "Thank you for letting me come here," she said.

Like a little girl remembering her manners, August thought.

"Thank you for coming," Eugene said. "August and I have become quite dull rattling around in the house. We needed someone to liven the place a bit."

She stared at him for a moment without answering and then went with Mayline.

By the time Ann had been with them a month, August was ready to admit—to himself, at least—that she was a complete enigma. She remained quiet and withdrawn, and he often wondered what thoughts went through her mind. Soon after her arrival he had suggested that she take some courses at the college to help fill her time and also give her a chance to meet some of the young people. But she dismissed the suggestion with a wave of her hand.

"Not now," she said. "Maybe later."

He could tell by her attitude that she had no intention of ever going to school again.

Several of the professors' wives had come to call on her, and some had brought daughters of Ann's age. Ann seemed interested enough, was polite to them, and never failed to invite a caller to return. But she never returned any of the calls.

Whenever he or Eugene suggested ways she could spend her time ("Why don't you have a party?" Eugene had asked her. "August can invite some of his students. Mayline will help you with everything."), she smiled and nodded as though pleased with the idea, and there it ended.

She spent most of her time sitting in the big chair in front of the fireplace in the living room reading. She had discovered Eugene's library the second day she was there, and it would be impossible to estimate how many of the books she had already gone through. The odd thing about it was that they were all books of philosophy. Hardly what one would expect to interest a child of seventeen.

In the afternoons she went for a walk, always alone. When August asked her one night at supper where she went, she seemed surprised at the question and said, "Just around town. Sometimes through the campus."

To August, though, the strangest thing of all was her obvious dislike of him. He could not imagine the reason for it. He had tried hard ever since she arrived to make her feel at home. He had invited her to drop in on his classes, to which she replied curtly, "No, thank you." One Sunday afternoon he had offered to go with her walking and she had said, "Don't trouble yourself. I know my way quite well by now."

He knew that Eugene felt helpless in his role of guardian. Since Ann was not a blood relative, he could not bring himself to issue orders to her as though he were a parent. And perhaps he knew that to issue an order would only bring about her open defiance.

Perhaps, August told himself, he was being an alarmist. The girl quite naturally was still upset over the recent death of her mother and her new surroundings. In another month or two she would feel more at home and be more natural. But for the moment she was far beyond either his or Eugene's understanding.

15

ANN CLOSED THE BOOK AND burrowed deeper into the big chair, staring at the fireplace. There was no fire now, for spring had come to Brandon. Outside the world was awakening—to what? Reading philosophical discourses gave her a feeling of superiority. For what did they know, the philosophers? One said ultimate reality was this, another said it was that, and there was no way of proving anything. The philosophers were only guessing, even as she did.

She glanced up at the portrait of her cousin, Angela. Sometimes she stared at the portrait for a long time, envying the girl whom she resembled. Angela was dead; she had returned to the nothing from which she came. She had died before she had a chance to find out what the world was like.

Ann left the living room and went upstairs to her room. The house was quiet except for Mayline's occasional hymns emanating from the kitchen. Uncle Eugene was in his tower, another philosopher trying to solve the mystery of ultimate reality, and August was at the college telling his impressionable students that God was in His heaven and all was right with the world.

She threw herself across the bed and stared out the window at the green buds on the trees. She hated spring because it was in spring—only last year—that everything had started. And ended.

In April her mother had gone to the hospital. Ann had not known that she was sick. She returned from school one afternoon to find Ward Claymore waiting for her. This, in itself, was not unusual since Ward had taken care of her mother's business affairs for years. Often, when she was a little girl, Ward would take her riding in his buggy, and when he came to the house to see her mother on business, he always brought her a gift.

On this day his usual smile was missing. "Ann," he said as soon as she was in the house, "Your mother is ill. We took her to the hospital this morning."

"But," Ann said, "she couldn't be. She was all right this morning."

"She has been ill for a long time, but she didn't want you to know."

"What is it?" Ann's hands, still holding her books, were shaking. "She'll be all right, won't she?"

He did not answer.

"Won't she, Ward? Won't she?"

He walked across the room from where he had been standing by the window and put his arms around her. "No, she won't be all right," he said softly. "It's only a matter of time now. She may be able to come home from the hospital, but—"

She pulled herself away. "How much time?"

"I don't know, Ann. No one knows. Maybe a few weeks, maybe less."

She sat down on the sofa, still clutching her books. "Why didn't she tell me? Why didn't I know before this?"

"I'm sorry I had to be the one to tell you," he said. "But I thought you should know before you see her. I'm going to take you to the hospital now. And Ann, your mother doesn't know that I've told you, so please . . . I think she would be happier if she thought you didn't know."

Ann nodded. She walked over to the drop-leaf table and placed her books upon it, rearranging them carefully as though that were the most important thing in the world. Finally she turned to Ward. "Thank you for telling me. I'm ready to go."

Her mother smiled at her and said, "You can come closer, Ann. I don't have a contagious disease."

Somehow she managed to carry on a conversation about all the things that meant nothing to her. "Miss Allen wrote 'excellent' on my English theme." "Do you want me to clean the house tomorrow?" And "When you come home I'll fill your room with jonquils. They're blooming now"—as though her mother had been away for a long time instead of just one day.

Somehow she managed. But when she left the room she flung herself into Ward's waiting arms and cried and cried. He stroked her hair, saying nothing for a while. Then he cupped her face in his hands and said, "Don't, Ann. We must go now. Laura said for me to take you to our house while your mother is here. We'll go get your things."

She stayed with the Claymores for a week while her mother was in the hospital. When she went back home the atmosphere had changed. It was a different place. A new and sterile world filled with the smell of sickness. There was a day nurse and a night nurse for her mother, and always neighbors dropping in, bringing flowers, adding to the funereal quality the house had taken on. Ann spoke in hushed tones to the visitors, answering their questions: "Yes, she is resting now. No, the pain is not as bad today."

And often the preacher, Mr. Talbot, came to call, his face long and sorrowful as he told her to be of good cheer because the Lord was with her in time of trouble.

Ward came by every day now after her mother returned from the hospital, and Laura, his wife, came sometimes at night. But it was only with Ward that she felt any link with her old life, her life before "it" had happened. Without Ward the long summer would have been unendurable. As he had when she was a little girl, he took her for drives in the country. "You need to get out of the house, Ann," he said.

"You can't stay with her every minute. If you do, she'll know that you know."

On a Sunday afternoon in October he took her with him to a farm to look at some collie puppies. "I'm going to get one for Laura for her birthday," he said. "You can help me pick it out."

She looked at the little balls of tan fur and chose one with a white mark on his face like a star. "We'll come back and get him next month," Ward said. "He's too young to leave his mother now."

On the way back to town something went wrong with the automobile. Ward stopped and got out to look at the motor. "I don't know anything about these contraptions," he said. "They'll certainly never be as reliable as the horse and buggy."

She watched him bending over the motor, only the top of his dark head visible to her, and she felt a sudden tenderness. All of her life, when she had needed someone, her mother and Ward had been there. Now, soon, there would be only Ward. She knew now that she loved him, had loved him all her life without recognizing the love for what it was. And on her discovery her first thought was Laura!

"I think I found the trouble," he said. "Maybe we'll be able to make it home anyway."

She spent the rest of the drive reflecting on the hopelessness of love, and life—and death.

Ward took her home with him after the funeral, and even her grief did not obliterate certain new attitudes that formed in her mind and made her more and more uncomfortable in the presence of Ward and Laura. She could not look at Laura objectively now and think of her as a friend. She could only view her subjectively—as the wife of Ward.

"Ann," Ward said to her when she had been with them for a week, "what about school? Would you like to go to Miss Phipps's as a boarding student?"

"I never want to go to school again," she said quickly. "Ward, I feel a hundred years old. I could never go back with those babies."

He nodded as though he had known that would be her answer. "Have you thought about what arrangements you're going to make? It isn't a question of finances, Ann. But you can't get the money your father left until you're twenty-one. You'll have to have a legal guardian now."

"You be my guardian, Ward."

"You have relatives, Ann. They should—"

"Only an aunt," she said. "My mother's sister who lives in Brandon. I've never even seen her."

"I think I'd better get in touch with her," he said. "Did you notify her of your mother's death?"

"I never once thought of her."

Later that month he called her and told her to come to his law office to discuss some business with him. She felt a momentary elation, thinking he was going to tell her something he did not want Laura to hear. But when she arrived at the office, he was holding a letter.

"I've heard from Professor Bryant, your aunt's husband," he said. "It seems your aunt just left home—a number of years ago, and no one ever heard from her or has any idea where she might be, or even if she's still alive. But the professor has a large home in Brandon and says that he will be glad for you to come to live there."

"Leave Richmond!" she gasped. "I won't go."

He came around the desk to her. "Ann, I've thought about it and there's nothing else you can do. You're underage, and—"

"Do you want me to go, Ward? Do you want to send me away?" She reached for his hand.

Oh, my God!" he said, and his arms were around her, his hands caressing her, and not gently, not for comfort. She clung to him until he pushed her gently away. "You're just a child," he said.

"I'm not a child." She looked at him steadily. "And you know it, don't you?"

"Yes. I know it."

She went on, relentless. "And now you know you can't send me away. Oh, Ward—"

"You're wrong, Ann. Now I know you *must* go."

And nothing she could say or do would change his mind.

Mr. Talbot, the preacher, stood in the aisle of the train. "Miss Ann, I heard you were leaving today but I didn't realize we would be on the same train. Good morning, Mr. Claymore. I'll be able to look after her for you. I'm going all the way to Atlanta."

"Thank you," Ward said, moving so that the preacher could sit beside Ann. "I think it's about time for the train to leave. I'd better get off."

"Ward . . ." But he was already making his way down the aisle. She looked out the window and saw him as he crossed the platform of the station. He did not once look back at her.

He'll come for me soon, she thought. He'll miss me as much as I miss him, and then he'll come . . .

"Miss Ann," Mr. Talbot was saying, "Mrs. Claymore told me you'd be living with your uncle in Brandon. I've been through there, and it's a beautiful town. A college town."

"I'll loathe it," she said.

He looked at her as though he had not understood. "I know how you must feel now—so soon after your dear mother's passing. But God will not leave you comfortless, my dear. Blessed are they that mourn, for they shall be comforted."

There was only one way to make him be quiet.

"Mr. Talbot," she said, "you're trying to dispense religion like pills and your pills have no effect on me. My sickness, like my mother's, is incurable and I don't need some religious medicine man to tell me what God wants."

It worked. Mr. Talbot did not open his mouth again during the journey, and when she got off the train at Brandon, he only looked at her and shook his head sorrowfully, a gesture she would always associate with preachers.

She hated spring and the budding trees outside her window. The season made it all come back to her, and she knew now that Ward would never come; the new beginning of the earth did not mean, as she had thought it would, a new beginning for her and Ward. If only she could find a place where there was no springtime, where she would not have to look out a window and see the world starting all over again without love.

August stayed late at the college for a meeting of department heads with the dean. The dean, as usual, had asked him if he was sure he wanted to continue with his full class schedule next year as well as his duties as head of the department, and August, as usual had said yes, which brought laughter from most of the other professors present.

He thought about the meeting as he walked home. Only a few of them understood why, on taking over the administrative details of the department, August had also wanted to continue with all his classes. But to August it was very clear. Teaching was his job and he liked it, and if it had come to giving up his classes or giving up the small amount of prestige that went with being a department head, he would have chosen to be merely a professor in the department again. As a professor he dealt directly with the students; he understood them, and, he supposed, sometimes influenced their lives as his had been influenced by a professor. As an administrator, he was bored with the myriads of details that seemingly had no connection with human values.

When he reached home the house was quiet. It was almost time for supper, but there was no sound from Mayline in the kitchen, and neither Eugene nor Ann was in the living room.

He went to the kitchen where Mayline was sitting by the table, apparently waiting for him. "Where is everybody?" he asked.

"Professor Bryant, he still upstairs, and Miss Ann is in the basement. I expect they be here time I get supper on."

He went back to the living room and sat down. Eugene was working longer than usual today, and Ann . . . He still worried about her a great deal. Although she seemed content enough with her life here—she never complained or tried to make any changes either in her own life or in theirs—he could not imagine why she was. A girl of her age and beauty should be with young people, should be beginning to get interested in the college boys. (He had heard the head of the English department on the subject of his young daughter and her antics to attract the attention of the college students.) He kept thinking that there should be some way he could reach Ann, talk with her, but on the few occasions when he had tried, she had either clammed up and said nothing or had left the room on the pretext of helping Mayline with household chores. He knew she did not like him and that was something else he could not fathom. She and Eugene had established rapport to a certain extent in that they enjoyed talking about the books she read.

"I didn't know you were home yet. I'll tell Mayline."

He started as she came to the door. "She knows I'm here."

"Then I'll tell Uncle Eugene."

It was as though, he thought, she could not bear to be in the room alone with him. "I'm sure he'll be down when he reaches a good stopping place," he said. "Sit down, Ann. Have you had a busy day?"

She sat down on the red sofa, and he was reminded of the first time he had come to this house and Angela had been sitting in the same place.

"Yes, quite busy," she said. Her tone of voice with him was always polite. "I didn't even have time for my walk."

"A new book?"

She shrugged. "I think I've had just about enough of those books. The authors write authoritatively—they tell you this or that is the way things are, and since you're reading them instead of talking to them, there's no way you can refute what they say."

"Do you want to?"

She shrugged again as though the subject were hardly worth going into. "Not particularly. I know what I know, and I guess they know what they know."

"And how do you think things are?" he asked.

"What things? Are you asking me what I think life is?"

"Yes, I suppose I am."

She hesitated. "You'll be sorry you asked me, because you're a preacher—or were. You think all we have to do is believe in God and our lives will be all sunshine."

"I don't think that at all, Ann," he said quietly.

"I'll tell you what life is," she said. "It's a long series of little tragedies, day after day. And sometimes the monotony of the little tragedies is broken by a big tragedy. God, if there really is a God, has a macabre sense of humor, and He's playing a joke on all of us—a dirty joke, at that."

"Ann!" Eugene stood at the door, his expression one of shock. They had not heard him come downstairs.

August himself was deeply disturbed by her words, and by the violence of the feeling behind them.

"You can't really believe that," he said.

"I never believed anything quite so much," she said. "I'd better go help Mayline now. She's late with supper." As she reached the door, she turned. "By the way, what I was busy with today, August, was moving. I found a nice little bedroom in the basement, and so I've moved my things down there. It's just what I—"

August felt as though he had received a blow in his

stomach. He got to his feet and started toward her. "No," he said. "No, you can't use that room!"

She looked at him coldly, not quite believing the outburst. August knew that Eugene was also staring at him, and he tried to calm himself.

"I'm sorry," he said, "but it's out of the question, Ann. You'll have to take your things back upstairs."

"But the room isn't being used for anything. I don't see why—"

"I said no, and you'll have to accept that as reason enough. Take your things from that room and then don't go in it again." He felt, rather than saw, Eugene's eyes upon him. "Your room upstairs is much more comfortable," he added weakly.

She looked at him for a minute and then ran from the room. They heard her feet on the stairs as she fled to the basement.

"August . . ." Eugene began.

"If you'll excuse me," he said quickly, "I'd better get ready for supper." He hurried up the stairs to his room.

16

IT WAS A LONG WAR, OR so it seemed to August, even though Brandon was not touched by it directly. There was a decrease in enrollment at the college, and a number of young men from the town enlisted, two of them sons of professors. Occasionally August heard or read in the newspaper of the death of a former student, and even when he remembered only the name, he felt a heavy sadness as well as a certain amount of wonder about it all. He supposed there was a cause for the war, that the country had been forced to fight, but how many of those former students—youngsters who did not yet know what life, let alone war, was all about—thought about the cause as they were being shot down?

He and Eugene discussed it, but August found no satisfaction in the discussions. Eugene sought to find a reason for war in the abstraction of philosophy, but in August's mind the abstract and the concrete were separate, and the one could not always account for the other. Again and again, though he tried not to think of them, Ann's words came back to him: "God is playing a joke on all of us."

The one good that August could see about the war was the change it made in Ann. She came out of her shell and worked every day at the local Red Cross headquarters. He was not sure what she did, but from the comments he heard, he knew that she worked with a fervor that he would have thought foreign to her ("She's dedicated," Mrs. Belaski had told him). Her dedication, he remembered, had begun shortly after the United States entered the war, on the day she received a letter from someone in Richmond.

She was standing in the hall, and he was on his way out to go to his classes. She opened the letter in his presence, and at once she paled and began trembling.

"He's dead."

"Who, Ann?"

When she did not answer, he picked up the letter she had let fall to the floor. It was from a Laura Claymore, who told Ann that Ward Claymore was one of the first men in Richmond to enlist. He had become ill with influenza on the ship to Europe and had died before reaching France. "He was always very fond of you and your family," the woman wrote, "and I thought you would want to know."

"It wasn't necessary," Ann said. "It wasn't necessary for him to go. Why did he do it?"

August could only say, "He must have thought it was necessary, Ann, or he would not have gone."

For a week she stayed in her room, and he wondered about the friend for whom she grieved. After that, she never mentioned the letter or the friend again, but that was the beginning of her long days at the Red Cross center.

It seemed ironical to August that as Ann took an interest in the war effort, Eugene appeared to go into the shell she had vacated. He seldom left his tower room except for meals, and even then he often called for Mayline to bring him a tray. On the rare occasions when he joined August and Ann in the living room after supper, he sat in his chair, staring across the room while they talked, and August knew he never heard a word that was said. When addressed directly, he sometimes nodded or answered a question, but soon he would pull himself up from the chair and say, "There is work to be done—so much work."

"Why do you push yourself so, Eugene?" August asked. "You can work tomorrow."

"The book must be finished, August. Already it has been too long in the writing." And he left them.

When news of the end of the war spread through the town, whistles were blown, people ran out into the streets to embrace their neighbors, and students left their classes and paraded through town. And then, unbelievingly, they learned that the war was not over after all. It was a false armistice. Dazed, the people left the streets.

On the eleventh of November, shortly after eleven o'clock in the morning, August's lecture on Old Testament literature was interrupted by the sudden ringing of the bell from the chapel tower. He closed his book and looked at his students. "I think," he said, "that it is real this time. The war is over. Class dismissed."

As they had not been able to believe that the other had been a false armistice, now they could not believe in the real one. There was no wild whooping, no disorder. The boys filed silently out of the room.

August hurried home, his steps quickened by the constant ringing of the bell, joined now by the ringing of church bells.

As he reached the porch, he saw Ann hurrying down the street. "August!" she cried. "It's over, it's really over!" She rushed to him and kissed him, and in their elation this seemed a normal gesture, even for Ann. "We must tell Uncle Eugene."

Eugene was standing by the staircase in the hall when they went in. He seemed confused. "I hear bells," he said. "Are there bells ringing, August?"

"It's over, Uncle Eugene," Ann said. She clapped her hands like a child. "This time it's really over."

Eugene took a step toward them. "I haven't finished my book yet." He looked at August pleadingly, alarming him. "I haven't finished my book yet, and it is ended." He fell by the newel-post, his arms stretched out in front of him as though he were reaching for something.

"Get the doctor," August said.

He picked up the frail form and took Eugene to the red sofa. While he waited beside Eugene for the doctor to arrive he heard, far down the street, a band playing and voices singing in the distance, "We won't come back till it's over, over there."

Eugene never regained consciousness after his stroke. He died two days later in the tower room, with August and the doctor at his bedside. Outside, the white branches of the sycamore, blown in a gentle breeze, scraped the window like small spirits trying to penetrate the glass. On the desk beside the window were the pages of his manuscript, some stacked neatly, others in disarray about the desk, as though the last act of Eugene's life had been to try to put the pages of the book he never finished in order. August could not bring himself to look at the manuscript.

In the days that followed the funeral he felt, for the first time, close to Ann. He could not have borne staying in the house had it not been for her presence. It was not so much anything she did or said, merely the fact that she was there.

Finally, when he felt he should put it off no longer, he went to the tower to go through Eugene's things. The books, hundreds of them, would be given to the college library. He thought that this was what Eugene would want. He went through the desk, finding everything from old lecture outlines to student examination papers. He also found Eugene's will. Still, he would not touch the pages of the manuscript spread out across the top of the desk.

He had never given any thought to the disposal of Eugene's property, and as he read the will he was stunned to find that everything had been left to him, including the house and Eugene's personal effects. There was the stipulation, however, that "should my wife Angela ever return, or should she be found, then my estate is to be divided between her and August Fielding, each to get a half." He had added a codicil in his tight little scrawl, obviously years after the will had been written. "I have made no mention of my wife's niece, Ann Elizabeth Randolph, and I find no reason now to rewrite my will, though I wish her to be remembered and have faith that August Fielding will be fair in her behalf."

After reading the will, he left the room. Eugene was still too much in it. All that August saw, the books, the papers, even the furniture, spoke loudly of Eugene. He could almost hear his voice saying, "You have walked to my house on a cold night, Mr. Fielding. I would be both disappointed and mystified if you left so soon." It was strange: Now that Eugene was gone, he thought of him more as he had been in those early years.

It was a long time before he could force himself to go back to the tower to try to put together the pages of the manuscript. Eugene had never talked much about it, but from the occasional comments he had made, August had the impression that the book would be not so much a philosophical treatise but philosophy as applied by Eugene to his own daily life. On the other hand, the manuscript might be in the form of a textbook, something worthy of being published. Perhaps that was why Eugene had worked so feverishly toward the end—to see the book published before he died.

He sat down at the desk and picked up the pages gingerly. There were more than a thousand, all written in black ink in Eugene's tiny scrawl. It took him nearly an hour to put them in order numerically, and then he went back to the first page and began reading.

After the first few pages, direct quotations from the *Dialogues* of Plato, he skipped some pages and continued reading. He pulled out a page copied from the *Symposium*. "Of the god's beauty much more might be said, but this is enough; the virtue of Love comes next. Chief is that Love wrongs not and is not wronged, wrongs no god and is wronged by none, wrongs no man and is wronged by none. Nothing that happens to him comes by violence, for violence touches not Love; nothing he does is violent, for everyone willingly serves Love in everything, and what a willing person grants to a willing, is just. . . ."

He skipped again and read further, and then began to thumb through the entire manuscript, reading at random. He could not believe what he saw. It was incomprehensible that this was what Eugene had been working on so laboriously day after day. He had not been writing a book at all. He had been copying the dialogues word for word.

Why? August put down the manuscript.

Dear God, why had he done it? Day after day, year after year, writing the words that had already been written.

August turned to the last page, hoping to find there some

reason. But the last page was as the others—copied. It was from *The Apology*, Socrates' speech when he drank the hemlock. The handwriting was much dimmer, as though not enough pressure was brought to bear upon the pen, but August made out the last sentence on the page, the end of the apology:

"And now it is time to go, I to die, and you to live: but which of us goes to a better thing is unknown to all but God."

17

THERE WAS SOMETHING HE knew he would have to discuss with Ann, but because of its delicate nature he put it off from day to day. Finally, at breakfast about a month after Eugene's death, he decided he could put it off no longer.

"Ann, you know since Eugene's death, things have changed somewhat here in the house."

"Oh?" She raised her eyebrows and the deep violet eyes stared at him.

"I was thinking of the propriety of our continuing to live here together," he said. "While Eugene was alive, well, he was your uncle and—"

"In other words," she said, "you're worried about what people will think. Here we are, not related, and for all anyone knows we're reveling in sin. Funny, I wouldn't have thought a thing like that would enter your pure, religious mind."

He let that remark pass without comment. "Of course, Mayline is here during the day and—"

"And that's all right," she interrupted. "But at night, with just the two of us here . . ." She broke off in a laugh.

He felt the blood rush to his face. "I was thinking," he said quickly, "that perhaps we should have a housekeeper, someone who would live in."

"Is that what you were thinking?" she asked. "Or were you

thinking how much less complicated everything would be if I went away."

"This is your home, Ann," he said. "Eugene wanted it that way, and you're welcome to stay here as long as you like. I want you to understand that this is your home, too."

She looked at him seriously now. "Sometimes when you are talking I want to stop you and say, 'Please, August, don't go on pouring out just words; tell me what you really mean, what you really *are*.' But I don't think you could do that, could you?"

"No, I guess not. No more than you could explain yourself to me."

She smiled. "I guess you could say then that in not knowing each other at all, we know each other very well."

He was becoming embarrassed at her insight and was relieved when Mayline appeared to remove the dishes. Ann folded her napkin into the silver napkin ring and stood up. "I don't think a housekeeper is the answer, August. It would be unnecessary expense." He followed her out of the dining room and she added, "Besides, it would hurt Mayline's feelings."

"We wouldn't have to let her go," he said. He picked up his books from the table. "We'll talk about it again tonight."

"There's an easier way to fix everything," she said. "We could get married."

He replaced the books on the table. "Be serious, Ann. We must—"

"Do you think I'm not serious, August?"

"But . . ." He was too dumbfounded to go on.

"Oh, you wouldn't have to worry about sharing your bedroom with me," she said. "Only your house. You made it quite clear to me which room was mine, and under no circumstances would I leave it now." She gave him his books again. "You'd better go now or your students will think you're not coming. As you said, we can talk about it again tonight." She gave him a playful push toward the door, and he, only too glad to escape, hurried out of the house.

She had surprised herself as much as she had surprised him. After he left she stood motionless in the hall for a long time, her eyes focused on the open door through which he had all but run. She could not imagine what had possessed her to say it unless, as had happened sometimes in the past, she had had a perverse desire to shock him, to shake him out of his placidity. She had never given the first thought to marrying August Fielding.

The old antagonism she had felt toward him in the beginning, when she had thought he would be constantly spouting biblical passages at her, had disappeared. She had not been conscious of its going; it had been gradually lessening during the three years she had lived here, and only now had she stopped to think that not once had August tried to inflict his religion or his philosophy upon her.

She might be beginning to like him a little, but love him? Never! She was still in love with Ward, whose death she had accepted as one of those big tragedies that come along to break the monotony of the little tragedies. It was part of the joke God was playing on her that she should spend the rest of her life in love with a man who was dead. But had he lived, would he not have been forever lost to her anyway? I'll never know, she thought. And that, too, was part of the joke, one of the things so vital to her that she would never know about.

She tried to remember Ward's face, the expression in his eyes the day he had kissed her in his office, the kiss itself. And though she had a blurred image of his face in her mind, there was no memory of the kiss. Much clearer was her picture of him that day at the train station as she watched him walk across the platform and out of her life without a backward glance. She now found that the ache she had nourished through the years had diminished without her knowledge and against her wishes. Its place had been filled with a new bitterness, and that also died now as she rationalized. If he had loved her, he would have come to see her. Or he would have written to tell her he had enlisted. Was his response, then, only a form of kindness to a young girl whom he considered to be suffering the pangs of first love? Had she, during those first months in Brandon, built her hopes on nothing more substantial than a small act of kindness? He was much older than she—almost as old as August—and it could have been that he thought her a young thing who for want of excitement had thrown herself at him. When he was alone with Laura, had they talked about it? "I think Ann has a crush on me." She could almost hear his voice now. And Laura: "Well, she shows good taste, my dear." And, of course, they had laughed.

For three years she had nursed an illusion of love and played her role daily like a tragedienne. Now it was almost with a feeling of sadness that she let the illusion go. It was time to get back to the world of reality.

The words that she had said to August in jest (no, she could not honestly say they had been in jest, for to jest implies previous thought) had popped out so unexpectedly that to recall them, to pass it all off as a joke, would only have added to the outrageousness of the situation. She had known as soon as she had spoken that she would have to go on and say, "I was never more serious in my life," or he would instantly have wondered about her mental stability.

She had known about August's marriage years ago to a woman who had died only three weeks after the wedding. But somehow the fact that he had once had a wife had never fully registered in her mind. She could not imagine August with a woman—the thought that he might actually kiss a woman as Ward had kissed her was utterly ridiculous. She had never analyzed her thoughts about it, but if she had she would have said August was like a Catholic priest, forever celibate, forever dismissing knowledge of carnality as sinful and beneath human dignity, certainly beneath *his* dignity. She could not visualize him in the actual act of love, abandoned to passion. Would he be gentle and tender or . . .

She arose quickly and went to help Mayline with the housecleaning. She must curb her thoughts if she was going to continue to live here. She could not stay in the same house with August if every time she looked at him in the future she was going to wonder . . .

She put on her coat and swept the porch, then dusted the furniture inside. (He was attractive in a strange physical way she had not thought of before.) When she finished dusting, she surprised Mayline by taking over the kitchen and baking a cake. (He was tall, perhaps a bit too tall, and certainly too thin, and his hair, that off-shade of red streaked with gray . . . But there was something about his face that was arresting.)

That afternoon she cleaned the bedrooms upstairs, going to his last. His room was neat, like his life, she thought. There was nothing out of place. She touched his hairbrushes

as she dusted, and a sensation went through her as though she
had touched him.

She went for her walk when she finished the cleaning,
hurrying along Faculty Avenue toward the stone wall. She
hesitated briefly and then went through the campus, passing
the Religion Building. Inside he was teaching, or perhaps
having a conference with some of the students who occasionally came to the house to talk with him.

When she went back to the house, she threw her coat
across a chair in the hall and hurried to the living room to
look at the portrait. August had told her she looked like
young Angela. The girl was beautiful, young and innocent
and beautiful. Was this the way August saw her, Ann?

She sat down in the chair and continued to stare, aware
now of the seriousness of the confusion inside her. Had she
convinced herself now that she was in love with August? Had
she talked herself into it, or had love been there all the time,
unknown to her, in disguise and lying dormant?

During the day August went through the mechanics of
teaching two classes, conferring with four students in his
office, and when it was time to go to his third class, he knew
that to give a coherent lecture would be as impossible for him
as flying to heaven in a chariot of fire. Instead of lecturing, he
gave his students a surprise quiz, something he almost never
did.

Later, as he walked across the campus, the cold air of the
wintry afternoon seemed to carry him along without any
effort on his part, hurrying him toward the north entrance
of the stone wall. But he did not want to hurry. All day he
had dreaded, even feared, the moment when he would have
to go back to the house. And yet, he admitted to himself, the
situation was not without humor. Here he was, forty-four
years old, a middle-aged man, stewing because a twenty-year-
old girl had jokingly suggested that he marry her. By now he
had convinced himself that she had been joking. Surely, she
must have been, for she had always acted as though he were
only a fixture in the house, like a piece of furniture which
was not particularly useful but could not be discarded. Or else
she endured his presence because, since he had arrived first,
she considered that he had squatter's rights.

But what on earth had made her say such a thing? What

had put it in her mind? There had been no sarcasm in her voice. Her words had been delivered in a flat monotone as though she were only stating an obvious fact. Perhaps it would be better not to bring up the subject again, even though the question of getting a housekeeper remained unanswered.

Not once since Mary's death had he considered marrying again. He had made for himself a busy and satisfying life in Brandon, and since he had known little of female companionship he could not honestly say he missed it. True, he had wanted children of his own, but now he had his students.

By the time he reached Faculty Avenue he felt better, but then he thought again of Ann at home waiting for him. Would she open the door and see his distraught expression and laugh at him, saying, "Oh, August, you didn't really take me *seriously?*" Once again the thought that had bothered him the most all day returned. He had put it aside, time after time, but she had planted the thought there, and all day it had grown in spite of his efforts to dismiss it. What would it be like to be married to Ann? In the past three years he had assumed, naturally, that someday Ann would marry, and he had wondered what type of man she would choose. She was distractingly beautiful, with a look of youthful innocence, but there was something about her personality that belied her looks. It was almost as if she purposely tried to give the appearance of being completely unfeeling. That, he supposed, could mean that she had once been hurt, or possibly rejected, but at her age it was possible to get over the little hurts amazingly fast.

He was fond of Ann; he had grown used to her being at the house and he knew that if she left he would miss her very much. But *marry* her! And again his mind was off on that pilgrimage, exploring the unknown of Ann, and again he reproached himself for thinking of her in *that* way.

But of course she had only been joking, and he would treat the matter as such. In fact, there was no reason to refer to her outlandish statement again. Tonight he would tell her, in an offhand manner, that he had begun to look for a housekeeper, and that would be the end of that.

If only she hadn't put the thought in his mind.

After supper he followed her into the living room. "Ann,

I've begun looking for a housekeeper. I thought tomorrow I'd ask some of the faculty, perhaps they know of someone who . . ." He paused, studying her expression.

Finally she said, "Suit yourself, August. It's your house."

"I don't want you to feel that way about it," he said. "As I told you, this is your home for as long as you want it to be."

She was staring at her hands in her lap now, but she was very still. He got up and stirred the logs in the fireplace. When he looked at her again he saw that her eyes were wet, and that she was not trying to hide her face from him. "I'm sorry, Ann. But you must understand that we can't continue like this."

"No, we can't," she said softly.

"I suppose," he said, "we could ask Mayline if she'd stay here at night."

"Mayline has her own house," she said, "and where would she sleep, August? In that bedroom in the basement?"

He pulled back from her chair, and by the time he had control of himself he knew that she had noticed his discomposure. She stared at him for a long time, her eyes narrowing, and he wondered what she was thinking. When she spoke, she changed the subject completely.

"Were you ever in love with anyone, August?"

"Yes."

"With your wife?"

He nodded.

"And when she died did you decide you could never love anyone else ever again?"

"No, I didn't consciously make any such decision."

"I did," she said. "I made a decision like that once. But I found out I was wrong." She stood up suddenly and to his amazement burst into tears. He grasped her firmly by the shoulders. "What is it, Ann? What is wrong?" She leaned against him, crying quietly, her face hidden against his chest. He put his arms around her and held her.

She was tall, but his height towered above her, and as he held her he thought, How vulnerable she is, how easily hurt. "Ann, if I said anything that . . ." Now she looked up at him and the violet eyes seemed darker, obscuring all the mysteries that were Ann. Still she did not answer him. He held her tighter. "Ann . . ."

She stood on tiptoe, raising her face to meet his lips. And

when he had kissed her she cried even more. He could not understand what had caused her to cling to him as though he were the only one left to her in all the world. And yet, was he not the only one? In her need for protection she turned to him, and he could protect her from everything except his own ignorance of her needs. And because she needed him, she was very dear to him.

"Don't cry, Ann."

His words had no effect. He stroked her back as he would a hurt child, and he felt her shiver beneath the silk of her blouse. In that moment she changed again in his mind from child to woman and he knew how much he wanted her. "Ann, this morning you said . . ."

She looked up at him.

"Ann, will you marry me?"

Dear God, he had said it! The words, unexpectedly, had come out of him and now they seemed to hang in the air like tiny dirigibles without a landing field. He could not recall them, nor was he sure he wanted to.

She drew away from him, her eyes narrowing as she looked at him. "You asked me to marry you."

"Yes."

"Why?"

"Why?" he repeated, somewhat stunned by her reaction. "You need me, and I—"

"I thought so. You're just the type who would consider it a privilege to make some sort of personal sacrifice."

Speechless, he stared at her.

"The answer is yes," she said. "Yes, I'll marry you. That will set your mind at ease about what people think, and you won't have to bother with a housekeeper. But I don't want your sacrifice to be too great, August. It should be enough that you're marrying a woman who means nothing to you. We'll go on just as we have been. I promise I won't disrupt or interrupt your life in any way."

"Ann, you don't understand." And certainly he did not understand *her*.

"Oh, yes, I do. Though I think I would have had more respect for you if you hadn't made the sacrifice at all."

She left him then, still standing in the center of the room, staring helplessly after her retreating figure. He had in some way touched a nerve with her, had wounded her pride badly, or hurt her feelings. He did not know how, and he wondered, as he had many times before, if he would ever in his lifetime understand Ann.

They were married quietly at the parsonage a week later by Laurence Gavin, the pastor of the First Baptist Church. During the short ceremony he glanced once at Ann, but her eyes were focused on Laurence throughout. She spoke her vows as though she were speaking them to Laurence and he, August, was standing by only as a witness.

After it was over, Laurence perfunctorily kissed Ann and said, "You are a beautiful bride," as indeed she was. She wore an ivory-colored wool suit with matching accessories, and her long blond hair looked almost the same color.

Then Laurence shook August's hand and said, "This is one of the happiest moments of my life. I rejoice with you." August thanked him, thinking, If you only knew, and then added mentally, If *I* only knew.

During the past week his and Ann's conversations had been entirely businesslike, preparing for the marriage as though it were a necessary inconvenience to them both. As they walked the few blocks home, he could not help comparing the occasion with his and Mary's walk from the Catholic church to their hotel. To him the first marriage was even clearer in his mind than the ceremony just performed, and for the first time in all these years he had a clear vision of Mary's face as they walked together. She had linked her arm and looked at him as though nothing else in the world mattered but this moment when they were together, and the other moments to come.

Ann walked beside him neither touching him nor speaking. Once, as she was striding along, her arm accidentally brushed his coat and she said, "Excuse me," and the space between them grew by several inches.

When they reached the house, Ann went immediately to the kitchen and he heard her say, "Mayline, Mr. August and I were just married." He arrived at the door in time to hear Mayline ask, "You all want anything special for supper?"

"No," Ann said. "We'll have the veal chops as planned."

"Yessum." She looked as puzzled by it all as he felt, August thought.

Mayline did, however, rise to the occasion. For dessert she

brought in a large cake, which though obviously an after-thought, was elaborate to the point of gaudiness. The white icing was decorated with what was meant to be pink rosebuds, but the coloring had run and was concentrated in big blobs on the cake mingled with splotches of green, ostensibly the leaves of the roses. Mayline set the cake in front of Ann and then stood behind her proudly.

Ann looked at it for a moment in bewilderment.

"I hope you all going to be very happy," Mayline said.

Ann continued to stare at the cake, then she pushed back her chair and left the room.

Mayline watched her, the whites of her eyes growing larger, then she looked down at the floor. "It ain't much of a cake for looks," she said, "but I thought maybe Miss Ann would like it."

August folded his napkin and arose. "It's a beautiful cake, Mayline, and we thank you. I think Miss Ann is a bit over-come by it all."

"Yessuh, I understands." She picked up the cake and went back to the kitchen.

August followed Ann to the living room. "You hurt May-line's feelings," he said. "She was only trying to please you."

"I'm sorry." She stared into the fireplace as though she wanted to jump in with the burning logs.

"I agree with Mayline," he said. "I always thought weddings were cause for celebration."

"The ordinary wedding is," she said, "but ours could hardly be called ordinary."

"Ann, why are you being like this? What have I done to hurt you?" He approached her chair, but the look she gave him stopped him midway across the room.

"You really don't know, do you, August? I don't suppose you'll ever understand."

"Not unless you tell me," he said.

She stood up. "August, it's been a rather tiring day. If you'll excuse me, I think I'll go up now."

She left the room before he could answer and he heard her going up the stairs to her room. There was a pause, and then he heard the door close.

He sat down before the fire and spent his wedding night staring at the slowly dying flames.

18

In the years following the war, August concentrated more and more on the college and the students and their respective growing pains. By 1922 the enrollment had reached an all-time high, and so had the number of students who came to August's office with their problems. Sometimes he wondered if he took an even greater interest in their problems because they kept him from thinking about his own—and kept him on campus long after his classes were finished.

If Ann noticed that the hour of his homecoming grew later and later, she made no mention of it. In the four years of their marriage Ann had changed—certainly not inwardly, August thought, but in her appearance. She now wore her long hair pulled back into a bun, adding years to her age, and starkly revealing a face that most of the time wore an expression and strain. The inner conflicts that caused the expression, of course, were never confided to him. He had tried everything in that first year after their marriage to get through to Ann, to penetrate the wall she was building around herself. Once he had even tried to make her angry, thinking that in an unguarded moment she would be herself. But she had remained distant, unruffled. As his efforts increased, so did the tension (or maybe the tension was his and he only attributed it to her). When he finally gave up trying, they both seemed to relax visibly and slip back into the old relationship, he as householder and host and she as a guest in the house. This was, he thought, the way she wanted it, and he vowed he would do nothing more to try to change her or to find out why she avoided him.

He never made comparisons now with his first marriage, for there was no basis for comparison. He no longer even questioned whether he loved Ann. Long ago he had accepted the fact that he did, just as he accepted her strange behavior, and he had learned to live with the fact without consciously thinking about it. Any overtures toward change, an unlikely prospect, would now have to come from her.

On an afternoon in late fall he left his office early. College had been in session for nearly two months, and the newness he felt with the beginning of each fall semester was wearing off. The freshmen no longer looked lost, and classes had become routine again. He hurried along Faculty Avenue, hoping to get home in time to go with Ann for her afternoon walk. The bright colors of the street were beginning to fade, and a heavy frost was forecast for the night. This might be his last chance for what he termed his "autumn ramblings and revelings."

He called to Ann when he went inside the house, but there was no answer, so he went to the kitchen. "Has Miss Ann already left for her walk?" he asked Mayline.

"No, Mr. August, she don't go walking out no more, not for a long time. She stays shut up like she's sick."

"Where is she?"

"In the basement, where she is every afternoon."

August caught his breath. He went to the stairs leading to the basement and called to his wife.

He waited, then he went down the dark steps. There was not a sound from the basement. He hesitated again and then opened the door to the room. In the light from the tiny window near the ceiling, he saw her sitting on the bed. She stared when she saw him and stood up quickly.

The room was exactly as he remembered it. Nothing had been changed in all the years since that April afternoon. The iron bed, the chiffonier with its cracked mirror, the leather chair—it was all as Angela had fixed it for him. He looked again at Ann. "What are you doing here?" His voice sounded harsh, even to him.

She looked frightened.

"What are you doing here?" he repeated. "I told you years ago you were not to use this room."

Her composure returned immediately. "I came to see where Bluebeard hides his wives. His *other* wives. . . . What are you afraid I'll find, August?"

He was glad there was not enough light for her to see his face. "Why do you come here? Mayline said—"

"So Mayline keeps you informed, does she?"

"She only said—"

"It doesn't matter what she said." She allowed him to take her arm and lead her out. "You're shaking all over, August. Perhaps you'd better stay out of that room if that's what it does to you. It doesn't affect me that way. I can stay there for hours, but then I don't have some kind of phobia about the—"

"Ann, promise me you'll never go there again."

They had reached the top of the stairs, and he closed the door firmly. As they stood in the hall he noticed for the first time that she had been crying.

"No, I won't," she said. "I see no reason why I should make any promises at all."

He was still shaken, but he tried to match her composure. "I came home early to see if you would like to go for a walk. The leaves won't last much longer, and—"

"I've heard that nothing lasts forever," she said, "but sometimes I wonder if that isn't a mistake. Some things seem to. No, thank you, August, I don't believe I want to go walking this afternoon."

He turned and left the house almost before she had finished speaking, moving quickly along Faculty Avenue as though he were hurrying to keep an appointment.

After he had gone she started back toward the basement, then changed her mind and went to her bedroom upstairs. She cried until her eyes ached, then got up and went to the bathroom and washed her face and applied fresh rouge. It didn't matter how she looked, she thought, because August never noticed.

She had known as soon as they were married that the marriage was a mistake, but even now, after four hopeless years, she was still unwilling to admit to herself the hopelessness of the days—and nights—stretching in front of them.

In a weak moment (and she was well aware that she had created that moment with her tears) he had committed himself to marry her and then because of his righteousness or gallantry or pride or whatever you want to call it, he would not take back the proposal, even though he did not love her in the least. And she, because she loved him and thought that maybe in time he would love her, had gone through with the marriage. But her feelings about it had been mixed from the beginning. If only he hadn't been such a *gentleman* about the whole thing.

She could not tell him that sometimes while he was out she went to his bedroom just so she could be close to the objects that were close to him.

She crossed the hall and went into his bedroom now. Always before she had been content to sit quietly or to wander aimlessly around the room, gently fingering the objects on his bureau. Now this was not enough. She went to his bedside table and opened his Bible to the place where he had left a blue marker. It was the Book of Psalms and he had underscored three of the verses.

Put thou thy trust in the Lord, and be doing good; dwell in the land, and verily thou shalt be fed.

Delight thou in the Lord, and he shall give thee thy heart's desire.

Commit thy way unto the Lord, and put thy trust in him, and he shall bring it to pass.

And what is your heart's desire, August? she thought. You have put your trust in the Lord and what has He brought to pass?

She replaced the Bible on the table. Some people managed to live through the little tragedies of their life by turning to God, others by turning to drink. She had neither a religion nor a thirst, and so there was nowhere to turn.

She opened the drawer of the table and was surprised to find it contained a great sheaf of papers, page after page in Uncle Eugene's tiny handwriting. She skimmed through them, reading at random from the *Republic, Ion, Symposium, The Apology* . . . Why on earth had Uncle Eugene copied the works of Plato, and why did August keep this great bulk of papers beside his bed?

She put the papers back into the drawer and left the room. She would never know why, any more than she would ever *know* August.

August had been asleep only a short while—in fact, he wondered if he had really been asleep—when he heard footsteps in the hall. He sat up in bed and listened. Yes, the loose board beneath the carpet outside his door was squeaking. He got up and put on his dressing gown. It was probably Ann, going downstairs to get a book. He did not know what he would say to her now—in the middle of the night in a house where the fires had long since been allowed to die—but he suddenly wanted to be with her, even if there was no conversation.

He opened the door of his room quietly so he would not startle her, then he drew back quickly. It was not Ann in the hall. Going toward the staircase was the shadowy outline of a man, and in the man's hand he saw the silver candlesticks, taken from the small walnut table outside Ann's door.

He rushed out into the hall and grasped the man by the shoulders spinning him around. The man tensed and struck out in the darkness, the blow grazing August's cheek. August tried to catch his hands and failed, and another blow threw him against the wall. He recovered quickly and went toward the man, who was now at the head of the stairs. He heard Ann's door open, and then the hall was flooded with light and Ann screamed. He struck quickly, his first blow going to the man's stomach, the second to his head. The man crumpled, bending slowly toward the floor as though going down on his knees to look for something. Just before losing consciousness he dropped one of the candlesticks and threw the other toward August. The sharp heavy silver object hit the back of his hand, cutting a gash across his knuckles. He felt warm dampness as the blood spurted out. Ann screamed again as the man finally hit the floor and lay still.

"It's all right now," he said, sucking his hand. "Call the police."

Ann, shaking, stepped over the inert body on the floor to go to the telephone downstairs. Before she was halfway down, the man stirred, sat up, and shook his head several times. Ann stopped as though paralyzed.

August picked up the candlestick and held it threateningly. "Don't move," he said. "Go on, Ann. Call the police."

"No, please," the man gasped. "Don't do it. I won't come here again. I swear to God if you'll let me go, you'll never see me again."

Ann looked at August almost as though she expected him to change his mind about the police.

"I swear to God," the man said. "I didn't want to steal, but I had to."

"Go ahead, Ann. This is no Jean Valjean."

It was at least ten minutes before two policemen arrived and took their prisoner in custody. "There's been a series of break-ins," one of them said. "I think you've got our man for us, Professor." They led him away, handcuffed. August and Ann watched until the car had disappeared, and then Ann noticed his hand.

"It isn't a deep cut," he said. Suddenly his calmness was gone and he felt sick at his stomach. "I think I'm going to be sick."

She pushed him toward a chair. "Sit down. I'll get a pan of water and some bandages." She returned with the pan and knelt beside him, bathing the injured fingers. He noticed that her hands were trembling.

"Were you frightened, Ann? You didn't seem to be."

"When I saw you in the hall with that man I . . . Here, hold this in place while I look for some tape."

He held the bandage until she applied the tape. "There, I think that will hold," she said. "Are you still feeling sick?"

"I'm all right." He shivered, realizing now how cold the house was. "You'd better get back to bed before you catch cold," he said. She had on only a thin wrapper over her nightgown.

She nodded and took the pan back to the kitchen. "You're not afraid now, are you?" he asked when she returned.

"No, August, I'm not afraid." She looked at him for several minutes, then she bent and kissed his bandaged hand. "Good night." And she went quickly upstairs.

He turned out the light and followed her, thinking, Why didn't I build a fire in the living room? Why didn't I say, "Let's stay down here for a little while?" For a moment, when she said good night, he had felt a closeness that had been so surprising he almost had not recognized it for what it was.

He went to his room and got back into bed, but he knew that he would sleep no more that night. His thoughts were no longer with the burglar. If only he could keep that moment, like a still life, Ann kneeling beside him, her long hair falling over her shoulders, her eyes registering concern and . . . And what else? There was another expression in them which he had never seen before. In that moment she had dropped her guard.

"Oh, God." He sat up in bed, his hands covering his face. He felt ill again, but the sickness was from wanting her.

He got up and crossed the hall and knocked on her door. His left hand, the one not bandaged, felt damp with perspiration, and his face was burning as though he had a fever. He knocked again.

"Come in, August," she said clearly. She was not, as he was afraid she might be, asleep again. He hesitated briefly, and then as he went into the room, she said, "That door never has been locked."

19

THEY HAD HAD THEIR USUAL quiet, happy Christmas Day, and now they sat together on the sofa, content to watch the fire blazing in the fireplace and the Christmas-tree lights shining through the boughs of the tall cedar.

"August," Ann said softly, "I have one more gift for you."

"Impossible," he said. "You're already given me—"

"This is for both of us. August, we're going to have a baby."

He looked up slowly, unable to speak. He was fifty-five years old. He thought of Abraham and Sarah, of Zacharias and Elisabeth. Jehovah hath remembered. It seemed a miracle now, as much a miracle as it had been in biblical times. He and Ann had waited through the past few years, never speaking of their desire to have children, afraid that mentioning the desire would only tempt some pagan god to laughter. This, he thought, was the way Ann might feel about it. And his bringing it up might have been construed as an accusation of failure on her part.

His eyes filled as he look at her. "When?"

"Next July." She put her head on his shoulder. "It was all

I could do to keep from telling you earlier, but I wanted to save it for Christmas."

He could not answer her. He sat very still, holding her hand.

"Oh, August, please say you're happy."

"Ann . . ." He pulled her into his lap and held her as he would a child. "Ann."

She sighed deeply with contentment. "We'll name him August and he'll be just like his father."

"No," he said suddenly and emphatically. "If it's a boy, I want to name him Eugene."

As they had not talked about their former childless state, so they did not talk about the coming child after that first night. Both were so deeply touched that it was impossible to put their feelings into words, and they found the experience more meaningful for being shared in silence. Occasionally, when it was necessary in planning ahead, one would bring the subject up lightly, as though it were something of a joke, and the other would laugh, settle the point in question, and immediately change the conversation.

To August's knowledge, Ann had said nothing to Mayline, and yet she knew. Her dark face wore such a knowing smile that every time he looked at her he wanted to burst out laughing, and she was as solicitous of Ann's well-being as he.

One morning in late February when he was eating an early breakfast in the kitchen before Ann was up, he turned to Mayline. "Well, do you think it will be a boy or a girl?"

Mayline laughed as though he had paid her a great compliment. "I guess it ain't a secret anymore," she said. "I reckon it will be a girl. Miss Ann's carrying it low."

"I think you're wrong this time, Mayline. I think it will be a boy. We're going to name him for Professor Bryant."

"I expect you're right," Mayline said, not looking at all convinced.

On Commencement Day, after he had closed his office and said good-bye to the last student, he was hurrying across the campus when a booming voice stopped him: "It can't be, but I do believe it is. Good God from Goldsboro!" He would never have recognized the man, but that gently profane expression pulled him back through the years immediately.

"Ellis!"

"Brother August, the preacher! My God, what a surprise."
Ellis pumped his hand, beat him on the back, did everything
but jump up and down on the grass. "My old preaching
roommate! What are you doing here? You know, I almost
didn't recognize you, then I told myself that nobody but
August Fielding could be so skinny and walk in a perpendi-
cular position."

"I'm not all that skinny," August said, patting his middle.

"No, I guess it was your hair. Even with the gray it's still
like a carrot. But you didn't answer my question—what are
you doing here?"

"I teach here."

"Sweet Jesus, since when? I thought you were preaching
in some little town . . ."

"Found I couldn't stay away," August said quickly. "I came
back in '99."

"Bet you're president of the college by now, dean at the
least."

"No, only head of the religion department. But what about
you, Ellis?"

"It took a while but I finally got that M.D. I'm a sawbones
now. Cut up people in Philadelphia. Lord, let's go find a
place where we can talk."

They sat down on the stone bench in front of the chapel.

"What brings you down from Philadelphia?" August asked.

"My God, you mean you've been on campus with him for
four years and you don't even know that Brantley Lloyd is
my son?"

"The football player?" August asked. "I know the name, of
course, but I never connected him with you."

"Well, I guess there's no reason you should. He doesn't
look much like me. He's pre-med, though. Graduated today."

"I wish I had known—"

"No reason you should. Brantley probably never went near
the religion department. Chip off the old block," he laughed.
"Tell me about yourself, Preacher. You got a family?"

"Yes, I was married ten years ago—for the second time.
My first wife died right before I came back to Brandon."

"Sorry to hear that. Any children?"

"Not yet, but we're expecting a baby in about six weeks."

"You're going to be a father for the first time—at your

age?" Ellis roared. "Congratulations, Preacher, you finally learned how to do it, huh? Me, I've got five."

August flushed. "How long are you going to be here, Ellis? I'd like for you to meet my wife. Could you bring your family by the house—we live in Professor Bryant's house on Faculty Avenue."

"Oh, yeah, the strange professor with the wife who put out. What happened to them?"

"They're dead," August said quickly. "Do you think you could come by?"

"We're leaving as soon my wife gets Brantley packed, but that'll probably take at least another hour. I could go with you now."

"Fine." August stood up. "Ann will be surprised."

"Surprised? She'll be dumbfounded when she finds out her proper, preaching husband ever roomed with the likes of me." They went across the campus, laughing together. August felt suddenly as though he were again an undergraduate, and he realized he probably had the same effect on Ellis, who certainly would not greet his patients the way he had his former roommate. As they turned to Faculty Avenue, Ellis said, "August, do you realize it's been thirty-one years? Good God from Goldsboro!"

Suddenly, he felt his age.

For days after Ellis's visit, August found himself enjoying his friend's brief visit all over again. Ann, charmed by her unusual guest, had laughed and laughed at Ellis's tales of August's undergraduate days. "And then there was the night he took me to a meeting of the M.S.A.," Ellis had begun, and then proceeded to make a hilarious story out of the tame little meeting. August smiled through the recitation without correcting the exaggerations.

But several weeks later a feeling of depression began to grow inside him over something Ellis had said just before he left. On finding that Ann was the niece of the Bryants, he had said, half-jokingly, "Professor Bryant's God was Plato, just as August's is Brandon College."

Those words came back to him often now as he walked through the campus. Was it true that in the years since he had come back to the college he thought less and less about God and more and more about Brandon? He had never been embarrassed about nor denied his great love for Brandon. It was with him always, as natural as breathing and just as involuntary. But it bothered him that during his student years, although he had loved the college then, he had been more concerned with spiritual things than he was now. Your God is that which you worship, he thought, that which you put above all other things. And he realized it was true: Brandon had become his god as surely as Plato had become Eugene's.

He returned from the grocery store late one afternoon to find Mayline in a state.

"Lawd, Mr. August, I thought you won't ever coming back!"

"Where's Miss Ann?" he asked, suddenly frightened.

"We taken her to the hospital," Mayline said. "That is, Mrs. Grierson taken her. She started getting her pains right after you left and—"

"But it's not time yet."

"There ain't no telling 'bout babies, Mr. August. Specially first babies. When I had my first one . . ."

He did not wait to hear her recall her first labor. He rushed from the house, running the three blocks to the hospital. When he reached the reception room he was so out of breath he could not speak. The receptionist stared at him in alarm.

"My wife . . ." he said finally.

"August, you finally got here." Estelle Grierson laughed as he turned to her. "Sit down and catch your breath."

"Where is she?"

"Upstairs. They just took her to the delivery room."

"Can I see her?"

"No, not now. There's nothing you can do but wait and play the role of the typical new father. I was with her until a few minutes ago. She said to tell you little Eugene would be here most any time now."

He could not think straight. "I should have been with her, but I had no way of knowing—"

"Just relax. Dr. Farmer says everything is all right, but it may be hours yet. I remember when my son was born . . ." She looked at his face and laughed. "Mercy, August, you'll be a patient yourself if you keep this up." She stood up. "Well, now that you're here, I think I'll run along. Call me when it's cigar-passing time."

"Thank you for all you've done, Estelle."

After she had gone he went back to the receptionist. "Is there somewhere I could wait—closer to my wife?"

"There's a sun-room on the second floor. Go up the stairs here and turn right at the top."

He found the room and sat down beside a large window. The hospital had opened only a month ago, and it was the pride of Brandon. Through the open doorway he could see nurses scurrying about carrying supper trays into the rooms along the hall. The odor of ether was oppressive, and he felt like a stranger, or a child, lost and frightened.

Each time a nurse went by the door he got to his feet, thinking she was bringing him news, and each time he was disappointed when she passed without looking in his direction.

Through the window he watched the sunset. The sky was cloudless and the sun sank slowly at first, then disappeared rapidly. By the time the sun rose in the morning, he thought, his son would have been born, a new life beginning with the new day. It seemed a long time, but tomorrow he would not mind or even remember the length of the wait. Tomorrow, he would see his child and offer a prayer of thanksgiving. . . .

He must have dozed off, for he jerked suddenly to attention and looked at his watch. It was after midnight. Something must have happened, or else they had forgotten he was here. He went quickly to the desk in the center of the hall.

"Mrs. Fielding, has she—"

"She's still in delivery. Why don't you go home and get some sleep, Mr. Fielding? You probably won't be able to see Mrs. Fielding before late morning anyway."

"No, I'll stay." He went back to the sun-room, put his head back against the coarse upholstery of the chair, and slept again, this time heavily.

When he raised himself stiffly he noticed first that the light had been turned off and the room was gray. He stood up, stretching himself, trying to get rid of the stiffness.

As he rose to look out the window, he saw Dr. Farmer standing in the door. "Come with me, Professor Fielding. I have something to show you."

August followed him down the hall, his mind confused as he tried to decide between a feeling of panic and one of elation. At the other end of the hall the doctor stopped before

a glassed-in nursery. In four of the boxes on the other side
of the glass were tiny red sleeping faces.

"Which one is my son?"

"The one on the end, the right side, is your *daughter*."

August looked at Dr. Farmer in disbelief and then looked
again at the baby. The face seemed old and wrinkled.

"Is there anything wrong with it—her?" he asked.

"She's perfect," he said. "Six pounds, six ounces."

He looked back at the tiny red face, studying each gesture.
The hair was brown, an indefinite shade. At least, he thought,
it isn't orange. Dear God, that's my daughter.

"Eugenia," he said.

"A nice name," Dr. Farmer said.

"May I see Ann now?" he asked.

The doctor's withdrawal was so obvious that August
imagined he saw him take a step backward.

"Professor, there were complications. She hemorrhaged.
We did everything we could, but it was impossible to stop
the bleeding."

In his mind he saw the doctor's face contort to monster
dimensions. What he was saying was not true. Ann was waiting for him in one of those rooms along the hall, waiting
for him to come tell her their baby was beautiful and that
he did not mind because it was a girl, that a girl was what
he had really wanted all the time. "We'll name her Eugenia
Ann," he would say.

"I'm sorry, Professor. I can't tell you how sorry . . ." The
monster face moved and the voice sounded again. "We did
everything we could, but Mrs. Fielding died fifteen minutes
ago."

PART FOUR

20

THE FORTY-TWO CANDLES in the six tall candelabra flickered spasmodically, giving the impression that the heat in the chapel was overpowering them. The flowers, basket after basket of them, carefully arranged across the sanctuary and beneath the choir loft, were wilting.

August stood behind a bank of white roses, wanting at this minute more than anything in the world to mop his forehead, which he knew was glistening in the candlelight. Instead, he held the Prayer Book rigidly in front of him and tried to concentrate on something besides the heat.

Behind him in the choir loft the organist played the last strains of "To a Wild Rose," and there was a brief silence. This, he knew, was the organist's dramatic pause before she began the march from *Lohengrin*. Right now he would have settled for dispensing with the dramatics and getting the wedding over as quickly as possible.

As the first chords of the wedding march pounded through the chapel, he straightened automatically, his eyes focused on the end of the long aisle where the bride would follow the bridesmaids through the large double door and, slowly, down the aisle to the bank of white roses. She and the groom would enter together and walk down the aisle together because that was the way she wanted it.

"We want you to marry us," she had told him, "and it would look silly for you to go in with me and then run around to the preacher's place. So Charles and I will go in together."

She also wanted to use the wedding service from the Book of Common Prayer, and August did not object, though he thought it rather odd for the daughter of a Baptist minister to have an Episcopal ceremony in a Baptist chapel on the campus of a Baptist college.

224

It was an all-white wedding. The six bridesmaids appeared in their waltz-length white bouffant dresses, two by two, their smiles seemingly stamped on their faces. When the last two reached the sanctuary and took their positions, there was another pause before the organist boomed out those six preliminary chords which meant it was time for the spectators to crane their necks to see the bride.

When she appeared at the double doors, her hand resting lightly on Charles's arm, she stopped and stared straight ahead at August. Then she looked at Charles and they proceeded down the aisle.

They stood before him now, and Gena looked up at him, waiting. She was like and yet unlike her mother. Her hair was pale brown with blond streaks which the sun had burned in. Her eyes were not the dark violet of Ann's, but her face was shaped the same, thin with high cheekbones.

He opened the Prayer Book at the ribbon marker. "Dearly beloved, we are gathered together here in the sight of God, and in the face of this company . . ."

Ann would have been proud of Eugenia. So poised, so sure of herself and her world. And Ann would have been glad that her daughter was marrying Charles Grierson.

"Charles, wilt thou have this Woman to thy wedded wife . . ."

Charles also seemed sure of himself. And why shouldn't they both be? They had grown up together—Estelle Grierson's son was only two years older than Gena—childhood playmates, high-school sweethearts, inseparable even in college.

"Eugenia, wilt thou have this Man to thy wedded husband, to live together after God's ordinance . . ."

Gena's face, uplifted in the candlelight, framed in the white veil, was like that of a Madonna. He thought of Ann, who had always had the look of a—no, it was not Ann who had reminded him of a Madonna, but Mary. It was the first time in his life that he had confused Ann and Mary in his mind. I am old, he thought. Seventy-five years old, and there can't be much time left.

"Forasmuch as Charles and Eugenia have consented together in holy wedlock, and have witnessed the same before God and this company, and thereto have given and pledged their troth, each to the other . . ."

It was over. He had given them his blessing and the blessing of God, and they had turned their backs to him and, to the joyful strains of Mendelssohn, had almost run down the long aisle and out of the chapel. He closed the Prayer Book and watched while the bridesmaids and ushers followed the bride and groom. Then he went slowing to a side door and slipped out of the chapel. He walked to the street just beyond the stone wall and waited for George and Estelle, who would take him to the reception at the Community House.

As she stood in the receiving line, just inside the door of the Community House, calmly and graciously greeting the guests and receiving their compliments, Gena knew there was not one thing she would have changed. Except maybe the weather. It was much too warm, and she was uncomfortable in the long white dress and veil, but better to have it too warm than to have rain. What mattered most was that everything that was *humanly* possible had been done to make her wedding perfect.

Between handshakes and kisses and compliments, she glanced at Charles out of the corner of her eye. His face was getting red, as it always did when he was too warm, and she knew that he was more uncomfortable than she. But the reception wouldn't last long, at least not for them. They had already spoken to more than one hundred people, and there were probably about a hundred more waiting their turn at the receiving line. Then they could leave the line and go to the punch bowl; she would cut the cake and the photographer would snap a picture of her feeding the first slice to Charles. Then they could leave.

"How many more?" Charles whispered as Mrs. Wayland, the dean's wife, proceeded down the line to the bridesmaids.

"We're about half through," she whispered back. "It won't be long now."

"Good. My shoes are too tight and my feet hurt and I'm ten degrees hotter than hell."

"My feet hurt, too," she said. They really didn't, but she thought it would make him feel better if she shared his pain. And then to Mrs. Latham, wife of the man who owned the drugstore where Charles was pharmacist, "Why, *thank* you, Mrs. Latham," getting just the right amount of surprise in her voice as though she had not just said thank you a hundred times to the same compliment.

"John doesn't know what he's going to do at the drugstore while you children are away, so hurry back, you hear?" Then with a wink at Gena, "But don't hurry *too* fast."

Professor Joe Peterson, who had replaced August as head of the Religion Department, pumped August's hand vigorously. "You're a lucky man, Feilding. You really *are* gaining a son. Isn't it good news that the young couple will live with you?"

"The best," August agreed, smiling at Gena.

And Gena smiled at Peterson. "We wouldn't have it any other way," she said. "And we'll be right next door to Charles's parents."

Just as we've always been, she thought. The only change being wrought by the marriage was that Charles was moving from the parental home to the house next door. And adding to the overall perfection of everything was the fact that she got along beautifully with George and Estelle. They were as happy about the match as she and Charles . . . and August. August *was* pleased, she was sure, even though he had not said so in so many words. He had had long talks with her when they first told him that the wedding was planned for July, and the gist of the talks was that they were both quite young, and wouldn't it be better if they waited awhile?

But there was no reason for waiting. She had finished college in June, and Charles had gotten his state license to practice pharmacy at the same time. There was nothing to wait for.

It wasn't that August disapproved of Charles, he was very fond of him. And his arguments in favor of waiting had diminished considerably since the night she told him that she wanted to live at the house with him. She knew that he was secretly delighted with that arrangement; that his protestations were only perfunctory. "I always thought," he said, "that young couples wanted to have a place of their own, not be bothered with in-laws and such."

She pooh-poohed the statement and hoped he did not think she was just being polite, or worse yet, self-sacrificing. The truth was, she really did want to stay in the house. That was home and she wanted her home, and Charles too. That it was possible for her to have both was one more thing which added to the total perfection of everything.

"How much longer?" Charles whispered again.

There was a lull in the onset through the door. "Let's go cut the cake and have some punch," she said. "Then we can go."

He had moved everything to the tower room: clothes, books, personal belongings, all the things that had been in the master bedroom. Now there was only one thing left in his bedroom—his former bedroom—to take upstairs, and that was Eugene's manuscript. He took it out of the drawer of his bedside table and made his last trip to the tower. He held the papers for a minute before putting them in a top drawer of the rolltop desk: tonight he needed to feel close to someone, for he felt very distant from himself, as gauche as the young student who had come here to see Eugene to ask his advice about going into the ministry. Now Eugene's room was to be his—his surprise present to Gena. In spite of her insistence that she and Charles really preferred to live in the house, he was not convinced that they wouldn't rather have a place of their own. And so he was giving them the house. The tower room would be his domain, the rest of the house theirs. The room was small, but after all, Eugene had lived in it for years. The view from the window, overlooking Faculty Avenue, was lovely in autumn and spring, and the sycamore just outside the window was an old friend. He would be content here; it was all he wanted or needed.

For a long time he sat at the desk, staring at the pages of Eugene's cramped handwriting.

"I say then that all gods are happy, but if it is lawful to say this without offense, I say that Love is happiest of them all, being most beautiful and best. And how he is most beautiful, I am about to describe. First of all, Phaidros, he is youngest of the gods. He himself supplies one great proof of what I say, for he flies in full flight away from Old Age, who is a quick one clearly, since he comes too soon to us all. Love hates him naturally and will not come anywhere near him. But he is always associated with the young, and with them he consorts, for the old saying is right, 'Like ever comes to like.' "

He tried to discipline his mind to think objectively constructive thoughts, but he was tired and all his thoughts were subjective, as they had been for the past two days. The many trips up and down the stairs today had been almost too much for him. And the weight on his mind in knowing that Gena would be away for a week was like bereavement. Of all the work he had done in his life, the sermons preached, the lectures given, the counseling, he was proudest of Gena. She was his masterpiece.

The panic and utter helplessless he had felt at being left alone to rear an infant had long since abated. He, with the help of Mayline, had done the best he could, and his best had been good enough. Now Mayline was gone, replaced by her daughter Annabel.

Twenty years, he thought. In some respects it seemed that not much had happened to him during those years, that their passing had been marked solely by Gena's growing from babyhood into a young woman. And yet in other respects the years had been eventful, not so much because of things that had happened to him but because of happenings around him. True, he had grown old. There was no longer any mistaking the signs: His hair was completely white, without even a trace of orange left. He was still thin, but now the thinness took on a look of fragility rather than youthful leanness. The biggest change, however, had been in his mind. It took him longer now to make decisions, and then he worried more about the decisions he made. It seemed to him that his entire process of thinking had slowed to match his slower reflexes and motions.

Though his life had been calm through these years, the world around him had not. World War II had brought changes to Brandon never dreamed of during the first war. Where August had concerned himself then with every battle, with the students who went away and those who came back and those who never came back, he found he could not bear to think of these things in the new war: the devastation to mind and body seemed too painful for him to dwell upon.

The war had brought one radical change to the campus of which he heartily approved. The student enrollment, in a year's time, had dropped from two thousand to eight hundred, and at a special meeting of the Baptist State Convention and college trustees the necessity of closing the college until after the war was discussed. August knew that once the college closed its doors they would never be reopened, and when it was suggested that in order to survive, the college should become coeducational, he supported the idea. To the alumni and to most of the professors, allowing girls on the campus which for more than a hundred years had known only the heavy male tread across the scattered stepping stones seemed nothing short of sacrilege. August's own enthusiasm for the plan was, he admitted freely, partly because he had a daughter he would like to see attending Brandon, but even more because he was willing to do almost anything that would mean survival for the college.

By a narrow margin the convention voted to admit women, and in 1942 the plaque above the arch was changed from "Brandon College for Men" to merely "Brandon College." August's effort on behalf of the co-eds was among the last of his active involvement with the college. In the spring of 1943, after forty-four years of teaching, he had moved his books and his few personal mementos out of his office and given the key to Peterson. Later, at a testimonial banquet, he listened to the words of the president of the college and his colleagues, and even some of his former students who had come back for the occasion, but the banquet seemed unreal and anticlimactic. It was, he told Peterson, like attending his own funeral. But there was no sadness in him at the time. The sadness had come the afternoon when he closed a textbook, looked almost hungrily into the faces of his students, and then dismissed his last class. That had been the real ending, the severing of his connection with the college.

And yet the connection was not entirely severed. During the past five years his home had become an unofficial gathering place for faculty and students alike. Even the new students, those he had never taught, sooner or later found their way to his house. They sought his advice on everything from classwork to personal problems, even matters of the heart.

Gena entered Brandon as a freshman in 1944, and August was delighted to observe during her years there that her feeling for the college almost matched his own. She had graduated with honors with the class of '48, and now, a month later, she was married.

Gena. Only yesterday she had been climbing the umbrella tree in the backyard and picking the purple blossoms to show Charles—and then not understanding why the blossoms wilted within five minutes even though she put them in water. And, now, not understanding why her father had wanted her to wait before marrying Charles.

He had to agree with her that a nicer young man than Charles was not to be found. Yet he had felt there was something missing: the elements of surprise and delight in sudden, unexpected love. Oh, he would have wanted her to marry Charles eventually, and it certainly was not in his heart or mind to wish her the youthful heartbreak of either unrequited love or love gone sour, but still . . . He could not help feeling that to everyone at one time or another there should come, unbidden, a love that was not quite so settled as Gena's love for Charles.

But now they were married, and he could only think that it was for the best. Young people today, he reflected, are wiser and more knowing than they used to be; oftentimes more knowing than their elders.

He sighed and rolled the top down over the desk, then went downstairs to turn out the lights. When he reached the foot of the stairs he was startled to see Estelle standing just inside the door.

"August, I wasn't sure you were here. I called and got no answer. Are you all right?"

"Sorry, I didn't hear you. I was upstairs moving a few things." He motioned toward the living room.

"Not tonight, thanks. I just wanted to look in to see that you're all right—not too lonesome—and to invite you to dinner tomorrow night. Maybe we'll have a card from the children tomorrow and we can make it a celebration."

"Thank you," he said. "That would be very nice."

After she had gone through the hedge to the house next door he stood for a long time looking out at the dark street. Tonight he felt very old—a feeling accentuated by the knowledge that his neighbor had come to "look in to see that you're all right." He smiled to himself. Well, she could hardly have said, "I just wanted to check to make sure you hadn't dropped dead during the day." But that was what she meant. To feel that you're old enough for people to be concerned about your survival when you're in a house alone is to feel very old indeed.

I'm tired, he thought again, knowing that the limit of his fatigue could be measured by the length of his thoughts on the subject of old age and death. He seldom thought about dying except when he was very tired, when the exertions of the day had not brought about much that was constructive.

He went back inside the house, closed the door, and started to lock it, then changed his mind. If he should die during the night, poor Estelle would have to break down the door tomorrow. And that was not a very dignified activity to precede a dignified funeral.

As he went up the two flights of stairs to the tower, he laughed aloud at the though of Estelle heaving her considerable bulk against his front door.

21

THEY HAD BEEN MARRIED for four months before Gena discovered that she knew Charles so well that she hardly knew him at all.

Marriage brought no change into her life. About the only discernible change was that Charles now shared her bedroom —only it wasn't her old bedroom, it was the master bedroom which had been August's until the wedding. And now, instead of receiving August's visitors at the front door and ushering them into the living room, she directed them to the tower. Most of the visitors, though, did not have to be directed. They soon learned where the new sanctum was and did not even bother to ring the bell, going straight to the tower without disturbing her.

She had no more household responsibilities than before. Annabel did the cooking and most of the cleaning. But for the first time in her life she felt like a child playing house. August and the Griersons, the Griersons particularly, continually referred to her and Charles as "the children" and she, who had always been treated as an adult by August began actually to feel like a child. She thought that if she heard Estelle say "the children" one more time she would let her know how she felt about it. August, she knew, would never have used the phrase if he had not heard George and Estelle do it so often. It annoyed her all the more when she remembered that their life together, hers and Charles's, was almost exactly the way they had acted it out as children. Each morning she went downstairs and put the coffeepot on before Annabel arrived, and then went back upstairs to dress. They ate breakfast together (August had breakfast in the tower and joined them for the other two meals), sometimes talking animatedly, sometimes saying very little. Then she went with him to the door and kissed him good-bye when he left for the drugstore. This was almost the identical routine they had acted out years ago in her dollhouse in the backyard, with Charles coaching her in the ways he had learned from observing his parents.

Still, she liked being married for the most part; liked the new status it gave her. Of course, it had taken her only a very short time to realize that her ideas about sex gathered from books hardly matched the actuality. She enjoyed making love with Charles, but it was not exactly an all-consuming passion.

She played her part well and was reasonably sure that Charles would never know that sex, to her, was not the rapturous delight he apparently found it to be.

She remembered the day she had been summoned next door, a week before the wedding, to find an Estelle nervous and unnaturally formal. "Sit down, Gena. I thought we might have a little talk while the men are all out."

Gena sat down and waited, filled suddenly with an awful premonition as to what the subject of this little talk might be.

"Your mother and I were great friends, Gena," Estelle said. "I think she would be as pleased as we are that you're marrying Charles."

How stiff can you get? Gena thought, wanting to say something to make Estelle feel more at ease but not knowing what to say. She thought about her mother but the thought could not go very far because she had never been able to picture Ann Fielding as a person. August had told her that the girl in the portrait over the mantel, Angela, looked exactly like her mother, so she had never been able to visualize her mother as anything but a pretty little girl with long yellow hair and deep-blue eyes. That she could ever have been a woman who had chatted with Estelle or taken care of a household or slept with August was so utterly impossible to imagine that it seemed ridiculous to try.

"Gena, I know you and August are very close and all, but I thought perhaps you'd like to talk to me. After all, the wedding is next week, and there are things that are probably bothering you. I thought you might like to discuss them with another woman."

The idea of talking about sex with Charles's mother repelled her. You'd think, she thought, that Estelle thinks I'm about twelve years old and ignorant. But then Estelle had no way of knowing of all the books she and her friends had read about sex—how to have a happy sex life, marriage manuals, even Havelock Ellis (though by the time she got to him he seemed a bit outdated)—always putting the books in a *War and Peace* or *Pride and Prejudice* dust jacket. The absolute ultimate had been a long poem entitled "This Is My Beloved." The only thing left now was to *experience* sex. And certainly with Charles she would feel no shyness.

"I don't think so," she said to Estelle. "The invitations were mailed two weeks ago. My dress is finished, and so are the bridesmaids'."

"That wasn't exactly what I meant, dear." Estelle played with the silver beads around her neck. "I thought you might ask me about—well, about the intimate side of marriage. Just pretend for a few minutes that I am your mother."

"I've always thought of you as practically *being* my mother," Gena said.

"I'm glad, dear. That's the way I wanted it."

"And I want to thank you for all the things you've done for me all my life. I feel almost as much at home here as I do next door." She stood up. "And I want you to know how much I appreciate everything . . ."

"I've tried, Gena. And now . . ." But Gena was going toward the door.

"I really must go, Estelle. I have to call the bakery to see about the cake. I'm afraid the caterers—"

"But Gena . . ."

"I'll come back when I have more time. Thanks for everything, Estelle." She bolted across the porch and through the hedge. And she had not found it convenient to go back to have the talk with Estelle, knowing that Estelle must be as relieved as she that their mutual embarrassment was thus dispended.

She thought she had known Charles before, known him to the point where she could tell what he was going to say before he said it. Now she wasn't sure whether she had not known him as well as she thought—or whether it was herself she had not known. But now they hardly ever talked about the subjects that had interested them before, and they had both found almost as soon as they returned from their wedding trip that they had very little in common with the college students or their unmarried friends. Inevitably, they had become a part of the young married set in Brandon.

Admitting to herself that, after all, she could be the one who had changed involved an added effort in attempting to remain the Gena Charles had known before. For if he had loved her the way she was, or had been, then it followed that he would not love her if she were different.

Just as she was getting used to the game she was playing—no, not game, for that kept her in the category of "the children"—she found that the biggest change of all was coming. She had no idea whether she was happy or unhappy or merely apprehensive about it, but she thought that perhaps after all she had better have a talk with Estelle.

When Gena told him she was pregnant—and that was the way she said it, "I'm pregnant," as though stating a medical fact which could have no possible bearing on their personal lives—Charles was first stunned and then delighted. He was on the verge of expressing his delight when it dawned on him that perhaps he had better find out how Gena felt about it first.

"You are?" It was as noncommittal a response as he could summon.

"Yes. The doctor said it would probably be an anniversary present for us."

There was still nothing in her face or voice that told him what he wanted to know. "Next July? That means it may also be a birthday present for you."

"Yes, I guess so. Well, shall we celebrate or spend the evening consoling each other?"

She looked like a little girl waiting to see whether she was to be praised or scolded. "I think a celebration is in order," he said carefully. "Have you told your father?"

"No, I haven't told anyone but you."

"Oh, Gena!" He could contain himself no longer. "I'm glad, glad, glad." He hugged her tightly—then, remembering her new condition, drew quickly away. "Aren't *you* glad?"

For the first time she smiled. "Yes, if you are."

"Let's tell everyone right away. Oh, Gena!"

"I thought maybe you'd think we shouldn't have a baby until we've had more time to get used to each other."

"My God!" he laughed. "We've been used to each other all our lives."

It may have been something of an overstatement, but he truly believed it. He could not remember a time in his life when there had been no Gena next door. Almost since baby-hood they had been utterly dependent upon each other, probably because both were only children and did not have to divide their attention to accommodate the demands of brothers and sisters. Then, too, because she had no mother and he did, and because her father had been since Charles's earliest memories an old, old man, he had unconsciously felt the need to protect her, even assuming the role of parent and going so far as to reprimand her on occasion when he thought she needed it. This invariably brought forth the same re-sponse: "Charles Grierson, you think you know so much." But he knew that she really liked it, and he had continued in the role of occasional parent until they were married. After that, there was a subtle change which was so gradual that it took him several months to realize a change was taking place. She didn't exactly *mother* him now, nor was she condescend-ing about what he assumed were his foibles, but somehow in the few months they had been married he seemed to have become, if not a child, at least younger than she, and though she never reprimanded him, he would not have been surprised if she had, and more or less expected it momentarily.

For that reason if for no other, he was delighted about the baby. With a baby in the house he would be reestablished as an adult, head of the family. He did not want to rule as a dictator; he only wanted their relationship to return to the same easy basis it was on before they were married.

Marrying Gena had seemed, from the outside, the easiest

and most satisfying arrangement for his future. Since they had known each other forever, they would be spared the many adjustments that he had heard imperiled most marriages. He had never considered marrying anyone else, had never, in fact, seriously dated another girl. His only qualms had concerned moving into the house with August. He would rather have had a home of his own. But since Gena wanted to stay with August ("I just can't go and leave him all alone, Charles. He's old—and lonely."), he had put up no argument.

Now, from the inside, nothing seemed quite as simple or as easy as it had before. Sharing the house with August had turned out to be the easiest part of marriage. They seldom saw him except at meals, and he could never accuse his father-in-law of interfering in any way with their lives.

He wasn't quite sure what it was, but there seemed to be something—some intangible, unnamable *something*—missing from their marriage. The more he thought about it, the more convinced he became that the baby would be the best thing that could happen to them.

They went together to the tower to tell August. He was sitting at the desk reading, his thin form hunched over as he rested his elbows on the desk. He looked around with a smile when they entered, and his expression did not change when Gena told him the news. He was silent for a minute, then he said, "I never thought I'd live long enough to see my grandchildren. There was a time when I thought I'd never have a child, certainly not a grandchild. God has been very good to me—better than I deserve."

They smiled back at him, neither knowing exactly what to say now that the first breathless announcement had been made.

"And what do the young parents think?"

"We think it's perfect," Gena said, her face quite serious. "Just perfect."

Jennifer Grierson, two weeks overdue, was born on the twenty-fourth of July in the Brandon hospital. She had deep blue, almost violet eyes, and dark hair which by the time she was a month old had turned white-blond. "She is the image of your mother," August told Gena. And Gena admitted that the baby did look like the portrait of young Angela.

Annabel appeared to be the only one in the house who treated the advent of the baby as a normal occurrence. When Gena returned from the hospital, Charles was even more solicitous than he had been during her pregnancy, and although she enjoyed the extra attention at first, she found her nerves were becoming frayed by it.

"For heaven's sake," she said to him. "I'm not helpless. You seem to think I can't do one single thing for myself."

Whereupon Charles made it a point to let her do almost everything for herself, and then wondered if this, too, annoyed her. To him the baby was little short of a miracle. He was quick to admit he had never seen a more beautiful infant (although, truthfully, he could not remember having really *noticed* a baby before). She was, as Gena said, just perfect.

Jennifer seldom cried, but when she did it brought August from the tower immediately.

"What's the matter with her?" he would ask, as though while his back was turned someone had allowed a catastrophe to befall his granddaughter.

"Did you get upset every time I cried when I was a baby?" Gena asked.

"When you were a baby, I was at the college every day. Besides I don't think Mayline ever let you cry. She spoiled you."

"It doesn't show now, if she did," Charles said gallantly.

"Well, no one's going to spoil Jennifer," Gena said. "Not even her doting father. You know, I think she's already beating my time with him."

"That's a crazy think to say," Charles said quickly.

Gena did not answer Charles, but later when they were in their bedroom he said, "You didn't mean that, did you, Gena?"

She hesitated, not sure what he meant, then she remembered the conversation downstairs and laughed. "Of course not, silly. I just like to tease you now and then. You shouldn't take everything so seriously. And anyway, I wouldn't mind at all if you loved the baby more than you do me. Think how awful it would be if you thought Jennifer was a nuisance, and I was constantly having to defend her."

"That could never happen," he said. He sat on the side of the bed, watching her as she undressed. "Your father certainly thinks the world of her."

"Charles, we've been married for more than a year and you've never called Daddy anything since we got married. You mention him to me, you say 'your father,' and when you're talking to him, you don't call him anything."

Charles laughed. "I know. I haven't known what to call him. He was always Professor Fielding before, but now that he's my father-in-law . . ."

"I call your parents by their first names—always have."

"I can't bring myself to call him August," he said. "It doesn't sound right. I thought about asking him what I should call him, but I've waited so long that it would be embarrassing now."

"You might as well call him August," she said. "Almost everyone else does, and he doesn't mind." She slipped a white nightgown over her head.

"You look like a bride," he said.

"I don't feel very much like one. Not with a six-weeks-old baby sleeping across the hall."

He reached out and pulled her down beside him on the bed. "I hope she grows up to be as pretty as her mother." He kissed her neck and hesitated above her lips. "Gena?"

"Yes," she nodded.

She had thought having a baby would make a difference in the way she felt when Charles made love to her. But nothing had changed. It was still a pleasant enough experience, but no bells rang, no fireworks exploded, no thunder roared. The novelists and poets, as usual, had grossly exaggerated an emotion.

August looked thoughtfully out of the window into the branches of the sycamore tree. Gena sat on the ground under the tree, the baby carriage beside her. Then he turned back to his visitor, Dean Wayland, and said, "I don't know that I favor it. I think firing him is a rather drastic measure."

"But what else can we do, August?" The dean scratched his bald head. You've got to remember that Brandon is a denominational school. His behavior might be overlooked at a state school, or even a private one, but not a church school where young men and women expect to get a Christian education."

"Sid Fleaky is the best football coach Brandon ever had—

in fact the only good one I can remember, and my memory goes back almost to the year of our Lord."

"Flea's a good coach, no question about that. It isn't his coaching ability that's under fire, though."

"Let me get this straight," August said. "Parents are complaining because Flea's language during football practice is . . ."

"Colorful enough to make a sailor blush." Dean Wayland sighed. "Profanity, obscenities—there isn't a word he doesn't know and use." He seemed on the verge of revealing some of the words, then remembered who his host was and said nothing.

"I think," August said, "you could remedy the situation simply by getting the dean of women to declare the football field off limits to the co-eds during practice. Interesting though it may be to watch the boys go through their workouts, that may be the only way to spare the girls' delicate ears. I daresay the players don't turn pink every time Flea comes forth with a goddamn."

The dean's eyebrows went up somewhat. "*I* daresay they're getting their vocabulary increased. But that isn't the only thing that bothers me. You remember that Sophie has a twin sister named Sylvia, identical? One of the boys asked Flea how he could tell his wife from her sister, and Flea is reported to have said, 'Oh, that's simple enough. Her sister has a mole under her left breast.' Now, I ask you, August, is that the kind of thing you expect to hear in a Baptist college?"

"It's the kind of thing I'd expect to hear from Flea," August said, smiling.

"Lord knows I don't *want* to fire him," the dean said. "We'd probably get someone in his place who couldn't win a game and then the alumni would be unhappy and cut down on their contributions to the college. Sometimes I wish we didn't have a football team."

"Well, why don't you have a talk with Flea, and ask him if he can't tone down his language a bit, both on and off the field. And keep the girls away from practice."

"I'll try it," Dean Wayland said. "I'm willing to try almost anything at this point—you should read some of those letters . . . Oh, August, I happened to mention your name to the new history professor, Ian Caldwell, the other day, and he said his grandfather or great-uncle or some relative was at Brandon when you were a student. Ferris, Farris, something like that. Anyway, Ian Caldwell would like to meet you, and I think you'll enjoy him."

"Tom Farris," August said. "My word, I haven't thought of him in a thousand years. He was a ministerial student. Yes, bring your Professor Caldwell by sometime. Was he ever a student here?"

"No, he went to the state university and Columbia. I'll bring him next time I come. And thanks, August, for listening to me spout off—and for the advice. As I said, I didn't want to fire Flea."

"You talk to him," August said. "Flea's not exactly what you'd call a reverent man, but there's no real harm in him." He went downstairs and out to the yard with Dean Wayland, and after the dean had gotten into his car, he joined Gena under the sycamore. He peeked over the side of Jennifer's carriage. "Is she asleep?"

"I don't think so, but it's about time for her to go in for a nap."

"Let me hold her a minute." He picked up the baby. "You know, Gena, she doesn't look as much like Ann as she did. Still has the same coloring, but her expression is more like Charles now. Had you noticed?"

"Yes, and remember Charles has light hair, too."

"Little Miss Jennifer," August said. "My first grandchild. Someday—who knows?—maybe you'll have a little brother or sister to play with."

"Not too soon, I hope," Gena said. She stood up and took the baby from him. "Anyway, being an only child isn't the worst thing that could happen to a person. Both Charles and I can testify to that."

She took the baby into the house and August went to the porch and sat down. No, he thought, it wouldn't be the worst thing that could happen if they didn't have any more children. But he hoped they would. Charles and Gena were such a good match that it would be a shame to share their happiness with only one child. And he knew without having to be told that Charles would like to have a son—and he, a grandson.

22

Ian Caldwell was shown into the house by Annabel, who told him to go up two flights of stairs to the tower. "Mr. August stays up there," she said.

When he entered the room, the old man seated at the desk stood up. "How do you do. I don't believe I know you."

"My name is Ian Caldwell, Professor Fielding. I came here this fall to teach in the history department. My . . ."

"Oh, yes. Caldwell. Dean Wayland said he was going to bring you to see me—I'm glad you didn't wait for him. Sit down, Caldwell. I understand you are related to Tom Farris, but I must say I don't see the slighest resemblance."

Ian, tall and trim and auburn-haired, smiled at the thought of being compared with the rotund, balding Tom Farris.

"He's my great-uncle," he said, "and he sends you his warmest regards."

"And you are to send mine in return. Your great-uncle did me a big favor once, without ever knowing."

Ian was afraid the old man would go into tedious detail about his and Uncle Tom's student days, but almost immediately his eyes seemed to snap to, preferring present to past.

"And how is it that you chose Brandon, Caldwell? Because of Tom?"

"Not quite." Ian laughed, beginning to like the professor. He was willing to bet that somewhere beneath the aged exterior there was a modern sense of humor, and now that he was safely away from the "reason" he had chosen Brandon, he could see certain aspects about it. Thinking of it all now, for the first time in weeks, he decided to tell August Fielding at least part of his strange background.

"You might say," he said, "that I'm here because of an overabundance of women in my life . . ."

He came, he said, from a college for women in Virginia.

There were only two male professors besides himself: Dr. Therbold in biology, and Dr. Lesgood in English, both of them well past fifty. The remaining members of the faculty he would have described as frustrated spinsters. At least four of them, he thought, were sapphic, and several seemed to be neuter.

The students, almost without exception, were the products of wealthy parents and exclusive boarding schools, and their main interest was in the Saturday night dances in the gymnasium to which students from the University of Virginia, Virginia Military Institute, and Virginia Polytechnic Institute were invited. It was a good thing, he decided, that the girls *were* wealthy and would never have to earn their living, for upon graduation there was not one thing that they were qualified to do except possibly bring up daughters in the same mold.

There was one exception on campus. Betty Ankers, a history major, was a scholarship student who expected to do a year of graduate work at the University of North Carolina and then go into social work. As it turned out, she never finished her undergraduate work, because Ian married her at the end of her junior year. To him she stood out among her social-minded sisters because she actually studied and because she was a loner—he was never quite sure whether from choice or necessity.

As far as Ian was concerned, Betty was the one bit of sanity in that insane college. When he was offered a position by the head of the History Department at Brandon College that spring he accepted immediately, without ever having seen Brandon and without knowing anything about it except that it was an accredited four-year college in his home state where a great-uncle, an overly religious preacher, had gone.

He and Betty went immediately to Brandon, where they spent a quiet summer getting to know the townspeople and the college people. And it was during the summer that they got to know each other.

Ian at first could not understand his growing disillusionment with marriage, and for that reason he attributed the disillusionment to the holy state of matrimony rather than to Betty herself. But by the time autumn came and his teaching job began, he could see a great many things that had been too close to him during the summer for understanding. In congenial surroundings among people who stimulated him he and Betty were no longer allied against uncongenial forces, and their former spirit of camaraderie slowly vanished. Then, too, on that near manless campus he had been the only single male —fully aware that this was the reason for the undue popularity of his classes—and she, apparently, the only student with either brains or personality. What was left to them now was the slow realization that they had little in common—and a refusal to admit so soon that the marriage was a mistake.

Ian frankly blamed himself for the change Brandon had made in their feelings. He was, after all, nine years older than Betty and should not have been carried away by romantic foolishness brought on solely by an overdose of flighty females. He made no predictions, not even to himself, as to how long the marriage would last. He knew only that if it ended, she would be the one to terminate it . . .

Ian stopped suddenly. He was talking much too much. He had told this man, a perfect stranger, things he had never told another living soul. Professor Fielding had laughed with him when he related his adventures at the college in Virginia, and he had somehow found himself going on, further and further into details of his private life.

Ian looked now at August, thinking that he had never met a man he liked so much so soon.

"Professor, I'm afraid I have been presuming upon a friendship which doesn't yet exist. I didn't mean to give you my whole life history, particularly certain aspects of it."

"You are being presumptuous in presuming that you are not my friend," August said. "Don't be embarrassed or have regrets later because you've told me the things you have. Many people come to me and tell me many things. I try to advise them objectively when my advice is asked, but I think really there is no such thing as objective advice. We can only measure by our own experience." He paused, then said, "You haven't asked me for advice because I think you've already decided to do what you can to make your marriage succeed. I suppose, as a preacher, you'd expect me to say just leave everything in the hands of God and stop worrying. Frankly, I don't think God has much use for people who leave everything to Him."

He gave a long sigh and stopped talking. When he spoke again, his words were almost whispered. "I sometimes wonder if there are any happy marriages—and by happy I don't mean continually exuding joy. I was married twice, the first time for such a brief period that when my wife died, I still did not know what did and did not make a good marriage. My second marriage lasted for ten years, the last six of which were wholly satisfying. But it took four years for my wife and me to . . . to overcome serious difficulties brought about by a lack of understanding on both our parts. From my own experience, I can only say to you to give your marriage time to grow up."

They sat quietly for a few minutes, and then Ian stood up. "Then I won't apologize for unburdening my personal problems, because you've made me feel that I've known you for a long time. Thank you. May I come to see you again—often?"

"I'll be disappointed if you don't." August held out his hand and then went with him to the door. "I'm almost always here and I like to have company. Talking with friends keeps me from feeling that I'm no longer any use to the world."

Ian left the house feeling better than he had in weeks. Probably, he thought, talking to anyone would have been a relief, but talking with August Fielding not only brought a feeling of relief but also hope.

On his way home he stopped by the furniture store and bought the matching table lamps Betty had said she wanted.

On a warm spring afternoon in 1951 the door of the tower room was flung open, and Sid Fleaky, puffing from the exertion of running up two flights of stairs, said loudly, "You here, August?"

"I am that." August removed some books from the extra chair so Flea could sit down and catch his breath.

"It's been a long time, Flea. What brings you away from the field during spring practice?"

"I gave the boys a holiday," Flea said. "Truth is, I needed one myself. And because it *has* been a long time, I said to myself, 'Flea, you'd better go see how August is getting on.'"

"I'm glad you came," said August, hoping that the visit was to be purely social and not the result of trouble, which Flea had an uncanny talent for getting into. "Everything going all right? Have you got a winning team ready for us next fall?"

"It looks good now." Flea undid his shoelaces and sat back, propping his feet on the side of August's desk. "Most of the old boys are coming back, and I've got several hotshots lined up for fall. Just got back from a recruiting trip."

Flea's recruiting trips were of campus-wide reputation. It was impossible to know whether the stories told about them were true, but August was inclined to believe they were. (Supposedly, when Flea was looking for a strong line, he went to the coalmines of Pennsylvania, stuck his head down a shaft, and shouted, "Any of you dumb bastards down there want a collitch education for free?" And out would come what would probably turn out to be the star fullback for the next season. Giving credence to the story were the unpronounceable names of some of the players.) True or not, the Brandon team was rated number one in the conference at least three out of every five years.

"I got a kid coming in the fall who beats all I ever seen," Flea said. "He can . . . well, I won't go into the technicalities since you ain't much of a football man. But take it from me, we'll even beat the living hell out of Duke this year."

"Glad to hear it, though that will make the Methodists unhappy," August said.

"Yeah, and speaking of that, you know there's going to be a new church in Brandon?"

"Methodist?"

"No, we're getting a Catholic church here. Been needing one for a long time."

"I didn't think there were many, if any, Catholics here," August said, hardly believing the turn this conversation had taken. "And as far as I know, none of the students are Catholic."

"Yeah, there're Catholics here. You know that Assyrian family on South Poplar Street? They been having to go to Raleigh every Sunday to mass. And in the fall there'll be some Catholics in the student body."

"Go ahead, Flea. Tell me about it. You've done something and you can't keep it to yourself any longer."

Flea grinned. "You damn right, August. I'm getting 'em to build that church here, but it might not be so good if anybody finds out I had a hand in it."

"Are you thinking about becoming a Catholic?"

"Jesus no! You know I'm a Baptist, if I'm anything. At

least on my records in the dean's office it says I'm Baptist. Change religions, I'd have to change collitches. No, it's like this. I found this kid up in Pennsylvania, Fred Sercek, the one I was telling you about. Well, I just about had him all signed and sealed when he found out the nearest Catholic church is twenty miles away from here. 'I can't go,' he says, and that left me in a fix so I told him there'd be a church here by fall, so now he's coming. And there *will* be a church, by damn."

"How in the world did you arrange that, Flea?"

"Well, it worried me some, making a promise like that, specially knowing that if he came and there wasn't a church, he'd probably take off for Duke or maybe go to Penn State. I thought and thought and then it came to me. I went to Raleigh and talked to the head man—the bishop or somebody—and I says, 'Bishop, I ain't a Catholic, but I'm here to tell you we need a Catholic church mighty bad in Brandon.' I told him about the people having to go all the way to Raleigh to church and about the new Catholics moving in town, and he says he'll look into the matter. Well, I don't know what kind of looking he did, but he called me the other night and thanked me for my interest and said the dioce-something was going to put a mission church here."

August held back his laughter. "Is that the truth, Flea?"

"As I'm sitting here, August, that's the truth. I'm getting a little nervous about it, though. What if those Catholics start investigating and find out there's hardly enough here to fill one pew?"

"I'm sure if there's to be an investigation, it has already been made," August said. "If the bishop agreed, you're off the hook."

Flea breathed a sigh of relief. "I'm glad to hear you say that. God's teeth, August, I didn't want to have them papists mad at me."

Now August did laugh. "I think in time they'll thank you. Who knows, maybe they think they can win over a few Baptist souls?"

And that was how the town of Brandon, with one hundred and twelve Methodists, and one thousand two hundred Baptists (not counting the student body), and five Catholics, came to have a Catholic church.

Jennifer was a practical, serious-minded child who by the time she was three had established what Charles called "thinking habits." She was often found alone in her playroom, not playing but sitting in a doll chair with her chin resting in her tiny hands, and when asked, "What are you doing, Jen?" the invariable answer was, "I'm thinking."

Her favorite pastime was having August read to her. She would go to the tower, climb into his lap, and say, "Read to me, August." And Gena began a campaign to break the child from calling her grandfather August, although August seemed to find it amusing.

On her third birthday August gave her a book of illustrated Bible stories and this book became her favorite. She requested some of the stories so often that while August read, she recited along with him, never missing a word and imitating to perfection the inflections of his voice.

"Jonah had a flashlight, didn't he?" she asked.

"A flashlight, Jen?"

"Inside the whale. He had to have a flashlight so he could see how to get out, because it was all dark in there."

"Yes, I suppose he had a flashlight," August said.

"Daddy," Gena scolded, "don't make the story any more impossible to believe than it already is. Next thing we know, she'll go to Sunday school and tell her teacher about the flashlight."

August smiled. "If she can believe Jonah spent three days inside the whale and got out alive, I don't think she'll have to strain her imagination too much to believe he had a flashlight. It sounds reasonable to me."

"Run outside and play, Jen," Gena said. And after the child had gone: "That's the trouble, I'm afraid. She's too reasonable for a child her age. Sometimes she acts like a little old woman instead of a child."

"Because she's around adults so much of the time," August said. He was quiet for a moment, then he said, "Now, if she had a baby brother . . ."

Gena stood up. "I'd better call Estelle. She called this morning while I was out and told Annabel she wanted Jen to go over for dinner tonight. I'd better let her know it's all right."

She hurried downstairs, so preoccupied with her thoughts that she almost collided with the man at the foot of the stairs before she saw him.

"Good afternoon. Is Professor Fielding in?"

"Yes, he's in his room."

"Thank you. I'll just go up." Gena watched him until he disappeared around the corner of the second flight. He seemed to be familiar with the house yet she had never seen him here before.

She made the call to Estelle, then went out to the front porch and sat down in the swing, keeping her eyes on the yard where Jennifer was playing. In a little while the man who had gone up to August's room came out on the porch. He started when he saw her in the swing, then smiled and said, "This is the kind of weather that makes it almost impossible to stay indoors."

"I hope it lasts," she said. "I hope winter won't come too soon."

The smile disappeared. "Winter always seems to come too soon, doesn't it? Well . . ." he hesitated. "Good afternoon." And he walked briskly toward his car parked at the curb in front of the house. His hair was almost red in the fading sunlight.

A good face, she noted. Honest, with nice gray eyes.

"Don't go near the street, Jen," she called, although the child was nowhere near the street.

The shadows of late afternoon were beginning to fall across the porch. Almost time for Charles to come home, she thought. I may as well wait for him here.

23

SHE PUSHED HER DARK HAIR away from her face, and, irritated by a gesture she made dozens of times a day in his presence, he thought: For God's sake why don't you either cut it or buy some bobbie pins? What he said, in answer to her question was, "No, I didn't stay to grade papers. I went to see August Fielding after my last class."

"What is it with that man?" Betty asked. "You must find him absolutely enchanting."

"I suppose in a manner of speaking, he is," Ian said. "Certainly I enjoy talking with him."

"Apparently a lot more than you do me," she said lightly. "Anyway, if he's so wonderful, why can't I meet him?"

Ian sat down at the dinner table and began carving the roast beef. "I'll take you with me sometime," he said, knowing that he did not particularly want to. "He's a remarkable character."

He was silent during the meal, his thoughts rambling back over the afternoon. This afternoon he had met August's daughter. No, that was not entirely correct. He had seen a woman he assumed was August's daughter and he had spoken a few words to her and she to him. She had seemed so placid —perhaps serene was the word—as she sat on the porch watching her child at play. He tried to visualize Betty sitting quietly, an expression of contentment on her face, seemingly at peace with the world. It was not possible to imagine her that way.

I wish, he thought, that it could have been my wife sitting there watching our daughter.

"Ian," Betty was saying, "would you mind if I went home for a little while?" She paused and looked at him. "I think perhaps it would do us both good."

He was surprised, and yet not surprised. "Why do you say a thing like that?"

"It's just that— oh, I don't know. I'd just like to go home for a week or so. Do you mind?"

He put his fork down. For a moment he thought of the student he had married, the young girl who felt she was suffocating in the atmosphere of the girls' school. Well, why shouldn't she want to get away for a while? What had he given her that was any better than what she had left to be with him?

He got up from the table suddenly, surprising himself, and kissed her. "I'll miss you," he said. "Don't be gone too long."

She looked at him as though she did not understand his unexpected show of affection. "If you'd rather I didn't go . . ."

"No, I think perhaps you should. After all, it's been a long time since you've seen your family, and I can't very well get away now, not until Christmas anyway."

"Do you want me to wait until Christmas so you can go, too?" She pushed her hair away from her face.

There were no big things; it was the little things that drove him crazy. "No," he said. "I'll probably have to spend the holidays making out examinations, as usual. Go now." He left her with the dishes and went to the living room.

When she became bored with the everyday sameness of life, Gena moved into a dream world, not completely losing touch with reality but mixing just enough of the real with the make-believe to make the new world compatible with her sense of practicality.

Ian Caldwell's looks had appealed to her. That combination of openness, honesty, and yet something held back had intrigued her enough to make her wonder what he would be like to live with.

She did not ask August who he was; knowing his name, what he did, the circumstances of his life, would somehow spoil the little game she played in her mind. And so she created him exactly as she wanted him to be. As the days passed and she did not see him again, the image of him became more and more real to her, and she found that without willing it so (even willing it *not* to be so) she could carry on long mental conversations with him as easily as Jennifer could talk with her imaginary playmates.

And then she began to feel guilty about the game and decided that the way to end it was to see him again or find out something about him and let the mundane reality of him spoil the image in her mind.

Before, she had never paid much attention to the goings and comings on the stairs to the tower, but now when she heard the front door open, she went mechanically, hardly aware of her reason, to the hall to greet the caller. She also made a habit of walking around the campus with Jennifer, often stopping to sit on the stone bench in front of the chapel.

"But I'm not tired," Jennifer protested. "Why do we have to sit here? I want my ice cream."

"In a minute," Gena said. "Let's rest for a while."

It was on a cold day in early November that the full realization of what she was doing swept over her, leaving her profoundly shocked. She took Jennifer by the hand and said, "Come on. We'll get the ice cream now—and we won't come here anymore. It's wintertime and much too cold to sit out like this." *Winter always seems to come too soon.*

Seated with Jennifer at the table near the prescription counter in the drugstore, she watched Charles give a bottle of medicine to an old man in overalls.

"I can't pay you yet, Mr. Grierson. I don't—"

"Your credit's good here. You can bring the money in later, when you have it."

When the old man left, Charles came back to the table and sat down. "I have tickets for Saturday's game," he announced. "Do you think Annabel with stay with Jen?"

"If she can't, we'll just leave her with Daddy. It's home-coming, isn't it?"

"Yes, and there's a party at the Clawsons afterward if you want to go. I told Ted I'd let him know at choir practice tonight."

"Fine," she said. "We haven't been out for a while. We'll pretend we're students again, whooping it up after the big game."

Suddenly she wished they *were* students again, living what had seemed at the time complicated lives and looking forward to a marriage that would put an end to the complications. True enough, their lives had become singularly uncomplicated, but the very lack of complications had added new frustrations. Charles must feel it, too, she thought, but he doesn't worry about it. At least so far as she knew, he didn't worry.

She looked at his blond head, bent now over Jennifer as he wiped her mouth with a paper napkin, and she felt a new tenderness for him, and the guilt that she felt before about her fantasies returned. Charles had an outgoing, giving nature. "Your credit's good here," he had told the old farmer, knowing that he would probably never be paid for the medicine. Was her credit still good also? For the love he gave her, she had given little in return. But from now on it would be different; no more fantasies, no more imaginary conversations with men she didn't know, no more guilt.

She felt as though she had been away from him for a long time. "Homecoming," she said softly.

"What?" he said. "Oh, yes, maybe some of the old gang will come back. Trust Ted to round everybody up."

"We have to go now, Jen. Put on your coat." And as

Charles started back to the prescription counter, she held his arm for a minute and whispered, "I love you."

She could see the surprise in his face. How long had it been since she had said the words? Had he taken it for granted that he, not she, was the demonstrative one and accepted with gratitude as much of her as she could spare—herself, parsimoniously given in few words, quick looks, small gestures?

The look of surprise vanished and he gave a low whistle. "Give Jen her supper early and put her to bed," he said. "I'll be home as soon as I can get away."

She felt her cheeks burning as she and Jen left the drugstore. Why couldn't he have said, "I love you, too," and let it go at that?

August pulled up his overcoat collar and walked a little faster as the wind whipped down South Main Street. He had walked farther than usual today because he had wanted to see the homecoming decorations in front of the fraternity houses, but now he was in a hurry to get back home and stretch his legs in front of the fire. He heard a cheer go up from the stadium and thought, Flea's boys are doing it again, and it gave him a certain amount of satisfaction to know that this time they were doing it to a so-far-undefeated Duke team. He smiled at the banners across the street, some saying merely "Beat Dook" and others showing the Duke blue devil falling on his pitchfork.

As the cheer went up, August paused momentarily in front of St. Catherine's Church, R.C. They may call it St. Catherine's, he thought, but to me it will always be Flea's church. Saint Flea. And he almost laughed out loud at the idea, knowing full well that Flea had never so much as set foot inside his church.

When he reached the stone wall, he cut through the campus, stopping again to look up, as he always did, at the spire. The campus was deserted and the only sound was the distant noise from the stadium. The old question, "If a tree falls in a forest, is there a sound if no one is there to hear it?" had always seemed totally irrelevant to him. But now as he looked at the spire he was sure that, like God, it was there and always would be even if there was no one to see it.

He continued his walk, feeling better for having looked up.

He had been depressed for the past few days. All was not well with Gena, though he had no idea exactly *what* was not well with her. Last night, in answer to his question, she had assured him that everything was fine.

"Why shouldn't it be, Daddy?"

"You've seemed . . . well, preoccupied lately. I thought something might be bothering you." Seeing her face, he went on. "Do you want to talk about it?"

She shrugged. "There's nothing to talk about, really. But you know, sometimes I don't think I'm a very good person."

"And what terrible sin have you committed? Have you been impatient with Jennifer, or maybe gotten in Annabel's way in the kitchen?"

She smiled. "No sins so terrible as those, but . . . I must go put Jen to bed. Good night, Daddy."

He knew that in all probability he would never know what was disturbing her. Gena would keep it to herself; it was doubtful that even Charles would suspect she was not entirely happy at the moment.

He reached the north side of the stone wall and had started down Faculty Avenue when he heard his name called.

"I see I'm not the only one who didn't go to the game," Ian Caldwell said as he hurried to catch up.

"To tell you the truth, I don't understand the first thing about football, though it's sometimes necessary to pretend I do," August said. "I'm always interested in the outcome, of course."

Ian laughed. "I'm not athletically inclined myself. And there's nothing like a quiet football Saturday for getting caught up. I've spent the afternoon reading term papers. I was on my way to your house when I saw you cross the street."

"Come along," August said. "I was just thinking how good it would be to sit in front of the fire, and it will be even better with company."

They continued down the street together, commenting on the homecoming decorations as they walked.

Charles cupped his left hand over his left ear, while with his right he steered Gena up the concrete steps of the stadium. Their progress was slow because of the crowd and because every three or four feet they had to stop to speak to old friends who had returned to Brandon for homecoming. He had looked forward all week to the game and the party afterward, but now he wanted nothing so much as to get home and give in to the pain in his ear. Ear ache was a child's sickness; he had forgotten how painful it could be, but sitting all afternoon in the cold wind had served as a reminder.

"What's the matter?" Gena asked, noticing his hand over his ear.

"Nothing," he said. She had been in such high spirits all afternoon and was now so happy over Brandon's victory that he did not want to spoil her fun. She looked, he thought, exactly like a co-ed. She wore a large yellow chrysanthemum on her coat and carried a Brandon pennant, both of which he had bought for her on the way to the stadium. "Aren't you cold?" he asked.

"A little, I guess. I hadn't thought about it. Let's hurry to the Clawsons'. They'll have something to warm us up."

Because of traffic conditions on a football Saturday, they had walked to the stadium, which meant that they now had a three-quarters-of-a-mile walk to the Clawsons'. Surely his head would explode before they got there.

Gena, like a little girl, was almost skipping along beside him, trying to keep pace with his long strides. She babbled on about the game, and he only half heard her. By the time they reached the Clawsons' rambling old house he was sure his disposition was in as foul shape as his ear.

Ted Clawson met them at the door with a cup in each hand. "Hot buttered rum," he said. "Merry Christmas."

"You're getting your dates confused," Gena said.

"Any time we beat Duke it's Christmas—to say nothing of Thanksgiving. Come on in."

Charles took a quick gulp from the cup and then began shaking hands, slapping backs, and pretending he was glad to see everybody, while Gena disappeared with Martha Clawson in search of some of their classmates.

It took nearly an hour and four buttered rums before the pain in his ear subsided a little. By that time he had spoken to so many people he could hardly remember who was there and who wasn't. Twice he had spotted Gena going from group to group, and once he heard Buck Yarder call out, "Hey, Gena, now you and Charles are married you don't have to spend all your time with him. Come here, sweetheart; you know when we were in college I voted you the girl I'd most like to neck with."

Charles wondered what Patty Yarder thought of that. He himself didn't think much of it and he thought even less of it when he saw Gena stand on tiptoe and kiss Buck's cheek.

"I'll bet if you really put your mind to it, you could do better than that," Buck said.

Charles went back to the punch bowl and deposited his empty cup on the table, then went back to the other room to collect Gena. He didn't know how much she had had to drink, but she was acting unusually gay. He pushed his way to her and said, "We'd better be going."

"Oh, Charles, everybody's going down to Ricardi's to eat later, and I told them we'd go, too."

He shook his head. "I don't think we should leave Jen with your father that long. He'll get too tired."

When they were outside she said, "What's wrong with you? I thought you wanted to go to the party and now you drag me away before it's even started good."

"You seem to have started pretty good," he said. "No telling where you would have finished."

"Charles, for heaven's *sake*. What's wrong?"

He knew he was making too much of the whole thing and that if he had been feeling well he would have thought nothing about it. "I have an ear ache," he said finally. "I couldn't stand any more of that noise and confusion."

"An ear ache!" The way she said it made it seem that to her nothing short of acute appendicitis should have forced them from the party. Then her face softened and she said, "Poor old Charles, suffering in silence all afternoon. Why didn't you tell me sooner?" The tone of her voice this time made him feel better.

"I'll race you to the corner," he said, and almost before he got the words out she was running ahead, looking back at him and laughing. His ear throbbed as he ran after her, but that did not keep him from the happy thought that Gena had been the prettiest one there, and that she was *his* wife.

They were both out of breath when they reached the house and rushed into the living room to find August sitting by the fire and a strange man on the floor riding Jen on his back.

Gena stopped. "Oh!"

The man helped Jen off his back and stood up, and August stood up also. "Gena, Charles," he said, "this is my friend Ian Caldwell. He's in history. Ian, my daughter and son-in-law, Gena and Charles Grierson."

"How do you do?" Charles shook hands.

"I'm glad to meet you both," Caldwell said. "I think maybe I'll kidnap Jen."

"I hope she hasn't been disturbing you," Charles said.

"On the contrary. I'm having the time of my life with her. I wish she were mine."

"Do you have any children?" Gena asked.

"No, I don't." He looked at his watch. "It's later than I thought, Professor. Betty will be wondering what happened to me."

Jen and August went with him to the door, and Charles sat down in the chair August had vacated. "Whew, that heat on my ear feels good."

"What?" Gena looked around at him as though he had just come into the room.

"I think I may have to run down to the drugstore and see if I can find anything for a bad ear," he said. "I won't get five minutes of sleep tonight with this pain."

"I liked him," Jen said. "He was nice."

"I think Dr. Caldwell liked you, too," August said. "I wouldn't be surprised if you became the main drawing card for him around here now."

"I'll be back in a few minutes," Charles said. He went to the hall and put on his coat, then looked back into the living room. "Can I bring you anything, Gena?"

"What? Oh, no thanks." She was staring into the fire now, all of her gaiety gone, replaced by a sad, pensive expression.

I'll never understand her, Charles thought as he went out. I guess I should have stayed at the party. The pain in his ear roared like a locomotive as he got into the car. Two blocks down the street he saw Caldwell walking and stopped. "Can I give you a ride? I'm on my way downtown."

"Thanks," said Caldwell, "but I live only a couple of blocks from here, just around the corner on Elm."

Charles nodded. "See you again, Caldwell." He drove off, wondering why a young professor would rather spend an afternoon talking with an old man and playing with a little girl than attending a football game with his wife—if the

Betty he had mentioned was his wife. Strange, he thought. Very strange indeed.

24

IT WAS DEAN WAYLAND WHO broke the news to August on a warm afternoon early in April. August sat very still, staring out the window into the branches of the newly budding sycamore tree. The dean had known it would come as a shock to the old man, but now he wondered if August's mind had wandered and he had not fully comprehended, or if perhaps the shock was so great that there would be no reaction. He waited for a few minutes and then he said softly, "August? Do you understand?"

He started to explain all over again, but August stopped him by holding up his hand. "I heard what you said. I just don't understand how anyone could take it seriously or give it a second thought. You don't think anyone will, do you?"

"Twenty million dollars is not to be taken lightly, August. And a great many people are giving it more than second thoughts. I am myself."

Then August exploded. "Sell Brandon College! That's the biggest fool thing I ever heard of!"

"It wouldn't mean selling the college, August," the dean said patiently. "The college would still belong to the convention, still come under the convention's rule. It would merely be a matter of moving the college to the town of Winslow."

"And how in the name of God do you move a college? Do you tear it down, brick by brick, and rebuild it exactly as it is, a hundred miles away from the place where it has stood for one hundred and twenty-three years? And how do you go about moving one hundred and twenty-three years of tradition?"

"The college is growing, August. We need money and we need it badly. The money from tuition and the money from the convention are not enough to take care of the growth. If we want to expand at all, to keep up with the growth of other colleges in the state, I don't see how we can turn down the offer."

August said nothing. He was still trying very hard to digest the facts the dean had given him. He understood only that the Winslow Textile Foundation had offered the college a twenty-million-dollar endowment on the condition that it be moved to Winslow.

"The offer was made several months ago, but we've kept it quiet while our attorneys looked into the matter," Dean Wayland said. "The attorneys' report came in this week. They find nothing amiss, and the matter will be presented to the convention at a special meeting next month. Of course, there is no assurance that the convention will accept the offer, but frankly, I would be surprised if it were turned down."

"Does money mean so much to the Baptists that they can throw away . . ." August stopped, realizing that he had referred to the Baptists as "they," unconsciously disassociating himself from the denomination.

"I've seen the terms of the agreement, August, and they look almost too good to be true. There are no strings attached. All the Winslow Foundation asks of the college is that it move. It can, according to the agreement, even keep the name of Brandon."

"And what's in a name? Brandon College certainly represents more than just a name, and if it moves, no matter what they call it, it won't be Brandon College. It will be a new college with no history, no tradition, no memories. Only a few ghosts from the past trailing around to haunt the minds of those who will remember it as it was."

"There'll be a new campus, all right," the dean said. "New buildings with every modern facility and convenience. You've got to admit, August, that some of the buildings here— Philosophy, for instance—are inadequate, to say the least. And the alumni building has been a firetrap for years. In addition to the new campus, which will take care of almost twice as many students, there'll be an increase in faculty as well as a general raise for the faculty."

"You're talking only in terms of money," August said. "Is that the only consideration?"

"Not the only one, no. But the main one." The dean

seemed to be losing patience. "We can't be completely impractical, August."

"I'm sorry," August said. "I can't seem to get my thoughts together. I know what I think of this business, but I find it hard to express myself. If Brandon needs money so badly, there should be some way to raise it other than selling out to a textile mill."

"We can raise money, yes. Maybe a million or two in an extended all-out drive. But that's a far cry from twenty million. And, August, we need more than a million or two."

August was silent again.

"If the offer is accepted," the dean said, "we have five years in which to build the campus in Winslow—on a beautiful site which the Winslow Foundation is *giving* to us—and make the move."

Five years to do away with what had taken one hundred and twenty-three years to build. "I suppose I'm just a sentimental old fool," August said. "But I would rather see Brandon remain a small college with its academic excellence and its sound traditions. I know you think I'm unprogressive and speaking only from the point of view of a maudlin old grad. But I want my college to stay *here.* If it moves, I think in the long run it will lose more than it gains."

The dean looked at him for a long time. "I couldn't agree with you more, August. I was appalled when I first found out about the offer, and I can think of hundreds of reasons why it should not be accepted. But I can't admit this to anyone but you. I have no vote at the convention, and to call the offer ridiculous would make me seem to be—as you said—unprogressive. As a member of the faculty, all I can do is keep my mouth shut and listen. I've tried to convince myself the offer is a good thing. I know all the arguments in its favor—you've just gotten them—but I'm against it. I've heard it discussed among the trustees and those I've heard have, to a man, been in favor of accepting the offer. And they *will* have votes at the convention, as well as a great deal of influence."

"Blinded by the dazzle of money," August said. "Brandon is a great college and can become even greater right here."

"August, the convention will have an open meeting where all arguments, pro and con, can be heard. As I said, I'm in no position to say anything. But as a former Baptist preacher and a department head emeritus, *you* might carry a great deal of weight with the convention. Would you consider being one of the speakers against the move?"

August thought for a moment, then shook his head. "If it were physically possible for me to do so, I would. But I can't stand up for more than a few minutes at a time, and then I'm exhausted. Anyway, I'm eighty-three years old and not likely to sway anyone's vote. I would be looked upon, as I just told you, as a sentimental, impractical old fool."

"I don't think so, but—"

"I will write a letter, giving my views on the matter, and you can take it with you. If the opportunity presents itself, read it to the convention." He looked across the room, his eyes misting. "That is about all I can do for my college now."

The dean stood up. "I don't think there's really much any of us can do, August. I'm convinced the offer will be accepted. But I hope at least there'll be some good fighters for our side."

August rose stiffly and walked the few steps to the door with his guest. "One more thing: What's to become of the old campus if the college moves?"

"The plan, as I understand it, is to put it up for sale, and use the money to help with the construction of the new campus. At any rate, this"—he gestured toward the south—"is still ours for five more years. And, August, we can always hope there will be enough preachers at the convention who will see things as we do and—"

"I'm afraid to hope," August said. "The whole thing seems to have gone too far already to allow much room for hope."

After the dean left, August, holding to the sides of his desk, leaned over as far as he could and looked out the window. At the end of Faculty Avenue he could see the spire rising above the newly green trees. He looked at it for a long time, and then, exhausted and aching from the effort of bending over, he put his head down on the desk and wept.

The following morning the Winslow Foundation offer to Brandon College was on the front page of the newspaper, and when Gena read the story, which included comments from some of the trustees, she was as positive as August that the college would go. This, she thought, must be the way you feel when someone you love dies suddenly with no forewarning symptoms of illness to prepare you for the shock.

She left the house, not wanting to see the bereavement in August's eyes, nor answer the telephone which she knew would be ringing shortly as her friends called to discuss the news with her. It was not to be talked about. She walked to the end of the avenue and turned down Stadium Road, wandered past the stadium and all the way into the woods before a new thought struck her with even greater impact than the original news. If the college moved, all the professors would go with it. *Ian would go.* She stopped short, her mind screaming, *No!*

She sank down on the cool, damp moss beneath an oak tree, then tugged at the moss, pulling up a small handful, turning the soft green over, and scrutinizing the dark brown soil beneath it. Life was like that if you examined it too closely, she thought. Under a soft, colorful exterior were dirt and ugliness. It was better to accept everything at face value without probing beneath the surface. Her love for Ian had remained beautiful, idealized, because they both knew and accepted and did not look for the ugliness that might be found in a cruel moment of investigable weakness. For whatever else they had been, they had not been weak. Every declaration of love they had made to each other during the past few years had been accomplished only by the words they had left unspoken. It was as if they had agreed that what they felt when they were together was too strong—and too hopeless—to be expressed in words.

"Good morning, Mrs. Grierson. How is Professor Fielding today?"

"Fine, thank you. You must come to see him. It's been a long time."

"Yes it has. Very long . . ."

She had never imagined that love could be like this. Without a word, without a touch, he made love to her, and she responded with all her being.

"And how is Jennifer?"

"Growing like a weed. Now that she's in school . . ."

"It's hard to believe she's started school already. It seems such a short time ago that . . ."

"That you were riding her around the living room on your back and saying you wished she were yours."

"I wish that more now than I did then . . ."

She did not know when it was that she first became aware

that he returned her love. There had been no sudden revelation; no one time when she looked at him and knew. In her fantasies he loved her, and gradually she came to know that his love extended beyond the fantasies.

At a faculty tea she had met his wife, an attractive girl who tried too hard to say the right things to the older faculty wives. She had felt sorry for Betty Caldwell and had gone out of her way to talk to her. But later, in her mind, the girl who was Ian's wife had no real connection with him, just as her life with Charles was entirely separate from the imaginary hours she shared with Ian.

The twinges of conscience that bothered her when the fantasies had first begun were now laid to rest. She had found she could be a good wife to Charles, a good mother to his child, and still love Ian with all her heart. She could think of Charles and Ian simultaneously and still keep them apart and beautifully clear in separate compartments in her mind.

It was not possible, though, to think of Ian, of his strong hands, the love in his eyes, and think about August simultaneously. Where her conscience failed, a mental picture of August sometimes succeeded in destroying some of the perfection of her fantasies. I am a good wife, she told herself over and over. I have never been unfaithful to Charles. And August's voice, from an echo chamber in her mind, said, "As a man thinketh in his heart, so is he."

Her hand shook as she pulled at the moss. If Ian went away, part of her life would be gone, and it was the best part. Since there was no help for their situation, they had been content with what they had, but now even that little contentment was to be taken from them. She had never asked for more than was possible. She would no more have thought of deserting Charles and Jennifer than she would of asking Ian to leave Betty. That would have been sinful, trying to make two wrongs add up to one right. There was no sin that could be marked against them. Only that voice coming unbidden at the end of her fantasies, "As a man thinketh in his heart. . . ." And the words spoken were, by constant repetition, losing emphasis.

She looked up, surprised and yet not surprised to see him standing beside her, looking down at her with eyes full of quiet misery. She had willed him to be there, conjured him up as she did in her fantasies.

"From my office window I saw you walking down Stadium Road. I followed you."

His voice sounded different. It was deeper, gentler, and had a tone of sadness like the chapel bells ringing a knell. She could only stare back at him, knowing now that it would be necessary for them to speak.

"You've heard the news, of course?"

She nodded mutely and he sat down beside her.

"There's no chance," he said, "that the offer will not be accepted. The college will go."

"And you'll go with it."

"I have to," he said. "There's nothing else. Gena—oh, God, Gena!"

"My love." The words were wrung from her as they turned at the same moment and found each other's arms. "Ian, oh, Ian, Ian."

There was no warmth in the embrace at first, only hunger and cold deprivation as they kissed frantically, trying in desperation to end the long fast with a feast. Wordless again, they struggled together on the moss like animals of the woods, clawing, holding, possessing, and finally relinquishing, each retreating into self again.

It was over. She lay upon the moss strangely at peace, thinking nothing. Except that it was over.

He sat up and looked down at her. His eyes said nothing. The words in them now, if they were there at all, were unreadable. He stood and helped her to her feet. "It's getting dark. The day is almost over and we—"

"No," she said quickly. Whatever it was he was about to say, she did not want to hear it. "It's still light. We'll be home before dark."

Slowly they walked out of the woods together, not speaking, not touching, passing the deserted stadium, turning from Stadium Road to Faculty Avenue, stopping at the corner by the campus. She was the first to turn away.

"Good night, Ian."

"Afternoon," he said. "It isn't night yet."

"Almost, though." *The night always seems to come too soon.*

He went toward Elm Street and she continued down Faculty Avenue, still at peace, still thinking nothing. Except that she had known love. Known it well, known it completely.

After dinner she and August and Charles sat in the living room. Her mind was still curiously blank; the voices of her husband and father reached her as though they came from a great distance. They were discussing the Winslow offer and the effect it would have on the college and on the town. She did not enter into the discussion, and although she heard what they were saying, the words did not register in her consciousness.

"The convention will never let it happen," Charles said. "Every Baptist in the state will be up in arms at the thought of moving Brandon."

"You're forgetting that a large number of Baptists live in and near Winslow and they'll be only too happy at the prospect of having the college there," August said. "No, Charles, I'm afraid there's no cause for optimism."

Charles was silent for a while, then he said, "What do you suppose will become of the old campus—"

"You see," August interrupted, "you're already thinking of it in terms of old campus and new campus."

"It isn't every day that a college, a ready-made college, goes on the auction block," Charles continued. "What on earth could it be used for—except another college?"

Gena blinked. This time the words had reached her. "You think another college could be started here?"

"I don't know," Charles said. "I just can't think of any other use that might be made of classroom buildings and dormitories."

"When will we know?" she asked.

"The convention meets next month," August said. "We'll know then what will be done about the offer. As for selling the college, it may be some time before a buyer is found."

"And," Charles said, "it will be five years before Brandon is moved to Winslow."

Five years! She sat bolt upright. She couldn't possibly have heard him right. "Did you say five years?"

"It will take that long to build some semblance of a campus in Winslow," August said. "So we have five years of grace. I think it unlikely at my age that I'll be here to witness

the move, and thinking that is the only reason I am able to
think about it at all."

They went on with their discussion, neither noticing that
Gena was crying. Large tears ran down her face and her
blouse, leaving dark circles on the blue silk. Five years! She
had thought—or rather, she had *not* thought, but the thought
had been in the back of her mind—that if the convention
accepted the offer the college would be moved immediately.
Five years! It made a farce of what had happened this afternoon. There had been no reason for urgency, no reason for
a frantic farewell, no reason to cling to him as if they were
about to be separated forever.

Had Ian known this? If he had, then the afternoon had
been doubly a farce. A bad joke, and the joke was on her,
for of course he must have known.

Oh, my God, what have I done? Charles, oh, Charles. If I
had known it could have been different. Ian and I could have
gone on as we were for five more years. There was no reason
to hurt you.

But, she asked herself, had she really hurt Charles? He did
not know, so how could he possibly be hurt?

As a man thinketh in his heart. . . . It was no longer in
her heart, it had happened in actuality. It was herself she had
hurt. Five years. And if they had gone on as they were,
would it have happened during those five years? Probably not,
for she would have had the time to get used to the idea of
separation from him. The panic she had felt today would have
given way to resignation.

Now there was nothing left of the afternoon but a memory
of burning shame. Thou shalt not commit adultery; it was
as basic as that. That is what August would have thought,
but thank God, August would never know. Even the echo
of his voice would be stilled inside her now, for since he
could not comprehend a sin so great, there would be no words
he could say about it. Ever since her childhood, when he had
read stories from the Bible to her, she had imagined that God
must look exactly like August, must *be* exactly like August,
tall and straight and kind and always right in the things he
did and said. And when, as a child, she had been reprimanded by August, it was the same as having God say, "You
have done wrong; you must not do that again."

Five years. What had seemed beautiful and compelling and

inevitable at the time had, in the space of a few hours, become shameful—a sin against Charles and August and God.

"Gena, you're crying!" Charles said suddenly, leaving his chair and going to her. "Don't let it upset you. The convention may not accept the offer. We may not lose Brandon after all."

She could not look at him or August. "I think I'll go to bed now. I have a headache."

"I'll come, too," Charles said, and followed her out of the room. "It's been a long day and I'm tired. Good night, sir," he called to August.

In their bedroom she fought to keep back the tears, at least until the light was out and Charles could not see her. She undressed quickly and got into bed, waiting for him to turn out the light. When he did, she knew that she could not cry while he was lying beside her.

"Oh, Charles." She shifted her weight to be close to his warm body, suddenly more frightened than she had ever been in her life. "Hold me," she said. "Please. Just hold me." She wanted to lie quietly in the comfort of his arms and feel that everything would be all right again. But she knew, when he mistook her trembling fear for passion, that nothing would ever be all right again.

The convention met the second week in May. It took four days to dispense with the business at hand: the Winslow Foundation offer to Brandon College. Memorial Auditorium in Raleigh was packed and overflowing with messengers (those who had been delegated to attend from the Baptist congregations throughout the state), trustees, college officials, interested Brandon townspeople, and as many Brandon students as could get up enough nerve to cut classes and go.

August sat by his radio during the afternoons, waiting for news of the meeting on local newscasts, and he read avidly a full account of each day's activities in the morning newspaper. On the fourth day he heard on the radio that it was all over but the voting, which would take place that night. When he went to bed there was no further report on which way the voting had gone. It would take a two-thirds majority to carry the vote either way.

At midnight he was suddenly awakened by the ringing of a bell, and he sat up in confusion. Then he realized that some-

one was tolling the chapel bell. Through the night the slow
bonging reverberated through the quiet town. He lay back
again with a sigh, knowing only too well the reason for the
knell: A college had just died.

25

EVEN AFTER SHE WAS CERTAIN, even when there was no longer
any possibility of doubt, Gena would not go to the doctor.

It never occurred to her that it might be Charles's baby.
Her mind was beclouded by many thoughts, many doubts,
but she never doubted that it was Ian's. Each morning she
awoke with a heaviness in mind and body that was unlike
anything she had ever experienced before, and each night she
went to bed wanting to scream, to cry out against Ian, against
her guilt, and even against Charles, whom she could not bear
to look at now. But she dared not; at all costs, she must be
herself.

The warm days of June turned into the hot days of July,
and finally she went to the doctor and he congratulated her,
told her how happy he was that she was going to have
another child, how happy Charles would be when he learned.

She had not seen Ian since that afternoon, and she did not
want to see him, for he had only to take one look at her face
and he would know. She could not imagine why Charles
could not do the same, but she decided that Charles saw so
much of her that he no longer noticed the changes in her,
mentally or physically.

There was only one consolation through those long days
when she agonized over how to tell Charles that she was
pregnant: her fantasies ceased. Although she knew she still
loved Ian, she no longer dreamed of him. She did not spend
long afternoons weaving stories in her mind of how it would
be if they were alone together with time and the world stretching endlessly before them, and without the existence of
Charles and Betty. But in place of the fantasies came the

guilt. Every time Charles looked at her, every word he uttered, turned her thoughts into scathing invectives against herself. He had loved her all his life, trusted her because between them they knew no other course to follow—and she was going to have another man's child. The voice of her conscience—August's voice—would not be stilled. *You have sinned against God and man, and the wages of sin is death.*

She could not tell Charles nor August.

One afternoon she went to the tower, not knowing exactly what she wanted of August, knowing only that she wanted him to talk, to keep talking, and perhaps out of some of the words she could pick a few that might be comforting.

"Daddy," she said, "I heard you've been asked to speak to the students at chapel next week. Are you going to?"

"At first I didn't think so," he said, "but Dean Wayland said I could sit down to talk."

"What are you going to talk about?"

"I haven't decided yet. I suppose they'll want something that will tie in with the move, something encouraging, but I can't think of anything to say. I think," he added, "I may talk about love."

"Love!" she exclaimed. "I didn't think college students needed any encouragement along that line."

"I don't mean one specific kind of love," he said. "When I was a student I preached my first sermon—the trial sermon in Fairmont—on love. I don't know why, but lately that sermon has been on my mind. I think it is still relevant and I may use parts of it for my talk. In the sermon I pointed out—"

She interrupted. "I should think sin would be more appropriate now. I don't think people are as good as they used to be. At least, the world seems more geared to sin now."

August laughed. "Gena, you're behind the times. Don't you know there's no such thing as sin anymore?"

"What do you mean?"

"Any good psychologist can tell you," August said, "people don't sin anymore—it's old-fashioned. If a sixteen-year-old boy murders his parents, that isn't a sin; he's had some traumatic experience in his early childhood which led him to the act. Murder, theft, fornication—they aren't sins. They're the natural result of feeling unloved, deprived, rejected. No one seems to believe in sin anymore."

"Do you?"

"Yes," he said. "I'm old-fashioned. To me a sin is still a sin, no matter what fancy name it goes by, no matter what lies behind it. Anyone who isn't completely insane knows right from wrong."

She was quiet for a moment, then she asked, "What did you say about love?"

He smiled. "I think my premise was that there isn't enough of it in the world."

She got up slowly. "Is that what you're going to tell the students?"

"I think so. At least, I'm going to rework the sermon and see what I get. It's possible that I may be able to tie it in with the convention's decision after all."

She left him and went downstairs to wait for Charles. She could not put it off any longer. Tonight he would have to be told.

"Jennifer is going to have a new playmate, Charles. A brother or sister."

For a minute his face held only disbelief. Then he picked her up and swung her around in the air, and just as quickly, put her down again. "You're sure? You *are* sure, aren't you? When? Oh, Gena, that's the best news in the world!"

"In January."

"January!" Why didn't you tell me before?"

"I wasn't sure myself. I guess I hadn't noticed the calendar."

"Let's tell August. Right away."

She knew she was going to cry any minute. "Later," she said. "Right now I have to help Annabel with dinner." And she ran toward the kitchen.

After she left the tower, August stared for a long time at the door, then he turned to the desk. Why, suddenly, had Gena asked so many questions about sin? What was bothering her? That Gena could really commit a sin was, of course, inconceivable. But in her mind she was worried about something that she had misconstrued as a sin. If only she would talk to him openly so that he could set her fears at rest. But she would not, and he could not pry.

He opened the top drawer of his desk and took out Eugene's manuscript. When he laid it on the desk it fell open at the *Meno*. He remembered immediately that day in class—how many years ago? Sixty some—when Eugene had called upon him to read the part of Socrates. ("Can you tell me, Socrates—can virtue be taught? Or if not, does it come by practice? Or does it come neither by practice nor by teaching, but do people get it by nature, or in some other way?") He laid the manuscript aside remembering too well his anguish that day as he read Socrates' lines, struggling to understand the meaning of virtue and knowing that virtue was a thing he did not possess. There had been nothing in him then but guilt.

And Gena had, not only this afternoon but also on several occasions in the past, acted just the way he had that day in class. Was it possible that guilt could be passed on to one's children? Like some diseases or a keen mind or a dull one or the color of one's hair or complexion?

"*. . . for I the Lord thy God am a jealous God, and visit the sins of the fathers upon the children unto the third and fourth generation. . . .*"

Quickly he put the manuscript away and closed the drawer. He straightened his tie, put on his coat, and went downstairs to the living room where Charles was waiting with a broad smile upon his face.

Day after day after endless day. July wore into August. Long and listless days in which she endured the good spirits of her husband and her father. Their joy was almost more than she could bear. Even Jennifer was the epitome of impatience. "When, Mama? When are we going to get the new baby?"

Now she knew why the fantasies had stopped. Her mind was so taken up with new thoughts, new feelings, that there was no longer any inclination to think of Ian as she had before. Also, the dream had become reality, and reality scared her. If the reality could have included bitterness toward Ian which could grow into a consuming, purifying hatred, then she felt her mind would be free of all but that, almost washed clean by the hatred. Instead, she loved him still, not in the quiet way she had always loved Charles, but with a feeling of frantic hopelessness.

And then she saw him again. It was a hot afternoon late in August when she took the shortcut through the deserted campus to South Main Street. She was looking down at the stepping stones and did not see him until he was less than three feet from her. Surely they would not go back to their early insane conversations—"Good afternoon, Dr. Caldwell, isn't this weather terrible?"—although she wanted to desperately.

"Good afternoon," she said softly.

"Gena . . ." He broke off and stared at her, his eyes going over her figure, then meeting her eyes. "You're going to have a baby."

Of course he would notice and of course his first thought would be that the baby was his. "Yes, I'm pregnant," she said, deliberately using the harsh-sounding word. "And it's Charles's baby, there's no question about that!"

"Of course," he said. "Of course."

He knew. She could tell by the way he said it that he was as sure as she that the baby was his.

"Gena," he said, "I've wanted to see you . . ."

She did not listen. She turned and almost ran away from him, half stumbling on the stones in her haste. She must never see him again, must never meet him again, not even accidentally as she had today. She almost called out good-bye to him, but didn't. And later even that small involuntary act held meaning for her. Between them there would never be a parting that was final, and therefore her mind would never again be at peace.

It was late that night as she lay wide-eyed beside her sleeping husband that she knew what her punishment was to be. She would lose the baby—or even worse, the child would be born mentally or physically defective to serve as a reminder every day of her life of the thing she had done.

And into her consciousness again came August's voice, muffled, as though from a great distance, as though she were seated far back in a congregation listening to him read from the pulpit.

Lord, have mercy upon us, and keep all these thy laws in our hearts.

. . . for the Lord will not hold him guiltless. . . .

There are they fallen, all that work wickedness; they are cast down, and shall not be able to stand.

26

CHARLES HAD NOTICED FROM THE first that Gena's reaction to her pregnancy was not the same as his. It was even different from her reaction the first time when they had gone together to tell August. This time she had left it to him to tell August, and although that had not seemed strange at the time, now he wondered about it. As far as he could tell she was not sick, the pregnancy was going well (he had asked the doctor about that), and there was no reason for Gena to worry. So there could be only one reason for her melancholy moods: She did not want another child. But when he asked her about this she looked at him with a stricken expression and said, "Charles, you're imagining things. Of course I want the baby. I want it to be a perfect baby."

That reminded him of the night they were married. "He'll be perfect," Charles said. "After all, he already has a perfect mother and sister." She looked at him again and he expected her to retort, "How do you know he'll be a he?" But she said nothing, just bit her lower lip and looked away.

"Gena, what's wrong?" he asked. "Why aren't you happy about the baby?"

"Nothing's wrong," she said quickly. "My goodness, Charles, can't I be happy without having to babble like an idiot to show it?"

And so he decided to say no more to her about it, assuming that this was the way pregnancy affected her and that as soon as the baby came she would be all right again. But it was strange, he thought, that before Jennifer was born he had expected her arrival to change their lives, which it had not. But this time there had to be a change; Gena could not continue as she was.

He talked to August about it, and August admitted that he, too, had been worried about what he called Gena's decline.

273

"She never smiles anymore," he said. "She seems lost in another world most of the time—and not a very nice world at that."

"Will she talk to you at all about it?" Charles asked.

August sighed. "Gena and I haven't had a really good talk for months. When she comes to the tower now, purportedly to talk, she asks me about sermons I have preached. It's odd, she wants me to go back and try to remember sermons in their entirety—and it's all I can do to remember the texts I used—and all but preach them to her. I don't understand this sudden interest."

Charles did not understand it either. All he understood was that Gena *must* become once more the way she was before, free from those black moods which apparently tore her apart during the day, even when there was no visible outward sign, and which at night left him lying tensely beside her waiting, listening for the almost inaudible sound of her crying.

August waited in the living room for word from the hospital. Charles had promised he would call as soon as there was anything to report. August stared up at the portrait of Ann. He never thought of the girl in the painting as being young Angela anymore. To him it was Ann, and sometimes, without thinking, he called her Jennifer. There were times even now when he wanted to talk to Ann (he suspected that sometimes he *did* talk to Ann unconsciously), but now, more than ever before, he wished she were beside him. He had not felt this way when Jennifer was born, probably, he thought, because Gena's mental attitude had been so different. Now he knew he needed her.

He heard the front door open and close and footsteps in the hall, and then Charles stood at the door, looking happier than August had ever seen him look. "It's a boy, and he and Gena are fine."

August stood up slowly, holding to the chair. "A boy?"

"Almost seven pounds' worth," Charles said. "They wouldn't let me see Gena or the baby yet, so I came to take you back with me."

They did not talk on the way to the hospital. When they reached the main waiting room August hesitated, flooded by the memory of the night Ann had left the world, and

Gena had entered it. As his eyes scanned the room, he saw Ian Caldwell sitting in a corner.

"Professor, I've just heard the good news. Congratulations. And to you, Mr. Grierson. If your son turns out to be anything like Jennifer in personality, you're a lucky man indeed."

"Thank you," Charles said.

"Ian, what are you doing here?" August asked. "I hope no one is ill. Your wife?"

"She's in the emergency room," Ian said. "Nothing serious. Cut her finger while peeling potatoes. I think the cut will require a few stitches. Oh, by the way, Professor, I suppose you've heard the news?"

"What news?"

"The campus site was sold today—to the state."

"The state?" August was perplexed. "Is the state going to operate a school here?"

"No. I'm sorry, but I assumed you knew. The state is going to use the campus for a mental institution."

August stared at the younger man as though he had been struck. "A mental institution? You mean an insane asylum where Brandon College is?"

"Apparently," Ian said. "I guess there isn't enough room in the one at Raleigh and Brandon seemed to be—"

"Oh, Lord, no!" August closed his eyes.

"Well, I suppose there are only so many things a college campus can be used for," Ian said, "and they seem to think Brandon—"

"Is this final?" Charles interrupted. "Or just a rumor?"

"True, I'm afraid," Ian said. And as Betty appeared at the end of the corridor, "Here comes my wife now. Congratulations again. To both of you."

As August and Charles waited for the nurse outside Gena's door, August thought, Why is good news always tempered with bad? A mental institution! The thought of it hurt almost as much as had the news that the college was moving to Winslow.

The nurse appeared. "You may go in to see Mrs. Grierson now," she said. "No, Mr. Grierson," as Charles started to follow August. "She asked to see her father first. I'm sure she'll want to see you later."

Stunned, Charles stepped aside, and August went into the

room. Gena looked so pale without makeup, and so tired.
Her eyes were closed.

"Gena," he said softly, and she opened her eyes.

"Daddy, have you seen him?"

"No," he said. "But the doctor said he was a fine baby.
Gena, Charles is just outside, waiting to see you. Shall I call
him?"

"Are you sure he's all right—normal, I mean?"

"He's fine," August reassured her. "A normal, healthy
baby."

"But are you sure? Please, Daddy, go look at him and then
come back and tell me. Ask them to bring my baby to me
now—while you're here."

He leaned over and kissed her. "Of course I'm sure, Gena.
Charles Junior is a beautiful baby."

She sighed and her head fell back to the pillow. "Not
Charles Junior," she said. "I want to name him David."

He plainly showed his surprise. "Why David? There's no
one in your family or Charles's, so far as I know, named
David."

"That's why," she said. "I don't want a name from either
family."

"Shall I get Charles now? He's waiting to see you."

"No, not now." She turned her face away from him. "I'll
see him later." Then she looked at him again. "Daddy, are
you sure there's nothing wrong with the baby?"

"He's perfect," August said.

A smile lighted her face and her lips moved, but he could
not understand what she said. "I'm going now," he said,
"but I'll be back this evening and so will Charles."

As soon as he was outside, Charles grasped him by the
arm. "What is it? Why didn't she want to see me? What's
wrong with her?"

August took a deep breath. "She's all right, Charles. I think
she has been worried about the baby all along. I don't know
why. But now that she knows he's a normal, healthy baby,
she's all right. Now let's go see if we can have a look at your
son."

When the nurse brought the baby to her, she held out her
arms, but closed her eyes. I can't look at him, she thought.
I'm afraid to look. But when she opened her eyes and saw
the fierce little face, the tiny clenched fists, she knew that

August had been right. There was nothing wrong with him. She was to be punished in another way.

She ran her hand gently over the top of his head, which was covered with silky wisps of red fringe—almost the dark auburn shade of Ian's. Every time she looked at him for the rest of her life, she would see Ian. And so would everyone else.

Charles, kind and thoughtful and unknowing, who had never deserved to suffer for what she had done, would know. He would have to go through life with the humiliating knowledge that the child who bore his name, whom he called son, was the son of another man.

She gave the baby back to the nurse without saying a word. As soon as she was alone, she put her pillow over her face and screamed into it silently over and over. No, no, no, no.

Oh, Charles, if only he were your son. I'd give my life if he were your son.

When Charles came that evening, his first remark was, "He's going to look exactly like his grandfather, and I only hope he'll turn out to be like his grandfather."

Later, when George and Estelle came in, George said, "Well, he certainly takes after the Fielding side of the house and not the Grierson side."

After they had gone she rang for the nurse and asked for a sleeping pill. She could not stand consciousness any longer.

27

AUGUST WAS BECOMING ACCUSTOMED to the quiet house, although there was still something unnatural about the long morning silence. At first, when David started school nearly two months ago, August found himself listening constantly for the little boy at play, for the sound of his footsteps on the stairs to the tower. A dozen times during the morning he would lay aside whatever book he was reading and cock his head in an attitude of listening. But now he was growing used to the silence while the child was in school—a silence broken only occasionally by the sound of a vacuum cleaner on the first floor, or the distant voices of Gena and Annabel. At night, of course, when all the family was home, there was enough noise to keep anybody company. He went to the window and looked out to the street. Autumn in Brandon, the burst of color on Faculty Avenue, still amazed him, though it had been two years since autumn in Brandon had had any real meaning for him. Brandon College was gone now. After the 1961 commencement, the move had begun. He had not wanted to know about it; he had hoped that overnight the army of movers would come and quietly take away everything while he slept, unknowing. But it had been a long process. The big trucks came, and day after day Gena and Charles reported on their progress while he listened and asked questions with painful and morbid curiosity.

The classroom and dormitory furniture was the first to be loaded, then the small things, which to August comprised the soul of the college, were brought out from the buildings. "They took the pipe organ from the chapel today," Gena said. "Everything else has been moved."

The library was the last to be stripped, and August, scarcely knowing why, asked Gena to drive him to the campus. There, parked just outside the stone wall, he watched while carton after carton of books was taken from the building and loaded onto the trucks. And I once wondered, he thought, if I would ever be able to read all those books. When the last carton was loaded, he turned to Gena. "Let's go home now. I want to go home."

But after the move, home was not the same either. His steady procession of callers ceased—the professors and students had gone to Winslow. Of his old friends from the college, only Dean Wayland was left in Brandon, and now when the dean came to see him, August felt as though they were holding a wake. Some of his friends among the townspeople came occasionally, but nothing had been the same since the college left.

He had seen pictures of the new campus, the buildings, the students in their quarters, everything that made up the new Brandon, but he had no desire to go to the site and see for himself what the college had become.

Almost before the last truck had left the old campus for

Winslow, workers had begun their job of dismantling, renovating, rebuilding, changing, and making over the campus to fit the needs of the new state hospital. And a year ago that job, also, had been completed. Now dormitories whose corridors had rung with the sound of boisterous students had become quiet hospital rooms and wards; and classroom buildings (he thought of the Philosophy Building, which had been the center of his life for more than forty years) housed doctor's offices and therapy rooms. To the three-foot-high stone wall, more stones had been added, and now it was six feet high, massive and forbidding. Since the day it was finished, he had never wanted to go beyond that wall.

Only two things remained unchanged: the arch and the spire. The graystone arch still marked the east side of the grounds, but the Brandon College plaque had been removed, leaving the place where it had been on the stone white and naked. *Pro Humanitate,* he thought, and he no longer tried to analyze his thoughts. The bitterness and the blame were gone. He had learned to live with the knowledge that Brandon was gone, just as he had learned years before that there is a time for everything but mourning.

But the years since the college had gone had been neither empty nor unhappy ones for him. Where his interests had been divided and scattered, they now centered solely on his family. It was impossible to nurse loneliness or regret in a house where there were children.

In two days he would be ninety years old. He had a feeling that Gena was planning something for his birthday. There had been too many whispered conversations which stopped abruptly when he appeared, too many times recently when Jen had clapped her hand over David's mouth. He had pretended not to notice anything, and whatever family celebration appeared he would act as surprised as they wanted him to be.

He closed the book that he had been holding in his lap and put aside the magnifying glass that he used for reading. Downstairs Gena and Annabel were probably even now discussing what kind of cake to bake for him.

Gena. Of all his blessings, she was the greatest. And yet he would never think about her without worrying. There was nothing wrong he could call by name, and if he asked her, she would deny, almost vehemently, that she had her mind on anything more serious than planning the next meal. But there was an "awayness' about her—some indefinable, indescribable state of mind which she could not, or did not, share with anyone.

At times he could hardly recall the self-confident, high-spirited girl who had always wanted everything to be "just perfect," and he had been mistaken in thinking that David's birth would precipitate a return of this girl. Gena, of course, was not a girl now and he could not expect her to remain childlike—indeed, did not want her to. But the difference in her personality during the past six years could not be entirely explained either by her motherhood and maturity or by her devotion to Charles.

After David's birth, she became quiet and thoughtful and more devoted to her husband than ever before. That was as it should be, August thought. Not that she hadn't loved Charles before, but she showed that love more now in little ways. August watched and noted that when they sat in the living room her eyes seldom left Charles's face.

"Are you busy?" Gena came into the room.

"Hardly. Unless you can call trying to read and not succeeding the height of industry."

"Then would you mind trying downstairs? I want to clean in here."

He laughed. "I'll get out of your way. But this isn't cleaning day, is it?"

"Since I'm cleaning, I guess you could call it cleaning day," she said. "No, I have something else to do tomorrow so I thought I'd get to your room today. Do you mind vacating for a little while?"

"Of course not. I'll wait downstairs for the children. Isn't it time for school to be out?" He held to the banister as he went downstairs, more convinced than ever that Gena had plans for his birthday.

Looking around the room after he left she almost groaned. It was the hardest place in the house to clean, not because it was dirty, but because the room was constantly cluttered with books, papers, letters—all of the paraphernalia among which August spent his days and nights. And to move one book, one paper, would bring about a cry from him, "Gena, what did you do with . . . ?"

The desk, of course, was hopeless. How he ever found

anything on it was beyond her. Only the top corner had any semblance of order and that was where, under scotch tape, he kept faded snapshots of Jen and David. She dusted carefully around one taken when David was a baby.

Since it was not in color, his red hair appeared sandcolored: this was her favorite picture of him because in it he looked less like Ian. And she uttered the prayer that was constantly in her mind: Please God, don't let Charles ever find out.

Yet even as she breathed the prayer, she knew that the day would come—maybe soon, maybe not for several years—when Charles would look at David and suddenly *see* him and know that he was Ian's son. And then he would share in her punishment. The thought left her with a sickness so real that the pain almost caused her to double up in agony.

When he thought she had had more than enough time to finish the cleaning, August went back to the tower. He was astounded to find Gena sitting on the side of his bed, clenching and unclenching her hands and staring at the window as though she expected the sycamore outside to disappear suddenly.

"Gena."

She did not turn, she did not even blink when he called her name. He stood in front of her and took both her hands in his. Only then did she raise her eyes slowly to his face—and, almost immediately, look away.

"Tell me." He said it roughly, not asking now but demanding to know.

She shook her head.

"Tell me," he said again in the same tone.

Now she looked him straight in the eye and said, "I can't tell anyone—ever." Then she burst into tears, and through the choking sobs he understood her to say, "What I've done is so monstrous that . . ."

He sat down beside her and stroked her hair, wanting to say, "There, there," as he had when she was a child. What could she possibly have done that she saw as "monstrous?"

"No one would ever forgive me," she was saying. "Any more than I can ever forgive myself."

"There is nothing that can't be forgiven, Gena. But nothing *can* be if you keep it all locked up inside you."

She sat up very straight and stared at him for a minute. Then in a toneless whisper she said, "David is not Charles's son."

It was a minute before the full impact of her words registered and even then his first thought was: No, I misunderstood. His overwhelming concern was to keep his face from showing any emotion whatever, not shock, nor disbelief, nor even surprise.

"I wasn't unfaithful to Charles but once," she said, still in a monotone, "except in my mind. I used to imagine . . ." There was a long pause. "But when it happened—it was an afternoon in spring—I thought that . . . the person . . . would be going away soon, out of my life forever, and I couldn't bear the thought. Later, I found out it would be a long time before he would go away."

August drew in his breath. "Ian?" he asked, knowing the answer.

She nodded slowly, and then she was crying again, heartbreakingly. This time, as he stroked her hair, he did murmur, "There, there."

Finally, when all the tears were spent and she leaned against him, exhausted, she said, "You see? Not even God can forgive you when you hurt someone so terribly. Even if that someone doesn't know about it, it doesn't lessen the sin." Her whole body shuddered. "I'd give my life to change it—and I've even considered that, but it still wouldn't change what I've done to Charles."

And August thought: *The Lord is longsuffering and of great mercy, forgiving iniquity and transgression and by no means clearing the guilty, visiting the iniquity of the fathers upon the children unto the third and fourth generation.*

The sins of the fathers . . .

"You see?" she said again, more a question than a statement. "I decided I might as well go on living, even though nothing would be right in my life again. I suppose to go on living is my punishment."

"Gena, don't. Don't ever say or *think* such a thing again."

"How can you tell me what to say or think?" Her face was completely open now, open and angry. "You wouldn't know what sin was if it walked up and shook hands with you. All you know is what is good and right and—"

"Gena!"

The sharpness of his voice stopped her.

"I know," he said. "I *know*."

Somehow, he had to find the right words to say to her. Gena *must not go* through her life as he had, must not spend the rest of that life paying for one April afternoon.

"Listen to me," he said. "When I was a student at Brandon, I betrayed the man who was my greatest teacher, the man who guided me, befriended me, helped me in every way imaginable. I betrayed the man who became the closest friend I would ever have on earth," and he added softly, "with his wife."

"But . . ." She looked at his face, and was silent.

"You see, I do know. I know what it means to sin greatly."

"But you're so *good*," she said finally. "The best person I've ever known. Ian once said," she lowered her eyes when she mentioned his name, "that you were the closest thing to a saint he had ever known."

August smiled. "Then I find it gratifying that my terrible misdeed has not kept me from influencing others in some way."

The bewildered expression was leaving her face. He could almost see the tension going out of her as she relaxed a little.

"But what am I going to do?" she asked. "Every time I look at David, I'll see Ian. Every time Charles takes pride in his son . . ."

"Gena, are you absolutely *sure* that David is not Charles's son? Isn't there even a chance that he might be?"

"Yes, he *could* be. That very same night . . ." She caught herself and looked down, horribly embarrassed. "But I *feel* he's Ian's. And anyway, I just couldn't stand to live with not being sure."

"Well, now, that's something you'll *have* to live with," he said. "But you don't have to let it ruin your life, Gena."

She nodded, and he could not tell how much acceptance or understanding lay behind that nod. He did take comfort in the fact that her eyes were clearing of tears.

In all these years he had never told anyone. He had lived day in, day out with his sin and his guilt inside him. Now, in confessing out loud and thereby—he hoped, he believed— helping to take some of the hurt out of Gena, August felt for the first time that perhaps it had not all been in vain. He could even, without cringing, think about that long-ago April afternoon when he had first seen through a glass darkly.

28

SHORTLY BEFORE NOON ON THE day of August's birthday, there was a rap at the tower door, and then Ian Caldwell's auburn head appeared.

"Ian! What are you doing in Brandon? Come in."

"I came to wish you a happy birthday, sir," Ian said.

"Thank you. I don't get many visitors now, especially from Winslow."

"Everyone sends regards," Ian said, and he went into a detailed account of news of August's friends on the "new" Brandon campus. Then he said, "I have some news also. Betty and I are going to adopt a baby."

"But that's wonderful!" August said. "When?"

"The agency says it won't be long now. We decided almost a year ago, and it has taken all this time. I've thought for a long time that a baby would make a great deal of difference, but you know, it was Betty who suggested adopting one."

"We haven't talked for such a long time," August said. "Is everything going well with you now, Ian?"

"Yes, and I have to say that talking with you during those years really helped. I think," he said slowly, "if it hadn't been for you, we never would even have thought of adopting a baby. Who knows, we might not even be married."

There was nothing August could say to that, and anyway his imagination was busy with the information Ian had given him. Finally he said, "It's all right now, then? With you and Betty?"

"Yes. A little better than all right, I'd say. And it's going to be a boy, Professor. Would you mind if we named him August?"

August smiled. "That's the nicest birthday news you could have brought me."

Gena had told him that dinner would be a little later than usual and that she would call him when it was ready. So he waited in the tower to be summoned to his birthday meal, knowing what he would find when he went in the dining room: the smiling faces of Gena and Charles and the children, and a stack of presents by his plate.

It was after seven o'clock when Jennifer came to the tower. She had on a blue party dress and her blond hair was tied back with a blue ribbon. She was so much like Ann that for a minute it took his breath away.

She held his hand going down the two flights of stairs. The house was very quiet, but at any moment he expected to hear David break into an off-key rendition of "Happy Birthday."

Then he stood at the open door of the dining room, his eyes blurred. The room was full of people; he had never seen so many people, and suddenly he was conscious only of a great noise as the people began applauding.

"Happy birthday, August! Congratulations, Professor! Many happy returns." The cheers blended into one voice as he tried to focus his eyes on the group. Charles and Gena and David stood by the sideboard, all smiling broadly. And then he began to make out other faces in the room. George and Estelle Grierson, Dean Wayland, Flea—my Lord, he thought irrelevantly, how Flea has aged.

Gena came to him and took him by the arm and led him to the head of the table and he looked down the long table at other dear, almost forgotten faces. The heads of almost every department at Brandon were there. He choked as he thought of his friends coming from Winslow to celebrate his birthday.

"Are you surprised, Daddy?" Gena asked.

"Yes," he whispered, and he could say no more.

"Well, August, we're all half starved," Flea said, "so why in hell don't you ask the blessing and let us pitch in?"

August laughed and bowed his head. "O Lord, I thank thee—we thank thee . . ." His voice broke and he tried again. "For all thy blessings . . ." He could not go on and there was a moment of embarrassment while those at table sympathized with his emotion. Again, it was Flea who broke the tension.

"Lord, we thank you for this food," he said, "and for August, and Lord, for God's sake give him back his voice because there are a lot of us who have come a long way to talk to him."

During the meal it was hard to focus on any one person for more than a second, or to listen to any one conversation. Everyone talked and laughed at once. August ate, hardly aware of what he was eating, his eyes moving constantly from face to face. He had been hungrier for the sight of his friends than he knew, and here they were, back in Brandon. It was as though the college were still here. For a few minutes he could indulge in the thought that it had not moved, that these people were still very much a part of his everyday life.

After dinner Gena said, "Coffee in the living room," and it was to the living room that Annabel, with the able assistance of David, brought the huge cake. And then they all sang "Happy Birthday."

Afterward, he moved about the room from group to group. If only there were time, much time, to spend with each person.

"How is it going in Winslow, Flea?" he asked. "Have you built any churches there?"

Flea gave him a scathing look and August laughed. "I'm not telling tales out of school, Flea. Everybody knows the story. You couldn't keep a thing like that quiet."

"I guess not," the coach said. "And you were right about one thing, August. I hear they got quite a sizeable congregation over at St. Cat's now."

"St. Flea's, you mean," George Grierson said.

Suddenly Dean Wayland rapped on the coffee table for silence. "I want to say a few words," he said, standing up beside August, and then pushing him to the seat he had vacated on the sofa. "Tonight we have come here to celebrate the birthday of a man who has meant . . ."

August held up his hand. "Please, no speeches," he said. "No hearts and flowers, my friends. I was given a testimonial dinner when I retired and one such dinner is enough, indeed, more than I could expect in one lifetime. I don't deserve all of this attention, and certainly I don't rate any speeches. It's enough for me to know that you came—to have you here with me tonight."

"All right," the dean said, "I won't make a speech, but you

know how I like to listen to the sound of my voice, August, and you're depriving me of a long anticipated pleasure." He took a large book from the table and gave it to August.

"This will say all that I was going to, and more. A few months ago when it dawned on some of us that your ninetieth birthday was approaching, we wanted to do something to try to show you what you have meant to each of us, as well as to hundreds of others who've had the privilege of knowing you through the years. We tried to think of a gift we could present to you, but everything we thought of seemed inadequate as an expression of what we thought. Then Ian Caldwell had an idea for a memory book. 'Why don't we get in touch with as many of Professor Fielding's friends and former students as possible and let them write birthday letters to him?' he said. August, I knew you had friends, and I knew the place you held in the hearts of your former students, but even I was surprised at the response. You'll find that response in the book—letters to you from all of us here, and from more than three hundred others, your friends and former students now scattered all over the world, but all together in their personal tributes to you."

There was applause as August opened the thick book. On each page was pasted a letter, some handwritten, some typewritten. His eyes blurred again as he turned the pages rapidly, looking at the signatures. Then he closed the book. It would take days to read all the letters; tomorrow he would begin.

He tried to speak, but he could not. "Thank you," he finally whispered. He looked for Gena, wanting her to help him, wanting her to say the words he was too moved to say. She was standing at the window besides Charles, standing just a shade closer to him than was necessary.

After the party, David helped him back up the two flights of stairs. And as he looked at his grandson, he thought: I never noticed before. How could I have seen the child every day and not have noticed? David looks exactly like me, even to that funny-colored orange hair.

How could he have looked at that skinny string bean of a kid with orange-red hair every day for six years and not have seen the young, intense August staring back at him?

Too close to see, he thought. We're always too close to see.

"You know what I decided today, Grandfather?"

"No, David. What did you decide today?"

"I decided I'm going to be a preacher like you were."

August smiled. "That's fine. But between now and, say, next year, you may decide you'd rather be something else."

"Probably," said David. "But by the time I'm old enough to be *anything,* I'll have decided to be a preacher again." The young eyes looked at August imploringly, asking for something.

August gave it to him. "David," he said, "I think probably you will make a very good preacher."